Dear Elly,

If you're reading this, I'm gone. It must have been unexpected, and I apologize for leaving you and upsetting you.

Forgive me for not going on and on about how I've loved you—how valuable a friend you've been to me. I hope I showed in my life what I'm omitting in my death. Likewise, tell the girls I treasure them.

The purpose of this letter, Elly, is to ask an enormous favor of you. I have often wondered what would become of this office—the papers I've collected, received, written, condemned to dead files.... Here I am, sitting in the middle of mountains of junk—some of it precious and some of it idiotic. I can't think of anyone who would know better than you which is which. This letter is an official codicil. I am asking you to be my literary executor. It will be by your discretion that letters, papers, stories, contracts, diaries, etc., be burned or passed along to someone else or published.

I have a suggestion, though you are by no means obligated to take it, or even to share this letter for that matter. You might ask Barbara Ann, Beth and Sable to participate, to help you sort and file and decide.

Thank you. I feel better knowing you're in charge.

Love, Gabby

The House On
Olive
Street

Robyn
Carr

MIRA

ISBN 1-55166-545-X

THE HOUSE ON OLIVE STREET

Copyright © 1999 by Robyn Carr.

Visit us at www.mirabooks.com

Printed in U.S.A.

For Bonnalyn H. S. Carr, with love

Part One

ONE

April 16
Fair Oaks, California

Elly sensed something was wrong immediately, but since she was not a woman who lived by her instincts, she did nothing. She pushed the dark, ominous feeling aside and made believe that it was her abhorrence for surprise parties that brought on this edginess. She held the grocery bag that Sable had given her and stood, obediently, on the walk leading to Gabby's front door.

This was Sable's idea—the surprise birthday party for Gabby's fiftieth birthday. It was April sixteenth, the day after taxes were due. Gabby was an Aries, but lacked many of the typical character flaws of the astrological sign. She was neither arrogant, nor selfish, nor controlling. She possessed a raw courage, and she had a rare zest for life. Gabby turned fifty today—a beautiful, vibrant, exciting fifty. Fifty on the brink of still greater things, not on the declining side of life. Elly, fifty-eight, had not had such youth or vibrancy at twenty.

Something was wrong.

Elly heard the ticktocking of Sable's heels on the flagstone walk. She, too, carried a grocery bag. There were two more bags in the trunk, all filled with the makings of a lavish champagne brunch. The idea was to arrive just prior to Gabby's waking hour—somewhere around 11:00 a.m. It was ten-thirty. They hadn't even considered coming earlier. Gabby, for all her joy of life, was as mean as a junkyard dog in the early morning.

"Don't get Daisy barking," Sable commanded in a whisper, though they stood several feet from the front door. "We don't want Gabby to know what's up until the others arrive." The others were Barbara Ann Vaughan and Beth Mahoney. The five of them formed an intimate little writers' group who relied on each other for support, critique, industry news, celebration and whatever the publishing industry threw at them. Their works were diverse, ranging from mystery to romance to academic. Gabby's house was where they always met.

Daisy. *That* was the trouble, Elly realized. Gabby's nine-year-old golden retriever was whining at the door. Not much more than a miserable squeak. Added was the occasional scrape of her heavy paw; she wanted out. This was not typical. If Daisy heard people outside the door, she usually got all excited. She'd woof politely, but loudly.

"Listen," Elly ordered. "That's Daisy. She's not barking."

"She probably knows it's us," Sable suggested.

Elly put her bag down on the walk and crept nearer the door. Daisy had known them all since puppyhood and it had never stopped her from barking before. She was *crying!*

"Eleanor!" Sable whispered furiously. She rushed

up behind Elly, snatching at her sleeve. "Come away from that door! You're going to spoil it!"

"Something's wrong," Elly said loudly, punching the doorbell.

"What the hell are you doing?"

The dog still had not started barking. "Listen," Elly said. "Hear anything?"

"Not yet, but any second we're going to hear Gabby cursing on her way to the—"

"Daisy *still* isn't barking. Listen to her fuss. Something's wrong." Eleanor began digging through her enormous shoulder bag for her keys. She was the only one among the women who had a key to Gabby's house, given to her years ago so she could check on things while Gabby was out of town. She'd had it ever since, but never had an occasion like this in which to use it.

"Eleanor," Sable groaned. "Shit. You're going to ruin everything. What do you think you're doing?"

Elly rang the bell a couple more times, but didn't wait for a response. She slid the appropriate key into the lock. Daisy came bounding through the door, rushing past the two of them, not looking back. Out into the freedom. Out onto the grass. She looked back over her shoulder guiltily as she squatted to pee not three feet from the front walk. She'd been ready to explode, obviously.

"Jesus," Sable muttered.

"Gabby?" Eleanor called into the house. "Gabrielle? Gabby?"

"She's probably still asleep," Sable said, but she said so hopefully. "Slept through the doorbell and the yelling. Just like her. She sleeps like the—" Sable stopped herself.

Elly frowned over her shoulder briefly, then walked into the house ahead of Sable. Daisy bounded past them again, in the other direction, into the house. The sound of talking could be heard inside—television talking. Elly called out a couple more times, but softly, suspiciously.

They found her in the family room. She was lying on the couch, eyes closed. One foot was on the floor and she had a sheaf of papers on her lap. Probably manuscript pages. From a distance of three feet she could be mistaken for a sleeping girl; she was slight of build, fair complected and had hardly any gray streaking her curly, honey-blond hair. On the sofa table beside her was a can of diet soda, a glass of water and a bottle of aspirin. By the time they got there Daisy had taken her place again beside the couch, guarding. She looked up at them mournfully, as though she knew.

Eleanor gasped and rushed to Gabby's side, her large purse slipping off her shoulder and crashing to the floor as she knelt. She frantically touched Gabby's brow. Sable's hand rose to cover her mouth, her eyes disbelieving and her head already shaking denial. Eleanor touched Gabby's cheeks, her neck, her hands, muttering over and over, *My God My God My God,* then, *Oh No Oh No No No,* while Sable, stunned and terrified, stood frozen, not breathing. Elly stopped touching Gabby after a few seconds and straightened herself stoically. She turned toward Sable as rigidly as a soldier. "She's dead, Sable. She's been dead for some time."

"No," Sable whispered.

Elly nodded, frowning, because by then she had noticed there was a smell of some kind. Eleanor had talked to Gabby the previous afternoon; it wasn't as though she'd begun to decompose. There were no visible signs of blood, bruises or marks. It was the smell of death and it's accompanying atrocities.

"Go back outside," Elly said calmly. "Wait for Barbara and Beth. Don't let them come in. I'm going to have to call the police."

"The police?"

"It wasn't old age, Sable," Eleanor said, her voice cracking. "What would you suggest?"

Sable's eyes had taken on a stricken, panicked gleam. She hugged herself to keep from shaking or being sick. Not sick with disgust, but sick with horror. Her dearest friend. Dead before her very eyes. Sable couldn't answer. Her face went white.

"Don't fall apart on me now," Eleanor instructed calmly but firmly. "Just don't. Hang on for a while. I'll join you outside in a minute. Now go."

Eleanor walked to the kitchen phone, picked it up and dialed 911. She figured whatever had killed Gabby hadn't been homicidal…and even if it had been, it was safe to use the phone. She didn't care very much about fingerprints and all that. The cause of death, she had already decided, hadn't been murder, but rather theft. Elly's dearest treasure had just been stolen. "Yes, ah, my name is Eleanor Fulton and I've just let myself into my friend's house to find that she's…she's…expired. *Expired*, I said. Dead. Dead for some time, I guess. She's very cold and white. I think it must have been natural—a heart attack perhaps. What I mean is, there doesn't seem to be any…any *sign* of anything. No, no, she's only fifty." She did not add "today." She noticed that the message light on Gabby's answering machine was blinking madly, something that would no doubt help the police determine how long her dearest friend had been gone. She wanted to play the messages, to hear what final words had been spoken to Gabby while she lay on the sofa, dying to late-night TV. Birthday well-wishers? Instead, she gave the police dispatcher the address and asked that there please be no sirens. This was all bad enough without flashing lights and sirens.

When she replaced the receiver she realized her hand was shaking almost violently. She tucked it under her arm like an annoying old sock and took a deep breath. She would have to call Don, Gabby's ex-husband, but she'd wait until after the police had come to the house. She might even be the one to tell the children—David and Sarah—but not without Don. She would see to that. Don would manage, somehow, to be civil to his children, or Elly might physically make her point about it. Maybe just coldcock him, something she'd had an impulse to do for years now. Gabby was much more forgiving than Eleanor.

But before she would let herself enjoy the prospect of decking Don, she went back to Gabby. She stared down at her. Over twenty years, she thought in desolation. They were young together, even though Elly felt she, herself, had never been young. They had survived things that should have killed them. The others—Sable, Barbara and Beth—might love Gabby equally, but they hadn't had her quite as long. Hadn't been through quite as much with her.

Eleanor picked up her heavy purse and looped the strap over her shoulder before she dug inside for a handkerchief. She felt her eyes and nose drip before she was even aware she was crying, and she sopped up her leaking pain as best she could, dipping the linen under her glasses.

Gabby didn't look particularly peaceful to her, or maybe that was just her own emotions projected. Was that a slight frown? Had Gabby's face recently taken on those lines without Eleanor noticing? It was lividity, she finally realized, the color drained from Gabby's face, her lips falling slack and drying out. It was outrageous that Gabby be the first to go; she was the youngest at heart of them all. Everyone depended on her to a fault. Her children still needed her desperately, and Don, divorced from her for over fifteen years, relied on her constantly. And God, not even Gabby knew how Elly needed her. Maybe we wore her out, Elly thought. But no. Gabby had never seemed worn. Nor even tired. Never.

"Goddamnit," she whispered to Gabby. "I wasn't done with you yet."

A prominent character trait of Eleanor's was her complete lack of sentiment. She was rarely emotional, and if she was, it was usually about something political or intellectual. It was one of the things that made her an exceptional book critic. Finding Gabby, however, made her feel twenty years older and as vulnerable as a prepubescent girl all at once. She didn't actually cry so much as her eyes kept leaking and dripping beyond her control. Her voice remained steady and her words precisely clipped, but everything inside her quivered. She'd never felt so weak.

She stooped, hunched, as she walked out of Gabby's house. Her legs and arms were heavy and aching. Her stomach, a problem anyway, was twisted around. Being the eldest, the one who had known Gabby longest, she would be expected to take control of this situation. To know what to do. It was doubtful, she thought.

The first thing she saw was Beth Mahoney being comforted by Sable. They sat on the edge of the planter box in Gabby's front yard. Beth was the youngest of their group, girlish for her thirty-two years. She leaned her elbows on her knees and wept into her hands, the sound of her crying like distant bird-chirping. Sable was turned in Beth's direction, one of her hands gently rubbing the young woman's back while she patted her knee with the other.

Sable turned instinctively toward Elly and stood to look her over. With great relief Elly could see that Sable had composed herself on cue. It was no wonder. Sable had taught herself this trick years ago. Who knew how she was falling apart inside, how she'd fall apart later, when she was alone? If there was a vulnerable side to Sable, she kept it private. But for now, while Elly visibly sagged, Sable stood erect and assisted her toward that same planter box like she was the little old lady she felt she'd suddenly become.

"You'd better sit down," Sable instructed. "You're white as a sheet. You're wobbling. You're—"

"Please, that will do," Eleanor said, but her usual bark was barely a growl.

"Do you need a glass of water or anything?"

"No. No. I'll be all right in a minute. What have you told Dorothy?"

"To stay in the car," Sable said simply. Dorothy was Sable's housekeeper and cook. Part of the birthday surprise was to be Dorothy's preparation of brunch followed by a thorough cleaning of Gabby's house. Housekeeping was not Gabby's forte. And Dorothy would get a handsome bonus from Sable for the day's work. "Look at her," Sable said in a low, irritated voice.

Eleanor had to once again wipe the liquid from her eyes and blink to clear her vision. Dorothy sat in the back seat of Sable's Mercedes. She stared straight ahead, her hands poised atop the purse she held in her lap. She had tightly curled silver hair, a sharp nose and no chin. "Did you tell her what we found?" Elly asked.

"No."

And the sight of women weeping on the planter box had not moved her to ask if anything was wrong? Would the arrival of the police and coroner cause her to turn her head? Sable had long referred to Dorothy as the kitchen witch.

"I should have learned by now, you never exaggerate," Elly said.

A horrible insult of putts, grinding gears and angry growls caused all three women to look down the street. A partially sanded 1967 Camaro jerked noisily toward them. Barbara Ann Vaughan had a frazzled, tense look of concentration as she edged the car, gears sticking, to park behind Beth's late-model Ford. Once there, the car died. But it got real sick first, coughing and choking. Barbara actually had a car of her own; a nice, fairly new one that she rarely drove. Someone else in her household always needed a better car and it was anyone's guess what that would leave her to drive. Her sons were aged sixteen, seventeen, nineteen and twenty-one. They would not leave home while the food held out.

She had to reach outside the car to open the door and let herself out. She gripped a screwdriver that had some function to driving, pitched it back into the car and took a few seconds to gather up purse, gift and some papers. She kicked the door closed with her foot and called the car "you piece of shit" while her friends looked on. Barbara didn't immediately see that anything was wrong; she was preoccupied with her own ever-present set of problems. Plus, this was approximately the scene she expected—Sable, Beth and Elly waiting outside while the cleaning lady, who wouldn't be expected to yell "surprise," sat in the car.

Barbara's round cheeks were flushed as she approached the gathering at the planter box. She held a wad of crumpled papers in one hand and a brightly wrapped birthday gift and purse in the other. Without taking any note of the prevailing mood, she put down the gift and purse and began to sift through the papers, her expression irate. "Bobby's car," she said. "He's taking a test for trade school and wanted a reliable car. Look at this. Speeding, failure to yield, failure to stop and discordant behavior. Court date is tomorrow... I wonder if he'll need a reliable car? And what the hell is discordant behavior?"

"From what you know of that particular young man, what do you imagine that means?" Elly asked, poking her sopping hankie under the rims of her eyeglasses again.

"He probably called the police officer a dickhead," Barbara Ann admitted. "Elly, what's wrong? Are you sick?"

"Barbara," Sable said, grabbing her upper arm as if to keep her from running away. "It's Gabby. We found her. She's dead."

"*What?!*"

The papers fluttered out of Barbara's hands.

"I know. It seems impossible, but it's true. She's been dead for a while."

"Several hours at least," Eleanor said. "Probably since last night."

"It seems to be natural, if death can be natural on your fiftieth birthday," Sable added.

Beth had not yet made eye contact with Barbara. A tiny breeze blew through the front yard and one of the tickets tumbled over itself, threatening to get away. Beth pushed herself off the planter box and retrieved them all, muttering, "You'll probably need these," in a soft, absent tone.

"This isn't funny," Barbara said.

The sound of sirens could be heard. "Damn fools," Elly muttered.

"It's not a joke, Barbara. It's true. Elly called the police."

"The *police?*"

"I think it's what you do," Elly said. "They might frown on us making a direct call to the mortuary." She looked up at Sable suddenly. "Jesus, are we going to have to call a funeral parlor?"

"Maybe Don will do that. Or David. Let's wait and see."

"I've got to see her," Barbara said, lighting off for the house.

Sable, quick as a fox, had her arm. "Wait a minute. Wait for the police. We'd better not be poking around in there until they've had a look. You never know."

"But you said natural..."

"Yes, well, there didn't seem to be anything suspicious," Elly said. "Except that Gabby is dead. And Daisy is sitting vigil at her side."

"But she can't be," Barbara said, trying to talk some reason into the rest of them. "She's in perfect health. She's never even had the flu."

They all looked at her, watching the flood of realization slowly wash over her as it had each one of them.

Her cheeks grew pale, her nose pink, and her eyes glistened.

"Nonetheless," Elly said.

"Well, did you try to resuscitate her?" Barbara demanded in an impatient, tear-filled voice.

"Barbara, she's ice-cold," Elly said.

"And there's a smell," Sable added.

"Well, she can't be," Barbara insisted. "There's been some mistake." She shook herself free of Sable's grasp and, with her back straight, stomped toward the opened front door.

"Let her go," Elly said wearily. "You just don't tell Barbara Ann she can't fix it. She has to see for herself."

They were a writers' group, they told the police. Close friends drawn together because of their shared avocation. Eleanor, an academic who wrote nonfiction and reviews, had known Gabby very closely for twenty-two years. It took her a while to count them in her head. Sable, rich and famous for writing women's fiction, stumbled and hesitated before she claimed to have known Gabby for at least ten years. Barbara Ann, a seasoned series romance writer, reported eight years and Beth, author of mysteries, said six. They gave their home addresses and phone numbers. Gabby had talked to at least one of them every day. Eleanor was the last of the group to speak to her.

Cowards all, they were relieved when the police agreed to notify Gabby's ex-husband, Dr. Donald Marshall, who would then notify his children. None of them said anything. All of them were thinking the same thing. Don was in constant conflict with his children—his grown children. What little relationship they had had been held together by Gabby.

The matter of carrying away the dead took an enormous amount of time, much of it wasted. The EMTs came first, not believing Elly's report. The police came next and then they called the detectives. The detectives called the coroner. The coroner called for a transport vehicle and announced that there would be an autopsy. The detectives, quiet, depressed, middle-aged men wearing terrible ties, advised that they saw no signs of foul play but would seal up the house in anticipation of the coroner's report. The women were asked not to walk around in there.

Eleanor went directly inside. No one attempted to stop her, if they even noticed her. She had always looked like an anonymous older woman—plain, stern and unapproachable. She went into the kitchen and pushed the button on the answering machine, amazed that the police, who were supposedly looking for the time of death or signs of foul play, hadn't yet listened to the messages.

Hi Gabby. Don. *Are we on for tomorrow night? Dinner? It's your birthday so you pick the time and place. Call my girl at the office and give her the message. I'm thinking around seven…maybe Christopher's? I'll meet you. Oh, and if it wouldn't be too much trouble, do you think you could pick up my shirts on your way? And remember the briefcase you took to the shoe repair for me? Think that'll be ready yet?*

He hadn't gotten much better at letting her pick the time and place, Elly thought. You could hardly blame Don, she reminded herself, if Gabby allowed him to take advantage of her. Gabby would argue that she was most willing, under the circumstances. The circumstances being that Gabby shamelessly manipulated Don into taking care of any financial need she had. Gabby had told the group that she planned to hit Don up for a new transmission at her birthday dinner, and predicted that Don would say, "You can just take it to my guy." Don had a girl for this, a guy for that, a lot of people to do things for him.

One of the police detectives was suddenly beside Eleanor. She glanced at him.

Well, I should have known you were out. Gabby's mother. *Why else would you forget to even call me on what you know is the most difficult day of the year for me? I would have expected more from you. Don't call me now—it's too late. I'm going to the club with Martin and pretend that nothing is wrong.*

This would be pitiful and heartrending if Ceola weren't so comically self-absorbed. They laughed with Gabby out of respect. Ceola had lost her fourth husband, the one she claimed to have loved the most, the day before Gabby's sixteenth birthday. So long ago. Likely, it was the same date on which Gabby had died. Ceola would typically wait until very late on the fifteenth of April for Gabby to call to console her on her annual day of grieving, something she was keeping secret from Martin, her seventh or eighth husband. Sometime in June, Ceola would remember that Gabby had had a birthday and send her a fifty-dollar check.

Mom? Are you there? Sarah, tearful. *Well, it's probably better that you're out—I was just going to dump on you anyway and I really shouldn't the day before your birthday. You must be so sick of me! But, anyway, don't call me back tonight—it's already eleven and I'm going to try to get some sleep. Justin's been out all night and I'm so mad I could kill him. But I won't kill him until after I talk to you. Love you, Mom. Talk to you tomorrow.*

Sarah had dropped out of college and married a

grease monkey when she was nineteen, the chief reason for her estrangement from her father. Justin and Sarah had had their first child, despite their financial woes, six months ago. To add misfortune to misery, the baby had Down's syndrome. The marriage, Gabby had reported, became continually more strained.

That was the end of the tape. The detective popped it out of the machine and slipped it into his pocket. A little late, in Elly's opinion.

"Do you know the people on that tape?" he asked Eleanor.

"Her ex-husband, her mother and her daughter."

"Her ex-husband?"

"Yes."

"He was taking her out to dinner for her birthday? And he wanted her to pick up his laundry?"

"Gabby was a remarkable woman," Eleanor said.

"I'll say," the detective replied. "You have a key for this front door?"

"That's how I got in," Eleanor said, weary of this man's stupidity.

"Okay, then let's lock her up."

She peered at him over the top of her glasses. "And the dog?" she asked.

"Oh yeah. Can you take the dog?"

Elly shook her head and walked away from him, the power having returned to her step. The heels of her flat, brown shoes hit the floor with their usual purposefulness. "Thank God she *wasn't* murdered," she muttered. "Come on, Daisy," she called, heading for the door.

Daisy rose tiredly, reluctantly, her collar and tags jingling as she followed Eleanor. They exited and waited for the detectives so the door could be locked.

Beth and Barbara hugged each other in the street, saying goodbye. Sable stood by her car, the groceries returned to the trunk.

Elly didn't have anything more to say, certainly no more goodbyes. She walked to Sable's Mercedes and opened the door to the back seat. "Come on, Daisy," she called. The dog walked lazily across the lawn and then bounded into the back seat beside Dorothy. Dorothy made a face of utter disgust and slid as far away from the dog as she could. Her eyes behind her wire-rimmed glasses widened to saucers and her little bit of a chin withdrew even more. She must cook and clean like a dream for Sable to put up with this shit, Elly thought. Sable had fired people for forgetting to sharpen the pencils. But if anyone could match nasty scowl for nasty scowl with Dorothy, it was Eleanor. She leaned into the car before getting in and glowered at the housekeeper. "Everything all right?" she inquired in a tone that clearly forbade reply. The housekeeper backed her chin yet farther into her skull. "Good," Elly confirmed, positioning herself in the front seat and closing the door.

Sable backed out of the driveway. Just as they were about to drive past the house and away, Elly touched Sable's cashmere sleeve. She said nothing, but Sable brought the car to a stop in front of Gabby's house.

They all lived in a wide circle around Gabby and had always met here. Gabby had lived in this house for twenty-five years. She'd raised her children here. Gabby and Don had built the house on Olive Street when the children were babies. After the divorce, Gabby began having guests, writer friends from all around the country, and she slowly began to realize that she'd turned her home into a sort of writers' retreat. To Elly, Sable, Barbara Ann and Beth, this house had become a second home. A refuge. In good weather they gathered on the covered redwood deck. The backyard was dense with trees and the Sierra Nevadas rose in the east. When the weather was inclement, they met in the kitchen, spread around the large antique oak table. On winter evenings they would light a fire and recline in Gabby's overstuffed chairs or against large pillows in the family room. But it was always here. This house and Gabby had welcomed them, embraced and encouraged them, celebrated with them, commiserated with them. And some to-die-for gossip had been traded here.

They'd tried meeting in other places, but it hadn't worked. The women were uncomfortable in Sable's plush, white manse, being served off a tray by the kitchen witch; it made them feel rigid and starched. Elly's little house, as if designed for an old maid schoolteacher, was piled with the indulgence of thirty years of books and papers. Barbara Ann couldn't tame her wild beasts long enough for them to talk, much less read their works in progress. Her husband invariably blustered into the kitchen, bearlike, dirty from a hard day and growling sweetly, "What's for dinner, darlin'?" even though it was obvious no one was hovering over the stove. And with Beth it wasn't the size of her town house, per se, though it was uncomfortably small. It was more that one never knew when her commercial airline pilot husband would be in residence. If Jack Mahoney was home, Beth waited on him, like a geisha, and seemed nervous the whole time, as if the presence of her friends might disturb him.

Gabby's house was the kind you could drop into anytime. There were very few rules: you shouldn't wake her too early, never leave the toilet-paper roller empty, and if you want something special to eat or drink, you had to bring it. Otherwise, she wanted people around her. Sarah and David still called them Aunt Elly and Aunt Sable—Barbara Ann and Beth having come along too late to become aunts. Even holidays, from the Fourth of July to Christmas, found the place a haven for family and friends. Since Beth's husband traveled often and both Elly and Sable were unmarried, it was only Barbara Ann who was booked for all family occasions. Gabby's had become a writers' house, a women's house. They had somehow managed to keep each other pumped up and productive despite the fact that no two of them wrote in the same genre...or perhaps it was that very diversity that kept them stimulated and interested in one anothers' work. And their mutual support had gone far beyond their works; they shored each other up through every personal crisis of their daily lives.

The house on Olive Street, Elly assumed, would be sold. And the friends, altogether too different to be close friends in the first place, would scatter without Gabby to hold them together.

"I don't even want to think what all we're losing today," Elly said.

"Looks like you're stuck with me," Sable consoled.

Elly peered at her over the top of her glasses. "But look at what *you're* stuck with."

TWO

Sable didn't speak to Dorothy after they dropped off Elly and the dog. She left her in the back seat, clutching her purse like someone was about to steal it, and drove in silence all the way back to Hidden Valley, forty miles from Elly's. Sable had always taken extra pains to treat Dorothy companionably, something she hadn't done for other employees, but her efforts went unrewarded. The woman never responded.

Sable had hired Arthur and Dorothy, a retired couple, four years ago. In addition to a little house on her property, she gave them a good salary and benefits. Arthur was sweet, handy with the yard and simple household repairs, friendly and a little too talkative. He often voiced his appreciation for this arrangement. Arthur was not the greatest gardener and handyman, but he was kind. Dorothy, by comparison, was the best housekeeper and cook she'd ever had. It was a challenge to find a speck of dust, a smear or smudge. But Dorothy did not stretch herself. There was nothing extra to be got from the woman. She frowned from morning to night; she rarely spoke; she never said thank you—not even for gifts. On those evenings when Sable told Dorothy she was not very hungry and would fix herself some salad later in the evening, Dorothy would nod and walk away. Sable did not once venture to the refrigerator to find that a salad had been thoughtfully prepared for her.

Sable parked in the drive behind her house. She popped the trunk and left Dorothy to worry about all the grocery sacks by herself. She grabbed her purse, slammed her car door and stomped toward the house. "She was my best friend," she said aloud to herself. "To not even offer condolences is just fucking cruel." Sable decided then, for the hundredth time, that she was going to fire them. Too bad about sweet old Art, but she'd had enough of that sourpuss. "Why couldn't I have hired a goddamn Hazel? Why the hell do I even try with her?"

She entered the house through the kitchen, the shining white kitchen. The house spread softly before her— thick white carpet, flashes of rose, violet, steel-gray, a tiny dash of soft blue and pale peach. And glass, lots of glass. Her house sat on a foothill lakeshore lot so that the great room and dining room, where she entertained guests, faced the lake. There were French doors along the lakeside wall that led to the deck, and from the deck there were stairs and walks that led down across the plush, manicured lawn to the lake. The back of the house contained the kitchen, laundry and a large, pleasant room that Sable could not bring herself to identify as a family room. All this faced the back property—yard, patio, pool, spa and sauna, guest house and Arthur and Dorothy's cottage. There were two guest rooms in the main house divided by a bath on the east end. The private drive came around the lake and up the west side of the house toward the detached five-port garage and ample parking area. Double doors led into a foyer in front of the open staircase to the second floor. Flagstone paths led around the house to the lakeside entrances or to the poolside entrances. Too many doors to be locked at night, but a glorious openness by day.

Sable did all her living upstairs. At the top of the stairs to the right were twin offices—hers facing the lake, her secretary's facing the pool. Between them was a roomy powder room. To the left was her bedroom suite, though it was almost a small apartment. There was the king-size bed and rosewood bureaus, a sitting area comprising settee, two chairs with ottomans, cocktail table and wall unit of television, VCR, stereo and wet bar. There was a master bath in which Sable could serve tea for ten should she desire, complete with sunken, Roman shower, deep, whirlpool tub, commode and bidet, massive closet and chaise lounge. She could rest between brushing her teeth and picking out her shoes. And of course, decks, furnished with chairs, tables and chaises, stretched the length of the second story, both poolside and lakeside.

It had been hard to find an architect to create the house from Sable's vision—a fantasy she had begun putting together in her head twenty years ago. It had sometimes been the vision of the house, to which she kept mentally adding rooms and furniture, that had gotten her through the hard times. The many, many hard times in her secret past.

No use thinking about that now. She went to her secretary's office; Virginia kept the Rolodex on her desk. Sable had expected to be at Gabby's all day and told Virginia she could have that time off. She ignored the pile of faxes and the blinking message light. It was only her business line anyway.

Before leaving Gabby's house, bereavement duty had been divided among the women. Eleanor was to

speak to family members—Don, Sarah and David,
Gabby's mother, Ceola. Plus she would take care of
Daisy temporarily and help with funeral arrangements. Barbara Ann was to call all the writers' organizations she knew Gabby to be active in. Beth, the shy-
est of them all, would go to work on writing obituaries
to be released to publications from local newspapers to
national writers' and booksellers' periodicals. Sable
was to call editors and agents.

Sable was perfect for the job. Her fame was such that
there wasn't an editor or agent in New York for whom
she would have to leave a message. Anyone within
fifty feet of a phone would take her call.

She began flipping through the Rolodex, calling
Gabby's last agent first. Then the last editor with
whom Gabby had worked. And then it began to snow-
ball. Odd that Sable hadn't foreseen this; Gabby was
both well-known and well liked in publishing. Although she'd never reached bestseller status, her
works were respected, her reviews had been good and
she was highly regarded as a bright, talented professional. Gabby's reputation in New York was sterling.
In her twenty years and twenty titles—five nonfiction
and fifteen novels—Gabby had worked with some of
the industry leaders. On each call she made, Sable was
given the names of two more people to be notified,
many of them publishers and presidents. As the California clock ticked on and business in New York
wound to a close, she was given home phone numbers
or extensions to bypass the publishers' switchboards.
Naturally, everyone wanted updated information—
the cause of her death, the date and place of the funeral, et cetera, something Virginia could follow up
later.

It was five o'clock when she found she couldn't go on. Her mouth was dry and her insides were cramped. She hadn't eaten anything all day and hadn't paused in her telephoning even long enough to get herself a cold drink. Of course, Dorothy wouldn't trudge up the stairs to ask if there was anything she needed. Sable dragged herself wearily away from the desk and down the stairs to the kitchen—the spotless kitchen. She browsed through the refrigerator; it was stuffed with the groceries for the brunch, including the champagne.

She hit the intercom button and waited for Dorothy's dry response from the cottage. "Yes?"

"Do you suppose you could make me something to eat? I'm quite done in from notifying people of my best friend's death."

"Yes." Not "Yes, dear," or "Yes, ma'am" or even "Yes, you bitch."

"I'm going to take a shower. I'll eat in the kitchen. In thirty minutes."

It was precisely a half hour later that Sable descended again. She wore satin lounging pajamas and silk slippers, chic even when in mourning. She entered the kitchen to find that Dorothy was already gone, her chore finished for the time being. There on the table, perfectly appointed for one, was a brunch. The woman had prepared the goddamned brunch food. If it wasn't bad enough that this was to be her dead friend's meal, how about the fact that this food—cream, eggs, cheese, sausage, mushrooms, melon and strawberries—had been sitting in the trunk of the car for two or three hours? Was she trying to kill Sable, or merely wound her emotionally?

Sable felt an ache in her throat but would not cry. Ever since the last time she had really cried, when crying had almost killed her, she'd vowed that she would never cry that hard again. Never. It was too dangerous. Too futile.

She left the brunch on the table and heated up a can of chicken noodle soup. She poured it into a bowl, leaving the can conspicuously on the counter for Dorothy to find and ponder. She grabbed the box of saltines, a diet soda, and took her dinner on a tray to her suite. *Goddamn her, goddamn her, why does she hate me so?* she asked herself as she trudged back up the stairs. *I've been good to her. Kind. Patient. What do I have to do? What right has she to hate me so?*

Her legal name was Sable Tennet, because she'd had it changed in court, but that was not the name she was born with. Only Elly and Gabby knew that, and now Gabby was gone. Elly would never tell. Sable had threatened her once and Elly said, "Why would I tell anyone? Secrets don't intrigue me."

Sable had met Gabby and Eleanor long ago, way before it had ever occurred to Sable to write her way out of her misery. Way before Sable bottomed out and ran away from everyone and everything. The only two people who knew her before and after were Elly and Gabby. Sable lived in constant fear of someone finding out who she really was and where she really came from, before she worked her way up.

Worked her way up indeed. She'd gone from a poor girl with a GED and one accidental year of college—where she'd met Gabby and Eleanor—to a world-famous novelist. She wrote fast—stories with emotional sting and happy endings. Women in trouble could identify with lonely heroines who were desperate, the odds being they would never get the job/money/recognition/man. She was a fixture on the *New*

York Times list; she was now worth millions. Her books were printed in more languages than she knew existed. She had rich friends, knew celebrities and socialites. She dined with famous actors, sports stars, publishers and producers. She had taken meetings on yachts, rested with friends in Nice between books and flown to Monte Carlo for dinner. She was much more than a writer. She was a star.

And alone. The golden ones she partied with were not her friends, they were business acquaintances. They helped her reputation and appearance. With Gabby gone, so was the one person who had loved her unconditionally, had never been jealous of her success—nor fooled by it either. Gabby, the nurturer and admirer and true soul mate, had known the facts of all that Sable had endured to get what she'd gotten. Gabby had respected her even though she was pretty sure she didn't deserve it. That was something she would never have again. No one, not even Elly, knew the extent of what Sable had lost today. Everyone else had people, it seemed. Barbara Ann had her husband and children, Beth had her husband and large, extended family, and Elly had her friends and colleagues from the college.

So on the evening of Gabby's death, Sable sat in her bedroom suite alone. She indulged in two vodkas, exactly, to take the edge off her internal pain. Fearing alcohol, she only partook with the greatest of care. She would not need the drinks if she could only cry, and loosen the coils of grief inside her. But it wouldn't come. Never again.

She would have liked to talk to Eleanor, but couldn't bear to hear the older woman handle this in her flat, direct manner. It would be even worse if Sable found

Eleanor crumbling; Sable might fall into the deep ravine of pain as well, and perhaps this time not claw her way back up. It was better, she thought, to imagine Eleanor coping than to know the truth.

She sipped her vodkas and thought about her life before and during her relationship with Gabby. She eventually slept from 4:00 a.m. to 6:00 a.m. She was in her kitchen for breakfast—showered, short blond hair perfectly styled, makeup tasteful, decked in tan slacks of light wool and crisply starched white blouse—at 7:00 a.m. She had examined her reflection and knew she did not even look tired. Dorothy had appointed the kitchen table for one. A plate and cereal bowl stood ready and Dorothy was busy at the sink, not looking at her, not saying anything, awaiting further instructions.

"It's a damn good thing I didn't see Gabby's brunch on my plate again this morning, Dorothy, or I'd have chewed your ass good," she said, the very first time she'd ever taken that tone with the grumpy housekeeper.

Dorothy stiffened as though she'd been knocked against the sink.

"I think fixing me the brunch that was to be prepared for my best friend's birthday was damned insensitive of you, Dorothy. You might want to think about my feelings once in a while. There's more to this job than dusting and vacuuming, you know. I am a human being."

All this was said without looking at her. Sable spoke while staring at her empty bowl. She was not a retiring person by any means and had reamed a few asses in New York in her day, but there was something about the housekeeper that held her at bay, that she wanted to beat, or win over. There was a reason why she put up with Dorothy, though it displeased her, though she wouldn't indulge another human being so much patience.

Finally, softly, "Would you like me to throw away the brunch food?" Dorothy asked.

"Yes. Or take it for you and Art. Just be sensitive for once. I'm tired of your nasty attitude. And bring me the cornflakes, please."

It made Sable feel much better to have been firm. Elated, in fact. She abandoned plans of firing them. She'd coach Dorothy, teach her common courtesy. Wipe that goddamn scowl off her face.

Dorothy was very, very much like Sable's mother had been. A soured, bitter victim who thought only of herself and how abused she was by everyone around her. Dorothy even looked a little like Sable's mother. Sable would recognize the likeness even better if Dorothy were lying on the sofa, blitzed, moaning about how badly men treated her or how unfair her boss had been or what a bad lot in life she'd gotten with a kid to raise alone. Poor me, poor me, poor me, while she did nothing to make her life better or love and nurture her child. Or her grandchild. But with Dorothy, her grim countenance present in her constant industry, Sable could only tell how alike they were in their unhappy eyes, their meanly set mouths, their silent, mistreated air. Sable put up with this in Dorothy because in a way, if she could change Dorothy, cure her, get her to show some love and compassion, it would be like succeeding with her mother.

She ate her breakfast in silence and when she finished and stood from the table, she looked at Dorothy. Dorothy did not turn from her chore of pulling the brunch food out of the refrigerator until Sable cleared her throat. Sable threw back her shoulders and lifted her chin. She'd try the next lesson with eye contact. "From now on, Dorothy, I would like you to speak to me as if you can abide my presence. You'll say good morning. You'll say good night. We'll start with those two things and see how you handle them. And you'll say them pleasantly, kindly, as though you actually give a shit whether I live or die."

They stared at each other for a long moment.

"Starting now, Dorothy," Sable said.

"Goo...Good morning, ma'am."

"You can call me Sable, you know."

"Good morning, Sable," she said.

There, Sable thought. We're making progress.

THREE

Barbara Ann's pulsing brood did the best they could with her delicate condition of grief. They restrained their voices to some degree, erupting now and then out of pure habit. Mike and the boys knew Gabby, but they weren't exactly close, so the loss was not theirs by any means. It was hers and hers alone. And none of the other women would ever know how much she had lost. Maybe *loss* wasn't the right word. *Ended* was closer. They would never know all that had ended today.

She cried through the afternoon and then at four o'clock, like an automaton, she zapped a roast and then threw it in the oven to finish cooking, boiled potatoes and carrots, heated buns and tore up lettuce, all through the narrow slits of her swollen eyes. Barbara Ann had the survival skills of a mother of four wild boys; she could do everything fast and many things at once. She could condense the cooking of a four-hour meal into forty minutes, and while the microwave purred, she collected a pile of dirty clothes. On her way to the laundry room, she wiped the hair and spit out of a bathroom sink with a T-shirt. On her way from the laundry room back to the kitchen, she picked up seven pairs of shoes and tossed them into their respective cages, then caught the potatoes before they boiled over.

Once everyone was informed as to the reason for her pain and tears, all she had to do was lift her chin with that injured air and purse her lips tightly together, and the din would subside.

For example, when Joe came home from basketball practice, about the time everyone else was going for their second helpings—

"Jesus Christ, get outta here with those feet, butt-face."

"Bite me! This is my house, too!"

"Not when you smell like bad cheese, it ain't!"

"Matt!" in a desperate whisper. "Mom!"

And then, warning taken, in a much smaller voice, "Sorry. His feet smell like goat shit. Jesus."

While Sable sipped her vodkas in her sterile environs and cautiously took herself back through the hard days before she was rich and famous, Barbara Ann Vaughan took a cup of coffee outside to the patio of her two-story home in search of peace. She had to kick aside a pile of wet towels to pull out a chair from the patio table. It wasn't yet pool season; they couldn't be there from last year! Car washing, perhaps. Used her good beach towels to dry off a greasy, tar-spattered car. She removed jeans and a T-shirt from the chair so she could sit. She pushed aside the mess from a partially constructed, radio-operated model airplane so she could put her coffee down. The craftsman, Bobby she thought, had probably lost interest by now; she'd been complaining about it for two weeks.

From the house she could hear her little darlings, the smallest of whom was six feet and a hundred and ninety pounds, and her loving spouse.

"Way to go, dickhead. I was gonna eat that!"

"It wasn't that great anyway."

"You wanna shut the fuck up, I'm on the phone here."

"Hey! Watch your mouth! I don't want to be hearing that shit outta you! Got that?"

"Got it."

Eat what? Barbara wondered. She'd just thrown a slaughtered cow at them. She rubbed the bridge of her nose, an odd habit she'd acquired somewhere, and felt the tears begin to trickle from her eyes again. She particularly loved it when her husband, Mike, disciplined the boys with statements like, "I don't want to hear that swearing shit outta you, asshole." There was a time, long ago, when his failure to see the irony in such a statement seemed precious in its simple, straightforward way.

Gabby, Gabby, Gabby, how could you leave me to this! I'll disappear into a blot of grease and never be seen again! I'll fall down the toilet in the middle of the night!

The sliding door opened and Joe and Bobby, seventeen and nineteen, spilled outside with their fight, a dish towel-snapping tussle. She splashed over some of the hot coffee and groaned. She glared at them meanly. They didn't see her right away, hidden as she was in the deepening dusk, alone on the patio. When they stopped long enough to take notice of her, they suddenly relaxed their weapons.

"Sorry, Mom."

"Yeah, sorry, Mom."

This was not the life she had envisioned when, twenty-three years ago, Mike Vaughan begged her to marry him and send him off to Seoul, Korea, as a fulfilled helicopter mechanic. "Marry me, Barbara Ann, and I'll come home, I swear to God, in one whole piece, and give you a shitload of kids." She had been twenty—barely. A naive, only child who had not done anything for herself since birth. So naive it never crossed her mind that there was no war in Korea in which Mike might be injured or killed, but Vietnam was fresh in her mind and she didn't take the time to differentiate between military bases and their functions. She married him to keep him safe. She had worked in a Realtor's office, answering phones, until he returned. Ten months after Mike came home, Matt was born. Then Bobby, then Joe, then Billy.

"As long as you make them comfortable, they'll stay," Eleanor said of her sons.

"Don't fight it, Barb. Just use your book money to get a small, tidy apartment nearby to write in," Sable advised. "And stop indulging them in everything. Force them to make their own lives. At least two of them are over eighteen." Sable—the voice of parenting experience.

"I would do anything to have four sons," said Beth, who'd been trying to get pregnant for years.

"You can change your life in many ways, Barbara Ann," Gabby said, "but people are permanent. And you have blessings in Mike and that half a baseball team of yours."

But people aren't permanent, are they, Gabby? she thought, tears running over.

Barbara Ann loved Gabby deeply and her feeling of loss was incredible, but the emotion that was pouring down her cheeks was combined with something else. *My God, I could die before I've done what I want to do! Gabby was only fifty, healthy as an ox! I could die before I make any real money on a book, before I succeed at this, before I'm known at all, before even one of these louts gets a life of his own! Before I ever live in a house where a single toilet seat is down!*

Barbara Ann was so disappointed in her life. Not that she didn't love her family. She must, she put up with a lot from them. Mike, though older and a little thicker around the middle, was still a handsome and lusty man. He could still get to her, easily seduce her, make her feel like a girl again, even with some of his inept flattery like "Honey, you're just pretty as shit." And the boys, each one of them damn good-looking, were just like their dad—rugged, masculine, athletic. Men's men. Romance-novel men. Rough, loud and big. God, were they big. They took up so much space; the smallest shoe she ever tripped over was an eleven.

It seemed to Barbara Ann that her life kept expanding without getting much better. The boys grew into men and required more space; they were in need of an awesome amount of fuel; their possessions became larger and more complex. She and Mike bought a five-bedroom house to accommodate them, but they kept adding on to it, in search of places to put people and things. They doubled the size of the family room. At least the result included an expanded master bedroom upstairs, a sitting room and dormer in which Barbara Ann could work and store her writing business. They built a detached garage—the original two-port garage barely kept the rain off their bicycles and athletic gear. Now they were a six-car family. Her driveway and the street in front of their house looked like a used-car lot. The boys had inherited their father's flair for mechanics, so every vehicle but hers was in a constant state of repair or improvement. They put in a pool and laid a slab of concrete for a basketball hoop. There was a lawn-mower motor that Mike had been meaning to repair all winter sitting in her bedroom, for God's sake. Every dime of her book money went to household improvements to make it seem as though they weren't stuffed into this large house.

Her income had grown without her work going better, without her feeling more successful. She had entered the business on a wild lark nine years ago. A friend of hers had taken up writing category romances and miraculously sold a book. Barbara Ann followed, quite literally. She joined a writers' group, attended several seminars and conferences, read dozens, if not hundreds, of romances, set up a typewriter in the bedroom and took on the challenge. Within two years she sold her first book. She sold a second before the first was out. Her income in three years' time was seven thousand. In four years it was twelve thousand. In five years it was twenty-two and in six years it was forty-six. Now, soon to release her twenty-sixth novel, her income this year would be in the neighborhood of sixty-eight thousand.

Wasn't that a lot of money?

Not for all that had gone wrong. Or, rather, had not gone. She had a twenty-seven-year-old editor who had insisted she revise and rewrite her last proposal twice, taking her three months to get a final, twelve-page draft that they would accept and pay her the first half of a ten-thousand-dollar advance. She was averaging three paperbacks a year and the woman who was accepting or rejecting her work was an art major who'd worked her way up to editor nine months ago. In her nine years of writing, struggling in this business, Barbara Ann had watched several acquaintances shoot past her, personally knowing too many who'd signed million-dollar multibook deals. Their writing was no better than hers! Their books were not that much different! And Barbara Ann was still toiling, writing her ass off at least forty hours a week, and begging for these ten-thousand-dollar advances.

"You haven't developed a strategy yet," Sable had told her.

"Great. Give me a strategy. Tell me how you did it."

"You're missing the point, Barbara Ann. There are fifty reasons why the way I did it won't work for you. Some of the things I did twelve years ago don't work now. The trends change too fast for you to catch up with them. The people in the business are all different. It's not as though you can write the same type of book I write and get rich and famous. There are already a million books like mine that aren't doing much."

"Then how the hell do you expect me to develop a strategy?"

Heavy sigh. "Everyone has a personal version of success, Barbara Ann. Are you sure you want the same kind I have? Maybe true success is a happy family?"

"Don't be patronizing, just tell me how. Please!"

"Well, I'll try, but it's just not the same for everyone, you see. You have to uncover what it is you can do better than anyone else, that hasn't already been done to death, and then you have to find the right people to help you do it and then you have to go about selling it in ways that haven't already been tried by every other midlist author. It's very cagey and creative and above all, individual. Plus, it is loaded with risks. You have to decide if you like where you are—which brings in dependable, if not incredible, money—or if you're willing to risk it all by walking away and hunting the big cats. It's a huge gamble. It doesn't always work. At the very least, it doesn't work fast."

Barbara Ann pushed Sable into going over all this again and again and she never quite followed it. It was too ambiguous. It might work for a certain type of author to fire five agents, change publishers, piss off a lot of people and stage a veritable raid on the publishers and finally get the money she wants. But another author could try it and find themselves disliked, avoided and basically out of work. One type of author with a certain type of book might be able to sell copies by developing a massive marketing campaign on her own while in another case it would only serve to bankrupt the author, annoy the marketing department and make the next book even harder to sell. It was all *individual*, Sable kept saying. Your strategy must exactly fit your ability, personality, type of work and potential.

Why the hell wouldn't Sable admit she'd just been lucky? And console Barbara Ann that she had not been?

"Of course there's luck involved in publishing, Barbara Ann," Sable relented wearily. "Lots of luck. Bestselling authors are always lucky. But they're not accidental."

Barbara Ann did *not* understand.

And then there was Barbara Ann's dirty little secret. She had conquered their group. She had pushed her way into Gabby's life because Sable was there and she needed what they had. It hadn't mattered to her whether or not she *liked* these women. She wanted Sable's help and influence because she wanted her own phenomenal success to come to her. She had too many obligations to take all these risks Sable talked about even if she could figure out what they were.

Nine years ago, in the very beginning of this writing endeavor, Barbara Ann had taken a short workshop course from Gabby because she heard that Gabby hung out with Sable Tennet. In fact, the little writers' group she belonged to kept trying to get Gabby to get Sable to come and speak to them. Sable was not easily got. She was very particular about where and when she was seen. Sable was single-minded; there had to be something in it for her. She drew a fee—something not many writers' groups willingly paid. They'd let you autograph books and they'd fuss over you. What more should you need? But Sable didn't hang out with other writers, unless they were sensationally famous. Her only regular friends were Gabby and Elly.

So Barbara Ann put the rush on Gabby. She phoned her, invited her to lunch, asked her many questions, made herself available. Gabby, being the friendly, approachable woman she was, gave in to the prospect of friendship. Barbara Ann knew that success was imminent. Before long she met the famed Sable, and Sable impressed the hell out of her. She was chic, elegant, arrogant and sought after. Sable would get important business calls while she was hanging out with the girls at the Olive Street house. Barbara Ann would eavesdrop as Sable went through various stages of wheedling, throwing a tantrum, cajoling or threatening, and everyone would eventually come around, give Sable what she hankered for. The advance would be upped, the advertising promised, the cover changed, the tour accommodations improved or the special invitation provided. Sable was psychic. She knew when to suck up, when to whine, when to scream. She always got what she wanted. Barbara Ann wanted that.

From the very beginning, Barbara Ann found the friendship between Gabby and Sable to be an odd one. Gabby was a very attractive, small woman who put more emphasis on her feelings and her intellect than on her wardrobe or lifestyle; Gabby valued things like friendship, honor, loyalty and sensitivity. Sable, you could tell after one meeting, mostly valued success and power. She was a classy, slender, gorgeously dressed blonde. She wore specially made suits and slacks and exactly the right amount of tasteful jewelry, all real. She drove a Mercedes, had a rich cache of famous acquaintances, and Barbara Ann met her at about the time she'd landed the biggest agent in New York and was beginning to sign contracts for a series of movies.

Not that Sable was shallow or superficial. She was entirely earnest. And her devotion to Gabby was one of the things she was most serious about. But they did make an odd couple—Gabby in her oldish Chevy, Sable in her Mercedes. Gabby in her blue jeans and Birkenstocks, raising two kids alone in an average-size four-bedroom house; Sable hiring servants, secretaries and publicists from her Hidden Valley manse. Gabby going to PTA meetings, soccer games, orthodontists' appointments and block meetings; Sable dashing off to New York for a book-release party, then on tour, starting with *Good Morning America* and *The Today Show*.

If the two of them were not an odd enough combination, Barbara Ann was introduced to their closest crony, Eleanor. A professor. A critic. A dour, drab, intellectual spinster. The three of them together looked perfectly ridiculous, and yet they were clearly thick as thieves. After a while, Barbara Ann began to see how timeless their relationship to each other was. She found out that the connection went deeper and had lasted longer than it even appeared, but they were, all three, protective of the details. That was the only thing that made Barbara Ann continually feel like a newcomer, but it was a significant thing. Apparently Sable had been a college freshman when Gabby was starting her master's program and Elly was teaching comparative literature when they met and became friends for the first time. They were aged nineteen, twenty-nine and thirty-six. (They must have looked even stranger then!) Sable moved to Los Angeles to finish studying and begin making her fortune while Gabby and Elly remained close and, of course, welcomed Sable home with open arms as a successful, bestselling writer. But there always seemed more to the story than they were telling, like they were all arrested for murder together or something.

Barbara immediately recognized the understated power of this trio. Gabby seemed to know everyone in the writing industry—the agents, the editors, the romance writers, the mystery writers, the president of the authors' guild. She'd collected these acquaintances through years of traveling as a correspondent, teaching, conferences, publishing and various writers' groups. Sable held the celebrity achievement award for fame and making money. And Elly provided the collegiate connection, the credibility, the brainpower. She had authored many little-known academic papers, but she also had written copious reviews of popular literature and articles for artsy-fartsy publications.

These women were the movers and shakers.

But they hadn't helped her. She was not so far from where she'd started, actually. More books under her belt, sure, but she wasn't exactly meteoring to fame and fortune. She was still a pudgy housewife who suffered under the constant stress of family obligations and found solace in Twinkies.

And now Gabby was dead. Gone. Gabby was the

one she had truly grown to love and depend on. Of the three of them, only Gabby really consoled her, tried to encourage her, kept her going. Barbara Ann wept as much for Gabby as she wept for the fact that their group would now surely fall apart. Though she had lost patience with the way every goddamn thing had gone Sable's way, though she felt simpleminded in the face of Elly's brilliance, though Beth seemed more a child in need of nurturing than an equal, she loved them. She needed them.

I love them and need them, but do they need me? Of course not! What could I possibly give any one of them?

It would be too much to say that Barbara Ann was going to give up or live in a vacuum. No, she was going to keep writing, keep in touch with Elly, Sable and Beth, and maintain her memberships in the writing groups where she had friends and acquaintances—and was pathetically most famous for being a close friend to Sable Tennet. But she was so unhappy. And tired. Frustrated by the mess and the noise and the blustering men who took her completely for granted while they trashed the house and made plans for how they'd spend the next royalty check.

"*I need a new engine.*"

"*Tough shit, artichoke brain, I'm going to electrician's school—that takes tuition money, y'know.*"

"*What about the ski gear I been promised since graduation?*"

"*I thought we were all going to take a family vacation. Hunting.*"

"*Hey! Does Mom have anything to say about this? Mom, what's more important, ski gear or electrician's school?*"

Take it easy, honey, Mike would say. They're just boys and we won't have them forever. They are animals, Barbara Ann would reply. And I think they'll pick my bones clean.

The message publishing was giving her was that she'd better resign herself to remaining one of those reliable, average romance writers, take her money (which was good money if you compared it to what she could make as a secretary, stinko money if you compared it to what she could make as a bestselling romance writer!), and accept the fact that she didn't have *it*. What she had was *some*. The skyrocket had left without her.

She felt she had failed. She felt doomed to stay right where she was. And it just wasn't enough.

FOUR

The autopsy revealed that a subarachnoid hemorrhage caused by a ruptured aneurism had taken Gabby quickly, probably causing her only brief pain. The aspirin bottle on the sofa table suggested she may have had a headache, but the fact that she hadn't attempted to call anyone indicated the pain had not been severe or protracted. Although Gabby hadn't had any religious affiliation for years, the memorial service was held in the First Presbyterian Church because of its size. The front of the church was covered in such an array of flowers it became gaudy. No one, not the family nor Eleanor, had had the presence of mind to come up with an alternate way for people to show their sympathy, such as a trust or benefit. They simply hadn't been prepared for this outpouring. They should have been—Gabby had many friends and admirers—but they weren't.

Writers tend to have more long-distance friends—brought together by their books, conferences, guilds and necessary networking—and fewer local friends, because they work in isolation. Even so, Gabby had exceeded the norm. There were cards, flowers and calls from hundreds of people in publishing. Writers and editors had traveled from far away to attend the memorial and the subsequent reception. It was not just that she was loved and admired. She had impacted the lives of those she knew.

Sable had been the first to realize the gathering to memorialize Gabby was going to include authors and publishing people from out of town. Sable's secretary, Virginia, was flooded with calls requesting information about the time and place of the service.

Barbara Ann, who had called names from various writers' groups' rosters, found the same response. Her phone rang for two days. Then, something that often takes place in anticipation of conferences and conventions began to surround Gabby's memorial. Writers, editors, agents and booksellers planned to add a day or two and made plans for dinners and lunches. They had set themselves up in little enclaves all over Fair Oaks and Sacramento. Something had to be done with them.

Opening up Gabby's house was out of the question. Her personal effects had not been sorted through and it would not be appropriate to attempt to entertain over a hundred mourners there. Even though Don and Gabby had remained amicable, he couldn't manage the after-memorial reception in his condo. Her kids, Sarah and David, hadn't the time, energy or room. Elly's, Beth's or Barbara Ann's homes—not even worth considering. Sable was the only person capable, and capability was Sable's middle name. She would host the mourners in her Hidden Valley manse.

Sable and Elly met at the church at one forty-five. Beth came in alone, and after saying one or two hellos, she gravitated to her friends. Barbara Ann arrived with her entire family. She looked like the grieving widow in her navy blue dress and dark glasses, flanked by her five huge men. She saw Beth, Elly and Sable standing in the aisle beside their pew and hesitated. Sable lifted an arm to her, a gesture welcoming her to the remains of the group, and Barbara's handsome husband leaned close and softly mouthed, "Go ahead." Barbara Ann tearfully joined them, unable to express her relief that they wanted her still, unable to admit the fear that it was only for today. Mike and the boys took their places behind the four women who had taken their places behind Gabby's ex-husband, mother and grown children.

And then Eleanor spoke, her voice mostly strong, her words more carefully chosen than at any other time in her life.

"I've known Gabrielle Seton Marshall for over twenty years, but I think there's another reason I'm before you today. I tend to draw assignments like this because I have worked so hard to establish a reputation as one who is absent of sentiment, as one who cannot be broken by anything of this world. Well, Gabby is no longer of this world. And I am no longer unbreakable."

Elly faced a gathering of over two hundred, five days after Gabby's death. As per Gabby's wishes, she had been cremated and her remains scattered over her beloved Sierra Nevadas, mountains she'd gazed upon from her deck or writing loft.

Elly spoke of Gabby's greatest life project, the mothering of Sarah and David, and her great pride in having raised "people of high standard." She described the years before Gabby's career as a novelist began, when she was traveling the world as a correspondent, from Bangkok to Africa to Belfast, in search of human rights stories of women and children that she witnessed firsthand, from infanticide to female mutilation to the agony of mothers who watched their eight-year-old sons bear arms. Eleanor described Gabby's work during that period as "largely overlooked and desperately good." She told of Gabby's near brush with death nineteen years ago when meningitis struck her, when she emerged from that nightmare stronger and more determined than ever. Gabby had given so much of herself, she reminded them, when she taught or supported or mentored other writers. And, of course, her heart and her home were always open to countless friends.

"Oddly, I thought until today that Gabby belonged to me," Eleanor said. "But that was her way, to make each one of us feel, on some level, that we were the only ones. Not one of us, I suppose, was more important than another…but then, neither were we ever less. I wish at this moment there was one stranger here, someone I could approach and convince, with my vast training in literary criticism and my extensive experience in debate, that I have not idealized this woman in her death.

"But, it is apparently unnecessary. If you were ever left in need of encouragement, you didn't know Gabby Marshall. If you ever felt forgotten, if you've longed for loyal friendship or a steady hand or compassion or understanding, you didn't know Gabby. If you ever found yourself trying to overcome a character flaw while you were Gabby's friend, she was utterly useless to you. She had an uncanny ability to accept the worst attributes in people as though they were charms. She saw us all in good light, rest assured.

"And if you ever thought you were alone, you never met Gabby."

Eleanor's voice croaked then, but she recovered herself instantly and admirably.

"Gabby's life was not easy, but you'd never know it. For as many years as I've known her—twenty-two now—whether she was on top of the world or had just suffered some magnificent defeat, she believed that her life was good and her future glowing. That, more than anything, is the tribute we can give our friend. To have a glass half-full and occasionally lift it to her continued success. Because wherever she is, she is making friends and making waves.

"Here's to you, Gabby," Eleanor said, lifting a mock glass in the air. "Good journey, my friend. Godspeed."

When Sable looked around her house at what her swift, efficient hand had wrought, she was pleased. She had made maps of the route to her Hidden Valley home and gave five small stacks to key people, asking them to pass them out with discretion. This reception was limited to those who were legitimate friends of the departed. Even making that firm assertion, she was still prepared to deal with curious tagalongs or, worse, opportunistic deal-makers. She'd be goddamned if she'd have someone make a book deal at her best friend's memorial service.

Caterers served a light buffet dinner and drinks; tables had been set up around the lakeside deck and pool area; the spring weather cooperated beautifully. She'd hired a valet parking service because, although there was an extensive drive and parking area, she thought she'd keep the traffic moving in and out, and it would serve as her first line of defense against letting anyone out of her house who'd toasted Gabby's memory too often. And, though Sable didn't expect any trouble, she called Jeff Petross, her personal security consultant. He owned a company that offered alarm systems, investigations, protection for celebrities and, for a handsome fee, a variety of other security services. He'd traveled with Sable on book tours, not as a visible escort but rather as an adjacent traveler who was always nearby in case there was any problem. At her reception for Gabby's memorial, he and one of his employees were present, appearing to be bartenders.

"Barbara, I don't know many of these writers on sight. Please introduce me and help host them. And Beth, please...? The ones you know?" Sable was neither antisocial nor unfriendly. It was her concealed fear, insecurity and lack of trust that caused her to refuse to join any of the national writers' organizations, despite the fact that she was frequently invited. She was most often begged by Barbara Ann, who, she suspected, wanted to take her to a conference or convention and show her off. She couldn't see herself chumming with them; she always assumed people had ulterior motives. Because Sable attended so many muckety-muck doings and eschewed the gatherings of ordinary writers, all in the interest of promoting her own success, she had set herself apart. Unintentionally, above. The resultant effect was that many writers considered her a snob.

Barbara Ann, in her glory, provided most of the introductions. But Sable once again stunned her. And left her slightly embarrassed. Sable had rarely discussed other popular writers or their works. "Oh yes, Elna, I've enjoyed your books," Sable said. "Particularly the pirate series." "Rosemary, a pleasure. I've often wondered what kind of woman can capture those Wild West tales with such erotic adventure. I'm curious to know if you have some Native American blood yourself." "Maggie, hello! You had a protagonist named Gabrielle once. Tell me, was any part of that wild, bright little sprite based on our friend?"

"You've never said anything about any of their books," Barbara Ann whispered, annoyed by this surprise. "I didn't know you even read them."

"Now and then," Sable replied. Sable had an uncanny memory and her reading speed was untimeable. But she had learned, long ago, to be careful what she said. No one but Elly would believe the number of books she read. Criticism was deadly and casually tossed-out compliments would cause her to be besieged by requests for endorsements. Her silence, however, had only caused her to be viewed as arrogant. She had no idea how greatly her few, well-placed comments had softened that impression.

By six, everyone had arrived, eaten from the light buffet, had their wineglasses or coffee cups refilled, and contentedly strolled the property. For some of the writers present, a reception at Sable Tennet's home was a treat of rare and special significance. Not that she was the lone success story; several of these writers had staked their own claims on bestseller lists, owned large, beautiful homes and drove expensive cars. But Sable was an icon, whether she knew it or not. Her success had been quick and fabulous, and had preceded them all.

She was exceedingly pleased with the way the reception had turned out. Sarah and David were down by the dock with their father and Beth, talking. Hopefully, not arguing this once. Barbara Ann's husband and four sons, all suited up stunningly, shared a table by the pool and did not betray the slightest itch that they longed to get away. The fact of their presence and behavior showed great respect and sensitivity to Barbara Ann, and Sable hoped her friend saw this. Gabby's mother, Ceola, and her latest husband, Martin, had drawn a small, sympathetic crowd. There were groupings of people here and there, chatting softly; guests walked around the yard, the lake, the patio. To their credit, she had not witnessed anyone poking around, curious about her possessions, though she did see some admirers of her artwork. She was complimented—that's what art was for.

She had stretched a gold chain across the staircase at its top, an idea she'd gotten from an older woman, a society matron. There was no reason the group should not be confined to the ground floor—upstairs was only her private quarters and business office. But Sable went up to her bedroom to use the lavatory.

She was about to open her bedroom door when she heard something, a sound in her office. She should have known, she thought instantly. One of these people would find their curiosity too much and be compelled to look at Sable's work area. She knew just how to ask the offender to please not pry; the door was closed for a reason. But when she opened her office door, she found there was a man in there she didn't know. He'd been looking at her desk.

"Can I help you with something?" she asked icily.

He shrugged, not terribly embarrassed. "I must have lost my way."

"That would be hard to do. There was a chain across the stair indicating that this area is off-limits to guests. Who are you?"

"My name's Robert Slatterly, Ms. Tennet," he said, stretching out his hand. She declined to take it. "I was just curious. I wanted to see where you work."

"This is not a time for presumption like that, Mr. Slatterly. We're all a little—" She stopped herself. Slatterly. She knew that name. "How did you know Gabby?" she asked.

"I...ah...took a class from her at Sac State."

"When was that?" Sable asked.

"I don't know. Two, three years ago. Why don't you have any pictures of your family around your desk?"

Sable turned and depressed a couple of intercom buttons beside the office door, paging to the kitchen. "Will someone please send Jeff up to my office? Right away, please." She turned back to Robert Slatterly. "Why would you be expecting to see pictures of family?" she asked. She knew she didn't like what was going on, but she couldn't figure out why.

"I don't know," he shrugged. "I read somewhere that your parents were killed when you were young. I thought you'd have a picture of them on your desk, or mantel, or something. I mean, since you never married."

"What *are* you looking for?"

"Look, I'll just shove off and—"

Sable shut the office door, barring his departure. "You don't even know Gabby, do you? What are you doing here and who invited you?"

He pulled a crumpled map out of his shirt pocket. "A nice woman named Iris invited me."

"Gabby didn't teach at Sac State recently. Not in the last few years. She guest-lectured for a writing class now and then, but she'd stopped teaching on a regular basis. Now, why don't you tell me what you want."

There was a light *tap-tap-tap* at the door and Sable opened it to admit Jeff, a nice, big guy with no neck—even less of a neck in his tux shirt and bow tie. "Better still, tell Jeff here."

Slatterly, tall but thin and wiry, began to chuckle as though satisfied and amused. "Security? At a funeral? Rich."

"Can I see some ID please?" Jeff asked.

"You a cop?"

"No. Private security."

"Then I don't have to show you any ID."

Jeff slowly smiled. He seemed to flex slightly without really moving. "Yes, you do."

Robert Slatterly produced his wallet and seemed to do so with arrogance. Driver's license, credit cards, library card, a few dollars. Jeff examined the wallet and passed it to Sable. "Los Angeles?" Jeff asked.

"Kind of a long commute to Gabby's class at Sac State, wouldn't you say?" Sable asked. "Jeff, this guy's some sort of interloper. He wasn't a friend of Gabby's. And he let himself into my office. Can I have him arrested for that?"

"Wait a minute, wait a minute, take it easy," Slatterly said hastily. "I'm sorry, okay? I had no business coming in here, but I was curious. I didn't take anything. I didn't touch anything. I didn't even open a drawer. I just looked at the office."

Jeff turned him around and began to pat him down. This seemed like overkill to Sable, who just wanted his ass thrown out, until Jeff came up with a very small camera. He handed it to Sable. "Jesus Christ," she said. "A reporter." And not one interested in a story about the passing of Gabrielle Seton Marshall, but interested in the inside of Sable's house, and perhaps more. He probably worked for a tabloid of some kind. "Who do you work for?"

"I'm freelance."

"Who were you going to sell pictures to?"

"The highest bidder," he shrugged insolently.

"Wait a minute, that's it. You called my publicist and asked for an interview with me. You told her you were with *People*..."

He smiled and shrugged. He wasn't with *People*. It was a lie.

She was completely unprepared for something like this. She'd turned down a number of interviews, totally unimpressed with some she'd given, and had even had a couple of journalists get real pissed off by her penchant for privacy. But she had never had anyone stealthily enter her house, her office.

"Jeff, can you get him out of here with as little commotion as possible?" She handed him back his wallet, but kept his camera. "Mr. Slatterly, my best friend just passed away. I think your behavior here today has been shameful and I won't forget it. Please don't ever come near me or my home again."

That unfortunate incident put an edge on Sable's hospitality, having validated those misconceptions about people in general that she harbored. They always wanted something. It wasn't her that people wanted to be close to, but her success, her connections, her influence. Or they wanted to find something about her to dislike, to resent, to criticize. She had opened up a little during the introductions, let her authentic good nature show, but by the time her guests were leaving, she was closed off again.

"We'll be seeing you in New York at the conference next month, right?" someone said upon leaving. She was to attend this writers' conference to receive an award for her years of writing the most popular books women read and to deliver a banquet speech. She had labored long and hard with the decision, having been tempted to send her editor or publicist in her place. But pressure from the publisher and from her friends—all but Elly, actually—had induced her to accept the invitation personally. Now she was having second thoughts. She was scared to death of them. She didn't want to overhear their snotty remarks; she knew she was called the Ice Queen. She thought maybe it was Barbara Ann who had let that slip. Although her books sold better than anyone's, she couldn't take two steps without hearing that they were badly written. Bewildered by her good fortune, people were compelled to find all that was wrong with them.

"I hope so," she said without warmth. "If there's no schedule conflict."

FIVE

"What do you mean, *schedule conflict?*" Barbara demanded. This was *just* what she expected—for Sable to bail out on her without a thought! Without remorse! "You made a commitment to that group and now you've got Elaine Hardy all worked up. She's going to start making phone calls the minute she gets back to her hotel, panicked that her banquet speaker might be standing them up."

"Who is she going to call?" Sable asked.

"Probably everyone on her conference committee, getting them to start looking for an alternate. There are eight hundred people scheduled for that conference. There might be a couple of hundred attending just because *you're* going to be there."

"Why?" Sable said. "What do they want?"

Barbara sighed and shook her head. "They don't want as much as you think, Sable. They'd all feel a lot friendlier toward you if you'd get down off your high horse and admit you're one of them. You just need to say a few words about how seriously you take your writing, or how hard it is, or how difficult it is to get published in the beginning...something that makes them nod their heads in agreement. Why do you think you're so much better than they are?"

"Are you so sure that's what I think?" she asked.

"That's what you make people *feel*. They can't understand why you won't socialize. Gather with other writers. You're not shy, we all know that. You don't lack confidence. You haven't been burned by any of them—you've been *admired*."

"Oh, please. They say awful things about me all the time."

"You bring it on! You won't take their calls! You won't accept their invitations. You're cold, Sable. You'll clear your calendar for a dinner halfway around the world if the *right* people are going to be there, but you can't be bothered to say a few words to the very people who *buy* your books!"

"I do all my socializing for business. I sell millions of books a year—I can't start meeting with small groups of readers. I'd never get any work done!"

"Jesus. I'm at the end of my rope."

"All right, all right," Elly said. "That's not what we're here for."

"Don't you ever get annoyed by this, Elly? The way Sable refuses to participate?"

"Not everyone is attracted to these large guilds of writers, Barbara. I think there's good reasons for either bent—the group person, the private person. But there's something else I asked you to stay for. If you can put all your other squabbles aside for a while."

"We aren't squabbling, Elly," Sable said. And she almost said, "Barbara's safer in that group than I am—she doesn't threaten them." But she stayed silent on that matter.

It was just after eight. The caterers were finishing up in the kitchen and loading the tables and chairs into their vans. The guests had all departed, as had Don Marshall, David and Sarah. Mike Vaughan and his sons left Barbara behind when Elly asked if she could stay to discuss the disposition of some of Gabby's personal effects. Beth would drop her off later. Now they sat in Sable's living room, the French doors open to allow Elly's cigarette smoke to escape from the plush but sterile decor of that room. Elly had her coffee, Beth her diet soda, Sable her tea, and Barbara, a glass of wine.

"I have a letter," Elly said, beginning to dig around in her enormous purse and withdrawing a long, slim envelope. The women went suddenly still, shocked by this. In the five days since Gabby's death, no one had mentioned a will or a letter. "I'll just read it.

'Dear Elly. If you're reading this, I'm gone. It must have been unexpected, and I apologize for leaving you and upsetting you. Don't get the impression I knew I was going. I rewrite this letter to you every New Year's Day. It's part of my annual tradition of starting the year by organizing my desk and files.

"'Forgive me for not going on and on about how I've loved you—how valuable a friend you've been to me. I hope I showed in my life what I'm omitting in my death. Likewise, tell the girls I treasure them. If I could give you each a gift, it would be thus. To you, Elly, I would give a garden of virgins for you to tend and plow.'

"Hmmph," Elly snorted. "I've no idea whatsoever what that means. Maybe she was drunk when she wrote this. 'To Sable,'" Elly read on, "'I would bequeath the Girl Scout Creed—she would have made a great Girl Scout leader. To Barbara Ann, our love expert, I would dedicate 1 Corinthians, 13, my favorite chapter in the Bible. And to Beth, I would give a laser sword, like the one they had in *Star Wars.*' Fine," Elly said. "If you can figure that out, more power to you.

"'The purpose of this letter, Elly, is to ask an enormous favor of you. I have often wondered what would become of this office. The papers I've collected, received, written, condemned to dead files, kept handy in current files to deal with when there's time. Don wouldn't have the first idea what to do. David is too busy making his life, and Sarah isn't worldly enough. And here I am, sitting in the middle of mountains of junk—some of it precious and some of it idiotic. I can't think of anyone who would know better than you which is which. Since it's something I wouldn't even want to do for myself, I know what a monumental task it is. If you look through and decide the best fate is a match, so be it. Alternatively, if you find something of value, I'm sure you would be the one to recognize it and know what to do. Believe me, there is no hidden gem in here that I know of. But this letter is an official codicil. I am asking you to be my literary executor. It will be by your discretion that letters, papers, stories, contracts, diaries, etc., be burned or passed along to someone else or published.

"'I have a suggestion, though you are by no means obligated to take it, or even to share this letter, for that matter. You might ask Barbara Ann, Beth and Sable to participate, to help you sort and file and decide. I know everyone is terribly busy, on deadline, committed to personal lives and families, work and obligations. Maybe the job would be quicker and more efficient if each one took a drawer? Don will want to sell the house and furniture…give the things or the money to the kids. But if there's any memorabilia left behind by Sarah and David that you or one of the girls would like to keep, I know of no one better to wrestle it away from Dr. Don than you. And don't let him give you any shit. He's never known anything about my work.

"'Thank you. I feel better knowing you're in charge. I'll see you again. Love, Gabby.'"

There was a deep silence, some clinking of dishes in the background as the caterers packed up the last of their goods. Only Elly had had the opportunity to consider the impact of this request or to puzzle out the meanings behind Gabby's special gifts. Sable was the first to comment.

"I guess you read us the letter because you'd like our help."

"I think so. Not because I'm intimidated by the chore—I could do it. But because I might not recognize the value of certain things Gabby's been saving. She wrote in so many veins, tried her hand at such a variety of things. There are manuscripts that can go to the Special Collections Library at the university—Berkeley. Original pieces that she was unable to sell or complete that we should read. Letters from fans and writers from all over the world. She was a compulsive letter writer. Gabby was in touch with Pulitzer and Nobel Prize winners. Her letter collection alone is probably worth a fortune—the names are staggering.

"For myself, I'm thinking of doing a biography. Not because she was famous. Quite the opposite. Because she was both typical and extraordinary. It wouldn't be a biography of Gabby Marshall, per se, but rather a study of an American writer. A woman writer."

"Eleanor, that's brilliant," Beth said.

"Not a popular piece, Beth. A scholarly study. A retrospective. It could be quite dull. I don't envision any earth-shattering or scandalous revelations."

"It couldn't be dull," she said. "It would be wonderful. So apt. She was so special. Her accomplishments were highly individual. In a lot of ways she was the average—not so many awards, selling in the midlist range, teaching or speaking to make ends meet, just another woman writer, facing all the same challenges as any woman in the arts, supporting her family in the arts. But her acquaintances ranged from Chiam Potok to...to...me! I don't think it's understood how extraordinary is the life of *any* American woman writer."

Eleanor stared at Beth for a long moment, mute, remembering that Beth had given an album of works to Gabby as a birthday gift a couple of years before. Included were the covers of old, out-of-print books and some of their reviews. The research into Gabby's literary life had been thorough and intense in order for her to have done that. "Exactly so," Elly finally said. "I need reminding sometimes. I almost forgot you took your postgraduate studies in library science."

Beth's gaze instantly dropped. Her shyness was such a burden.

"Of course, I haven't decided yet," Elly continued.

"Then you would want a lot of Gabby's papers, while you decide," Beth said, her gaze lifting immediately. As long as she was not the subject, she could participate fully.

"Yes," Elly replied, clearing her throat. "Don gave me this letter. Gabby was more organized than she lets on. Don knew exactly where she kept her insurance papers, bank account information and regular monthly bills, the file on her house and her car, her will—for the kids, you know. Right off, that rattled David, that Don should do what he considers to be *his* job. This letter was with the will. I read it and explained it to Don and the kids. They were in the midst of a power struggle over who should play executor. Sarah and David thought it should be David, Don thought he should do the work and pass the worldly goods on to the kids. It was the first time in my memory Don didn't have someone in mind to do it for him.

"In any case, he showed excellent judgment in offering the whole ordeal to David, who in his turn, showed excellent judgment in giving it back to Don." Eleanor shook her head. "David might want the control, but he's doing his residency and shouldn't take it on. And Don may be an ass, but he's fair. He loved her to the end."

"He had a funny way of showing it," Barbara said. "Gabby told me he was having affairs when they were practically newlyweds."

"Don's always been self-important. His relationship with his kids is a testimony to that. The minute either of them makes a decision he can't personally endorse, he begins to harangue them and issue ultimatums. Gabby was the only person who knew how to deal with him. She always let him think everything he did for them was his idea, even though she'd planted it. It was some Southern thing.

"In any case, I told them about her request and took a very brief look at her office. Three file cabinets, boxes in the garage that are labeled books, manuscripts, letters, et ctera, sixteen bookshelves... It had never seemed that many when I was there. Did it to you? Sixteen *sets* of shelves. Everywhere. She had a bookshelf in the bathroom, for God's sake. Writers," she said, shaking her head again. "All compulsive.

"I think Don and the kids are genuinely relieved that they don't have to deal with Gabby's office, her papers. And I'm more than willing. But I can't do it now, I told them. I have to finish the semester. It's not going to be a weekend job. That's just as well. They're too upset to deal with all the other things Gabby left behind. Just going through her dishes, clothes, furniture and odds and ends is something Sarah isn't ready to face. And as I said, David needs to concentrate on work. I suggested a compromise and they leapt at it. I suggested they have someone get the perishable food out, give the place a thorough cleaning and close it up, as is. Don can hire a gardener to keep the yard manageable for later, when it's either sold or one of the kids takes it. The kids aren't desperate for money at the moment because Gabby had a life insurance policy. They'll each get a tidy little check. In a couple of months, it will be easier for Sarah and David to go through their mother's things. And after the semester, say, in June, I can begin on her office. If the house is left intact, water, phone and electric on, furniture in place, I'm thinking of moving in there as my summer sabbatical. To sift through the paper."

"Moving in?" Sable asked, shocked.

Eleanor shrugged. "I can't think of a more efficient way to do it. Despite Gabby's admission that this is a large task, my reason is more practical. Gabby would understand if I simply made piles and ran a fast glance through her accumulation, but I'm interested in what she has pigeonholed away. Some of her earlier work, I feel, was overlooked. She did some very courageous and vital writing in those years as a journalist abroad. She was one of the first to take on some of those subjects. As a woman, she was a pioneer. Besides, if I move in temporarily, I'll be there to lend moral support to David and Sarah when they go through their mother's things. And I'll be in residence if any of you has time to stop by and help."

"Won't it be hard for you?" Barbara Ann asked. "Living in Gabby's house, going through her things?"

Eleanor briefly closed her eyes. She'd lost her mother when she was twelve, her father when she was nineteen. She had a brief, catastrophic marriage in her twenties. She had one older sister with whom she was close, but they lived on opposite coasts and within opposite lives, Margaret being married for forty years, the mother of three and a grandmother. Elly had admitted to her alcoholism when she was forty-two after it had nearly ruined her career and left her academic reputation in tatters. She'd redeemed herself and been sober now sixteen years. It was not as easy a task as she let people think. But nothing, nothing, had been as difficult as losing Gabby. Eleanor's life had been hard at best. None of these women could possibly know the loneliness of being a dowdy, overly serious, spinster academic. And now, it would be lonelier still.

"You have no idea," she answered breathlessly. Then, stronger, "But, as I said, it's practical. If I'm going to do the job, I'm going to do it right."

"I'll be better able to help in June," Beth said. "I have a book due the fifteenth of May. And if you're living there..."

"I have one due in May and one due in September," Barbara said.

"Don't worry, Barbara Ann," Elly consoled. "This isn't an obligation. You also have the largest family to contend with. Gabby wouldn't have expected you to neglect your family or your work."

"Would you be offended if I didn't make a full commitment? If I promise to help what little I can? I've got to finish that September book...and if I have revisions..."

Sable reached across the deep, white sofa and put a hand over Barbara's. "Your work and your family come first, Barbara. You have more on your plate than any one of us. Don't add guilt to it. We already find it hard to believe you can do all you do."

It wasn't unusual for Sable to offer warmth and understanding. One of her rare gifts was that she could do that even with someone who, just a few minutes earlier, had been chewing her ass and accusing her of arrogance. But Barbara didn't take any special note of Sable's gesture. In fact, she wanted to snap back a question. *Are you going to do that damned conference or aren't you?* She wisely did not open that subject again. Instead, she nodded.

Eleanor looked at Sable and the eyes of Beth and Barbara followed. "Of course I'll be there," Sable said. "I'm not planning any kind of retrospective, but I care about Gabby's work as much as any of you. Maybe I can get something that's out of print looked at again. There could be a few bucks added to her estate for the kids."

"Good," Elly said. "I'm glad you're all going to have input. Gabby had more faith in me than I have in myself. I'll look at my class schedule, talk to the kids and give you an exact date for when I'm going to open the house." She sighed. "Maybe in a couple of months, this won't seem so emotional."

"Aren't we going to see each other?" Beth asked, moving to the edge of her chair with a panicked rise to her voice. She was answered by indecisive, mute stares. Her eyes began to water. "Oh God, don't tell me we're not going to see each other!"

Elly took off her glasses and began cleaning them with a napkin. "Beth, I don't feel like critiquing manuscripts. And I'm not very social to begin with." Her voice sounded tired. Worn. She was feeling her age; her spirit was injured.

"I don't care! We don't have to read to each other! Can we have lunch? Dinner? Meet for coffee or something?"

"Oh, Beth, of course," Sable said quickly, recognizing the fear in the young woman's voice—another thing she should have foreseen, but in her own grief had not thought of. Elly had the college; Barbara Ann had that brood and many friends—her long-distance bills could be staggering—Sable's life appeared hectic and full, despite the fact that it was filled with many acquaintances and business associates, and no friends. But Beth *needed* them. She had only her husband, and he was often out of town. Her family was in Kansas, and she was so painfully shy. Sable had guessed that Beth's life with her pilot husband was lacking. Troubled. "We can get together. At least I can, I know that. What would you like to do? Lunch? Dinner one night?"

Beth visibly relaxed. Now that she'd made her panicked plea, she was unable to go the next step, take control and arrange their meeting. Everyone waited.

"Anything," she said quietly. And everyone knew that someone else would have to decide.

Barbara was tired. She sighed.

Elly was unmotivated. She didn't want to think anymore.

"Okay," Sable said, "I've got that conference in New York next month...it's actually three weeks from now. Let's meet for dinner two weeks from Tuesday. Maybe you can give me some pointers on my speech." Barbara's mouth dropped open and she stared at Sable. "Yes, Barbara Ann, I'll go. You and Elly are both going, so I'll go. And I'll be charming. And you can call that friend of yours at her hotel tonight and tell her that you spoke to me and I said I wasn't expecting anything to come up. Only an emergency would keep me away."

"Thank God," Barbara said, hand to her breast. She had been the one, after all, to deliver Sable. She would stand humiliated if Sable suddenly reneged.

"Let's meet in Fair Oaks anyway, hmm? It's halfway between me and the rest of you. Beth, pick a place. Let's have a nice dinner. Let us know where."

"I'll have to check Jack's schedule. You know he likes me to be home when he's home. He's gone so much...."

Sable wanted to ask what would happen if she simply made her own plans, without checking with *Jack*. Instead, she said, "Any evening that week is okay with me, if you need to change it."

After a short discussion of possibilities, Sable was called into the kitchen to sign off on the caterers. Barbara Ann and Beth were heading out the kitchen door. Elly lingered, waiting for Sable to conclude her business. When she finally closed the door on the caterers and turned to Elly, the older woman seemed to sag as she leaned against the kitchen counter.

"I'm worried about you," Sable said. "This has really taken its toll."

"Don't worry about me. I'm tougher than I look."

"Those were beautiful words you said for her. Will you do that for me someday?"

Elly seemed to deflate. She let out a whoosh of air and her face took on more lines. "I hope to God that never becomes necessary! I don't plan to outlast you, too!"

"Well, in the event you do, promise me there will be no biography."

"I wouldn't dream of it. Why would I? You're writing your own life. Listen, I have something for you. I didn't say anything because there were no individual letters for Beth or Barbara Ann." Wearily, she pushed herself off the counter and headed back for the living room. Eleanor did not walk so much as clomp. Once there, she simply reached to the floor to retrieve her heavy purse from where she'd left it. She flung the strap over her shoulder before digging around in it. She presented an envelope.

"Did you read it?" Sable asked.

"No. It was sealed. In with her vital papers, like mine. I asked Don to let me give it to you personally. You know, because they didn't get one."

"Do you want to wait a minute? So I can show it to you?"

"How do you know you'll want to? It might say something like, 'Be sure to trick Elly into taking her Geritol every day.' No, not now. I'm exhausted by Gabby's last wishes. Funny, she never asked much in life. I've got to get going. It's a long drive."

"You can stay the night if you'd like."

Elly, who was never demonstrative, patted Sable's cheek. "Thank you, dear. But no. I want my own bed."

"Elly, I had some trouble here today." The older woman's eyes widened briefly. She hadn't any idea. "I had my security guy here, serving drinks. I had no idea what to expect. Most of these people were complete strangers to me. And I don't usually open my house to so many. I found a reporter in my office. He snuck in on the pretense of attending Gabby's memorial, and went into my closed office. He had a tiny little camera. He was taking pictures of the inside of my house."

"Oh God," Elly said in sympathy. "The rigors of fame."

"I guess that's what made me testy, made me behave as though I was threatening not to attend Barbara Ann's stupid conference. I couldn't believe it."

Elly shook her head. "Sable, I'm not surprised. I'm sorry, but not surprised. You've insulated yourself so well that, while you're safe from one kind of crackpot, you draw the attention of those god-awful starmongers. You've let yourself become too damn mysterious. And unattainable. By not pandering to them at all, you're a challenge. They're looking for a story."

"What do you suggest I do?"

"I don't know," she shrugged. "This is not my area of expertise. Ask your publicist? Sic your lawyers on him? I just don't know." Eleanor's eyes were droopy; she licked her dry lips. Sable felt panicked by what appeared to be Elly's deterioration. Eleanor was failing, looking sixty-eight instead of fifty-eight, and Sable needed her. "I've got to go home," Elly said. "Call me if you think there's any way I can help."

"Call me," Sable said, "if there's any way I can help you."

"Sadly, I don't think there's anything anyone can do for me. Like Gabby used to say, 'When I'm tired, sad and heartbroken, I take a rest and then I come back into myself and maybe write about it.'"

"She said that about him, didn't she, Elly? John Shelby. When she quit traveling the world, it wasn't because she was done with that kind of writing. It was because she knew she'd never have the man she loved, wasn't it?"

"It was all of it. She told him that she'd had enough, that she needed to be home with her children and couldn't stomach any more heartbreaking stories, that she couldn't maintain her low profile so that his wife wouldn't catch on. She had delivered him an ultimatum—to make good on his promises, or end the affair. That was the note on which they left it. You can imagine her pain. Which she bore alone, he having been married with children."

"You were there. She wasn't alone."

"I was very little help, I'm afraid. Who would listen to an old spinster's advice on the pain of lost love? I only hope I can persevere as well as Gabby did."

"You haven't been tempted...to...you know—"

"Drink? Oh Sable, you pure soul. I'm tempted all the time. Ninety percent of the time drinking worked tolerably well for me. It was that goddamned ten percent that got me into trouble. But don't worry. I won't drink. I don't think they distilled enough gin last year to numb the loneliness Gabby's left me with. And you? How are you dealing with this?"

"I don't know," she said honestly. "I never feel anything but fear. It's the only emotion I can actually identify. I'm afraid without her." Sable shrugged. "I was afraid before. And now I'm afraid of one more thing."

Eleanor gave a wan smile. "I know. And I don't imagine we're the only two. I'll call you within the week to find out about our dinner plans."

Sable stood in the kitchen for a long time after Elly left, looking at the precious script of Gabby's hand on the envelope. There was a light tapping at the kitchen door and Jeff Petross let himself in. "Everyone's gone and we checked the grounds. How you doin'?"

"Tired. But okay."

"I don't think you have to worry about that little wimp we threw outta here. I mean, you don't have to worry that he'll come back. I can stay over...."

"No, no. I'm sure you have better things to do."

He shrugged. "I'm free. If you'd feel better. I know sometimes you feel unsafe. You don't have to have a reason. It's hell being all edgy. Better you should sleep."

"Thanks, but I'll just lock up."

"Beep me if you change your mind. Want me to check around inside?"

She gave a sheepish shrug, she wouldn't mind. He smiled and walked past her, into the house. She waited in the kitchen. She could hear him in the distance, opening and closing windows and doors. It was a big house; it took him ten minutes.

Sable knew, had known for three years, that Jeff had some unspoken tender feelings toward her. He took care of her as though she were more than just another client. His eyes were soft when he talked to her and occasionally he would give her arm a squeeze of reassurance. He made himself personally available to her every need, armed her with his pager number, encouraged her to rely on him and had long ago worked it into the conversation that he was unmarried and not seeing anyone. He took care that his behavior was professional and proper; he never made any advances. But she knew. He knew she knew. And there had been times she'd been tempted to find out for herself just how deep his feelings ran, despite the fact that she did not trust men and felt she had no room in her life for a romantic relationship.

But not tonight of all nights. Not while Gabby's letter waited.

"Everything's secure, Sable," he said.

"I really appreciate that you do this yourself, Jeff. I know you could just send one of your guys."

"I consider this job one of my perks," he said, smiling again. "Try to get some rest. You don't look tired, but I can imagine."

"I also appreciate that you never make me feel foolish," she said.

"I don't think you are. Like I told you, I'll stay over if it will help you sleep better."

She shook her head. "You're a nice guy, Jeff."

"You're a nice lady, Sable. Lock this one here and you're all set."

Sable saved the letter for a while. She locked the door, assured herself that Dorothy and Art's light was on in their little cottage, retired to her upstairs suite and slowly peeled off her beige silk suit. She got into bed before opening the letter. She could see it wasn't very long. And it was dated September 19, four years old.

Dear Sable,

I hope it's been so long that you've forgotten the

day. We met, the five of us, and Barbara Ann was particularly tenacious in her questions about your life, your past and the history of our friendship. You and Elly and I had a brief discussion—which verged on an argument. The subject was your invented past. I wondered if it was good for you to carry around the weight of all that pretending. But you were adamant as usual. You said something I just can't let go. You said, "I'm better as I am than as I was."

No one on earth admires Sable Tennet more than I do, but there's something I want you to know. I admire that smart little Helen, too. You may have filed down some rough edges and refined your character, but you haven't created a whole new person. You only think you have.

I love you like a mother, sister, godmother, best friend. I love what you've done with your life, your work, your ambition, your spirit. But I don't love what you've done with your history, Helen. You can't wipe people out like that. Without the guts, smarts and strength of Helen, you could not have written as the hope of so many women readers.

I hope that by keeping Helen hidden you don't bring yourself undue pain. Helen deserves your respect and gratitude. Releasing her could help and inspire others.

You are by far the warmest, most sensitive, most generous person alive, and you keep it secret. Only Elly and I know a fraction of what you've really accomplished in your life. Please, be generous to yourself. Give yourself your due. Take pride not only in who you've become, but where you've come from. Be yourself. Your wonderful self.

With deepest love,
Gabby

Sable held the letter against her heart. She read it again and then held it against her cheek. She covered her face with it, breathing deeply, hoping to get a whiff of Gabby's smell. But it smelled like paper. Then she laid it on her lap, smoothing it slowly with loving hands.

Thank you, Gabby, she thought. I know you were always proud of me. But not everyone would be impressed with the life I led and the terrible mistakes I made. Not everyone would admire the willpower required to change from Helen into Sable. In fact, most people would gasp in horror. Some would even be delighted to know I wasn't such a big damn deal but really just a poor, stupid girl with unforgivably bad judgment. Gabby, Gabby, I wouldn't feel better unloading the secret. How to face the snickers from people who've always felt so inferior to me—though I never invited that—and have been waiting for *years* for my comeuppance! Or their pity? Or the sly, superior smiles of all the writers who have been asking themselves what's so goddamn special about Sable Tennet? No, no, no.

There was one thing Sable had understood from the beginning—people think that if you have money and success, you can't suffer pain and humiliation. She knew; she had believed that once herself.

She slept through the night without waking—for the first time in days. When she woke, the letter was under her cheek and the ink was badly smeared, but still legible. Upon rising and looking in the mirror, she found ink on her cheek and chin and temple. She had cried in her sleep.

SIX

It was already 9:00 p.m. and the dinner she'd gone to such lengths to prepare was drying out when Beth heard the sound of the garage door sliding open; her husband was finally home. She didn't let the lateness of the hour discourage her. She was married to a pilot and all kinds of things, from mechanical problems to bad weather, could delay flights. He was supposed to have been home at four and she *wished* he had called, but maybe he couldn't.

Of course, *she* had checked on his flight. It had arrived on time.

But never mind all that. She quickly lit the candles on the dining-room table just as she heard Jack come in. He dropped his brain-bag, suitcase and hang-up right inside the door. "Oh, Christ. What's all this?" he asked, looking through tired, reddened eyes into the dining room.

"Just a nice dinner," she said. "Would you like a drink first?"

"Yeah, why not. Sure. I stopped off for a drink, but I could always use one more."

He hung his jacket on the doorknob and pulled off his shiny black boots while Beth fetched glass, ice and scotch. His tie and epaulets had already disappeared and his shirt looked the worse for wear. She caught a whiff of perfume. Sometimes the flight attendants were squashed into the van with the pilots and their perfume clung to Jack's coat. She ignored it. The sight of him, his tall handsomeness, never ceased to make her shiver with desire. He had a boyish look for a man just over forty. With his tall frame, solid chest and legs, drop-dead smile and full head of thick brown hair, he was more man than she thought she'd ever have a crack at. And he was so playful—that was one of the best things about him. Of course, she wished he'd play with her more than with all his pilot pals. Or whomever.

"I hope this candlelight dinner isn't all about a prelude to hot sex, babe, 'cause I'm shot. My body doesn't know what day it is or what time it is. I could fall asleep without food, really, but…"

"No, it's all ready, Jack. And don't worry, I'll let you catch up on your sleep. Then once you're well rested…"

"It isn't our anniversary or anything, is it?" he asked, joking. He sipped his drink and suddenly the smell of perfume mixed with scotch and something musky made her nauseated. It seemed like a lot of perfume for just one van ride over five hours ago. And a lot of scotch for *a drink*. She knew that to bring up the subject would only delay the discussion she had in mind; she dare not make any accusing remarks. It's just that it bothered her so. To have another woman's smell on him, however innocent.

"Would you like to change?" she asked. "Get comfortable? And I'll get the food on the table." *Maybe get that slut's stink off you?*

"I guess," he shrugged. He grabbed one of his bags, pushed his hat back on his head in that sexy, devil-may-care way he had, and took his drink with him to the bedroom.

He'd been gone for six days and hadn't even kissed her when he came in the door. He was five hours late, had stopped off for a drink—or six?—and hadn't even bothered to call her. But Beth wasn't discouraged. She couldn't *let* herself be discouraged.

There were a few things Jack could almost always do. Eat, drink and make love. Even when he said he wasn't very hungry and was probably too tired to get it up. Beth assumed by the way he dug into his dinner that if she didn't waste too much time in the kitchen cleaning up afterward, she might catch him before he fell asleep. It could be one of the best ever, by her way of thinking. Because Beth had something on her mind.

"What's that sneaky little smile about?" he asked her.

"Oh, I don't know. I've missed you, that's all."

"You have? Well, I'm all yours for the next few days. I'm going up to the lake a couple of times—but you'll be working then anyway. Except for honey-dos, I should be pretty much hanging around here." Jack always referred to his chores as "honey-dos" but in fact, they had nothing to do with Beth. She did everything around the house except bill paying; Jack's "chores" would consist of upkeep on his Mercedes sports car, boat, lake lot, investments, et cetera.

"Maybe I could go to the lake with you?" she suggested.

"Naw. I'm just going to change the oil on the boat motor, maybe cut down the shrubbery on the lot, stuff like that. This is really good, babe. You sure are good at screwing up a chicken."

"I wouldn't mind going with you even if you're just

doing that stuff. Jack, I've been so lonesome lately. Since Gabby died."

"Who? Oh, you mean that woman you knew?" He shoveled in another mouthful.

Beth had become a master at overlooking all the little painful things Jack did or said, but on this subject it was hard. Could he really not remember who Gabby was? Or how important she'd been to Beth? "Gabby was a very, very close friend of mine. I loved her very much."

"Oh-ho, careful, babe. You're starting to sound a little, you know, lezzie...." He laughed at himself. Beth was insulted. Hurt. And it caused her to be a bit reckless.

"You know, I've been thinking. I'm ready to have a baby." His fork stopped moving but he didn't look up. Beth forged ahead bravely. "I've decided it doesn't really matter much that *you're* not ready. What difference does it make? I'm alone here all the time anyway. I can't even go to the lake with you. All I want is to be a little less alone. I want to have a baby."

"We've been over this," he said. The humor and playfulness was gone from his voice.

"You knew when we got married that someday I'd want a baby. You said we'd talk about it later and we've been putting it off for seven years. I'm thirty-two. I'm an aunt more times than I can count. I'm—"

"Not now, Beth. I'm tired."

"I've always gone along with what you want so we can have all this time to ourselves, but there's no *we*. No *our*. It's you going places, having fun, having friends, and I don't do anything but stay home and write. I'm almost a total recluse. Gabby was one of my only friends. And she's dead. Can't you even imagine how I might be feeling?"

"Look," he said, putting down his fork, picking up his drink. "I'm sorry about your friend, but it doesn't mean it's time to have a baby. That won't help you get over it any faster. And I'm not ready." He drained his drink.

"You'll never be ready," she said while he was drinking. "You can't control everything, you know."

He lowered the glass to the table with threatening slowness. When Beth looked into his angry eyes she jumped, but she kept telling herself not to back down this time. She was going to get what she wanted for once. It was her money, after all, that paid for most of his expensive toys. And trips. And hobbies. And probably friends.

"Just what do you mean by that?" he asked.

"I could stop using birth control and you'd never know the difference," she told him. "I'm getting a little tired of working all the time, never having any family life, never having any fun, never having any... I could have a baby and he'd be here six months before you even noticed!"

Jack pushed himself away from the table. "Didn't I tell you I was tired? Didn't I tell you I hardly had the energy to eat a meal? But you have to yammer at me about this now?"

Seeing such anger in his eyes caused her own to well up with tears. It was hard to stop and start things with Jack, especially when she never knew what to expect from him. She'd been planning this discussion for days, precisely because he was due home at four and should be rested. He'd been flying a San Francisco-New York-London pattern with a long layover in New

York before the last day of flying. That should help him unscrew his body clock and get on U.S. time again. Then, after a five-hour flight in the midday from the East Coast, he should be able to sit down to a good dinner and have a pleasant evening with his wife.

He wasn't too tired because of his job. He was too tired because he didn't come home from his job. He'd stopped off somewhere, had several drinks and probably a large meal, maybe a few other activities, and wasn't in the mood for this discussion because he was *never* in the mood for this discussion.

There was nothing she could do about it. She'd just have to try again some other day, sometime when he appeared to be a little less testy.

"Sorry," she muttered. Her eyes downcast, she picked up her plate and flatware and headed for the kitchen. It tasted bad anyway; she wasn't going to get anywhere with Jack tonight.

As she passed his chair she tripped over his foot. The plate sailed across the kitchen floor, bits of chicken and rice and peas scattering everywhere. The wind was knocked out of her with a loud *whoosh* and she couldn't breathe. She'd hit her chin on the floor and it began to throb instantly. Before she could even think about getting up she felt the unmistakable pressure of his foot on her back. He pressed down hard between her shoulder blades. She was afraid she'd never get another breath.

"But you're not going to do that, are you, Beth?"

"Ugh-ugh," she exhaled. He bent over and grabbed a handful of hair, pulling her head up. He banged her face against the floor a couple of times. Hard.

"We have bills!" he barked.

All bills for his boat and property and sports car.... She

pinched her eyes closed. She was afraid of what he'd
done to her face.

He let go of her hair, removed his foot from her back
and with his stocking-foot in her ribs, he rolled her
over. It took a second before she could take a breath;
she wheezed air into her lungs. Her eyes were glassy
with tears, her head throbbing and her nose bleeding.
"I'm thorry," she said in a coarse whisper. "All I
wanted wath to talk about it."

"But I'm not ready!"

Crying soundlessly, she crawled out of the dining
room and into the kitchen. Still on her hands and
knees, she gathered up pieces of the scattered food and
scooped the debris onto the plate. Drops of blood from
her nose fell onto the floor as she cleaned. Drops of
tears fell as well. She was a pathetic little cripple. Defeated. Again.

"I'm going to bed," he said. "I'm going to *sleep.*
Don't wake me up and don't pull anything. You hear
me?"

He didn't wait for a reply; he just left her there. Then
in a moment he was back, standing over her, staring
down at her. "I don't know why you have to take a
perfectly nice evening and fuck it all up," he said.
"Things were just real nice and then you had to start
pushing all my buttons again. Jesus, sometimes you
are such a stupid bitch."

He left for good that time.

Things were just real nice, she thought miserably. *Real
nice....* Let's see, what does Jack consider nice? He
comes home five hours late, the stench of his last
woman still on him, he's half-drunk, completely insensitive, planning what he's going to do with his days off,

spending my hard-earned money, making it clear I'm not included....

Beth held ice on her nose and chin for a while until the throbbing and bleeding stopped. She didn't think he'd actually broken either one. She didn't want to look at herself until the initial redness and swelling had gone down. This was something she'd learned—if you looked at your injuries too soon, you could really scare yourself.

She sobbed while she cleaned the dishes, but quietly, noiselessly. Her expectations were shattered. She cried at her own foolishness because she never should have had expectations in the first place. Jack wasn't going to give her *anything* she wanted. He wasn't going to ever want a family, and he'd knocked her around so many times on even less provocation, she should have expected this reaction. But somehow she hadn't. Somehow she'd allowed herself to think that this time he would say, "Okay, you're right, it's time to have a family...." Where had such insanity come from?

This was Beth's shame, that he abused her in every possible way and she still wanted him, still believed in him. Oh, not right away after a beating—she wasn't that far down the tubes. But by the end of the week she'd be thinking like a woman who had never been slapped. He was as predictable as a sunset and yet she couldn't see that he would do it again and again and again. It still crushed her that he had other women, still surprised her when he failed to act like a loving husband, and still amazed her each time he did some horrendously selfish or brutal thing with no regard at all for her feelings. And if all that was not insane enough, she still loved him. How in the world could that be?

Because I am mentally ill, she thought as she wept through her kitchen chores.

Earlier that evening she had talked to her mother on the phone and learned that one of her sisters-in-law was pregnant. "This will be grandchild number twenty-one," Elba Sherman pronounced. "Deborah, the career woman. Here she is, thirty-six, spoiled rotten, and now she's throwing up every morning. Remember when she used to get so mad at me for asking when the babies were coming? She called them 'Catholic' questions!"

Beth wanted a baby so bad she thought she would die from it. Her entire family thought she and Jack had been trying for years, but the truth was that Jack forbade her to stop using her birth control. Her little secret was that she'd been flushing her pills down the toilet for the past four months. If she could just get pregnant, she'd leave him and go back to her family in Kansas City, Missouri. The Sherman clan—Mama and Daddy, three married brothers, three married sisters and one brother-priest—would enfold her and her child into their lives and protect her.

Elba Sherman couldn't understand having a daughter who would have such trouble having a baby. "I was afraid to wash my unders with your daddy's, I was that fertile. God will bless you soon, sweetheart. Maybe you should go to one of those, you know, getting-pregnant specialists. It's nothing to be ashamed of. Lots of women go to them."

Mama, Mama, why do I hang on? Why do I stay with him, letting him hurt me like he does? What's wrong with me?

Beth's greatest quandary was what to do about the baby once she got herself secretly pregnant. She couldn't bear the thought of telling her family that Jack was abusive, but if she didn't, they would naturally encourage her to reconcile with him. No, she couldn't stay with him! Could she? It had been a long time since she'd suggested counseling. Maybe he was more agreeable to an idea like that now. Maybe—

She rubbed her chin where it had slammed against the floor. The hurt was still fresh and brought with it a fresh crop of tears—and a fresh bout of reality. *Jack's not going to any counselor! He's not going to let you have any baby! You need to get out of here, you big dope. So what if you love him? Your love is sick! Pretend he's dead and you just can't have him. Just go, you idiot! What is the matter with you?*

She had fantasies of stabbing him with his girlfriend's letter opener, hiding him in the trunk of his car, parking it in the long-term lot at the airport…. She wished she could dip his toothbrush in the toilet every morning, but somehow she was too decent. He was really such a cocksucker. How did she manage to feel tenderness for him? What mental illness was this and why did no one else in her family have it?

She hoped her face wasn't bruised; she didn't want to have to hide out. She'd already met Barbara, Sable and Elly for dinner, but if something came up and there was a chance to get together, she'd hate to miss it on account of bruises. It had happened that way before. She'd told the girls she was going on a trip with Jack, just long enough for a black eye or swollen lip to vanish. It seemed possible Sable was catching on. On two occasions, as Beth sat in her small town house with telltale facial injuries, listening to her answering machine before picking up the phone, Sable had called— even though Beth had said she'd be out of town. Sable, calling, saying, "Beth, you there, honey? Can you pick up, Beth? Oh, that's right, you're on a trip with Jack, right? And I forgot! Well, you'll have to tell us all about London when you get back!"

And she would—tell them about London or Madrid or New York or Montreal. Though she'd never been there. She'd never been anywhere. She'd never once gone out of town with Jack even though she could fly first class for free. The only place she'd ever used her free-pass privileges was to go to Kansas City to visit her family. Alone.

When her dishes were done she didn't want to go to bed and lie beside him where she would vacillate between wanting him and wanting to kill him until she fell asleep. Instead, careful to be quiet, she went to her small office in the second upstairs bedroom. She'd go back to work, something she was able to lose herself in. When she was working she managed to temporarily not think about all the lies she told to cover herself and her bruises. Or the way her mother, her entire family for that matter, would be thoroughly ashamed and appalled that Beth had let this happen to herself.

Beth turned on the computer and located the last chapter she'd been working on. She had created a tough, cute and sassy private investigator named Chelsea Dolan who had persevered and gained popularity through five books. It was better all around, Beth thought, that she pour herself into Chelsea's problems rather than her own. After all, Chelsea actually had a shot at solving hers.

It appeared the victim had been murdered at his desk, as though the perpetrator had wanted his full attention. He could have been killed in a variety of venues; swimming pool, driving his car, eating his dinner, sleeping in his bed. So why, Chelsea wondered, did the killer seem to want it made clear he/she could enter the victim's home while he was working, engage him in conversation so nonthreatening that the deceased never even rose from his desk chair, never reached for his phone? And then, the killer obviously took his/her leisure in putting that bullet in the victim's head. A relatively tidy murder. A power play? Oh yes. Because the killer was a woman? Perhaps a woman who'd been wronged.

Good, she thought, rereading it. It would mean changing around the plot a little but she liked the idea that a woman who'd been wronged could get even. Her readers would like it, too.

She thought about Jack briefly. How sad it was that he'd never change, that they wouldn't have a family together. He didn't know how wonderful it could be, growing up in a happy family. It was his loss, she told herself. Poor guy. He'd never know what he was throwing away.

She went back to her manuscript. She changed the single bullet to the victim's head to four. *Blam Blam Blam Blam.* There. That's better.

It was a good thing Eleanor had been teaching for so many years and could go by rote, because the zing was definitely gone from her lectures. She assigned voluminous papers for every class—she had for years—but at present she was having trouble reading them. Typically, she could return these papers to her students with amazing speed. She wasn't doing so well at that now.

It had only been a few weeks since Gabby's death, she reminded herself. Things would just have to go as they go. She wouldn't apologize or explain to anyone. Of course, the worst of it wasn't getting behind in work, it was the completely muddled way she felt in her head. Her total lack of concentration. Her mind would suddenly wander off, sometimes in the middle of a sentence, and she would completely forget where she was and what she was doing.

She was attempting to read students' papers in the evening, when the doorbell rang. It was only seven, but she was already in her robe. She checked the peephole. She wouldn't open the door unless it was a neighbor in need. But it was Ben! Oh God, she thought. How could she have forgotten that it was Wednesday! Their television night, as he so delicately put it. She flung open the door. "Oh, Ben, my God, I entirely forgot!"

"Sometimes you're not very complimentary, Elly," he said, but he laughed good-naturedly. "That's okay."

"It's my brain. It's gone to mush."

"Oh now, I can't believe that. I brought us some butter brickle ice cream. Can I come in?"

"Yes, yes, of course," she said, holding the door for him. He held a couple of grocery bags. He always brought some sort of fruits or vegetables and ice cream. "But Ben, I'm not sure I'm good company tonight. Gabby, you know. I'm still so out of it."

"Maybe you need a shoulder rub, hmm? And a nice dish of butter brickle?"

"I don't know...."

"Well, let's see. If it turns out to be a bad night, that's okay. We could leave the television off and play some music. Or maybe we could play cards...to take your mind off things. Or, I could just go home."

"No, no, you've come all this way. Let's at least have some ice cream. Can you put on the coffee while I go change into something less comfortable?"

He kissed her cheek. "You don't have to change, Elly. You look fine to me."

She considered this for a moment. She *was* comfortable. But he was all cleaned up, wearing his best pale yellow shirt with his favorite burgundy sweater. His face was smoothly shaven and his sparse, thin hair slicked from his right ear to his left ear in an attempt to partially cover his bald head. "I'll change," she said. "Be right back."

How could she have forgotten about Ben? She had hardly even thought about him!

Elly had met Ben years ago. Seven or eight, she thought. He ran a roadside fruit and vegetable stand that she'd found off the main drag between Sacramento and Berkeley, which she drove three or four days a week. She did a lot of poking around in the small towns off the freeway for diversion. She took various exits just to experiment. On one of the heavily traveled back roads around Davis, Ben had his stand. From April till at least October, she stopped there regularly for one thing or another. After four or five years of that, he asked her if her husband enjoyed all his fresh goods. She told him she had no husband and he said he was sure surprised at that. Then he said he'd been widowed a long time—about five years at that point. Then began his series of invitations—to a church function, to a potluck thrown by his grown children at a daughter's house, to a movie, to dinner at a cafeteria-style restaurant.

Eleanor continually declined, but she did begin to learn more about Ben. He was a farmer and had been farming vegetables for years. When he reached the age of fifty-five and his wife was gone, he faced an impasse—he could turn the farm over to his two sons or sell to Del Monte. With the blessing of his children, he sold the farm, except for one generous garden. He still lived in the farmhouse in which he'd raised his five kids—now aged thirty to forty-one—and he sold most of his vegetables at his roadside stand. It was meant to be a hobby, but the "dad-gum thing" not only required as much time and effort as a general store, it also brought him a handsome living. His house was paid for, his money from Del Monte was invested, and he earned more than he needed from his vegetable stand, which was open from noon to six every day, seven days a week.

Ben was ordinary and homely. His nose was too large, his eyes a little small and his teeth slanted into his mouth. He dressed funny—mismatched colors and old, outdated double knits. For Elly to notice this suggested he was a fashion disaster—she was no Donna Karan herself. He was thick around the middle and short—about five-six and one-eighty. And although he liked to read, he wasn't at all book-smart. He'd finished high school but had never gone to college. He was a funny-looking, odd-dressing little old farmer who wasn't very bright.

But he was kind, tolerant and compassionate. Eleanor was accustomed to hearing even intelligent men in her age bracket make insensitive, bigoted remarks, but Ben was completely innocent and unprejudiced. Sweet. Gentle. Patient. The most guileless man she'd ever known.

He was probably rich. And for some reason he was very fond of Elly.

She had finally agreed to have dinner with him and they went to some family-style place near Davis. He had a healthy appetite and ate his meal quickly and seriously. But when he was finished eating, he talked. And asked questions. She learned all about each one of the five children and all his grandchildren. He asked her questions about the courses she taught—question after question after question—until he finally thought he understood. And then he would say his favorite saying, "Well, Elly, I think you're the most interesting woman I've ever in my life known."

They had started spending Wednesday and Saturday evenings together at her house about a year and a half ago. Since they had discovered they didn't like the same kind of restaurants, movies, books or sports, they found that what they did like to do together was talk. They watched television together, ate some ice cream, drank a little coffee, talked about their respective days and weeks and went to bed together where they enjoyed satisfying, if Victorian, sex. In the bedroom, lights off, under the covers. It was not imaginative or creative sex, just standard stuff—missionary position. For Elly it was, well, fabulous. Ben was obviously not an experienced lover, which she didn't mind, but he was efficient. He had no trouble maintaining an erection at the age of sixty-five. Somewhere along the line someone, probably his wife, had informed him about foreplay, at which he was both adept and unhurried. Then they would get up, Ben would dress and Elly would put on her robe, they would have a final cup of coffee together, finishing the pot, and Ben would drive home. Seven to eleven p.m., twice a week. If Elly had other plans, they wouldn't reschedule. If Ben had something come up, which happened less often, he would invite her along and she would decline.

There was only one hitch in their relationship. Elly had told *no one* about Ben, and although Ben had told his kids he was seeing a woman named Elly, she had never met any of them. Ben made it clear, in his sweet, innocent way, that he didn't understand this and it hurt his feelings. "I hope you're not ashamed of me, Elly."

To which she had replied, "Certainly not! I'm simply private, and would like our relationship to be." But that was only an excuse.

Elly changed into clean underwear, a knee-length cotton housedress and slip-on flats. When Ben was coming over she would usually shower after school and put on a housedress in lieu of her skirts, hose and blouses or sweaters. Today, having forgotten him entirely, she hadn't primped at all. She was too tired to remember things, so wrung out she was off her schedule.

He was staring at the coffeepot, watching it brew. "There you are," he said as she walked into the kitchen. He put his arms around her and gave her a little squeeze. "Still having a hard time of it, Elly girl?"

"It's not even the sadness that's so hard," she said. "It's the confusion. I'm senile."

"That will get better with time, you'll see. Are you eating and sleeping?" He pulled the dress away from her waist, testing the give of it to see if she'd lost weight.

"I don't have much appetite, but it's more that I forget to eat. And I sleep in short naps all through the night." She chuckled. "Sometimes in class. Is this what happens?"

"When Syl died, I stared off into space so much that I decided to do something about the farm. It shouldn't go to seed 'cause some old farmer couldn't think straight."

"But she was your wife!"

"She was my friend, too. It's hard to lose a friend." He reached up into the cupboard and pulled down two mugs. "You want to wait a little while on the ice cream?"

"Please. But you go ahead."

"I'll wait a while, too. Come sit on the couch by me, let me see if I can loosen up your shoulders and neck muscles a little bit. I wish I'd known this Gabby," he said. "She must have been a wonderful person."

"She was fifty."

"Eww, Lord. Just a girl," he said.

They sat on the sofa together in Elly's stuffy little house—she'd lived alone in it for thirty years—turned sideways some so Ben could rub her shoulders. Elly continued the stories she had been telling him about Gabby since she'd died. She had already covered her marriage and divorce from Dr. Don, her travels, her affair with a Pulitzer prize-winning photojournalist, her brief but terrifying illness, various problems with her kids. Tonight she went way back, to Gabby's childhood.

"Gabby's mother, Ceola, is now married for the seventh or eighth time, I've forgotten which. When Gabby was born, Ceola had left her young husband, Gabby's father, and moved home with her own mother. Before Gabby was a year old, Ceola had found herself a new husband, but he wasn't interested in having children. He was a sax player in a dance band that traveled. So, Ceola left Gabby behind and went off with him. Then she was back a couple of years later—the sax man was a rover. Then along came another husband and again Ceola left. This went on until Ceola married for the fourth time, this time to a stable man who wanted

Gabby to live with them. Gabby was twelve by then, and living with her mother for the very first time—except for those visits. Ceola always said that one was her favorite husband.

"According to Gabby, Ceola was always beautiful. She's still a good-looking woman at seventy-two—a bit hunched, somewhat slower. She had flaming-red hair and bright green eyes, long, enamel nails, lots of makeup, lots of jewelry and an extensive wardrobe. But she was always fragile, Gabby said. When she did go live with her mother, she ended up taking care of Ceola. Then Gabby's stepfather died, the day before Gabby's sixteenth birthday—the same date as Gabby's own death. Gabby said Ceola nearly died herself, she was so depressed. Gabby would have to hurry home from school to make sure Ceola was out of bed, had something to eat, had bathed and primped a little so she'd feel better.

"Gabby always called her Ceola, from the earliest time she could remember. It didn't offend her mother. When Gabby was seventeen and Ceola found another man, she lied to him and told him Gabby was her younger sister, orphaned and in her care. Gabby said she thought it was hilarious. The only problem was, by that time Gabby's grandmother had died and Gabby had to stay with her mother. When she did go to college, Gabby's stepfather—or brother-in-law, as he thought he was—took on the expenses so that Gabby could live away from home. And she almost never went back. Ceola would make excuses about how busy they were.

"One Christmas, Ceola and her husband went to the Caribbean without her. They *forgot* to mention it to Gabby until the last minute. The dorm was closing up for the winter break and Gabby had to go somewhere. She finally went home with a friend for the whole month. She said it was the most humiliating thing she'd ever endured. From that point on she made sure that Ceola gave her an allowance that would afford an apartment. She wasn't ever going to have to admit that her own mother cared so little about her that she'd make plans for Christmas that didn't include her."

Ben made a tsking sound. "That poor woman missed the most rewarding part of being a parent…having your children come back home to you."

"I don't think Ceola was at all interested in being a parent. She's always had a man in her life. And when she's between men or having a little trouble with one, she gets on the phone to Gabby, her little mother, or visits her, until she can recover from the shock of being a woman on her own. She's loaded, Gabby had said. She's been divorced at least twice and widowed three times. She has quite a little nest egg. But she still never helped Gabby out or remembered the children much. Gabby used to put money in a birthday card and write 'With love, Nana.' Then one year David said, 'Doesn't Nana live in Atlanta? This card was mailed in Fair Oaks.' That pretty much blew the whistle on Ceola. The kids were onto her. I wonder if Ceola knows that David is gay?"

"It sounds like she's a woman who wouldn't pay much attention to what's going on around her. Your shoulders are tight, Elly girl," he said, massaging. "Maybe Gabby never bothered her mother with any of that. And it doesn't sound like the boy would tell his gramma."

"It's what drove a wedge between David and his father. David is doing his residency in internal medicine right now, but he wants to specialize in treating AIDS patients. Dr. Don almost flipped his lid. Don had envisioned something more along the lines of a suburban practice and country club membership for his son."

"Those folks are having a hard time of it, those AIDS folks. Seems like they need a few more doctors to specialize. It's not as if the boy hasn't found himself a challenge. You ever see anyone with that disease, Elly? It's the most pitiful thing I've ever seen. I saw a special 20/20 program on AIDS patients." He tsked again. "Would you like some ice cream?"

Elly didn't answer. She simply leaned back, relaxing into his hands. Strong, gentle, farmer's hands.

"I wish I had known your friend," he said.

But Gabby had died not even knowing that Elly had a man in her life. The first man in over thirty years. It was that fact more than the fact that Ben was a simple, uneducated farmer that embarrassed Elly. She reckoned her friends and acquaintances would have a very hard time picturing her with a man. And they might not appreciate Ben, innocent, unprejudiced, sweet Ben. She wouldn't be able to bear it if they thought he was a funny little man. As for his kids, well, she didn't want to get involved. She felt she was incapable of playing grandmother to the grandchildren. She had never been nurturing. Once Ben's children told him how cold and intractable they found her, the relationship might be over.

"Would you like to lie down for a while?" he asked her.

"I'm not feeling very much like—"

"We could just lie down," he said. "We don't have to be wild lovers every night."

"Maybe we could. Just lie down."

"I'll hold you for a while. Maybe you'll even fall asleep. That would be okay."

"You're the most generous man I've ever known, Ben."

He laughed. "Me? With my free tomatoes and butter brickle ice cream? You must not have known very many men."

"I didn't mean about the tomatoes and ice cream," she said, grateful. And guilty about the fact that she kept him hidden, as though he wasn't up to the scrutiny of her friends and colleagues.

SEVEN

Eleanor knew that Sable feared large gatherings of writers. The Hearts and Roses Annual Conference in New York was the first of its type Elly had ever attended with Sable; there would be mostly romance writers. There had been other workshops, conferences and conventions at which they'd both been present—Cal Writers at Stanford, the American Booksellers Association Convention, Southwestern Writers Conference. Sable was always particular about being shuffled into and out of such gatherings quickly. If she was to sign books for two hours, she'd appear from the back of the store with unobtrusive security behind her, sign, and leave by the same route, whisked away in a limo. If she was to speak, she would arrive in time for her talk and manage to slip out before any gathering could form around her prior to or after her speech. She minimized her contact with the coordinators or hosts. Eleanor frankly thought that Sable went to extremes.

For the New York conference—booked for eight hundred, predominantly women—Sable had convinced Elly to take a room at the St. Regis with her rather than the Hilton, which housed the convention. Sable had booked herself a suite between two spacious rooms on the tenth floor, one for Elly and one for Jeff

Petross, Sable's security man. Jeff's room connected to Sable's suite, their usual arrangement. Petross hung back until Sable introduced him to Elly at the airport and Elly found him to be a personable, fair-looking young man in his late thirties. He seemed to have a good sense of humor, though a cautious one. He was as protective of Sable as the Secret Service was of the president. He was always within sight, but he took care not to appear to be escorting Sable. There were two reasons for that, he explained to Elly. First of all, it wouldn't do to advertise her security—that would make it easier for a troublemaker to breach. And second, it might only serve to create adverse publicity for the subject. Petross had been in this line of work for years; it was his business and he had many employees he had personally trained. He was more than a bodyguard to the rich and famous; his small company could install alarm systems, provide safe transportation, even investigate anyone who threatened the safety and general well-being of a client.

The three of them flew to New York, first-class, Elly and Sable sitting beside each other and Jeff across the aisle. When Elly and Sable took a cab to the St. Regis, Jeff followed in his own cab. They checked in separately. At least they rode up in the same elevator.

"Isn't this just a bit over the edge, Sable? Do you expect to be kidnapped or something?"

"The good scenario is that I'm going overboard," she said. "I've had a problem or two. I told you about them."

But Elly hadn't really taken them seriously. Once, when Sable was in Los Angeles on a book tour, an off-balance couple with a cowritten book had hijacked her. They caught her coming out of a television station, herded her into a cab and took her to their hotel room where it was their agenda to have her read their manuscript and personally get it to her agent and publisher. They didn't actually have any weapons, but they had *suggested* they had a gun. She played along with them until she could break free on the pretense of calling her agent and having him fly out to meet them all for dinner. The couple was arrested.

Another time a prisoner in a federal penitentiary had written to her at her home address, knowing full well where she lived. When she didn't answer his first letter, a flood of eerie letters followed—he could picture her showering, reading, writing, sleeping. He never threatened harm, but there was definitely an invasive, frightening quality. So far, only the letters had arrived, but Sable did have to go to some trouble to find out about the man and keep tabs on the length of his sentence. Since Sable was not a victim or family member, the authorities were under no obligation to inform her when he was paroled.

"I hate to admit this," Elly had said during the flight to New York, "but I think Barbara Ann might be right. You hold yourself too far apart from other writers. Perhaps it would show better on you if you played along with them a little, wandered around their convention, attended a couple of their lunches or cocktail parties, acted like one of the guys."

Another thing that bewildered Elly was Petross. He was the president of his security company, yet he took on these little missions of protecting Sable as though he were just a simple bodyguard. She asked him about this, forthright as Elly is.

"Because it's a very light security job. I only travel with Sable when there's some publicity accompanying her trip, business trips, not when she's traveling to visit friends or for strictly social reasons. And I only go to her home when she has guests in. Those occasions are rare. It doesn't make for a full-time job. Besides, it's very good for the client to see the same person or team for every occasion. It makes them feel, pardon the expression, *secure*."

There was definitely more to it than that, Elly decided at once. The man was smitten with Sable. You could smell it on him.

"Has he ever made a pass at you?" Elly asked.

"Elly! He's just a very thorough, very thoughtful man!"

"Bull. How long has he been following you around, trying not to stare at you like that?"

"Like what? Heavens, for a woman with no imagination, you certainly—"

"And has he ever saved you from your crazed fans?"

"He cleared a couple of nonthreatening but too ardent book lovers out of my hotel hallway once, but he appeared to be just the guy next door, responding to some sort of trouble outside his door. The whole idea is that with Jeff around, and some careful planning, it should never get to that. And his personality is simply sweet all the time…so I never have to worry about being uncomfortable with him." Sable thought she answered that quite well, though she was a bit shocked that others might also see what she'd known for some time.

"Does Barbara Ann know about him?"

"She knows about the few problems I've had—some phone calls, letters, being chased down by people who think I can ensure fabulous publishing careers. And she knows I have a security company that monitors my house. But she doesn't know about Jeff. Barbara Ann thinks I'm crazy not to lap up the attention. A few crank letters or phone calls wouldn't bother her, she's been very vocal about that. But then, maybe they wouldn't bother me if I lived with five brutes. Remember, Elly, I live alone. And there's no one within shouting distance."

Elly lived alone, too. Gabby had lived alone the past three years, since her daughter had married and moved out. Beth was alone most of the time. But of course none of them had a name that was a household word. Perhaps Sable needed a security consultant, Elly conceded. But Jeff Petross was no ordinary bodyguard, Elly was convinced of that.

Elly, being fairly anonymous even though she had been one of over fifty workshop speakers, was able to watch from a close yet safe distance as Sable met her obligation at the convention. Barbara Ann and organizational muckety-mucks shouldered Sable from room to room, from workshop to signing to tea...and Sable was swarmed everywhere she went. When Elly wasn't conducting her own modestly attended class, she kept an eye peeled for Sable. She was fascinated. How could she hold up so well? Smile so naturally when her lips must be ready to fall off? Even Barbara Ann appeared to be wilting by the end of the day, but Sable dashed off via limo to primp for the evening affairs, and returned in minimal time looking smashing. Elly didn't put much stock in things like fame; however, something like pride began to swell up inside her, for Sable unquestionably did honor to the role. And by the glowing faces of the dozens of writers and would-be writers who mobbed her, she satisfied them with her friendliness, encouragement, charm and gratitude.

"The Ice Queen is mingling with her subjects? I'll be damned!"

The cutting remark came from behind Elly and she turned sharply. A couple of women closely watched as Sable entered the banquet hall amidst a happy throng.

"I wish I could get by with writing the same goddamn thing over and over. I don't know what keeps her on the *Times* list," her companion said.

"Momentum, that's what. She bought her way on in the first place, you know. She comes from money."

Elly was seized with a simultaneous urge to snap out some ugly retort in Sable's defense, or crumple to the floor in a fit of laughter. Money? She came from the poor section of Fresno! Jesus Christ, what a couple of vipers!

It was irresistible. "Hi," Elly said, sticking out her hand. "My name is Eleanor Fulton. I don't believe we've met." She eyeballed their name tags closely. The women cautiously introduced themselves, and with the most exquisite timing, Barbara Ann joined them. They may not know Elly, but *everyone* knew Barbara Ann.

"There you are, Elly! I've been looking for you.

Hello," she nodded to Elly's companions politely. "Come on, I have a place for you at the head table, beside Sable."

Elly kept her eyes on the women who had spoken so nastily of someone they didn't even know. This was the sort of thing that hurt Sable so deeply, and one of the reasons she avoided these large crowds. There was a prevalent misconception that if you made enough money, you wouldn't care if people hurled malignant remarks your way. What a crazy notion. There was a certain percentage of people in the world that would hate her simply because she'd made good.

"It was nice to meet you," Elly slyly told the women. They had the good grace to flush slightly, but Elly did not delude herself that they might have learned a lesson.

Elly looped her arm through Barbara Ann's, as affectionate as she'd ever in her life been, and moved with the happy throng toward the banquet tables. She would not let a small, negative experience mar what was, for Barbara and most of these people, a night of nights. "Give the spot at the head table to someone else, Barbara Ann. You know, someone who will think they've died and gone to heaven to have a chance to sit next to Sable Tennet."

"Why Elly, isn't that sweet of you!"

"I'm feeling generous," Elly said. And not in the mood to have eight hundred people watch me cut my meat.

Sable was the guest of honor and sat at the center of a head table while the awards were being given out. She was to receive her award at the end of all the oth-

ers. In a surprise move that she must have worked out
with conference coordinators, she rose in the midst of
these awards and acted as a presenter for one of the
categories. She held the plaque, smiling secretively, as
Barbara Ann Vaughan's name was announced. It was
quite an emotional moment; there was hardly a dry eye
in the house as the friends embraced. If Barbara Ann
had ever doubted Sable's friendship, Elly thought, she
must surely be convinced now.

Then Sable received her award for her contributions
to women's fiction. She gave what Elly considered a
roaring good banquet speech, complimenting them
one and all on their contributions to changing the way
women saw themselves in their relationships with the
culture, the gender, the arts and the opposite sex. Sable
urged them to write from their hearts with honesty and
continue to elevate the quality of women's fiction.
When the banquet was at an end and the chairs were
pushed back, Elly faded out. She didn't bother to say
goodbye to Barbara Ann, who was surrounded by her
many friends anyway and had plans, Elly knew, for an
"after the banquet party" in one of the suites. She had
seen Sable shaking hands and giving those abbreviated
hugs and kisses—and also shaking her head—perhaps
declining one of the many parties upstairs. It was already eleven. These people were inexhaustible!

Elly went to the hotel entrance. Jeff was standing at
the curb beside the limo. He must have been told that
Sable would leave the hotel immediately following the
banquet. After about fifteen minutes, Sable arrived at
the door, escorted by about ten people to whom she
must say goodbye again. Her agent, her editor, con-

vention hostesses. They all said goodbye so fondly, with such flowery compliments and thanks for her participation, that it was hard to believe everyone here didn't love her to death. "No, no, thanks anyway, but it's been a very long day and I'm worn-out. And I have to leave in the morning."

She made eye contact with Elly, inclined her head toward the car, and the dowdy little woman slipped into the limo with Sable. Jeff sat in front with the driver. Elly wondered what that left them all thinking. Was that her mother? Her secretary? Her masseuse?

"Whew!" Sable said when they were inside.

"You did an outstanding job, Sable. Your speech was excellent."

"Why thank you, Elly!" she said, surprised. "God, am I glad that's over! Do you think Barbara Ann will be satisfied?"

"She'd better be satisfied with what you gave today," Elly said. "I was exhausted just watching you!"

"Will you have a nightcap with me, Elly?" she asked.

"I'd rather go to bed. You can have a drink with Arnold Schwarzenegger up there."

"I just want a quick one. I could have it in my room, but I'd rather go to the lounge. And I'd rather have you come with me, than Jeff. I'll have a drink, you can have your decaf and smoke your brains out and I won't say a word."

"You'll cough and wave your hands around," Elly said.

"If I promise not to do that, will you come with me?"

"I'm sure you were offered drinks back there. Why didn't you join them?"

"I don't want to talk about myself anymore. I feel safe with you. I know you aren't going to smile in my face and then say something nasty about me when I turn away. Something I'm *bound* to overhear."

Elly wanted to know how much of that Sable had endured, but she was loath to ask. Neither of them could do anything about it. "From what I overheard, you made a very favorable impression on some of the people you signed books for. I was standing in the lobby outside the tearoom when they came out."

"That's nice to hear. I was invited to a brunch in the morning, but had to decline because of our flight, and I think it upset Barbara. She had expected me to—"

"Don't worry about Barbara Ann," Elly said grumpily. "You can't please all the people all the time." She huffed a little. "I hate bars," she groused.

The limo came to a stop. "It's not a bar, it's a lounge. A very nice one, too." She stepped out of the car. "We're going to have a quick nightcap, Jeff. You can go on upstairs if you want to."

"I'm in no hurry," he said. And he followed them by about twenty feet, taking a table near the door of the lounge.

Sable found a booth for them. "This hasn't been too bad, actually. Tiring. But I met some very nice people. One woman asked me for an address so she could write me. I gave her my business card, with my agent's address on it, and she handed it right back to me. She told me to write my home address on the back. She didn't ask me, she *told* me. I said I took all my mail through my agent and she then told me my home phone number would do." Sable shook her head and laughed. "What is it with some people? I have no idea who she is. She could be a serial killer!"

"Did you give her your phone number?"

"Sort of."

"How do you 'sort of' give someone your phone number?"

"I gave her several of the numbers." The waitress approached. "One vodka, over ice. Elly?" Elly ordered a cup of decaf. "Anyway, aside from her, I met some very nice people. How was it for you?"

"Interesting," Elly said.

"At least it put you in a good mood," Sable laughed. "Lighten up, Elly. I might have two drinks. You can manage to pound down about twenty cigarettes."

Eleanor was already digging in her purse. She looked up briefly to scowl at Sable. She continued with her task at hand and lit up. "So," she said, "you had a good time?"

"The conference was quite nice. Very busy, but not as grueling as it could have been."

But there had been pressure. Sable had rankled the conference committee by selecting her own hotel, and they told her so, even though she had paid for it herself. She arrived on Friday afternoon to find fourteen messages waiting when she checked in. Although she had been scheduled to sign books from two to four on Saturday and give a banquet speech that night, there were several other last-minute invitations she was forced to turn down. She had made arrangements to have a cozy dinner with her editor and agent for Friday night—just the three of them. She hadn't even invited Elly. But someone—her agent blamed her editor and her editor blamed her agent—had turned it into a dinner for twenty held in a banquet room. She was asked to attend the convention's opening cocktail party (which she declined because of the dinner), was invited to three other dinners (all declined), and was asked to attend the keynote address on Saturday morning, which added two hours to an already long day.

Sable had given the switchboard at the St. Regis a list of names of those people whose calls were to be put through to her room. This service was one of the reasons she liked to stay there. Several people she'd never heard of had left messages with the desk for her to call them at the Hilton; four had asked her to read manuscripts, one wanted to meet with her "at her convenience" to share the ways in which she had promoted her early books to stardom, one wanted an endorsement "whether or not she had time to read the book," and five thought she might be interested in joining them for breakfast, lunch, dinner, drinks, coffee, or whatever, so she could meet some other writers. She had a call at midnight Friday from a writer who had been trying to reach her all day—the name of the conference coordinator had finally been used to breach the switchboard screening. The writer had idolized her for years, had studied her style and patterned her own books after Sable's, and wanted to meet her to discuss a collaboration. And at seven the next morning a man had called—this time her agent's name had been used to bypass the operator. He claimed to be a producer interested in making movies from her books. When she told him to contact her agent he became irate and called back several times, insisting they meet alone. He was *intimately* acquainted with her novels, he said. She asked the switchboard to stop putting him through and told Jeff to be on the watch.

Some of these were friendly, well-intentioned people and some were crackpots, but there was no surefire way to tell the difference. This exhausted Sable. She didn't mention any of those things because you're not allowed to complain about fame and fortune. The bizarre thing, in Sable's mind, was that not every bestselling author went through this. She'd met several, of course, over the years, and she'd asked a few of them. Men, particularly, didn't seem to be followed around and pestered so much. She thought maybe the problem was that her novels were sexy. Or else she was handling it all wrong. But she didn't know what she should be doing differently. Whatever the problem, she had ended up with a life in which she had few close friends and the only other people she even half trusted were people she *hired.* They'd help preserve her privacy or she'd fire them.

"I've been thinking about retiring," she told Elly.

"How do you do that?" she asked.

"I'm not sure. Choose a pseudonym? But people find out. Stop writing altogether? I don't know if I could do that. It's the only part of the job I like." She sipped her vodka. "But since Gabby died, I don't enjoy even that."

"It hasn't been very long, Sable. None of us is enjoying things the way we used to."

"Maybe I'm just reacting to her death," she said. But it was more that Gabby's death had brought to a head something Sable had been grappling with for years. Not having any friends. Not trusting anyone. Having everything and nothing.

Sable noticed a familiar face across the bar. She looked at the man, slowly sipping her vodka and praying it wasn't so. What were the odds? Sable leaned out of the booth and stared. Jack Mahoney sat in a booth across from them. With a woman.

"My God," Sable whispered.

"What is it?" Elly asked, turning clumsily in her seat so that she could look.

"Don't look, Elly! Just wait a minute. God, that's him. Wait a minute, I'll tell you when. That couple across the bar, behind you a little. She's a blonde."

Eleanor puffed slowly. "Can I look *now?*" she asked.

"Be careful. Don't let them see you staring. You stare worse than anyone I know."

"I simply look directly at people. I don't call that staring." She glanced and looked back. "So?"

"What was he doing? Was he kissing her neck or something?"

"Do you know him?"

Sable finished her drink and signaled for the waitress. She ordered another one.

"Are you looking for a good night's sleep or a coma?" Elly asked.

"You know him, too," she said. "That's Jack Mahoney."

Then Eleanor did what she usually did. She stared. Hard and straight. Her thin lips tightened, her brows drew together, and she pierced him with her eyes. Sable half expected Jack to turn and see them, Eleanor looked at him so potently. But he didn't because he was kissing the woman's cheek and snaking his hand up her skirt under the table.

"Stop that!" Sable hissed. "God, you're the worst gawker. Don't let him see us!"

"Why not?" Eleanor asked. "I think we should go over and say hello. Introduce ourselves to the young woman. What do you think?"

Sable's drink arrived and she asked for the check. "No," she said to Eleanor. "We're going to quietly tiptoe out of here and escape before he sees us. Try, Elly, just this once, not to move the floor when you walk."

"Let him see us," Elly said threateningly.

"No! That would give him an advantage, knowing he got caught. If anyone's going to have an advantage, it's going to be Beth!"

"Do you have a strategy for everything?" Elly asked.

Sable disregarded the question. "Things are much worse at her house than we've ever suspected, Elly."

"I haven't suspected anything!"

"That's because you don't think too hard about things. You take everything at face value. Can't you see Beth is unhappy? She can't leave the house when Jack's home. She has to check his schedule before she can even go to lunch with her friends! There have been bruises—we've seen bruises on her. Not on her face or anything, but you know batterers don't hit their victims in places where the marks will show. She makes excuses. She keeps pretending to have this loving marriage with Jack, denies that he abuses her, but all you have to do is look in her eyes to know she's lying, covering up for him. He's an abusive, controlling fuckaround."

"I'm not so sure he actually hits her," Eleanor said.

"I am," Sable replied. The check came and Sable gave the waitress a twenty, telling her to keep the change. "Try to be casual," she said to Eleanor as she slipped out of the booth, carrying her second vodka with her.

Eleanor tamped out her cigarette. "You're so good at subterfuge. People don't give you enough credit." She followed Sable out of the lounge. "And now you have some plan, don't you?"

"Not yet I don't. I just knew that son of a bitch was a slimeball. Poor Beth."

The elevator came. Jeff caught up. "This isn't our business, Sable," Elly said.

"Whose business is it then? Theirs? You know what that usually means? It means this asshole gets to fly around the world collecting venereal diseases while Beth sits at home, alone, praying for a baby. Jesus. Beth is so *bright!* How can she not know? She knows. She must. She just isn't facing it."

"I've got the worst feeling," Eleanor said. "I'm getting a muscle spasm."

"Don't worry about it," Sable said. "If you don't want to take responsibility for what you saw, I'll handle it alone."

"Please think about this for a while," Elly said. "Don't do anything tonight."

They reached their floor. "I won't call her or anything. Tell her something like that and then leave her alone? For God's sake, Elly, I'm not that insensitive."

"Good. We'll talk about it tomorrow. Don't brew and stew all night. He isn't worth it."

"Maybe not, but she is."

Jeff opened Sable's door for her, letting her in, before walking next door to his room. Sable saw her flashing message light and ignored it. She finished her drink. She took a hot soak. And she brewed and stewed.

Why could men be such slime? Why should a sweet, innocent woman like Beth be stuck with this animal? Why did Beth keep pretending they were in love, trying to have a baby, living some idyllic romance in their little town house? In six years did she think no one noticed the inconsistencies in her stories? In her behavior? It came out sometimes. Beth became skittish when asked about her husband. Even when Jack had all those days off for which airline pilots were famous, he was often on his own. Beth couldn't think fast enough to cover up for him every time. Beth didn't go with him on his boat because she didn't like fishing that much? Jack had a speedboat! He liked to go skiing in Colorado with some of his pilot friends—there were no wives along. He had hunting trips, fishing trips, scuba-diving trips, card games. She didn't often go on his scheduled airline trips to places like New York and London because he didn't have that much time off when he got there. He didn't visit her family with her because, you know, he had to travel all the time with his job and didn't need more trips. In the six years Sable had known Beth, she had crossed paths with Jack a couple of times. She found him too flirtatious. Sable could smell a womanizer a mile off.

Beth had no one in her life but the girls. For Sable to be so alone was a different story; she had lots of hired help, lots of important functions and the demands on her time were extraordinary. Besides, Sable reminded herself, no one really knew how alone she was. What was Beth's excuse? She had a large, loving family in Missouri—but none of them ever visited California. And Beth's mysteries were gaining popularity. She was getting more and more attention from the critics, the guilds, and New York, but she rarely went to the conferences out of town. She had friends, Beth claimed, mostly pen pals. Pen pals couldn't interfere with Jack's schedule or threaten Jack's control.

Sable became more and more irate as she considered her six-year relationship with Beth. Gabby had brought her on, as Gabby had collected them all. She'd found her at an autograph signing where they were both signing books. Beth was new and Gabby wasn't famous, so they'd had plenty of time to chat, get to know each other. Beth was so quiet, so shy, that Gabby took it upon herself to introduce Beth to a few writers. But Beth was such a loner that the introductions stopped with their little group.

When Beth talked about her family, her beautiful dark eyes lit up and she became almost animated. When she was asked about Jack, she seemed to struggle with what to say.

Jesus, we're all a bunch of invalids, Sable thought. Gabby had surrounded herself with troubled souls, handicapped pretenders. Elly was an aging, solitary, egghead who had lived in the same cluttered little house for thirty years. Sable was a messed-up, abused teenager who'd somehow become a famous person—a fucked-up famous person who distrusted everyone and acted like a magnet to weirdos—without ever resolving the mess she'd left in her past. Barbara Ann was a raving codependent who controlled everyone around her by playing the victim, starting with her family of men and spreading the gloom of her daily disasters almost nationwide by long distance and conferences. And Beth was undoubtedly an abused wife who was trapped in some kind of secret tyranny that she shared with no one.

Sable lay in her bed, thinking about what a mess this small group was. Group therapy wouldn't be a bad idea, she thought. It's absurd that none of us is happy with what we have. I hate fame and something about the way I treat people is seen as regal and offputting rather than professional. Elly has become a curmudgeon, hiding within the walls of academia, fighting her alcoholism in a silent, solitary battle that she never talks about but is always conscious of. Barbara Ann's pursuit of success has blinded her to all that she has— family, friends, health, love, work. And Beth is being beat up, emotionally and probably physically.

Of course she couldn't sleep. She started thinking about the honor bar in her room and it frightened her. Whenever she wanted one more drink than she thought was prudent, visions of her mother came instantly to mind.

It was one-thirty when she crept to the door that adjoined her suite to Jeff's room. She opened her portion and leaned her ear against his door. It wasn't the first time she had done this much. Feelings of loneliness, despair and burnout had driven her to wonder what might be behind those kind eyes…or why that huge paw of his could feel so gentle on her arm as he escorted her. Most curious of all was that he would have those feelings and not push her one bit. Was this a man who actually *could* be trusted? Who would not hurt? Use?

Those other times that curiosity and temptation had pushed her to listen at his door she had caught herself in time, but Gabby's death had left her lonelier than ever. The conference had burned her out, leaving her weary and frustrated. She was more needy and less strong—a volatile combination. And…it had been a very long time since she'd let a man get near.

She could hear the faint, distant sound of his television. Why would he be awake? He must have nodded off with the set on. God, this was nutty. She should forget it. She was acting insanely anyway. This was probably going to end up being a big mistake. She should not open this door, literally or figuratively. Before, when she was much younger, sex had only numbed her to other pain in her life. She wasn't sure if she was past that even yet. After all, it was one-thirty and she was in pain, and his eyes had always been reaching.… She did not want to go back in time in that way. Still, she did not want to go back to bed alone. She decided to tap lightly and if he didn't come to answer her knock immediately—

He popped the door open and she jumped. He was

wearing only his trousers, his chest and feet bare. He was so large and muscled. Almost frighteningly so.

"You weren't asleep?" she asked.

"Not yet. Neither were you." He looked into her eyes, not down at her negligee-clad body. That was what had tipped her off in the first place, the way he looked into her eyes rather than appreciatively studying her curves.

"Did I make a mistake...or do I see something when you look at me...something that I could have misinterpreted...."

He entered her suite. He pulled her into his arms in answer to the question. He put his hands on her waist and drew her toward him. As he looked down at her, his eyes partially closed, she thought she saw him smile slightly. He'd never once made any kind of physical move on her. But when she made one suggestive remark to him, he was there, ready, eager.

"This could be a big mistake," she said.

He shrugged. "I doubt it. It's not as though you rushed into it."

She put a hand against his chest, laying it there lightly. "Have you felt this way from the very beginning?" she asked him.

He nodded. "It only got stronger as I got to know you. I knew you could tell. It's the sort of thing you can't really hide. But that's good, you see, because I wanted it to be up to you."

I just don't want to be alone, she almost said. "Are you sure? This isn't part of your job description."

"Sable, *this* isn't a job. This is an emotion." He bent his head, lifted her chin and kissed her lips. Slowly.

Tenderly. Then he embraced her, drew her against him and kissed her neck. "Why do I get the impression you're not going to feel any of this?" he asked in a whisper.

She turned her face away. He knew too much. He saw through her.

But she stayed in his arms.

She felt. Everything.

That his hands and mouth brought perfect physical pleasure was her first surprise, while at the same time she had always expected that would be the case. That a man so strong and physical in appearance could be so gentle and sensitive in bed, forceful at just the perfect moment, was a fantasy of hers. She wrote about such men. He had promised as much with his eyes long ago. And Sable, who usually needed her space, slept peacefully within his arms, feeling natural there. She was forty-one, and it was the first time in her life she had felt safe and wonderful after sex, cradled in the protective embrace of a lover.

"What if this doesn't work out?" she asked him.

"I don't know what you mean," he answered.

"I mean, can you still be my security consultant now that we've been...intimate?" His eyes narrowed and his brow furrowed in question. "Can you be as protective...as professional? Can you still take care of me in that way now that there's a personal side to our relationship?"

"I'll probably be even better at it," he said.

"And what if, for some reason, I don't feel it's right for me to be intimately involved with you any longer?" she suggested.

"I guess you'll tell me."

"What will you do? Have someone else come to my house? Travel with me? Et cetera?"

"Sable," he said, brushing his hand down the length of her body and sending quivers through her, "you don't strike me as the kind of woman who has trouble making a decision. You've obviously thought about this for a long time. Years. Why are you second-guessing yourself now?"

"I'm not good with men," she said matter-of-factly.

He laughed very seductively but grinned boyishly. "Nonsense."

The most wonderful thing about Jeff was his apparent ability to accept things the way they were without overthinking. During the next two weeks he dropped in on her twice, in the evenings. He called from his car and asked if it was all right. He brought wine and chocolates once, flowers the next time. He had no expectations, he said, except that she know he was sincere. He was unrehearsed and spontaneous; they talked about subjects that did not threaten her. He covered his childhood, she discussed her writing career and travels. He rose to leave when she yawned and it seemed he would be content with a kiss good-night. There was something about him, some dichotomy in his personality, that drew her even closer. He was innocent and boyish, yet he ran a company that pandered to the needs of people who were harassed by the worst of real world fears. He was proper, treating her like a virgin, when she'd yanked him into her bed on a whim.

Sable had had her share of come-ons. She was attractive enough to turn a head and a few men had given her the rush. But Jeff was in no hurry. He had no cagey lines. There seemed not a manipulative or malicious bone in his body. He was genuine and old-fashioned. He courted her. She had never been courted in her life.

Those times he called on her in the evenings with his candy and flowers and wine, and charmed her by his genuine interest in conversation, she asked him to stay over. And not because she was afraid to be alone.

Part Two

Part Two

EIGHT

June

Eleanor had begun reading through one of Gabby's manuscripts. By the time she'd read eighty pages, she had to stop and create a chronology of the events of Gabby's life that she'd been told so that she could place the work. Before she could tell the others what she'd found, she had to be sure. The manuscript was typed in three styles plus longhand on yellow-pad pages. A consultation with the computer index showed that some chapters were so old, they weren't even on the new computer. The novel, which appeared to be auto-biographical fiction, had been in progress for at least ten years. Even in the first eighty pages, Elly could see gaps and holes, but the scenes that were fully developed were stunning.

She re-created Gabby's life in a time line on a steno pad.

Gabby was twenty-three, a recent college graduate, when she met and married Don Marshall. He was finishing up his residency in OB-GYN in Virginia, with plans to return to California to open his own practice. Gabby did what so many young doctors' wives do; she became her husband's business partner immediately.

She left Ceola and the Magnolia blossoms of the South and followed Don. She shopped for his office space, hired his staff, managed the books and held down a job to pay the rent while he was setting up.

The children came along much sooner than they'd planned, but Gabby persevered. She worked until she felt the contractions start and was back to work before the babies were weaned. And Don's practice grew. Don spent very little time at home with his family; the business of doctoring was time-consuming. But Gabby managed; she was young, had energy, had faith, had love. She slowly began to notice that the only thing she didn't really have was Don.

After seven years of marriage, Don's income was good. They had a nice house, new cars, good clothes and even investments. But Don couldn't relax long enough to enjoy family life. He was too busy for school projects, birthday parties, family vacations and trips to the zoo. For all practical purposes, Gabby found herself a single parent on a good income. And then she found out about the nurse. All the excuses Don made and promises that he'd change were so quick, well-rehearsed and articulate, Gabby suspected that this had not been his first affair.

"I'll be damned if I'll give it all up that easily," she had told Elly. Gabby went back to school for a master's degree, held Don to a strict budget, monitored all his promises to be good, and was determined to save her marriage, her family life and her future.

But she got terribly sick. Meningitis. And almost died. Her recovery from that was tedious and difficult. In all the quiet hours that followed, Gabby realized that she was not cut out to compromise. She emerged from the darkness of her illness as a phoenix. On fire.

She was going to make every single day worth living fully and she was going to raise her children well. And she was *not* going to share her life with a man who was not as committed as she.

Don, as it turned out, could face down almost anyone but Gabby. Gabby appeared facile, but was something else. He never seemed to know if she was manipulating him, having a showdown with him, nurturing him or disciplining him. (Elly had always believed that Gabby inherited this ability to deal with men from Ceola.) Maybe it was just that he really loved her—although he couldn't seem to stop himself from carousing. It was obvious he had some kind of deeply imbedded guilt, as though his affairs almost killed her. In any event, she managed to get what she wanted out of him. She divorced him and got herself a writing job.

So began Gabby's trips—to India, Thailand, Iraq, Israel. She'd take six to ten weeks to prepare the groundwork and settle Don in his old house to care for the children for a two- to three-week stay. She approved of the housekeeper who came along as part of the deal and gave Don strict orders that he not have overnight guests.

Gabby met John Shelby on her third trip abroad. The manuscript Elly had found was so riveting in its detail of the year, the time. Mao launches a cultural revolution; Jacqueline Susann dies; OPEC oil embargo ends; Patty Hearst is kidnapped by the Symbionese Liberation Army; Palestinian terrorists seize a school in Maalot, twenty-one children are killed…and Gabby is in Cypress, hiding in a baker's dirty loft during an island-wide blackout with a cocky, impatient, irascible photographer when Turkey invades. John was born in America, but had lived almost all his life in Australia and England, and just happened to have won two Pulitzers for his work. That was where and how they came together. A group of reporters and photographers not smart or lucky enough to get off the island and are holed up, mostly terrified, in small civilian enclaves around an impoverished village. Gabby was the only woman. She and John started out as mortal enemies and were lovers at the end of three days. She was thirty-two, he, forty-five.

From that point on Gabby found she could do her work ten times as well by following John to the floods in Bangladesh, the famines in Africa, the evacuation of Vietnam. She was covering the worldwide plight of women and children, and he, the human politics of war.

Elly remembered what this had done for Gabby. Despite jet lag and deprivation, her eyes sparkled, her cheeks glowed, her energy was high. Their love affair was an adventure, but so was Gabby's work, which pealed with talent. Some digging turned up a box of photos, some of which were prize-winning in and of themselves. Gabby and John sitting on a tank, sharing a canteen. Gabby on the ground, flies swarming her, holding a malnourished African baby while the mother leaned over to gesture to her own mouth. John taking a picture of a photographer taking a picture of a smiling Ulster lad, while in the background, out of the first photographer's range, was a demolished city street. It was breathtaking—like looking into a mirror of mirrors. It was the same setting as the first Pulitzer photo, probably snapped before or after. And the most poignant photo of all, a gathering of darkly clad mourners standing behind a casket in the rain, umbrellas over their heads, a spray of lilies on the casket, a preacher's back to the camera, and far, far, behind them all and to the left, the slight figure of a jeans-clad, pea-coated, curly-haired girl. She looked no more than eighteen in the grainy black and white. Gabby.

Yes, Elly quickly realized, this was what she had done. Novelized her affair with John Shelby. Gabby rarely talked about it. Oh, she'd mentioned it, but she never named him when she discussed the details. Elly and Sable knew a lot more than the others. They'd caught her on melancholy nights not long after it ended. She would describe their travels, their fights, their reunions, their passion. She had never breathed a word of trying to get it down on paper. What Elly had read so far was phenomenally good. But from the piles and stacks of papers she'd rounded up, Gabby had over five thousand pages of written and rewritten and scribbled-on manuscript pages. Original stuff, duplicated stuff, edited stuff, X-ed-out stuff.

Elly was stunned. This was a secret gem. But pulling together a novel from this much of one's own writing was difficult enough; putting this extraordinary mess together into a cohesive, compelling story would take a literary genius.

Or four good heads, she thought.

Unfortunately, the group was in a bad place. Elly had been in Gabby's house for a week now, and much had happened since Gabby's death. Sable had confronted Beth about Jack. Beth refused to believe anything Sable accused, and the two of them were very distant, hardly talking. Even Elly, who had little interest in such domestic melodrama, had to admit that Beth was acting childish and something was awfully wrong in her life that she'd do well to look at. Sable's detective had finally turned up information on that

Slatterly fellow who'd snuck into her office the day of Gabby's memorial, and found him to be a gossip-monger who sold the dirtiest dirt he could find to the worst tabloids in print. Sable claimed she couldn't imagine what he was up to, but the prospect that he was even interested in her had Sable more uptight than Elly had ever seen her. Barbara Ann had had a run of bad luck—a book she'd done extensive revisions on, re-creating it again and again, had ultimately been re-jected, contract canceled, advance money owed back. Barbara Ann was devastated. The next proposal she submitted had been rejected as well, and her confi-dence was shattered. She was terrified that she'd sud-denly lost it after twenty-six books.

As for Elly, she was getting to know Gabby anew, reading her letters, her notes, her manuscript and her calendars. The other women had been over several times, browsing through things, making their own small files at Elly's direction, but each one was so ter-ribly distracted by her own set of catastrophes, they were no help at all. She had told Ben to pretend she was out of the country doing research. She didn't think it would be wise for him to come to Gabby's to see her since the women were in and out, David and Sarah and even Don dropped by, but she found herself calling him, missing him and wishing she could change her mind. It had only been a week of separation and she was already miserable about it.

It was going to be a long summer.

Sable was toweling her hair dry when she heard a heart-stopping scream from downstairs. It was so shrill and went on for such a long time that she was nearly to the bottom of the stairs before it paused. And then it started again, this time in shorter spurts. When she got to the kitchen to find the source, Dorothy was backed against the refrigerator with a stricken look on her face, staring at the kitchen window. There, on the other side of the pane, was a large camcorder, taping the screaming housekeeper. And Sable, who wore only a terry robe.

"Jesus," Sable breathed, at first frightened, then immediately furious.

Dorothy was holding her broom up as protection. Sable whipped it out of her hands and flew out the kitchen door, holding the wooden end of the broom like a lance. She rounded the corner of the house and took after the photographer with menacing intent. "What the hell are you doing?! Who are you? What do you want here, scaring an old woman out of her wits? Art! Art!" she yelled.

The photographer, apparently accustomed to this sort of response, backed away from her, camera running the whole time.

"Turn that goddamn thing off! What are you *doing?*" But as she walked toward him, broom handle out, he simply filmed her rage. He had no intention of answering her. When he had enough, he'd probably run off.

Sable fixed him. She quit asking questions and began jabbing him with the broom handle. This is my property, she thought. Let him sue me. She jabbed and jabbed, poking his gut, and he backed away while filming. Finally she gave him one serious lunge and he went backward into the pool, camera and all, and in a second came up sputtering and talking. "Hey! What the hell was that for?"

She stood over him and looked down into the pool.

"I wonder," she replied with as much sarcasm as she could muster.

Out of the corner of her eye she saw Art running out from the behind the garage with a hedge clipper in his hand, but he wasn't looking at her. He was looking down the driveway. She turned sharply. There were three men standing in her driveway. One had a camera and shot a couple of still pictures of her. Another one had a tape recorder hanging from his shoulder like a purse, a microphone in his hand. "Ms. Tennet?" he began.

"Art!" she yelled hotly. "Get the gun! Now!"

"Ms. Tennet, can you tell us a little bit about your marriage to William Parker?"

Art stood there, dumbfounded. Of course, there was no gun for Art to get. Sable, however, had a nice little midnight special that she kept in the bedside table. She was already telling herself that it would be a very undiplomatic way to end this interview. She could get in trouble.

"Art, goddamnit, get the gun! Shoot these bastards, or I will!"

"Ms. Tennet, what can you tell us about the death of your child seventeen years ago?"

She was already in trouble.

She whirled around to see the man with the videocam struggling out of the pool. With a foot to his shoulder, she shoved him back in. She whirled back toward the others. "I'm going to get my gun. You'd better run for your worthless lives."

She stomped into the kitchen, threw the bolt on the door, took the stairs to her bedroom two at a time and grabbed the revolver out of the bedside table. She was down the stairs and opening the kitchen door again with incredible speed. In all her life, nothing could possibly have prepared her for the audacity of tabloid reporters. The still photographer flashed a picture of her pointing the gun at him. The very idea caused her to smile. But it was the wickedest smile she'd ever worn. She fired the gun—always kept fully loaded and shot at a range at least twice a year—into the air over the lake.

At least they had the common sense to flinch.

"Put the camera down. And the tape recorder," she instructed levelly.

"Let me give you the film," the photographer, now nervous, pleaded. "The camera cost seven hundred dollars."

"And what do you think my private life costs, you lowlife son of a bitch? Put them down. Now. Very slowly and carefully. I'm all upset."

They did so. The soaking camcorder photographer was edging his way slowly toward the driveway. He had to go past her to get away. "Don't sweat it, babe," he said. "Film's ruined."

"Put it down!" she snapped. "And don't you *ever* call me *babe!*"

He wisely disengaged himself from the heavy piece of equipment, placing it on the ground.

"Now run," she advised. "Run!" she restated when they hesitated.

One by one they took flight, their gear lying on the driveway behind them.

Sable was distraught and took leave of her senses for a moment. She aimed the gun quite carefully toward the far edges of the drive. She fired once, then again. They ran all the faster. She longed to empty the gun into their skinny butts, but she knew she was already in for it. The first shot she'd fired over the lake had probably fallen and hit a fish and she'd end up being fined by the Environmental Protection Agency.

It's here, she thought with utter dread. They've got me.

Art had become a statue. He still stood right where she'd left him. He was in some sort of trance, his mouth open and his eyes disbelieving. "Art, put this stuff in the maintenance shed. Make sure it's locked. Bring me the film out of the camera and the tape out of the recorder. And hurry up, before any of them come back after their stuff. They're arrogant, and they're stupid." He simply stood there, looking at her. "Art," she said slowly. "Get a grip! Help me out here!" He began to move. He dropped the hedge clipper and proceeded toward the discarded equipment.

"Lock the door," Sable instructed Dorothy when she went back into the kitchen. "Don't let anyone in but Art or Virginia. They're tabloid reporters, I assume, and they're sneaky as hell."

"What do they want?" Dorothy asked.

"They want to ruin me."

Jeff Petross told Sable to lock up and call the police; he was on his way with some help to secure the house and grounds. Virginia arrived at eight to report there were a couple of cars and vans at the end of Sable's drive. She had thought something was wrong at the house. She stopped to ask them what they were doing and they began firing questions at her. What was Sable Tennet's real name? Where did she really grow up? How many times had she been married? Had she only had the one child? Had there ever been a police investigation into the death of that child?

Sable called her agent, Arnold Bynum. "What the hell is this? They don't do this to writers! What's going on here?"

"I was going to call you. They just notified me. It's the television tabloid *Twilight Truth*. They're airing an exposé on your life tonight. They've offered you an opportunity to make a statement and, if you desire, schedule your own appearance."

"What?"

"That's it. Now, why don't you fill me in on what we're going to see tonight?"

"Arnie, I have no idea! Didn't they tell you anything about what they're going to air?"

"No. Nothing. What kind of questions did they ask you?"

She was struck silent. She closed her eyes and tried to take deep breaths.

"Sable?"

She couldn't speak. They can't have found all that! How would they manage? Where would they start? No one knew but Elly and Gabby and neither of them would have divulged. Butch? Her mother? My God, why would anyone want to dredge that up? What would it matter?

"It's very personal," she said weakly.

"Not anymore."

"Arnie, listen, I'm not running for Supreme Court judge or anything. Why? Why would they do this to me?"

"Money, Sable. Smut sells. You'd better tell me now, before I'm put on the spot. This could cause us some problems, if it's nasty enough."

"What kind of problems?"

"With your publisher. They expect a certain kind of

image. You sold them your image as much as your stories."

"Bullshit! There's no image clause in any of my contracts!" But even as she said that, she knew it was untrue. *She'd* created an image for herself, just as all public personalities do. Jesus Christ, would it have been better in any way had she not attempted to be refined, classy? It was no different than taking the curlers out of your hair before going to the grocery store! She simply wanted to look her best!

"The fact is, if you have some sordid past that's now coming out, it's going to matter to your publisher. It could hurt book sales. If there's anything they might say on that program that's unsavory but true, I'd like to hear about it now. For both our sakes."

Book sales! My life is falling apart and our first concern is book sales! Not, Are you in pain, Sable? Does this hurt, Sable? How can I help, Sable?

"Don't worry, Arnie," she said tiredly. "There isn't anything sordid in my past. My past is simply pathetic, that's all. If they actually tell the truth tonight, my books should sell like hotcakes."

"What is the truth, Sable?"

"I'm sorry, Arnie. I'm simply not ready to talk about it." She didn't say goodbye. She hung up the phone and walked across the hall to Virginia's office. "Virginia, I'm only taking calls from Jeff Petross, Elly Fulton or…" God, she almost said Gabby. That had happened to her so many times! Something would happen and she'd begin to think, Gabby would get a kick out of this! or Gabby would have been so much nicer about that. Then she'd realize, with a stab of pain, that Gabby was gone forever. "Just Jeff or Elly. And Jeff should be here momentarily."

She would call her lawyer when Jeff arrived, when she began to assimilate what she was dealing with. First, the police came. As she should have expected, she was the bad guy. Not only were they responding to her call, but also to a call from reporters that they'd been run off her property with gunfire. "Did you shoot at those men, Ms. Tennet?"

"Absolutely not."

"But you did fire a gun?"

"Sort of."

"How do you 'sort of' fire a gun?"

"Well, they had me very frightened and upset and it did go off a couple of times, but I was being very careful with it—I know how dangerous firearms can be—and it wasn't pointed toward anyone when it accidentally went off. I think the whole problem was their trespassing and peeping in my windows at the crack of dawn. I wasn't sure who they were. They could have been a gang of murderers!"

"But you asked this gang of murderers to leave their cameras and tape recorder behind?"

"Is *that* what they told you? I think they simply got scared when the gun went off and dropped their things. Honestly, I would have apologized, but they just ran! If I'd known they were just a bunch of idiot reporters, I never would have found it necessary to get my gun!"

She briefly told Jeff what she was up against, without telling him the details. Jeff, practiced in the art of pandering to the privacy of celebrities and politicians, didn't push her in any way to bare her soul. He went about the business of making sure that no one set foot on Sable's property. Sable's lawyer said he'd try to get some kind of injunction to stop the airing of the television show, but he warned her that the prospects were doubtful. And Arnie called. Again and again, begging for some information or at least a chance to talk about it. Then her editor began calling, then her publisher, her publicist and various other people who had been seeing promos for the 6:30 p.m. *Twilight Truth* show that would reveal and unveil the *real* Sable Tennet. But Elly, Barbara Ann and Beth did not call. Elly wasn't involved in a good gossip tree, but Barbara Ann would surely have been notified by someone, somewhere, who had seen the promos. They must all be at Gabby's, sorting and reading.

Can my life really go down the tubes like this? she kept asking herself. I didn't mean anyone any harm by creating a new persona. I meant only to spare poor Helen the humiliation of reliving, over and over, the painful horrors of her short, pitiful life.

"Is there anything I can do for you, personally, Sable?" Jeff asked.

Sable felt a giant pang of doubt. Perhaps it had been too good to be true—a decent, honest and caring man, all hers. When he found out the truth about her, he would know, unequivocally, that she was not worthy of his affection. Jeff was pure; Sable was tarnished. She placed her small hand against his firm, square jaw. "I think you've gotten yourself in over your head, Jeff."

"How so?"

"I think maybe you've fallen for me."

"Don't hold that against me, okay?"

"Yeah, but I'm a bad bet. Trouble."

"More like you got trouble, the way I see it. Sometimes when trouble comes, it helps to know there is someone who cares about the real you. The you inside."

We'll see about that, she thought. "The program is on at six-thirty. Watch it with me?"

"Sure."

Virginia quit her job at 3:00 p.m. She couldn't take it. She was in tears, feeling guilty about running out on Sable with no notice in her hour of need, but the pressure of fearing her boss had some seedy past that was going to go public frightened her. She was afraid they were going to start hounding her for information.

Finally, out of survival, they unplugged the phones. She dismissed Dorothy without any further explanation. Jeff had three guys wandering around the property, keeping any reporters away from the house. But they could not be kept away from the end of the drive. Food was out of the question, but Sable quite needed a vodka for the viewing.

When one thinks of the books most loved by American women, there is a name that tops the list as the writer who has best captured the trials and triumphs of women as they struggle with their lovers, their families, their careers...Sable Tennet. She has more than sixty million books in print and has, through her very emotional, very melodramatic fiction, moved her readers to tears, given them hope and helped them dream. But is there a deeper reason why this extraordinary woman has been able to achieve such heartfelt empathy for her heroines who have overcome the very worst that life has to offer?

I think there was a compliment in there somewhere, Sable thought.

There was very little time to brace herself for what followed because the film segued to a photo of Sable, née Helen Gobrich, at the age of about twelve. She was already teasing her hair and wearing way too much eye makeup, her jeans fit like skin and her pubescent breasts strained against a low-cut knit top. She looked like a slut. An unattractive slut, with her crooked teeth, her bent, hook nose, her shaggy brows. The narrator gave her name—God, they had it down—the condition of her (now-deceased!) alcoholic mother. She was in and out of foster care, a promiscuous teenager who dropped out of school at the age of fifteen and liked to party. She was a boozer and an addict. (Sable stared into her vodka. She had not touched alcohol until the age of about twenty-five and had never been drunk a day in her life.) She married a local short-order cook, Butch Parker, and they had a volatile, dangerous marriage, filled with binges, fights and poverty. There were photos. One of her and Butch sitting on the hood of a car. One of Butch wearing a dirty, torn sweatshirt and tipping back a beer. Where the hell did they get the photos?

She could not look at Jeff.

They brought into this impoverished, disastrous life of drink, illicit sex and days-long parties (they had a photo of her mother's house—a recent one—it was not improved with age) a child. Thomas Adam. A beautiful, bright, healthy baby. And tragedy struck one night during a typical gathering of neighborhood partyers when someone, presumably Butch, lost his temper and beat his two-year-old son to death. He confessed to the crime and served four months. (Four months!!) And Helen Gobrich disappeared forever.

So how does a woman living in tragedy so poignant drag herself out of such a life-style? Not unlike the heroines in her novels, she…

That was when Sable stopped listening. Not on purpose. A kind of sensory overload had clogged up her brain and she'd heard all she could for the time being.

She felt Jeff's hand massaging the back of her neck in sympathy and she turned to look at him. Amazingly, she didn't see pity in his eyes. She wasn't sure what she saw.

"It didn't happen like that," she said. "Oh, Butch beat Thomas Adam to death, that's true. But we weren't having a party. We didn't have parties. I was working. At the hair spray factory. The three-to-eleven shift. I had to leave Tommy with my mother and Butch. I didn't very often. When I came home from work—" She stopped because she couldn't describe that. She could barely watch as that reel of memory film ran through her mind. "I didn't drink," she said.

"Let's turn it off," he said.

"Some of it's true. My mother was a drunk. Dead now, so I hear. I married Butch...don't ask me why. My name was Helen Gobrich. My nose was big and my teeth were crooked and I wasn't very attractive...but I sure tried. I was always thin. I wore the tight jeans. Well, you saw...."

"Sable..."

"I wasn't really ever bad," she said sadly. "But I was very stupid."

"You were only very young."

"I can't believe the timing of this. They're doing public vivisection on me...and I never hurt anyone. Who did I hurt? And all this just a couple of months after my best friend dies. My God. My God. It simply horrifies me that anyone would ever do anything like this to another human being."

"It makes a person want to cry," he said.

"I don't cry anymore," she replied, her wide, clear eyes looking at him. "I almost died from crying over Thomas Adam. I only weighed about eighty-five pounds when someone—probably a neighbor—called the ambulance for me. So I don't cry anymore." She did not even realize that was the most personal information she'd ever shared about herself with anyone. Especially a man. "Will you take me somewhere?" she asked him.

"Anywhere. Anytime."

"Let me pack a few things. I'd like to go out of here in your trunk, if you don't mind."

"We have the van..."

"No, no, that's too obvious. You could be hiding someone in the van. I want to go in the trunk. Will you drop off some luggage for me tomorrow? I don't want to hide in the trunk and have those assholes at the end of the road see your back seat full of suitcases."

He made a small smile. "You have a knack for this, Sable."

"Yeah. When this is over, I'll run for public office. You can be my bodyguard."

She filled several suitcases and left them in her room. With her she took only an overnight bag and change of clothes. Jeff offered to take her to his own house or a hotel, but only one place came to mind where she would feel completely safe. It had never occurred to her to phone ahead. When she arrived at Gabby's house, she asked that Jeff stay in the car and leave once she went inside. She did give him a kiss on the cheek and promised to talk to him more when he brought the rest of her luggage. There was a car she didn't recognize parked in the drive, but that didn't intimidate her. It was probably one of Barbara Ann's sons' cars. They could still be sorting and reading; Barbara Ann may as well hear the story from her. She'd have to tell it now. To her friends, at least. All three of them. So they could sift through the garbage of it and decide whether they could stomach knowing her.

She had to ring and ring. Elly wasn't answering. Finally, she saw a shadow cross over the peephole and the door came cautiously open. She waved off Jeff and entered. Elly was in her robe.

"Oh, Elly, you were asleep? I'm sorry! I should have called. I wasn't thinking."

"Sable? Isn't it a little late?"

"Elly, they know. Actually, that's the least of it. They embellished horribly. You can't imagine what they're saying about me! It's simply unbelievable."

"They *who*?"

"The tabloids. I was the subject of a television tabloid show tonight. You didn't hear about it? I'm surprised someone hasn't called…"

"Elly?" a strange voice called from the bedroom. There was a shuffling sound. "Is everything—"

A squat, bald man appeared in the foyer. He wore hastily drawn-up brown pants with an untucked fuchsia shirt. His feet were bare. His belt was open. Little wisps of hair stood out around his ears. Sable looked between Elly, who wore a robe, and the man. "Oh my God," she said in a breath. And then, idiotically, "Elly, do you *know* this man?"

NINE

"All this time you've hidden him!" Sable exclaimed to Elly when Ben had finally gone.

They were putting fresh sheets on the guest-room bed for Sable. "It's nothing to what you've hidden, so don't get started on me."

"But why, Elly? He's so wonderful!"

"You're hysterical," Elly accused. Had Sable met Ben under any other circumstances, she might not have noticed his finer qualities. But Sable had been in trouble; her life was unraveling in the most grotesque manner. Once everyone was clumsily introduced—and dressed—Sable had asked, "Can I talk in front of him? Will he take my story to the press or something?" Ben had offered to leave, but it was Elly who insisted he stay, vouching for his integrity. And then Ben wound his charm around her, as only Ben could do. It broke his heart to think what was happening to Sable; it wounded him personally to witness the cheap voyeurs we'd all become. "My daughter watches that program," he had said. "I'm going to insist that she stop!" There was not an ounce of recrimination from Ben for the young girl who'd lived shabbily and married stupidly and suffered unimaginably. Just his straightforward kindness. "Some people can be so cruel. How do they sleep, do you s'pose?"

"I'm not hysterical about him," Sable assured Elly. "Are you sure it's okay if I stay here?"

No one had spent the night with Elly in over three decades. She was already feeling claustrophobic. "You have to stay somewhere," she said.

"Do you think I brought this on myself, Elly?" Sable asked.

Eleanor was struck by the childlike quality of Sable's voice. She sat down on her side of the guest bed. She thought for a minute. "Your story, the true version," she said, "is not very different from what is often used as the inspirational fodder of political speeches and religious reformers. You grew up under the oppression of every social disadvantage and you somehow saved yourself. You overcame. The only problem I see with the image you created for yourself is that it consistently hid your strength. But I sympathize. Those things that are personally humiliating to us rarely have the expected effect of shock and disgust on others. People are remarkably sympathetic and forgiving. When we open up, we become more human. We're easier to relate to. Opening up about the secrets frees us from our false pretensions and people usually respond."

"That hasn't been my experience," Sable said. "I feel like there's an army of people out there who will be thrilled to find out I'm not such a class act after all."

"Well, I've been to a lot of AA meetings. My dear, you can't even compete."

"I've never heard any of your revealing, human stories, Eleanor."

Elly stood. "Well, that's the most dangerous part of my disease, Sable. My personal shame. I seem to run into it every time I turn a corner." She thought about Ben, of whom she had been ashamed, though she loved him and knew that he was inherently so good. She gave Sable a pat on the head. "I didn't change my name, that's all."

Sable wasn't her usual chic self. Her clothes were wrinkled, for one thing, because they'd been hastily packed. And the water in Gabby's house was slightly harder, which caused her hair to fall differently, and her makeup didn't go on as smoothly. Then she had to eat Eleanor's bran cereal for breakfast, which was a lot like eating a cardboard box. She'd find a way to get the right food in this place, if she was going to stay.

Although Barbara Ann and Beth had not phoned Elly, both arrived at the house early, bursting with the news. Neither had seen the program. Barbara Ann was called by several of her cronies after it aired; they were filled with questions, ripe with curiosity. Barbara Ann had called Beth, but Beth knew nothing about it. She rarely turned on her television before 8:00 p.m. They had both tried to call Sable, but of course there was no answer. And both were astonished, but greatly relieved, to find her at the house. Of course, they wanted the factual details.

"I think in a heinous sort of way, I owe that program a debt of gratitude. They might have ruined my career and cost me millions, but they made me out to be so much worse than I really was, that the truth isn't as terrifying anymore. Not that I'm blameless. Not that many people will be interested in my version."

"You had a catastrophic childhood," Eleanor said. "There's no blame in that."

"I was twenty-two when Tommy was killed," Sable reminded her.

"As I said," she insisted.

It was almost like old times, though Gabby was missing. The sky was clear and the morning cool, so they positioned themselves on the deck with steaming coffee cups in their hands. Sable didn't realize that she'd practiced a bit of this telling exercise with Jeff and then with Elly and Ben. But this was the first time she was willingly going over all the grim details with an honest desire to unburden herself of the load.

"I have vague memories of my mother dressing me in little tennies that matched my outfit. I remember her singing to me while I was in the bathtub. I think that when I was small, she wasn't as far down the bottle. I think maybe she loved me. I think she had some self-esteem then.

"Of course, I also remember the men. Oddly, my mother was never a prostitute. I say oddly because she was very critical of hookers—that women would take money for it! But my mother used to pick up men in bars and bring them home for the night. When I was little, she would take me with her. When I was older—four or five—she would tuck me in, warn me not to get out of bed or open the door for any reason, and leave me for several hours. Sometimes I'd be so scared, I'd lie there and just tremble. And then when I heard her come stumbling in, giggling and knocking things over, I could finally relax. Once, one of her men came careening into my room. I'm amazed it was only once. And my mother went crazy. At the time I couldn't imagine what had caused her to lose her mind like that—screaming, throwing things, hitting him, shoving him. Later I understood. That was when our life together changed, and she started leaving me alone too much, probably to avoid bringing men home so often. Shortly thereafter, when I was six, I was put in my first foster home."

"Was there no family to take you in?" Beth asked.

"There was family somewhere, but I don't know who or how many. My grandparents threw my mother out when she got pregnant and she moved in with Helmut Gobrich, who she said was my father. She later said he wasn't my father after all, but he believed he was and that was good enough for her since she had nowhere else to go. I have no idea what happened to that relationship. He might have been a loser who walked out on her. Or, she might have told him the truth and left him. We never heard from him. When I asked if my grandparents were dead, she said, 'No, Helen. I am.'"

"I can't believe no one would want to adopt you! No family would come forward and take you! Even this Gobrich guy!" That came from Barbara Ann, who won the prize for having the most people to care for in her life, immediate and otherwise. It brought a smile to Sable's lips because just considering the number and variety of doomed pets her sons had rescued over the years virtually guaranteed that Barbara Ann would not have left little Helen to flounder untended, had she but known. You had to love her for that.

"I wasn't a cute little girl, Barbara Ann."

"That's hard to believe. I mean, look at you."

"You're looking at about thirty-thousand dollars' worth of orthodonture and plastic surgery. I was ugly as a stump."

"That's not true," Elly said.

But it was. Ironically, that was probably the hardest part of the story to tell. Much of her early abuse derived from her looks. She was called the Ugly Duckling by her own mother. If that wasn't hard enough, foster families and schoolmates followed suit. If she'd looked then like she looked now—slim, blond, pretty—maybe parts of her life would not have been so difficult. Or, giving the human race the benefit of the doubt, if she'd had anything to smile or be perky about, maybe things would have been smoother. But added to her disadvantaged looks were downcast eyes, a grim mouth and withdrawn or skittish behavior.

"There was a social worker, when I was nearing eighteen and about to be dumped out of the foster care system. He was this nerdy guy named Boyd. He gave me some tests and I passed...."

"She excelled," Elly corrected.

"I did okay. He helped me get a GED and a scholarship and off I went to college, where I really didn't belong. But that's where I met first Gabby and then Elly."

"Didn't belong? Ha! You cannot imagine what she studied, this girl who hadn't finished high school," Elly said.

"You can't imagine what this woman threw at me. She tossed nine-hundred page volumes at me and said things like, 'If you had earned your place in this class, you would have read this two years ago, so read it now.' It was so much bullshit. Most of Elly's students hadn't read that shit in the first place and she knows it."

"They were supposed to have," Eleanor said, but her lips curved slightly. She had never before had a student like Sable. It had been intoxicating.

"Gabby had taken me under her wing and was pretending to ask me for help with her psychology course. She was studying me like a lab rat. When she thought I was interesting enough, she shared me with Eleanor, who then took over the grooming of the poor kid. Elly was wearing those tweed skirts, flat-soled brown shoes, and she even had that huge purse back then. She's been chain-smoking for forty years. She felt sorry for me, I think, sitting in her class day after day, auditing."

"That is categorically untrue. You fascinated and impressed Gabby, then me."

"I fascinated you? Impressed you? You never said that."

"I didn't think I had to," Eleanor replied, but inside she suddenly felt a huge stab of regret. Could things have turned out altogether differently had she outrightly praised Helen? "I should have."

"No, Elly, I liked you the way you were. I wouldn't have believed you any other way. The problem was mine. I was still mired in the old life. I couldn't believe I was really smart enough to be there, to do anything significant with my life, therefore I didn't. I went back to Fresno when my mother got in touch and said she needed me. My return was so ambivalent. I resented that she would draw me away from my one chance to have a life, but I was relieved to go back to a place I felt I belonged. Or deserved."

She didn't drag it out. She spit it out fast, sharp and clear. For a writer capable of dynamic, moving description, she stuck to the facts, which were bad enough. Stuck with a sick, drunk mother. Finding some solace in Butch. Having the baby. The death of the baby. Her near death from grief. Escape to L.A. Escape into women's fiction. Writing and working like a woman who had nothing to lose, because...

Beth was staring down into her coffee cup, her fingers tightening and relaxing around it at intervals. Barbara Ann got up from her chair. "Stop a minute," she said weakly, softly. She turned her back on Sable and walked to the edge of the deck, looking out at the trees. "Give me a minute," she said.

"Please don't cry about it," Sable said. "I can take anything but pity. Really."

"I'm not crying out of pity," Barbara Ann said, turning back to Sable and revealing the wet streaks on her cheeks. "I'm... You can't believe what I've thought of you. All these years."

"I know what you thought. I know what everyone thinks."

"No, you don't. I've been so jealous. I didn't want to be—it was at least as hard on me as it was on you. It just seemed that everything in your life went your way, no matter what! God, you designed the perfect life for yourself and pretended to be living it!"

Sable laughed hollowly. "Right from the time my surgeon father and designer mother took their fateful trip to Alaska and died in a plane wreck?"

"Even that sounded romantic. I gotta admit, Sable, you sure can tell a story."

"The critics don't agree," she dourly replied.

Barbara Ann wandered back, sitting down. "You were so hard to love sometimes. You were so—"

"But you see, that's what makes this even worse! Are there people out there who will be able to treat me with respect now? Because my life was such a disaster? Because I grew up as bad as any dog? How the hell is that fair?"

"That's not what Barbara Ann means, Sable," Elly said.

"Don't tell her what I mean," Barbara Ann protested.

"I'd better, because you're going to fuck it up. It wasn't your constant good fortune that made you distant, Sable. Nor does revealing your many hardships make you more lovable. There is a place between the truth and the lie where you became untouchable. Your life hasn't been perfect since you started making millions, but you didn't trust anyone enough to tell the truth about that either. You had problems. You've covered everything up for long enough."

"Are you suggesting that if I'd complained about business problems—like my tax bill—I'd have gotten *sympathy?*"

Elly sat forward and sighed. "Do you miss the point intentionally, or are you dense? I think it's pretty well established that money—taxes included—is not one of your problems. But you reveal *nothing* about your real self. And since you don't, I can't elaborate."

"Now, Elly, you have a nerve—"

"We'll expose my secrets another day!" she snapped. "This is about you! Do you want to understand this, or not?"

"Jeez," Sable said, taken aback. "Don't get huffy."

"Is there anything imperfect about your life? Do you sweat? Get pimples? Have hemorrhoids? Secretly take Valium in amounts not particularly recommended?"

Sable was stunned. She felt turned on. Cornered.

"Elly, that's not what I meant," Barbara Ann said quietly.

"Yes, it is, you just don't realize it yet. Well?" Elly said, looking at Sable.

"Of course there's stuff about my life that's hard.

You know that. I get trouble from fans sometimes. That prison guy had me pretty scared."

"You threw money at that problem; Jeff is taking care of it for you. He's in touch with the prison, correct? What about the way you live, Sable? What's going on inside your personal life?"

"I can't believe you're doing this to me," she said. "I've never known you to be cruel."

"Cruel? I'd just like to know who the hell you are. I've felt, for all practical purposes, like a mother to you. At least a favorite aunt. I've loved you, I've taught you, I've defended you, I've lauded your accomplishments. But most of the time I wonder who you really are. You know, I don't have the first idea how you're dealing with Gabby's death. And aside from hiding out, I'm not sure how you're dealing with this!"

"I'm terrified, all right?! I don't know if I'll have *anything left* because of this! I may not have a way to earn a living, I may not have any friends left, and I might never—sleep. I don't sleep anyway. I toss and turn. I have nightmares. I'm scared to death to be alone! That's why I have Dorothy and Art living on the property! Every single night before I turn in, I check the locks in the house fifteen times, and then I can't settle down until I'm sure the light's on in their cottage. Every time I made some money, I could at least surround myself with more people, to insulate me. To keep me *safe*. The secretary can shield me from the calls, my publicist can shield me from the reporters, my agent from the publishers.... I have to have *protection!*"

Elly sat back, satisfied. She gave Sable a minute to collect herself. Then she stood. "Well, I can't speak for Barbara Ann and Beth, but I'm not going anywhere. I can't help you fall asleep or protect you from the boo-geyman, but I will be your friend, one hundred per-cent, no matter what crap you reveal about yourself. Not your insulation, but your *friend*. I can't be scared off by your distance or this adverse publicity that's go-ing on all around you. Coffee? I'll bring the pot." She clomped off the deck and into the house.

There was a moment of silence all around. It was Barbara Ann who finally spoke. "I have never seen a display like that in my life!" She reached from her chair to Sable's, covering her hand. "Are you all right?"

"She was just making a point. I've been dishonest."

"I don't think keeping your worst problems to your-self is really *dishonest*. More like, private."

"That's the excuse I used, too," Sable said.

Eleanor came back in time to hear those last remarks. She began filling coffee cups. "I'd hate for you to mis-interpret what just happened between Sable and me, Barbara Ann. I hardly think anything can be gained by public sniveling or chronic complaining, but Sable's fears and anxieties come from the cradle. If she com-plains, they won't love her. If she isn't perfect, they'll abandon her. And above all, she'll be left alone and frightened, no matter what she does. Harboring fears like those keep people from being intimate. It's only through a willingness to be vulnerable—admitting to the weakness of such fears—that one can become inti-mate. With friends, with mates, with family. It's time, I think, to put that to rest once and for all. It's safe for you to be yourself now, Sable. You aren't as alone as you feel. There *are* people who will love you as you are."

"There are," Beth said softly.

"That was always the hardest part about being your

friend, Sable. You didn't need anything," Barbara Ann said.

"I apologize, Sable, if my timing was bad," Eleanor said. "I'm not very good at these things, but I do know the drill." She sighed heavily. "You can't imagine the things I've been forced to admit."

"Did it help you, Elly?"

She actually had to think for a moment. "Ultimately," she said. "I was a hard sell, but eventually I learned that it was more than gin that caused me to tuck the back of my dress into my hose before walking on stage at a baccalaureate ceremony. I mooned the class of '76. It was a magic moment, one of my brightest displays."

The women began to laugh, in spite of themselves. Barbara Ann was laughing through tears.

"Get ahold of yourself," Sable said. "Obviously, I've gotten through it."

"Oh, that's not it. I never thought there could be this deep, horrible reason you behaved like such a bitch sometimes."

"Funny, I thought that deep down inside you might be secretly relieved to know I wasn't so cool."

"Relieved? Gimme a break! It was hard enough for me to deal with all you had in your life! Now, in addition to everything else, you're *tragic*. Jesus, Sable. I've never felt so ordinary in my life!"

"Well, if it's any comfort, I'd prefer to be the way I was when people hated me."

"I never hated you, Sable. You didn't have to go through all this to get my sympathy. You could have just spilled chocolate syrup on your blouse to make me feel vindicated." She blew her nose. "You've always got some strategy," Barbara Ann said. "What's your plan now?"

"I have a non-plan," she said. "I'm not going to do anything."

"You could call your lawyers," Barbara Ann suggested. "I've always been so impressed that you had lawyers. And stockbrokers. And financial planners. All those little bunnies, hopping around doing things for you."

"I have a feeling that a lot of little bunnies could get rich off this without doing me much good, and I don't want to participate. What would happen if I didn't spend a lot of money trying to head off what I can't head off anyway?"

"Couldn't it all get a lot worse?"

Sable laughed.

"Couldn't they *find* you?"

"Now that's a problem. I'd really like to have a break. I want to think things over for a little while. I want to stay here and work on Gabby's office. I need to get some cereal and cold cuts—Eleanor eats like a prison inmate. I should do something about my house. I don't want anyone to hurt or upset Dorothy and Art. I don't want to watch any more television reports on me or read any of the shit they write.... I just want to rest for a while. Think."

"Is there any chance these media types could question *us*?" Beth asked.

"I suppose. Maybe even follow you. Do whatever you want."

"Come on, it's not like we'd *say* anything," Barbara Ann insisted. "We'd better make sure no one's following us when we're coming over here. Make a list of what you need, Sable. I'll run to the store. You can't change your life without good food. Then, I think we ought to head them off at the pass, if possible. Elly, I have an idea."

"This is Dr. Jerome Edwards, calling for Mr. Arnold Bynum," Elly said, deepening her already deep voice. Barbara Ann couldn't help herself; impossible-to-control laughter pushed its way roughly through her nose in a giant snort. Her head fell into her arms, which rested on the kitchen table. Her shoulders shook and she began to squeak helplessly. "This is in regards to his client, Ms. Sable Tennet. I'm her physician. Thank you."

Elly put her hand over the receiver and angrily demanded, "Why the hell do I have to be a *man?*"

But they'd been over this. Barbara Ann insisted there were only ten women in America who had a voice as low and raspy as Eleanor's. And Eleanor, known to be Sable's friend and having been heard speak in public, would be found out. She could sound like a young, male doctor or Eleanor Fulton, period. "Just do it!" Barbara Ann said through her laughter.

"Yes, Mr. Bynum," Elly was saying. "Dr. Edwards here. I've been asked by Ms. Tennet to give you a call. She's been hospitalized with…for…" Oh God, they hadn't come up with her medical problem. Six eyes widened in total panic and stared back at Eleanor, useless. "It's mainly a stress reaction that seems to have caused…diverticulitis. Inflammation of the bowel." Sable slid to the floor in shock, hugging herself. She could almost read the headlines now! Sable Tennet Succumbs to Stress-Induced Bowel Inflammation.

"Diverticulitis?" Beth said, confused.

"It's…the only…illness Eleanor's ever…had," Barbara Ann managed to choke out, trying to control herself. She sat on the floor beside Sable and covered her mouth to control her laughter, but tears ran down her cheeks.

"That's why she eats that shit for breakfast," Sable managed.

"You mean the forty gallons of coffee she drinks a day doesn't run right through her?"

"Sometimes," Sable answered. "That's the other symptom. God, why couldn't she just give me an ulcer? It's not as though I haven't earned it!"

"In fact, that's the purpose of my call," Elly was saying. "I've recommended that Ms. Tennet have no visitors and rest in a stress-free environment for a week to ten days." Sable began frantically waving her arms at Elly. "Actually, make that two to three weeks. To that end, I have been asked not to disclose the hospital or the location and to inform you that she is going to be fine and will be in touch with you when she's feeling better.... Well, Mr. Bynum, she didn't ask me to give you any instructions about how to handle her current business problems, so that indicates to me that she trusts your judgment...."

"Or she doesn't give a shit," Sable whispered.

"Even if she could discuss business right now, Mr. Bynum, I don't think it would be very useful to you. She's been medicated for pain and depression. She's silly as a goose...."

"Silly as a goose?" Beth whispered. "That didn't sound very medical."

"Great idea, Barb," Sable remarked. "I'm slayed with bouts of diarrhea and I'm silly as a goose. Arnie won't believe a word of this."

"Yes, of course I'll tell her. And I'm sure you'll be

hearing from her as soon as her symptoms subside. I think we can treat this nonsurgically. If the medication can induce shrinkage in the diverticula, that is.... Fine, I can do that. I'll give you a call in a week or so and keep you informed about her progress, but I can assure you, she's in good hands. Edwards...Dr. Jerome.... Very well, then. Goodbye." She hung up the phone and glared at them.

"Diverticulitis? You couldn't think of anything else?" Sable asked.

"It's the only disease I know how to treat," Eleanor replied self-righteously.

Later in the afternoon when Barbara was leaving for the day, she stole a moment alone with Sable. "Just tell me one thing," she whispered. "Did you have those perky little tits lifted, or do they stay on your chest of their own accord?"

"Lifted," Sable admitted. "And, tummy-tucked."

"Oh thank God," Barbara Ann sighed, embracing Sable warmly.

Sable had never been an overnight guest in Gabby's house, not even when she first returned to the Sacramento area. But now, as she sat in the guest-room bed, propped up against the pillows, she regretted that. There was something about the whole environment that was soothing. There was no television in the room, for one thing. It was early in the evening for her to be in bed, only nine-thirty.

She felt relaxed, though she couldn't imagine why. Her life was coming apart; she should be in a psych ward somewhere, sedated. But strangely, she didn't feel she needed it. What she needed—wanted—was to be away from everything. *Everything.* The phones, the faxes. The perfect white house. The servants. The jewelry. The clothes. In this guest room, cluttered with books, a little dusty, small and densely furnished, it was like burrowing into a cocoon. She felt safe.

Elly came into the room. She was wearing her old flowered robe, had a folded newspaper tucked under her arm and carried a steaming cup. She sat down on the bed beside Sable. "Cocoa," she said. "No caffeine, warm milk."

"Are you suggesting I forgo the two vodkas I usually take like a sleeping pill?"

Elly shrugged. "I'm a little sensitive to that. No reason to push your luck."

"It's really never more than two," Sable said.

Elly put the cocoa down on the bedside table. "That's not the point, really. The cocoa's there if you want it." Then, strangely, Elly opened her arms. Elly had *never* embraced Sable. Not really. The other women were all huggers and Elly allowed herself to be put upon in that fashion, but it always seemed as though she was going along with it, indulging them. Yet within Elly's strong arms was a great nurturing. Elly's bosom was soft and thick against Sable's; her shoulder was solid under Sable's cheek. "It's been a long, long day," Elly said, massaging Sable's back in slow comforting strokes.

Unbelievably, Sable began to quietly weep.

"It's going to be all right," Elly said. "Awful as it seems, this is going to pass. My dear, dear girl, there is no way I can explain the horrors of what's being done to you, but I do know that my own blackest days have often led to something I needed in the end. It will pass. It will."

"That's not what I'm crying about," Sable whimpered. "Thomas Adam," she said softly, sniffing. "And Gabby. And you."

Elly pulled back. "Me?"

Sable's cheeks were wet with the first tears she'd shed in twenty years. "My losses. You can't imagine how I loved that baby, how I loved Gabby."

"I can," Elly argued. "But have I hurt you so badly, Sable?"

"Oh no, Elly!" she said, falling back into the embrace, holding Elly close. "I had no idea you loved me so much!"

"Ah," Elly said, resuming her consoling massage. "That, my dear girl, will not pass."

TEN

The women made the decision to combine their efforts in sorting through Gabby's office with the understanding that it was Barbara Ann who had the most commitments with her writing and family. She had the least amount of extra time, yet she was at Gabby's house every day. She arrived in the morning by ten; she left by three-thirty so she could stop at the grocery store on her way home (if necessary...and it was *always* necessary), give her house a second straightening while she cooked dinner (it would already be a mess after her first attempt to tidy it in the early morning), run a load or two of wash, hose down the kitchen after dinner and then attack her evening reading and chores.

"Why don't you stay home and work on your book?" Sable had asked, offering Barbara Ann a way out, an excuse.

"Right now I'm just waiting to hear how they liked the one I just sent in, and what they want by way of revisions," she said, as though everything was business as usual.

"Don't you usually crank up a new proposal between books, while you're waiting?"

"Everything is mailed in," she said.

"Barbara Ann, you are absolutely amazing. I've always wondered how you do it."

"I'm well organized. Besides, if I don't help you, who knows what kind of a mess you'll make of things. Somebody has to keep things straight around here."

Barbara Ann had named herself custodian. You don't raise four boys in a relatively clean environment by being disorganized. Sable had apparently forgotten how to clean a house in her decade of full-time help, Elly had never learned and was comfortable in chaos, Beth, who was extremely tidy, seemed at odds with someone else's clutter, and so it fell to Barbara Ann. She started every morning by shopping from the list Sable had given her the day before; groceries, toiletries, odds and ends. Next, she cleaned the kitchen. Then she'd go around the house in search of messes that required a quick, capable hand. She didn't overtake them. She didn't bother their clothes, laundry or personal possessions. But there was no excuse for dirty dishes lying around, or scummy bathrooms, or filled trash cans. She couldn't stop herself from washing a couple of loads of towels now and then. It seemed so senseless to Barbara Ann to have a washing machine sit idle if there was anything in the house that needed laundering.

She attacked the paperwork in the same efficient manner. Beth was organizing contracts, royalty statements and out-of-print books. Those works that were still bringing in occasional royalties would have to be converted into payments to Sarah and David. On several works that were out of print, the rights could be reversed back to Gabby's estate for possible resale. Eleanor was working on the project that required the most space; she was putting together Gabby's early articles and nonfiction with photos, letters, old calendars and miscellaneous writings. She had also found some original unpublished work from Gabby's traveling years. Sable was organizing letters into files; some would be returned to senders, some destroyed, others saved for posterity through collection or publishing. Every single page of paper had to be read and considered for the job to be complete.

So, that left boxes and boxes of various manuscripts to Barbara Ann. She hauled them into the house from the garage and began the identifying and labeling process. Her job was also to arrange to have them donated to UC Berkeley's Special Collections Library. From just the volume of paper they'd already handled, it was possible to finish in another week or two, if everyone kept working.

But, not everyone was working. There was a lot of dawdling going on. Then there was lost time when someone found something she wanted to share; a special letter, an outline of a book idea that was never written in full, or their favorite—which cost them a whole day—the Vitriolic Prose File.

The VPF, subheaded the WBNM file—Written But Never Mailed—was Gabby at her absolute best. It was a shame not to share it with the world. These were the letters she wrote when she was angry; letters condemned to a dead file for her private and regular amusement. Barbara's favorite was the letter written to an editor fifteen years ago.

Gabby had written a wonderful book typical of her talent. It was constructed of many layers; a love story, a suspense and a lot of social commentary. Gabby was the only writer Barbara Ann knew who could pull off such a feat of blending plot types in such a stunning way. Gabby's editor had bought the book in a panic of thrill; she was going to hang Gabby's star. Then the publishing company underwent corporate changes; Gabby's editor left and the book was orphaned. The manuscript was finally assigned to a former cookbook editor who, it came to seem, didn't think the book had been worth publishing at all. The novel—which in the end was very favorably reviewed and sold a respectable number of copies—did not excel to the greatness it might have achieved because the editor never liked it and never pushed it. The editor then rejected the next novel altogether. She was finally fired, her superiors eventually recognizing her complete lack of aptitude for fiction. Too late for Gabby's book, of course. The letter was written—but not mailed—after the rejection of the second book but before publication of the first book, just when Gabby had had all she could take of being screwed around.

Dear Ms. Townsend,

It's quite clear you have been dealing with cakes and cookies rather than fiction. Even so, you should know enough not to pour salt into the wounds of those innocents you stab in the back. That the editing of *Simply Told* was atrocious, I could forgive. After all, it is my responsibility to provide a readable book. That the cover depicted a white stallion and white mare rather than *people*, or a tasteful alternative, I am forced to overlook as the horses *were* mentioned on one page in the novel. That the marketing plan was altered to reflect a 5,000 book-print run in lieu of the 50,000 hardcover copies your predecessor planned, though I object, I must defer to your greater publishing wisdom. We all have our opinions, after all. But to indict me of poor craft in your rejection letter is crossing the line of human decency. You wrote, "Unfortunately, you just haven't captured the clarity and complexity that I believe you capable of achieving...a problem I have found inherent in your work and something I *know* you can, with perseverance, develop eventually." You are full of shit, Ms. Townsend. You don't know your ass from a Bundt pan. And you wouldn't know decent fiction if it exploded in your oven. If you don't fucking like the book, say so. But don't give me this omnipotent complexity and clarity crap, since you're consistently oblivious to both!

Now, I'll be the first to admit I may lack some objectivity regarding the quality of my work. Emily Rothschild, my former editor and the very one who paid a considerable amount of money for *Simply Told*, may have been overly enthusiastic in promising that this novel would achieve bestseller status in nothing flat. But, allowing for such prejudice and/or inflated excitement, I still know that my work, my craft, my ability, is *competent*. What I mean by that, should you require an explanation, is that my work is as good as anything out there and better than a lot of it. What I mean is that my readers and critics have been consistently satisfied. I am trying to say, Ms. Townsend, that you're a stupid fool. And besides that, you're unforgivably mean.

You may have sold *Simply Told* short, and I can't do anything about that now, but you really missed out by cruelly rejecting *Banished Children*, which will be better published by someone with a working brain. By the way, who read it to you?

Yours sincerely,
Gabrielle Seton Marshall

Barbara Ann only wished a few nasty letters, written but not mailed, would make her feel better. Sadly, she wasn't as confident of her own work's competence as Gabby had been. Suddenly, they weren't buying her. God, oh God, she wasn't sure why. A finished, contracted, revised and rewritten book had been mailed back to her with the vague explanation that "It never quite got where we thought it needed to be." Immediately, her next proposal, a mere twelve-page idea, was ordered rewritten according to the editor's special needs. Twice. Then it was rejected out of hand. "It just doesn't do anything for me," the editor had said. "I can't feel the potential for enough romantic tension." Three weeks ago Barbara Ann had mailed in another finished novel and another twelve-page proposal. They were supposed to respond within thirty days, but they rarely made the deadline. If she didn't have this project at Gabby's house, she would go crazy. They were going to do it again, she could feel it. Throw her away. Chew her up and spit her out. She had no idea what she was doing wrong, and her editor—her sixth in as many years—had only vague explanations and quirky tastes. *This character is simply not multilayered enough.* Does that mean her hair should be frosted instead of brown? *There doesn't seem to be enough personal conflict to drive her forward.* What should I add to the fact that she was orphaned, abandoned by her first husband and raped by her boss?

Barbara Ann had been writing romances since the beginning. She began because she loved reading them. She wrote three, sometimes four, a year. It took almost all the time she had, but she'd braved a couple of leaps into mainstream publishing anyway. She'd somehow found time to attempt a couple of other proposals for longer, more complex romance novels than what she'd become known for. If she could just snag a second publisher, one who was excited about her potential, she would be on her way at last. She wouldn't have to write so hard, so fast, always hammering to keep up with the next deadline. True, she'd tried submitting to a new publisher only twice, but they didn't take. There were only so many hours in the day.

Now a second publisher was the least of her worries. She just wanted to keep her job.

She hauled in another box of old manuscripts from the garage and plopped them on the kitchen table. Through the kitchen window she could see Sable standing behind Beth, brushing out her long, black hair. Sarah and the baby—frequent visitors since Elly and Sable had taken over Gabby's house—were sitting across from Beth. There was a makeup bag on the picnic table. This was beginning to turn into some weird slumber party. She wanted to bark, "Let's get to work around here!" But she couldn't. A) You don't deprive a poor twenty-two-year old girl who has just lost her mother of the only comfort she has, which seems to be visiting her mother's friends in her mother's house. B) You can't snap at someone like Sable, who was going through a bizarre recovery from a lifetime of catastrophic problems. And C) Barbara Ann didn't really want this project at Gabby's house to end too soon because she, too, was feeling terribly lost and needed this to slow down time.

So, she got herself a soda and wandered onto the deck to join them.

"You didn't put the money into a joint account, did you?" Sable asked Sarah.

"No, I did what you said. I opened a new account. But I have to pay some bills with it. I'm behind on everything because of Lindsey's medical expenses. I need to catch up on the car insurance, for one thing. I can't let that get behind."

Barbara Ann put down the soda and reached for the baby. At six months, you could only tell around the eyes that the baby had Down's syndrome. Lindsey immediately smiled at Barbara Ann. She was the most pleasant, most precious baby. She still couldn't hold up her head. Barbara Ann felt her muscles immediately relax, her poor humor disappear. Babies did that to her. It was her doom.

"Of course, my dad wants me to move out on Justin, now that I have some money of my own," Sarah said.

"You know," Sable the wise said, "the only difference between your mom and your dad is that your dad wanted you to just listen to him and avoid all your problems, and your mom knew you'd have to do things your own way and come to your own conclusions. They were always both equally distressed by what you've been through lately. I don't think Justin is a bad guy, Sarah. But it appears he's just not up to all these responsibilities." Sable was starting to French-braid Beth's hair. Barbara Ann had *never* seen Sable do things like this.

"I know," Sarah agreed.

"But do you love him?" Beth wanted to know.

"I'm not sure anymore. Ever since I got pregnant with Lindsey, he's spent more time out with the guys than with me. I used to think it was just me, that when I wasn't pregnant anymore, things would change. But it hasn't. We fight all the time. I know it's my fault. The minute he gets home, I start in on him. So he leaves."

"Does he love you?" Beth asked.

"Beth, give it a break. What's the use of having all this love shit if they can't get along for five minutes?" Sable wanted to know.

"Because if they love each other, maybe it can be worked out," Beth said earnestly.

"If he *loves her,* he needs to spend an evening with her and Lindsey and not the boys. There is this little thing about actions following intentions, you know."

"But if he *does* love her, maybe she can find a way to make spending an evening with her more appealing than going out. Sarah, you have to stop needling him so much if you want him to hang around more."

"Maybe she should meet him at the door in a garter belt and push-up bra?" Sable suggested sarcastically.

"That isn't what I mean at all," Beth argued. "But there might be a way to make coming home and staying home more desirable than going out with the guys. If you think about it, you know?"

"I used to try that a lot," Sarah said. "But it hurt my feelings so much when it didn't work that I just got meaner and meaner."

"I don't know how he can keep his hands off this baby," Barbara Ann said, snuggling Lindsey close and breathing in the wonderful smell of her.

"He does love the baby," Sarah said. "She's the only reason we're still together."

"See," Beth said.

"See what?" Sable reacted. "That's not going to be good for the baby or their marriage. They have to work together to raise this baby. She's going to require a lot of special attention."

"It's a place to start. It's something to build on. People can change, you know."

"People can also become bigger assholes, given the opportunity. There," she said proudly, braid finished. "That's stunning. Now, take off those glasses and let's do your eyes."

Sable's dual tragedies—the horrors of her life as Helen and the subsequent public dissemination of it all—were having the most unexpected effect. First, Barbara Ann found Sable walking around the house barefoot. The perfectly put-together, chic and sophisticated Sable, barefoot. Barbara Ann didn't even know she *had* feet! She thought Sable's legs ended with Italian leather pumps—scuffless, new, shiny pumps.

Then, Sable had gone through Gabby's closet and found a couple of old sweat suits that were too short on her long legs, but she wore them anyway. Recently, she had graduated to some of Gabby's summer smocks—lightweight, gauzy, busily printed, flowing, midi-length dresses. And just yesterday, like a kid who lost her first tooth, Sable announced ecstatically, "Look! My roots are growing out!" She'd picked off her fake nails, quit drawing on her eyebrows and took to napping on the chaise lounge on the redwood deck.

Sable's luggage, filled with her expensive, tailor-made outfits, stayed packed and stacked up in the guest room while Sable wore whatever old thing she could dig out of the back of a closet. She no longer maintained fussy perfection in her appearance, either. The one thing Barbara thought would bring her pleasure caused only disdain as Sable ignored a salsa stain on the front of her sundress, stating that it blended in with the print. Barbara feared Sable was going through some sort of nervous breakdown over this whole thing.

And now she was playing makeup with Beth. Barbara Ann handed the baby back to Sarah. "I'm going to get out of here before Sable starts giving her a pedicure."

"Are you still working mainly in the kitchen?" Sable asked Barbara Ann.

"Yes, why?"

"We're going to take a break here and make some cookies. Want to help?"

"You're going to take a break from *what* to make cookies? Sable, we *do* have to get through Gabby's things," Barbara Ann impatiently reminded her.

"Oh, there's no hurry," Sarah said, repositioning the baby onto her shoulder. "I dread the day you're finally done. I don't know what I'd do without you all here."

Barbara Ann ran her hand over the baby's feathery hair. "I know, sweetheart, but we all have other commitments. I can't do this all summer."

"I know," Sarah said thickly, the sound of tears creeping into her voice. "But it's been such a help."

"I'm afraid that what it's helping us do is avoid facing the other ugly things we have to do—like going home and facing the music." Barbara looked at Sable. "Don't you think there are some people who are worried about you?"

She shrugged, putting a finishing swish of blusher on Beth's cheeks. "No. But I think there are a few who are planning my death. There! Why do you hide all this beauty behind those big specs? Why don't you get contacts? Put on a little makeup?"

"Jack really likes my skin natural," Beth said.

"But what do you like?" Sable pressed.

There was a slight hesitation. "I like what Jack likes," she said.

"Jesus, Beth, why don't you just give the guy a kidney! It would be simpler."

"Oh, stop.... There's nothing wrong with trying to please your husband."

"Beth, did it ever occur to you that it's a big mistake to—"

Barbara Ann went back into the kitchen. She couldn't take it anymore. She wasn't going to listen to the rest of Sable's lecture. She'd had enough for one day. She left the box of manuscripts on the kitchen table, picked up her purse and the list of items Sable had made for her to pick up before coming back the next time. She stuck her head out the back door. "Listen, I have things to do at home. Is there anything else you need on this list?"

"No, hon," Sable said pleasantly. *Hon?* God, what had happened to her? "Let me give you some money...."

"You gave me enough money on Monday to last me for the next two weeks. I'll see you tomorrow."

"Is everything all right?" Sable wanted to know.

"I'm just busy, Sable. I have a lot to do. I'll see you later."

"Hey, wait a minute," Sable said, following Barbara Ann back inside. "What's the matter? Is something wrong?"

She sighed. "I'm not used to you like this. All the time I've known you, you've never been this... this...*nice.*"

Sable laughed. "Stripped of my pretensions?"

"Yeah, well, some of your pretensions were admirable." She poked a finger at Sable's chest. "Like keeping food off your clothes. You're getting real weird."

"I know," she said. She pulled out the sides of the

thin, gauzy dress and twirled around. "I never thought of wearing anything like this before. Imagine, I worked in a profession I could do in private, at home, and I still got up every morning and primped, like I was going out to sell real estate or something. Like who was I going to impress?" She pulled the sides of the dress away. "I'm not wearing underwear. I feel like a nudist."

"Lord. It's bad enough watching your roots grow out. Have you thought about…counseling?"

"I'm going to try that later, when things settle down out there," she said, tilting her head to one side, indicating the mean old world at large. Sable had not left the house in almost two weeks. She refused to be told the latest tabloid gossip about her. There had been two more television exposés but she and Elly had not tuned in. "Look, Barb, you don't have to come over here every day. You don't have to devote yourself to this. The rest of us have more time."

"I want to do this," she said. It was something to take her mind off what could be coming in the mail. Ordinarily, she would unload about the stress of her present situation. It seemed that she, of all of them, had the most chronic of pressures and disappointments in this publishing life. She was always losing an editor she had just gotten used to. Or having someone mess around with her work until it hardly resembled the book they'd asked for in the first place. Or having deadlines moved up. Or waiting for weeks longer than she should have to for word on whether her latest effort was acceptable. Late checks. Disastrous copyediting. Unbelievable covers…the kind you want to hide behind a brown paper bag. But it had never been as frightening as this. Her charge cards were maxed out, she was going to have to borrow money for Bobby's trade-school tuition, and although she did have a book due in three months, she was afraid to sit at the word processor. Everything she wrote turned to dreck right before the editor's eyes.

But she couldn't say anything. Gabby was dead. Eleanor had virtually closed herself into the master bedroom with thousands of pages, pictures and notes, compiling some original text Gabby had left behind. Beth's husband was fucking around on her. Sable's life was coming apart in the press and Sable was coming unhinged before their eyes. Sarah, so lonely for her mother, so unhappy with her insensitive husband, had dropped in on them several times in the last couple of weeks, looking for love and support. And Barbara Ann was supposed to complain about a couple of rejections?

For once in her life, she told herself, she was going to be strong. No one was going to know how terrified she was.

"I'm just going to head out for today," she told Sable. "I'll see you tomorrow. If I leave now, I can stop at the store on my way home."

"I hope they at least give you your own parking space at that store. Hey, don't come tomorrow if there's something else you should be doing. We're slow, but sincere. We'll get it all done eventually."

"Don't worry, I'll be here," Barbara Ann said.

She found her house deserted—everyone at work or play. She hauled in four cases of pop, six bags of groceries, and then went to the mailbox. On her way back to the front door, she shut off the hose that had flooded the front yard because someone had left it running. There was a shoe on the breakfast bar and four pop cans—all half-full—in the family room. The sofa cushions were askew; she straightened them fifty times a day. Her sons were out of school and had one full- and three part-time jobs between them; you'd think they could pitch in a little. But no. They just created squalor as they moved through the house. She sorted through the mail. Bill. Bill. Bill. Bingo.

She stared at it. Letter? Her editor normally called. She'd been at Gabby's, of course, but no message had been left on the machine. She pulled a new box of Ding-Dongs out of the grocery bag and took it, with the letter, to her bedroom. She closed the bedroom door, ripped open the box of pastry, bit into one for courage and ripped open the envelope.

Dear Barbara Ann,
I'd rather have talked to you about this on the telephone, but when I couldn't reach you, I thought this news would be better placed in a letter than left as a message on your machine. I'm afraid the proposal you sent us isn't going to work. It's...

She read in disbelief. The book idea wasn't strong enough, the characters not believable. Barbara Ann skimmed the sentences that talked about the good writing and the potential for a similar story that might work better with different characters. And she barely saw the sentence that suggested she consider this only a minor inconvenience, that a writer of her experience and flair—and speed—would have no trouble creating just the right romance.

She stared at the letter through tear-filled eyes. She ate a second Ding-Dong and a third, thoroughly devastated. That was two rejections and one canceled book in a row. Three wallops. Not only did she not know what to *do* differently, she didn't know what she'd *done* differently. She'd love to sit at her word processor and pound out an angry letter about how her work was consistently competent, but she wasn't sure of that. She had never been able to discuss in the same type of academic, intellectual way that Sable, Gabby, Beth and Elly could, what made a book work and what made it fail. When she gave an opinion in one of those discussions, only she knew she was faking it. She knew what she liked; she wrote what she liked. It had worked fine once. And now it didn't.

It had been such a long time since she'd enjoyed her work. When she began this career, the writing had been fun. She believed in the happily-ever-after stories, silly as that sounded for an adult woman in a world where love fails more than it succeeds. But it just wasn't that simple anymore.

She ate twelve Ding-Dongs, carefully stuffing the cellophane into the box so she could take it sneakily to the outside trash can later. She was lying there on her bed, the letter on top of her aching belly, trying to decide what to do with the rest of her life, when she heard a couple of the boys come home. The door from the garage to the kitchen slammed, there was some scuffling and joking around downstairs, and then she heard someone yell, "Mommmm!" Well, no matter how old they got, no matter how many times she asked them, they would never learn to walk through the house to find her if they wished to speak to her. No. They would shout from the farthest corner of the house, garage or yard and expect her to shout back. She could be on the phone with her editor, on the toilet or hanging herself in the pantry. They never thought of her business being more important than running to them. Fat chance. She was done running. Struggling. Striving. Yearning to please. Fuck 'em. "Mommmm!" She heard his feet on the stairs.

There was a light tapping on her bedroom door. "Mom?"

"What?"

"Hey, there's groceries down in the kitchen. The ice cream melted all over the place. It's even on the floor."

"So?" she answered.

"Well jeez, what am *I* supposed to do? I didn't put it there!"

"Use your imagination, Joe! Wipe it up, maybe. Or finger-paint with it. Or, if you're hungry, start licking!"

ELEVEN

June grew old, the summer turned hot and humid, and Sable's luggage remained closed and stacked in the room that had become hers. She had taken to wearing mostly Gabby's old clothes until Barbara Ann, complaining that it gave her a very eerie feeling, stopped by Marshall's and bought Sable a few things—a couple of those lightweight gauzy dresses, some loose knit shorts and tops, some flip-flops and two terry-cloth beach cover-ups that were all-purpose. "I can't take it anymore," Barbara Ann had said. "I don't know what emotional stage you're going through, but it gives me the creeps to see you in Gabby's clothes every day."

"You should have said something sooner," Sable replied. "I just wanted to feel comfortable. I don't feel like wearing dress-up, fussy clothes and I don't have casual clothes. I don't even own a pair of jeans."

"These are comfy," Barbara Ann said, handing her the Marshall's bag. "And now they're yours."

"Oh, my gosh!" Sable said, opening the bag and making a big deal out of the inexpensive items inside. "This is wonderful! Oh, look at this. This is *perfect!* Oh, these shorts.... I don't even have a pair of knit shorts! Barbara Ann, this is wonderful!"

Barbara Ann watched this reaction calmly. When Sable was done oohing and aahing and holding each item up to herself, Barbara slowly shook her head. She looked at Elly. "She's lost it. We've got to get her to a doctor."

"It's a bit like living with Alice in Wonderland, this creature who is seeing the world for the very first time," Elly replied cynically.

But for the first time in Sable's life, she felt she didn't need psychological help. She slept. She had an appetite. She laughed. She had no schedule. She hadn't done any exercises since her story broke and she was eating all the fattening, junky food she wanted. She fell asleep in the afternoon, reading. On some evenings she took a couple of sodas to her bedroom and made herself invisible while Elly and Ben spent time together. She believed that her mere presence under the same roof had intimidated them into celibacy, even though she had privately promised Elly she would not open her guest-room door until morning. Just the sound of their faint, distant, indiscernible conversation going on in the family room gave her an odd sense of satisfaction, knowing that Elly had a man to love.

Of course, so did Sable, though she was moving very cautiously, being admittedly crippled in the relationship arena. Her behavior would confuse the dickens out of a man with any expectations, but Jeff continued to seem able to roll along without any confusion in his mind. She called him daily on the pretense of asking about her property, but it was really the calming sound of his voice that she craved. After she'd been at Gabby's for about a week, Jeff showed up one morning. He was wearing shorts and a polo shirt. He had a cooler, picnic basket and a blanket in the trunk and he invited her to drive into the mountains. She instantly hugged herself, afraid to go out there.

"Take a chance," he said to her. "No one will bother you. Except maybe me."

"What if someone *sees* me?" she had gasped.

"No one would recognize you," Elly stated flatly. "In fact, I hardly do. You look like a bag lady."

She had nothing to fear from Jeff, she realized. In fact, she didn't *know* any of the people she was afraid of! Suddenly she realized that all the people she feared were faceless strangers! She dug around Gabby's closet for an old, faded, wide-brimmed hat and off she went for a day of lying under the trees on a blanket, where someone cared for her for no apparent reason.

"Are you going to call your agent soon?" Elly had asked.

"I don't know," Sable said, pressing a hand to her once-flat abdomen. "My diverticulitis hasn't been feeling much better."

"This can't go on forever, Sable. Eventually we have to get back to our real lives."

"I know," she said. But she wasn't sure yet what her real life was going to be.

It was a Thursday evening at nine o'clock when things changed again. Eleanor was reading on the family-room sofa and Sable in the chair. The thing Sable had come to most appreciate was being quiet with someone. If Elly hobbled off to the kitchen for ice cream, she'd offer to bring Sable a dish. If Sable read something interesting, she'd mention it to Elly. But not too often. Sable liked to read the newspaper in the morning, Elly in the evening, so every morning Sable carefully folded the paper together for Elly's later use. Sable had never been happier. And then the doorbell rang.

Sable hung back until Elly could see who was there.

With a gasp she said, "Beth!" and threw open the door. It was not the sudden arrival of the young woman that shocked her, but the condition of her face. Her right eye was swollen nearly shut and a large bruise covered her cheek. She held a suitcase in her hand. "My God," both women exclaimed.

"Can we put my car out of sight in Gabby's garage, do you think?" she asked.

Sable met Barbara Ann at the door the next morning. She relieved her of one of the grocery sacks and pulled her in the house. "You aren't going to believe this. You'll have to see it with your own eyes."

"Oh, what now?" Barbara Ann wearily asked.

"Beth's been here since last night. We're at another crossroads."

"I can't take any more crossroads," Barbara Ann began to whine. And then she saw Beth sitting at the kitchen table, still dressed in her nightclothes. Barbara Ann gasped and almost dropped the grocery sack. "Dear God," Barbara Ann said in a breath. "Jack?"

Beth nodded, looking down into her teacup. Elly sat at the end of the table, trying unsuccessfully to blow her cigarette smoke out the open window. "I'll put away the groceries while Beth tells you what happened," Sable said. Elly merely lifted her eyebrows. She wore a look of unhappy resignation.

"Really, he's never hit me like this. I mean, this much. I think I finally pushed him too far," Beth said.

"Spoken like a true victim," Elly groused.

"People don't push people into hitting them," Sable said from the kitchen.

"What do you mean, 'like this'?" Barbara Ann wanted to know.

"If he lost his temper about something, you know, he sometimes lashed out at me. He could be rough, but it's not like he regularly beats me."

"When he 'lashed out,' Beth, did he ever leave any bruises?" Beth looked down at her hands. "Dear God," Barbara breathed again.

"It's too late for prayer, Barbara Ann," Sable announced.

"Be quiet a second," Barbara demanded. "What was it that caused him to lose his temper this time?"

She didn't raise her eyes. Large tears collected. "We had an agreement about having a family. I didn't keep my part."

"What? You've been trying to get pregnant for years," Barbara Ann said, confused. Actually, she thought the bastard had beat his wife because she'd failed to get pregnant as instructed.

"No," Beth said, shaking her head. "I wanted a baby so much, I lied about that. We weren't trying. I was on the Pill. I've been on it since we got married. Jack doesn't want any more children. He already has two children, from his first marriage."

"He was married before," Elly put in.

"Twice," Beth explained. "He has two teenagers from his first marriage, living in Texas."

"Jesus Christ, does any of us tell the truth about anything around here?" Barbara asked, dumbfounded.

"I just couldn't stand it. I wanted a baby. I didn't see how it mattered that much whether Jack did or not. Why should it? It's not as though he was going to take care of it. Besides, I knew what Sable said about him was true. I know he hasn't been faithful. He hasn't been around much and he's been in a nasty mood since Christmas, so I decided I was just going to go off the

Pill and when I got pregnant, I was going to go home. Back to Kansas City."

"Beth! You were going to get a baby out of him, then leave him?"

She shrugged. "I couldn't see any other way to have a baby. I'm thirty-two and I'm not going to get married again. I don't think I *want* to ever get married again! I come from a huge family where everyone has lots of kids. I have twenty-one nieces and nephews alone and it seems like there's a new one every year. I love kids and I was aching for a baby."

"There's always artificial insemination, if you're that determined," Sable said.

"There's only one way you get a baby in my family," Beth said quietly. "I wouldn't want to embarrass them. My brother's a priest."

Barbara Ann covered Beth's hand with hers. "But Beth, do you really want a baby from this man who beats you? Even if you're only going to leave him...?"

"That was my first plan," she said. "But things started getting so much better with us. I don't know what happened, really, but Jack was acting so sweet. I know you'll never believe this, but Jack can be so wonderful when he's in a good mood, when things aren't going wrong for him. It's only when he gets stressed out—with work, with his family. His father's a big problem. Now *there's* a mean man! But that's always been the hard part. When he's sweet, he's the most wonderful man in the world and I love him so much. I decided it was worth one more try. I'd tell him about the baby and—"

"You're *pregnant?*" they exclaimed in unison.

She smiled and nodded. It was a small, satisfied smile that even the bruise and her swollen eye couldn't diminish. But the smile faded quickly. "I told him about the baby and he got furious. I should have lied, but when he asked me if I'd done it on purpose, I just blurted out the truth. I thought maybe, just *maybe*, he'd understand how much I really need to have a child of my own! But he didn't."

"Obviously," Elly muttered.

"Does he know you're here?" Barbara Ann asked.

"Oh no! I didn't tell him I was leaving! I told him about the baby at dinner last night and he left at about eight o'clock for a midnight departure out of San Francisco. He's flying to London. He won't be back until Sunday night. I guess I could have just stayed at home."

"No, you need to be here. With us," Sable, the new housemother, proclaimed.

"What did he say? Or did he just coldcock you?"

"Oh, he said a lot. He screamed a lot, about betrayal and ungratefulness and sneakiness and jealousy and spite and— He had a lot to say. My mistake was yelling back at him. I just couldn't take it anymore," she said, beginning to cry. "If I'd just kept my mouth shut…"

"Beth, for God's sake, if he can yell, you should be able to yell back without living in fear of a beating! How did this happen to you?"

"I don't know, I don't know. I can't believe how I've failed! I've made a mess of everything! If I'd just thought of a better way to handle this, maybe we could have worked it out somehow!"

"Beth, my God," Barb attempted. "Honey, it's not up to you to *handle*—"

"I called him a cheap, lying, cheating cocksucker. I told him I didn't need him, and if he didn't want our child, that was fine with me. He could go fuck himself."

There was a moment of shocked silence in the kitchen. "Let me get this right," Barbara finally said, pausing to rub her temples. "When you decide to yell back at this Neanderthal wife-beater, you call him a cocksucker and tell him to fuck himself?" Barb turned around and looked at Sable. Sable simply lifted her thin, washed-out brows, a contrite look on her face. "Did he hit you anywhere else? Could he have hurt the baby?"

"No, I'm all right. This one knocked me off my feet, but I had a soft cushion to land on. I really didn't have to panic. I could have taken my time packing. I could have followed through on my original plan. I was going to load my computer and some of my favorite things—*my* things that I bought or got from my family—into a rented truck and drive back to Kansas City. I have a lot of brothers and brothers-in-law there who wouldn't let anything happen to me. But I can't let them see my face. It would kill them to think I let myself be treated like this. And even though he's going to be gone for a few days, I just had to get out of there as fast as I could. He was so threatening."

"Did he say he was going to hurt you again?" Barbara asked her.

"Not in so many words. He said that he would expect me to arrange for an abortion and hopefully have that taken care of before he got back. Or else, he said. So," she said, her voice rising in what was sure to be a whimper, "I guess that's that. It's over." And then she laid her head down on her folded arms and wept.

Barbara Ann rubbed her back. "You go ahead and

cry, sweetheart, it's going to be all right. We're all done with that cocksucker."

"But I love him so much," she wailed, not lifting her head.

"Aren't women amazing," Elly said, leaving the table to get a fresh cup of coffee.

"Beth, the man is unfaithful, physically and emotionally abusive, and he ordered you to abort the baby you're carrying. It is impossible for you to love him," Barbara Ann said.

"I know," she cried. "But I do."

Barbara Ann glanced over her shoulder at Sable, who responded by taking a deep, frustrated breath. Barbara turned back to her weeping friend.

"Beth, dear, I hope you don't take this the wrong way, but you're so fucked up, you're starting to make Sable look stable." She giggled suddenly. "Stable Sable," she said again. "Beth, how long has this been going on?"

"Since the beginning," Sable answered for her. She brought her own coffee to the table and sat down, gently stroking Beth's shoulder, speaking for her. "Seven years. Since this twenty-five-year old girl met and married Mr. Smoothie. This sort of thing usually runs in families, but she's a genetic throwback. There's no abuse in her family. The worst she ever got growing up was a swat on the rear with her mother's wooden spoon. And that, according to Beth, hardly ever happened."

"What about your father, Beth?"

"Daddy never laid a hand on any of us. Not that he didn't want to, he said, but Mama would have had the priest at our house every evening for the rest of his natural life. My whole family is in love. They're all happily married...even John, whose bride is the Church. I'm the only one who hasn't been able to make it...work."

"Come on, Beth, no one's that perfect. Surely there are a few marital problems in your family?"

"I don't think so. If anyone could spot it, it would have been me. I'm the only one—"

"Dysfunction like this doesn't always run in families," Elly said. "When there's no gene for it, it can be accomplished with lots of practice."

"I always suspected this," Sable went on. "He's been knocking you around for years. Some of those trips you took with him, those last-minute decisions to go with Jack to Amsterdam or Madrid or New York? It was because of the bruises, wasn't it? You'd hide in your town house and pretend you weren't there. Right, Beth?"

She slowly raised her head and nodded. "And I knew you knew. I thought that if I could make it *look* as though my marriage was good, it would be good. I always knew it wasn't. I knew the first month and I know it now. But if Jack walked in the door right now and said how sorry he was, how much he loved me and wanted our baby, I'd want to give him another chance. Because—"

"Because this time it would be different," Eleanor said. "I think you'd better go home, Beth. You're not ready to leave Jack. It's not bad enough yet."

"Elly!" Barbara barked.

"It's not," she shrugged, unperturbed. "Beth hasn't reached the bottom yet. She's got a lot more bruises in her. She might even be willing to sacrifice the baby to this jackass."

"We're not *letting* her go back to him!" Sable proclaimed.

"Beth, tell Elly you're not going to go back to him, even though it's tempting," Barbara insisted.

Beth didn't exactly comply. "I wouldn't ever let Jack hurt the baby, Elly. Surely he wouldn't hurt a child!"

Barbara groaned loudly and put her head in her hand, tousling her own short, curly hair in utter frustration. Sable pressed her hands flat to the table, closed her eyes tightly and ground her teeth, but Eleanor looked at Beth squarely.

"Beth, did I ever tell you how it was I decided to stop drinking?" she asked.

"I…I don't think so," she stammered, instinctively knowing she was in for it.

"Gin or beer is what I liked, unless there was only wine—or bourbon or vodka. The only thing I'd hate to be stuck with was scotch. I hated scotch. I *knew* I drank too much. Most alcoholics do. I'd had mishaps. I woke up one morning to find myself asleep on the couch and a cigarette had burned a ten-inch-diameter hole in the rug. I wonder why I didn't just go up in flames, I was so soaked in gin, living in that paper trap of mine. I had a couple of accidents. I hit a parked car once, rear-ended someone another time. I fell off my chair at a faculty dinner, tipped over a punch bowl at a function to welcome freshmen, and, of course, I mooned the class of '76. I fell asleep—a kind term for passing out—in the middle of a student's oral exam. You know, little upsets here and there. Embarrassing, but survivable.

"The president and the dean of students confronted me. I'd known these men for years. They were real clear about one thing—they knew I hadn't been drunk a lot in earlier years, but from what they could see, it was getting worse and worse. I was offered a choice—my job or my gin. The president's sister was a recovering alcoholic—so he wrote down her name and phone number for me. I was quite insulted, but I took it. He suggested three options—I could leave the college then and there, I could take a leave and go into a hospital treatment program, or I could go to AA. The bastard didn't allow me the option of just giving him my word that I'd do better.

"I thought I was capable of it, you know. I thought I could control my drinking, make a conscious decision to drink less gin. I don't know anyone who has more willpower than I do. So, I made an independent decision to drink less gin. I had to go along with him to some degree. I didn't have parents to bail me out, a husband, a savings account or a trust. All I had was the college.

"So, I went to AA meetings and brought my administrator little signed chits saying I'd been there. It wasn't easy, but I went to a meeting after work when I was at Berkeley or here on my days off. I liked the four o'clock meeting because I could get out of there by five. I did this very successfully for almost three months. I had no mishaps, I was alert during classes and student appointments, and I quit tucking my dress in my panty hose. I was happier than I'd ever been. I'd finally found a way to manage my drinking so that it wouldn't get me into trouble. And the president was very pleased. He wished I had called his sister, just to have a friend to talk to about this, but overall, he couldn't complain.

"There was only one problem with that four o'clock meeting—I had to drive home during rush hour. With my two-hour commute, it was a long time till I could get to that first drink. So, I found a little bar way off the campus where I could have one or two small ones. It took the edge off and it was much easier to wait until I got home where I could have a real drink. There was no chance anyone was going to see me for no one from the college would be there. It was in a seedy part of town, but I only stayed for a little while.

"I was leaving the place at about six-thirty one night. I'd gone about three blocks when I hit a woman. She was suddenly right in front of my car. I had no idea where she'd come from. I couldn't have fallen asleep. I couldn't have been drunk, at least, I couldn't imagine that at the time. But suddenly there was a terrible thump, a squeal, a crashing sound. By the time I realized what had happened, she was *behind* my car. She was a bag lady who'd been pushing a grocery cart full of all her worldly goods. The cart was way on the other side of the street and she was lying there, twisted and wounded and moaning. She began vomiting in the street. Another motorist came along right away and went for help. The police were called, the paramedics and the ambulance. I gave them all my ID and credentials, told them I'd been visiting a used-book store in the neighborhood, and was allowed to leave the scene. I wasn't even cited for the accident. And the reason I didn't get into any trouble was that the paramedics said the woman reeked so badly of gin that they assumed she had careened into the street in a drunken stupor. They were all making faces and fanning their noses. They couldn't smell it on me because she had fouled the air. I had only had two drinks, was certain I couldn't have been under the influence, but I *didn't even smell it!*"

Six eyes watched Eleanor as she closed her story. Everyone knew she was a recovering alcoholic, but only Gabby had been around when she was actually getting sober. She didn't tell her drinking stories to this group. In fact, Eleanor might not have told them at all except that part of recovery was unloading that stuff. She'd learned from the stories of others and told her own, but she'd never become a zealot outside of her AA circle. After sixteen years of sobriety, meetings were just a way of life and she rarely mentioned them. She went by rote, to keep a green memory, as they said.

"What happened to the woman, Elly?" Sable asked.

"Broken femur and dislocated hip. I'd have paid her hospital bills if she hadn't gotten good care, but they took better care of her than I could have. I easily could have killed that woman and the only thing that saved me was she was more pickled than I was. I called the college president's sister, at long last, and she became my first sponsor.

"Beth, addiction crosses all lines. Smart people, dummies, rich people, poor people. I don't care what your addiction is—booze, food, sex, domestic abuse, drugs—it doesn't matter. You are in denial at least as fierce as was mine. Understand this—the consequence is *always death*. Sometimes it comes real fast, sometimes it kills you slowly and by degrees. You need to end the denial and beat the addiction or someone will die— and it could be someone you love, like your child. You can kid yourself all you want, but you're done fooling me. I've met you before."

The women were quiet for a moment, then Beth weakly spoke up. "I feel so helpless."

"Then ask for help. There are dozens of agencies in the phone book. You have friends who will help you, and family. You have options. You can have your child and a good life, but the minute you say 'this time it will be different,' you have signed a death warrant. And I give you notice. That's when I withdraw my support. I will not be a party to suicide or murder." Eleanor stood up. "I'm going to get to work."

When Eleanor had walked out of the room, Sable reached across the table and covered Beth's hand. "Me, too. I'd do anything for you—whatever you need—but if you give him another chance to hurt you or the baby, I'm out."

"Oh, Sable, I won't just *let* him—"

"Me, too, Beth," Barbara said. "I'll only help you if you're willing to be helped. You have to give up the abuse, once and for all."

"But what if he...what if he..." She got a panicked look in her eyes as they darted between Sable and Barbara Ann. What if he what, Beth? she asked herself. What if he's sorry, as he's been before? What if he *promises*? What if he begs? What if he slaps the baby? Her eyes focused on Sable's and she almost gasped in sudden realization. Large tears were rolling out of Sable's funny eyes—funny, because without makeup and brows she looked so much like an inmate rather than her beautiful, chic self. And it hit her then; this wasn't the first time for Sable. She was reliving it through Beth. Perhaps Sable had nurtured the same denial for just one day too long.

"Just in case you're wondering if it can really happen," Sable said, "let me tell you, it can. It has."

"Oh God, it can. Okay," she said, taking a deep breath. "Help me."

Barbara Ann grabbed Beth's hand, Beth grabbed Sable's and Sable grabbed Barbara Ann's. "Okay," Barbara Ann said. "First things first. We get all your stuff out of your town house and store it in the garage here.

You might be entitled to the house but it's too risky for you to stay there and deal with him. Sable, can that security guy of yours get us a truck of some kind?"

"He can do anything," she said proudly.

"I'll call home and ask if any of the boys are available to help, but if not, we'll manage. You'll supervise, we'll lift and carry."

"Jeff can get us a couple of people from Petross Security."

"We'll get you an appointment with a good counselor. You need to meet some women who have gone through this. Whether you like it or not, you have to get proactive about this. We're tough old broads, but we're not professionals. You have to learn the ropes here and do something about getting emotionally untangled from this jackass."

"I know. I will."

"You'll call your mother," Barbara Ann said.

Beth looked stunned, reluctant.

"Yes," Sable concurred. "Inform your family. Tell them what's been happening and that you're out. Tell them where you are and that you're safe here until you *move* back home. We'll get on the phone with you, to give your mother some peace of mind."

"I do want to go home," she said, tearing up again. "But I can't think of leaving you."

"You won't leave us until it's time," Sable said, the strength in her voice reassuring. "But eventually you'll go home where you belong—with your brothers and sisters, your mom and dad, your nieces and nephews. We'll visit you twice a year and you'll come here. Everything is going to be all right now."

"It is, isn't it?" Beth said, considering it for the first time. He won't get mad at me again, she thought, because I won't be there. He can't hit me again because I won't be there to be hit. He can't threaten the baby, can't screw around on me, can't leave me at home when he goes off fishing or skiing. God, wouldn't it be good not to *worry?* Wouldn't it be good to stop struggling to make it right? To stop hiding out while the bruises heal? It would even be good not to wonder why he's being so nice to me all of a sudden. "Oh God, the plane," she suddenly realized.

"What plane?"

"His plane. That was it. That was why he was being so nice to me. He wanted to buy a plane." She laughed suddenly, but her tears overflowed again. "I bet if I could go back through old calendars, I could find the reason for every good spell we've had in our marriage."

"He was nice to you because he wanted to buy a plane?" Barbara asked.

"A sports car, boat, lake property, plane—all his toys. How could I pretend not to know that?"

"It's not as if he needed your permission...."

"He didn't need my permission, he needed my money."

"I thought airline pilots made a lot of money," Barbara Ann said.

"Oh, they do, but Jack never made enough money for all those things. Plus, he pays child support, and he's going to get stuck for half his kids' college costs. I've never made less than forty thousand dollars a year. In the last three years it's been even better than that. And I never bought myself anything. I didn't even pay for plane tickets to my mama's. I flew standby." She laughed hollowly. "That's how I got this baby," she said, her hand going instinctively to her abdomen,

not even swollen yet. "He wanted a plane. He wooed
me."

"Well, how interesting," Sable said, a devious light
coming into her eyes. "Looks like we'd better move a
little paperwork out of that town house as well. Then
we'll call one of my little legal bunnies. Congratula-
tions, kiddo. Looks like Junior has a half interest in a lot
of costly toys."

TWELVE

Barbara Ann was exhausted, aggrieved, anxious, rushed and bone-tired. She'd managed two entire households, two full families, for a month. She had her own brood—sloppier and hungrier in summer when their various jobs overlapped and they kept hours of which only the young are capable—and the family of women, with a menagerie of troubles and life-styles to strain the most patient housemother.

Elly had brought a long trestle table into Gabby's old bedroom upon which to line up and stack the pages of her project. She fled there each morning after her bran flakes and wouldn't let the others browse through what she'd found until she felt she'd organized it. Beth was moved out of her town house, a fiasco that took two days even with the help of a couple of Jeff's employees. She and Sable literally stole all the financial papers they could find—deeds, loans, bank statements and tax returns for the past seven years. Sable copied them, keeping the originals to be given to Beth's lawyer and returning the copies to the town house. Beth's bruises were fading, her worldly goods were stacked in Gabby's garage alongside her car, and she crept off to a support group for battered wives every afternoon. She slept in the guest bed beside Sable who reacted as though she had finally found herself a surrogate child.

Sable, at least, had been convinced to alter her hairstyle from two-tone to one shade of brown, something she had to do from memory. She still looked more like a health-spa escapee than her old self; her bare feet, baggy clothes and absence of makeup were so unlike her.

Sarah, Lindsey and Daisy, Gabby's golden retriever, dropped in almost every afternoon for moral support. Even after months, Daisy still ran sniffing through every room in search of Gabby before she settled down close to Sarah, a ritual that ripped Barbara Ann's heart out each time. Evenings, Barbara heard, were just as active, filled with drop-ins ranging from this elusive Ben she'd finally been told about, to David and his partner, Ed, Jeff, the security man who had somehow become more than a security man to Sable, Dr. Don on occasion, just to see how things were going, but really because he too missed Gabby, and often a second visit from Sarah and the baby if she was lonely, blue, or pissed off at Justin. "Maybe it's the house," Elly said. "This is more or less how Gabby lived, as a traffic director."

If Barbara Ann had an ordinary life, going home from that circus would be a rest. But there was no rest for the wicked, as her mother used to say. The boys, out of school for the summer, had more time to create their individual and group havoc. There was more time to work on their cars or various other projects; in every corner of the garage, drive, house, yard there was something in some stage of repair, renovation or construction. New wheels were being installed on Rollerblades; remote control airplanes, crashed, were being repaired; parts were being bought and collected to upgrade an old computer, mainly for games and online fun; someone was tinkering with the weed-whacker motor (For what? she wondered. No one had bothered to whack weeds in a millennium). And the kitchen was in constant upheaval.

Along with the four boys came their friends. If each one had only one friend over, it was eight large, hungry, sweaty, smelly young men. And then there was Mike, who seemed to be oblivious to turmoil. Who seemed to be able to sleep through music, television, laughter, shouting, and God knew whatever else through the night. And in the morning, when the tired ones slept in, Mike was already gone to work himself. He wasn't home to see the occasional presence of boys who didn't belong to them wandering into the kitchen in the morning looking for breakfast. Barbara Ann had announced that when some *girl* wandered down from upstairs, she was through. And there were girls, even if she didn't personally encounter them very often. She knew of their existence by the appearance of little square foil packages that had floated out of the pockets of jeans in the washing machine. "At least they're using protection," Mike had sagely offered.

The house paint was chipped and peeling, the yard overtaken with weeds, the driveway spotted with oil drips, the walls smudged with fingerprints, the carpet a sight of spills and stains. She begged. She threatened. She cajoled. She warned. She went on strike for a couple of days and found there was only one person in their household who couldn't live with the animal house atmosphere of her home—her. The backbreaking labor of taking care of them, keeping them fed and somewhat in line, had her just shy of blowing sky-high. It was a good thing she didn't know how to load any of the hunting rifles Mike and the boys possessed or she might lose it and start shooting. She was at the end of her rope.

It was in just such a frame of mind that she found the pot.

She had been on a mission in the detached garage to find the mousetraps she knew were stored somewhere; she had found evidence in Gabby's pantry that mice played there. She thought they'd last used them in that garage and that they might be in a box full of stored paraphernalia—one of many such boxes stacked against the wall. Once inside, she instantly remembered why she avoided the place. It was a disaster. They worked on their cars, bikes, skis, in peace here; Bobby and his friends "jammed" here on their ear-splitting guitars; they never bothered to straighten the place up. She had to blaze a trail through the scattered junk—pop cans, food wrappers, plates, glasses with permanent rings in them, discarded clothes, rags, paint cans, tools—to get to the storage boxes.

She hurriedly ripped through three or four boxes, glancing within for mousetraps, and closing them up as quickly when she didn't see them. Then she came upon a box that was neatly stacked with what appeared to be one-pound square packages of marijuana...six of them, skillfully wrapped in plastic, lining the bottom of a box...and on top of the pot, a bong. Unmistakable. Hidden there. Enough to keep them and all their friends stoned for a good long time. Out here, where the fumes would not alert their parents. Out here where they could pretend to be working on their various projects at all hours of the night when in truth, they were getting ripped.

Something snapped.

Barbara Ann placed the box of grass and equipment

by the door and began tearing through the other boxes with a vengeance in search of more evidence of drugs. She didn't bother putting things neatly away as she searched and discarded boxes. Were they sniffing the fumes from all these discarded paint cans? Were they all brain-damaged now in addition to being slovenly animals? She didn't find anything else in the garage, but that didn't bring her any comfort or calm her hysteria. When she was done in the garage, she took the box of pot and bong to the house, placed it safely in her bedroom and began on their rooms. She dumped out drawers, flipped mattresses, emptied pockets, cleared closet shelves with one swipe, looked behind furniture, dug under beds, searched behind shelved books. She didn't come up with much: some rolling papers, a roach clip, a pamphlet on growing marijuana, eyedrops and a couple of ordinary-looking pipes. She had thoroughly destroyed four bedrooms to collect a half shoebox of what she considered to be drug paraphernalia. Part of her was extremely relieved not to have found what she considered to be even more dangerous drugs—pills, cocaine, crystal methamphetamine, LSD, crack—but she was not naive about the seriousness of what she *had* found.

Barbara Ann was no wimp. She had not raised a group of quiet little Sunday school boys who wouldn't push the envelope from time to time. She and Mike may have hoped for more control, but they hadn't really expected it. Bobby and Joe threw a kegger at their house one weekend when Barbara and Mike had managed to get away. She knew it the minute she walked in the door upon her return—her house was cleaner than the boys had ever kept it. They were all grounded for weeks. Matt had been arrested once a couple of years before, the charge being something like "crawling with attempt to walk." He was nineteen, out drinking beer with his pals, and was too smashed to run from the police when their party was busted. Barb and Mike let him suffer till morning in jail, which seemed to alter Matt's level of respect for alcohol. There had been a few fights, though her boys were not typical thugs (in her opinion) but rather, loyal friends willing to take a side. And of course there'd been enough traffic violations and minor accidents to put Mike and Barbara Ann's auto insurance through the roof. A family of four could *live* on what she paid in car insurance. But all in all Barbara Ann considered them fairly typical boys—rough, messy, irreverent and irresponsible, famished and ungainly, uncertain about their futures and their talents, or the lack thereof.

That is, until she found the nice big cache of pot in the garage and her thinking instantly shifted. Right now she considered them spoiled goddamned brats.

She put all that she'd found in the middle of the table and set about cleaning her kitchen for what she considered to be the last time. Joe was the first of them to enter the house. Joe had just graduated from high school and was "taking a year off to find himself." She had wryly suggested he look under the bed. He glanced at the goods on the table, then his panicked eyes darted to his mother.

"Would you like to claim any of that stuff?" she asked him with dangerous calm. He shook his head, his mouth open and his eyes very big. "Fine," she said. "Then have a seat. I'll be with you shortly."

"Can I...uh...get a Coke?"

"To drink?" she asked sarcastically. "By all means, be comfortable."

Next, a half hour later, came Bobby. He was not interested in claiming the goods either. She invited him to sit down beside his brother while she went about the business of loading the dishwasher and opening jars of prepared spaghetti sauce. "You can get a Coke," Joe whispered to Bobby, "then she's going to kill us and feed our parts to the McCloskeys' dogs."

Barbara Ann lifted her brows. Not a bad idea.

When Billy came in, Barbara Ann felt her heart sink. Her baby. Her pretty, sweet boy. Billy was almost no trouble. He was good-natured and the quietest one of the group. He was equal in sloppiness most of the time, but he was seldom disrespectful. She hated to tie him in with this mob, but there was no question he was one of them. It almost brought tears to her eyes when she asked him if he wanted to take responsibility for the collection of stuff on the table. He checked eyes with his brothers; they warned him to speak up at the risk of his safety and he shook his head.

At five forty-five Mike came in; he was unconscious to the danger he walked into and did what he always did. He growled appreciatively at his wife and grabbed her in his bearlike embrace. He so loved seeing her in the kitchen, at the stove preparing his daily feast, that he treated her much like prey he had to shake to death before eating. Sometimes she loved this; Mike might be lacking in the many refinements of social graces, but she was smart enough to appreciate certain things about him. In twenty-three years he had never strayed, never abused, never lost his sexual appetite for her. He took her for granted, yes, but he worked hard, turned over his paycheck, was devoted to his family even if he wasn't responsible for much of the raising of them and never stopped adoring Barbara

Ann as much as the day he'd begged her to marry him. The only problem with Mike was that he seemed oblivious to the fact that she needed more than to be devotedly loved. She needed a little fucking *help.* "Go shower," she told him. "We're going to have a talk with the boys."

"About what?" he asked. She inclined her head toward the table. He walked over and studied the collection. "What the hell's this? Is this what I think it is? Who the hell is responsible for this? Well?" Six eyes stared at him in a combination of shock and fear, though the worst he'd ever done was blow his top and yell at them. Of course, Mike's yell was pretty impressive. "Well?" he asked again.

She put a hand on his shoulder. "Go shower," she said. "This is my party."

Matt was the last to arrive. Barbara Ann couldn't have planned it better. It was a rare night that all four boys were around at dinnertime. Matt was Barbara Ann's firstborn, the leader, the shining star. He was working full-time and going to college part-time, though it would take him years to finish at this rate and he still hadn't decided what he was going to do with his life. Matt was the most experienced and least hardheaded of the group. He was ready to slip into his father's role—done with child's play and ready to settle down. He'd probably move from his mother's house to some young woman's and do for her what Mike had done for Barbara Ann—love her intensely, work tirelessly, eat her meals with gusto and lie on the sofa to watch sports every night. Unless it was hunting season.

"Okay," he said, "it's mine. I'll take the rap. All this stuff. Mine. I did it." He was also fearless.

"You're too late," she said. "I collected it out of four bedrooms and you're too late. But it was a nice gesture. I'm sure your brothers appreciate it. Sit down."

"You can have a Coke," Bobby whispered. "Then she's going to cut your balls off."

In the time it took them to gather, Barbara Ann had heated spaghetti sauce, boiled noodles, torn up lettuce, cut up vegetables for the salad and heated French bread. She wasn't planning a dinner meeting, however. It was a Last Supper.

She couldn't go through this ritual without briefly considering all the boxes of memorabilia she had stored all over their bursting house. Handprints made in school. Mother's Day cards their teachers had forced them to make in which they listed all the things they appreciated about her. Photos by the hundreds—of birthday parties, camping trips and graduations. She remembered the times they tried to make her breakfast and the time they tepeed the front yard for her and Mike's anniversary. There were many times they cried and came to her for help. It was not a question of love. She loved them. Hell, she lived for them. It was enough to bring tears to her eyes, but she'd be damned if she'd cry. It was a question of limits. And they'd reached hers.

"You little bastards have had the last piece of me you're going to get," she began. "Do you know I have never shopped at the grocery store with one cart? I've never gone a week without doing laundry? I've never had a food bill that couldn't support a third world nation? Any one of you could live for a year on what I pay in car insurance alone!"

"Mom..." Joe tried.

"Don't even insult me with excuses. I've put up with

so much from you animals that it makes me wonder if I'm insane or just stupid." Mike wandered into the kitchen and took his place behind Barbara Ann, shoring her up. He was good at this. It was following through where he fell apart. He didn't realize that this time he was going to get it, too.

"I've given you everything I have—every ounce of energy, even when I thought I'd drop, every penny, even though I can never come up with enough, and every emotion, even when you crush me with cruel disregard for my feelings. I've begged you to help out, to just keep your *rooms* clean, but you can't even do that. You're all smart enough to rebuild engines, but not one of you knows how to operate a washing machine. My charge cards are maxed out and I don't have a single dime saved toward my own retirement, but you've all got enough money for new parts for your cars, trips you have to take to play with your friends and hot nights with your girlfriends. I have to get out the goddamned whip and chair to get you to wash the very plates you eat off of, and even that's a disaster. I have to hose down the kitchen when you're done anyway.

"Each one of you has so much talent and brains, you excel in what you love, but you can't be bothered to study in school. I've got a musician who can convince the whole neighborhood we're having an earthquake, but gets D's in English. I've got a mechanic so skilled that people come from miles to get help on their cars, but would never consider getting a *degree* in something so that he can get off my payroll and have a life. I've got a prize-winning athlete, a gifted radio-operated airplane pilot, a marksman and a champion diver…but not one of you will pick up your goddamned Coke cans or carry your cereal bowls to the kitchen. I don't know how long I would have continued to be your maid, but I'll tell you this right now, I am through catering to a bunch of ingrates who store enough pot to open a storefront operation. This tears it. I'm through with you. I'm through giving you my time, my hard work, my money and my life. You want to live in a pigsty? Fry your brains on this shit? Have it. It's all yours."

"Mom, this stuff isn't ours," Bobby said. "It's—"

"Bobby, have you ever used this shit?" she demanded.

"Mom..."

"Have you? Ever?"

"Well, yeah, I've tried it a few times, but I—"

"All of you have, right? Well, this shit is *drugs*. I know, we're supposed to be *modern* about all this, it's a new generation, after all. Well, there isn't anything new as far as I'm concerned! I've still got the same irresponsible slobs who could care less about their living conditions, never ask if they can help out, never offer to do anything to make the house your dad and I pay for a decent place to live, never go out of their way...and now all I've added to it is a bunch of lowlifes who think a little joint now and then is okay! Maybe that's why you were so unmotivated you couldn't remember to buy me a damn Mother's Day card, Joe. Or maybe that's why you got so many traffic tickets, Bobby. Or maybe that's why you forgot registration one semester, Matt. Or maybe that's what got you D's in English and history, Billy. All I can say is I know there are some things you care about and some things you don't. And I'm one of the things you don't care about!"

"Okay, you're all going to do some time for this

here," Mike said, stepping in at what he thought was his moment to play father. He was going to clip their wings, ground them.

Barbara Ann whirled on him. "I don't think you get it, Mike. I'm leaving. You seem to be content to live in a frat house—have at it. I'm through. I'm leaving you all. Forage for your own food. Wear dirty clothes. Pay your own car insurance. Eat off paper plates…if you can find anything to eat without me going to the store every damn day. There's just one thing I'd like you to understand about me leaving." This was where the tears began. "It isn't as though I haven't loved you. It isn't as though I haven't tried. I had this stupid idea that if I could *show* you how to live in a clean house, you'd learn to *be* clean, that if I *demanded* that you be decent, it would be automatic for you. But you've thrown it back in my face. My house is a hovel, no matter how hard I work. There are at least four cars being worked on in my driveway and half-done projects all over my house and yard, not to mention the dirty dishes, dirty clothes, trash heaps, overgrown lawn, algae-infested pool and chipped paint everywhere. There's a goddamned lawn-mower motor in my bedroom and I deserve better for all my hard work! If you're still not catching on, all I've ever asked for from any of you was *respect!*"

"Mom…we…"

"Joe, you're too late to say you respect me. You have time to spend hours tinkering with your computer for your own entertainment, but my lawn needs to be tended. Bobby can play rock music till four in the morning, but is too tired to pick up his dirty clothes. Matt's got a full schedule, sure, but there's time left over to work on cars for friends. Where's the time left over for family responsibilities? The house has needed to be painted for years now! Billy, all that's ever asked of you is that you get decent grades in school, but you're too busy with planes and sports and music to study for a test. And God forbid you should pick up after yourself to save me one-tenth of the work I do every single day.

"This is my fault," she went on. "I tried, but I somehow failed to teach you that you show respect by lending a hand, by treating the property of others with care, by keeping shipshape the surroundings that you live in and someone else pays for. I've tried to reason with you, I've threatened you, I've begged you. And you all blew me off. That," she said, pointing to the collection on the table, "was the ultimate fuck-off. You not only don't care about me, you don't even care enough about yourselves to steer clear of that dangerous, mind-altering, cell-damaging crap. You've really done it now. You've pissed off the help."

"Okay, boys, we're going to make a few resolutions around—"

"You're too late too," she said, turning on Mike. "You can't back me up now because by tomorrow, when I'm insane again because no one around here gives a damn, you'll be telling me they're just boys. You blow me off, too! How does a grown man expect to set an example by leaving his own clothes in a pile on the floor? I'm sleeping with a lawn-mower motor, for God's sake, and it's not as though I haven't asked you to get it out of my bedroom. The fact is," she said, turning back to the boys, "I'm the only member of this household who works two full-time jobs. I have a job as a writer—a stressful, difficult, time-consuming job—and I come off that job only to clean, cook, shop and do laundry for the rest of you. I don't come off my job to lounge around the house that *you* made clean, or eat the food that *you* bought and prepared, or wear the clothes that *you* laundered for me. And on top of this, I find drugs in my house. Enough drugs, if I'm not mistaken, to qualify for a felony!"

They all had the good sense to hang their heads in shame. But Barbara Ann was too far gone to be tricked into giving them another chance. She was done living on cupcakes and Snickers bars to dull the frustration.

"You're abusers, all of you," she said, taking Mike into their fold. "You abuse me every day that you neglect my constant pleas for help, for consideration. You aren't going to have me to kick around anymore."

She swept the collection off the table and into her arms. "Your supper's on the stove. After this, you're on your own." She stormed off to her bedroom. By now the tears were stinging her eyes and running down her cheeks. She almost screamed in agony when she recognized a familiar sensation—she was *hungry!* She could numb a lot of what was hurting her by eating a cheesecake!

She closed her bedroom door and got out the suitcases. She'd been thinking about what she would pack all afternoon while she was constructing her speech to them, but now that she had an opened suitcase on the bed, she couldn't remember. All she could think about were her babies, her little boys.

Sometimes when the house was sort of quiet and Barbara Ann was watching a television movie, Matt would lie on the couch and put his head on her lap. Twenty-one, six foot two, one-eighty, drop-dead handsome, and still her little boy. She'd gently caress his floppy blond hair and he'd turn those incredibly blue eyes up at her and say, "If I don't find a woman like you, I'll never be able to get married."

When Bobby, her most difficult and stubborn child, would find himself ecstatically happy about something, he would pick her up off her feet and whirl her around like she was just a girl. He'd squeeze her so hard she couldn't breathe, kiss her on the cheek and tell her how much he loved her. Even though he was a real jerk twice a week at least, he would *always* say he was sorry and that he loved her more than he was able to show.

Joe was Bobby's opposite; his emotions were hidden far beneath the surface. He was the tall, handsome, silent type. But when his girl had dumped him, he'd gotten Barbara Ann out of bed at eleven-thirty to say he had to talk. He'd leaned his head against her breast and wept because he'd lost love and his pain was too intense to suppress. She'd stroked his head, her grown boy, and told him he would find love again because he was so lovable.

And Billy, her heart, who had been left out of the older boys' games since the days he toddled, who had a dangerous case of mononucleosis when he was thirteen and had spent two weeks in the hospital, had brought her home trophy after trophy for football, basketball, baseball; team champions, most valuable player, player of the year, team captain in his junior year. And with his beautiful shining eyes had smiled and said, every single time, "I did it for you, Mom—my best girl."

Which one had rat-holed enough dope to stay stoned for a year?

She hadn't forgotten why she adored each one of them. Sometimes they really came through for her.

They'd been wonderful about Gabby's memorial—scrubbed, handsome, patient and sensitive. Too bad she'd come home that night to find her house a disaster and about five extra young men gathered around the big-screen TV for a basketball game.

Mike came into the bedroom. "You can't be leaving me," he said. When she turned to look at him she was struck first by his handsomeness. His once-blond hair had darkened over the years and was streaked by gray at the temples, but he still had a boyish, bearish look about him. The next thing that struck her was the weary, pained look he had around the eyes. It had always amazed her that a man so handsome, so strong and fit, could love her so thoroughly, even when she'd gained thirty unwanted pounds and her body showed the rigors of so much childbirth. This was killing him; he loved her so much. It stunned her even now.

"I can't do it alone anymore, Mike. You're willing to have me put up with too much."

"I'll help you get them in line," he said. "I'll whip the shit outta them. You'll see."

"Great," she said, turning back to her suitcases. "Call me when you've had them in line for a month or so. I'm not banking on any more promises. I'm not sure you'd recognize a dirty house if it bit you in the ass."

"Barbara Ann, baby," he said, hugging her from behind. "I know you're all upset, but you didn't give us any warning. You gotta give us a chance here."

That made her cry harder. "I warned you all for twenty-three years! I begged and pleaded and threatened! The best I ever got was twenty-four hours of cooperation! I can't do it anymore! I'm forty-three and I'm tired!"

"Honey, you've been through a bad time—"

"You're goddamned right I've been through a bad time! My best friend is dead, my other best friend is going nuts before my very eyes, my other best friend is being beat up by her husband *and* I'm losing my job! Do any of you care? You say, 'Oh, that's too bad, honey,' and then drop your dirty clothes on the floor and leave your dirty dishes in the family room! Jesus, Mike, no matter how much I love you all, even I have a limit!" She took a breath and pinched her eyes closed. "I want to live in a clean, well-repaired house. When I'm talking on the phone, I'd like respectful quiet rather than shouting and cursing in the background. I'd like my messages written down and rags used to wipe up spilled oil instead of my good towels. And I want to look at the young men I've raised with pride instead of shame. *That's* what I want."

"Barbara Ann," he asked sweetly, "are you getting your period, honey?"

The phone rang at Gabby's house and the only person who could answer it was Eleanor. Beth was hiding from Jack, Sable was hiding from the press, and for once, the ladies were the only ones at home.

"Hello?" Elly said. "What? You can't be serious? Where? How much? Oh Lord, I don't believe this. Fine, fine. We'll think of something. Call him and tell him what? Now, what's that? Yes, I can do that. Oh, I'm sure we'll come up with it somehow, don't panic. Well, I guess we can put you somewhere. Okay. Goodbye."

By the time Elly hung up the phone, Beth and Sable had been drawn to the kitchen, waiting for an explanation.

"Barbara Ann's in jail. We have to go bail her out."

THIRTEEN

"I'll pay you back somehow," Barbara Ann said to Sable.

"There isn't going to be anything to pay back," Sable said. "You aren't going to jump bail, are you?"

"Elly, what did Mike say?"

"He seemed thoroughly confused. I told him that the police picked you up for speeding and found a box full of drugs in your car that you found on the front lawn by the mailbox that you were just en route to delivering to the police because you didn't know what else to do with it. The police arrested you because you had it, even though you swore you'd only found it and your family knew nothing about it. By the time we were hanging up, the police were at his door."

"I'd better call him," she said. Barbara Ann went to the phone and had a very brief conversation. She returned a few minutes later. "Well, for once they were smart," she said. "They told the police they didn't know anything about any drugs and nothing was found in the house or garage. So I'm the only one in trouble. The police did tell Mike that it looked like the place had already been searched. Mike assured them that it was just the appearance of a house occupied by five sloppy men. When the police asked them if they knew where I was, Bobby told the police I left them because they're worthless pigs. And the police officer in charge said it looked like I was the only one around there with any sense."

"What were you going to do with the marijuana, Barbara Ann?" Beth asked her.

"Oh, I *was* taking it to the police. I sure wasn't going to leave it there. The boys would either sell it, smoke it or dispose of it in some stupid way and get themselves put in prison. I was so pissed off, I was speeding." She leaned back into the chair she occupied. "Well? Can I stay?"

"Barbara Ann, is this really what you want?" Sable asked. "After putting up with them for all these years?"

"It's more than that. I just don't have anything left. I've had one canceled contract and two rejections in a row. I feel like it's only a matter of time before my editor calls me and tells me *another* finished book isn't good enough...."

"You're borrowing trouble," Sable said. "The worst that's going to happen is they ask for some rewriting. They're not going to cancel another book on you before giving you a chance to revise it. Honestly, Barbara Ann."

"That isn't how it *feels*. It feels like I can't do anything right, like I've lost it. And frankly, I've lost too goddamned much lately. That stash of pot put me over the edge. Much as it killed me, I could live with turning four selfish slobs loose on the world, but I couldn't live with turning loose a bunch of dopers. If that's how far they're willing to go, they're going to have to go without me. I've had it."

"Poor Mike," Beth said.

"Yes, poor Mike," Barbara Ann mimicked with sarcasm. "You know, I love the man. In a lot of ways, Mike is a prince. He's faithful and decent and hard-working—and a total chauvinist. I'd scream my brains out at those boys and he'd back me up all the way...but all they had to do was watch him to learn their behavior. And they were watching a guy that went to work every day and came home to a big man-size meal, after which he'd take to his chair. A couple of times a year I'd be able to shame him into cleaning up the yard or digging out the garage. But a couple of times a year isn't enough. It takes more than that to run a household. What the hell kind of sty would we live in if I was motivated to take care of it twice a year? It's time for poor Mike to figure out there's a lot more to managing a family than yelling, 'Do what your mother says.'"

"So you're really just interested in teaching them a lesson," Elly observed.

"Well, Elly, that depends entirely on whether they're capable of learning one, which I seriously doubt. Wouldn't it be nice if they figured this out real fast? I love taking care of my family. I love filling up the shopping carts, covering the table with good food and watching them appreciate it. I even love making the kitchen and bathrooms shine. What I don't love is do-ing it over and over and over, only to have some incon-siderate baboon trash it right behind me. All I've ever wanted from any of them was a little help in *keeping* it nice.

"So, I figure they don't do it because they can't, be-cause they're domestically challenged. It's hereditary, and it comes from the Vaughan side of the family. Mike's mom and dad live in a cute little house that hasn't been vacuumed or painted or picked up in twenty years. Mike's dad has been saving an old refrigerator motor on the front porch since we got married. I've been fighting it for twenty-three years, and I've been fighting a losing battle. They're incapable.

"I'd like to stay here for a little while, finish going through Gabby's things and make sure the rest of you are all right. Then I'm going to get a job and an apartment—a nice, little, white apartment. It won't be much, given the kind of money I can earn, but it will be mine, it will be clean, the toilet seat will be down and there won't be axle grease on everything but my underwear."

"Don't you have a book due in September?" Sable asked.

She shrugged. "Screw 'em. I'm going to call my editor tomorrow. I'm going to tell her I need an extension because my best friend died and I'm separated from my husband. I may never write the book. I won't get any money for it anyway. Since they canceled my contract on the last book, I'm in the red. I now owe them five thousand dollars, which of course I don't have. They'll suck it out of my royalties, so I'll earn even less. I can't do it anymore. I work too hard to be treated like dog meat all the time." She took a deep breath. "All I want right now is a box of peanut butter crispies and a good night's sleep. I'm going over the edge with the rest of you lunatics."

"It's contagious," Sable said. "Are you going to let your roots grow out?"

"These *are* my roots! And incidentally, this is my ass, too! All sixty pounds of it!"

"Poor Mike," Beth said again. "He loves you so much."

"You do love love, don't you, Bethie? How is it

you're writing those bloodcurdling books? You should be writing all your cockeyed ideas about *love*."

"I'm passive-aggressive," she said. "That's what they told me in my support group. It's the only way I can express my anger. By murdering people in my books."

Sable threw back her head and guffawed. Barb looked at her earnestly. "Seriously?"

"Uh-huh. The only problem is, what's going to happen to my writing when I'm cured? Think I'll be unable to write the ruthless killer?"

Elly had wandered out of the room and when she came back, she was holding a small stack of papers. She handed them to Sable. "Read this," she instructed. Sable began to glance over the first page. "Read it to all of us," Eleanor said.

"What is it?"

"You'll see."

"But it says 'Chapter Twenty-One.' What's this from?"

"Just read it to us. Then if you have any questions, I'll answer them."

Sable began.

"Chapter Twenty-One

Clare pushed open the shutters to let the sun flood the second-story room of the little Donnelly inn. There came a groan of protest from behind her as the bright light scorched Brandt's eyes. She ignored him and leaned out the window. Ireland was possessed of a vivid emerald green to be seen nowhere else on the planet. A scent of grass, flowers, ponds and reeds filled her breast. Also in the air was the faint acrid odor of gunpowder and death.

The little village of Donnelly had the appearance of a Renaissance resting place—the aura of peace, tranquillity and security. Yet thirty miles away in Belfast four children and two women had perished in another terrorist bombing. It was rumored that Great Britain was sending more soldiers. The demonstrations would escalate, the shooting and bombing would tear through the city and rip open the flesh of innocents. Belfast was fast becoming a city of no windows. Brandt had taken a picture of a boy, no older than eight, aiming a rifle at him as he focused the lens. This sort of thing took her breath away.

'Come with me to London,' he said from the bed.

'I can't this time,' she answered, not turning toward him. She drank in the green, perhaps never to see it again. The most beautiful land on the planet, torn asunder for years by political unrest, hate and prejudice, poverty and murder. Clare often wondered if it was that small dash of her own Irish blood that caused her such sentimentality toward this land, these people. She did not feel the same deeply personal pangs for the land and people of Bangladesh or Cambodia. In Ireland, it grabbed her heart and squeezed; her fear was palpable and her grief piercing. And of course Brandt was always at the center of it, in the midst of the violence, waiting for that special shot. The perfect light—that was his gift. It was not the way he aimed the camera, but the instinct he had for being there at the most opportune moment.

'I've got to go to London, love. I can't possibly avoid it. Go with me.'

She turned from the window. 'Don't you mean, Go as well?'

He shrugged. He seemed to fill the bed. His head and shoulders rested against the pillows and he lay tangled in the brightly white, sun-dried sheets, one long leg bristling with blond hair sticking out. 'However you term it, I must go to London and so I would like it if I could see you while I'm there. Because I want you madly. Because of how you look in one of my shirts. Because I'm dead in love with you, I want you in London.' A fleece of golden hair covered his chest; the crop of curling blond hair on his head was growing thinner, but he still looked younger than forty-seven.

'I read a piece about you in *Newsweek*,' she said. 'Did you see it?'

'Aye. It was a piece, all right.'

'They call you something of a womanizer. I think it was meant as a compliment.'

'I wonder how they get off. It's not at all true. I'm a one-woman man.'

'Now that's pushing it, don't you think?'

'Oh love, come here. I can't bear it when you're out of my reach.'

'Not until you explain the article...and the womanizing,' she said playfully.

'I'm an unconscionable flirt, that's true. I do tend to take advantage of women who think I'm grand...but hell, I never lead them on. I don't lead them far, and I *never* sleep with them. I like the attention is all.' He reached a hand toward her. In a second, she knew, she would let him draw her back to the bed.

At four this morning she was pacing, beginning to sink into a familiar panicked, frantic thinking. What will I do if *this time* he is too close to the action? This could be the time she'd have to find her own way out of some country he photographed, alone, terrified, grief-stricken. Jake Friedman of the Associated Press, or some other crony of theirs, would find her in the Donnelly inn, tap reluctantly on her door and say, 'Clare, love, sorry, but it's awful news…in some random cross fire…'

Then his face appeared at seven in the morning, his beard coarse and stubbly, his eyes dancing as though strung out on some caffeine high. She tried to pretend she hadn't worried while he sat in some dangerous Belfast flat through the night, waiting for a good shot, hoping for perfect light. 'It was dawn when the women and their children came onto the streets, some trying to go about their lives and some cautiously looking for dead. Their faces are blank, the children are armed! God, Clare, it's a nightmare they're living!' His passion stored on the film in his camera, he grabbed her up in his arms and spent the rest on her, like a victorious warrior returning from battle to his woman.

She let him draw her to the bed. 'Will you come?' he asked.

'If you touch me in the right places,' she replied, smiling.

He pinched her butt. 'To London!'

'Not this time, Brandt. I'm going to go home.'

'I don't like the way you say that. It sounds suspicious to me. Is this because of some piece in that American rag of yours? About women?'

She laughed at him. 'No, no. I know you don't sleep with other women. Well, I *assume* you don't…you spend too much time writing, calling and seducing me. If you do sleep with them, you don't give them much attention beyond that.'

'Then why are you sad? You hide it not at all,' he said, pronouncing it "at-tall" in his clipped, Aussie accent that had tidied up to near British over the years, nary a trace of his American roots left. 'Is it just that you're tired? I know something's wrong.'

'I did rather well, considering. If you had asked me three years ago how long I'd be content to follow this romantic figure around the worst places on the globe, I never would have guessed three years. David's playing soccer now, did I tell you? He's brilliant at it. He has a temper, though. It's hormones—he's eleven. His feet grow a size every month and he doesn't know what to do with his arms and legs unless he's on the soccer field. And Sarah, I noticed, is starting to blossom into a young woman. She's too young for that, I think…but she's becoming physically mature. She's so graceful, so beautiful. She won't need braces on her teeth.'

'What are you saying?' he asked, frowning.

'I have to go home to my children, Brandt. I'm away from them too much.'

'You won't give us up. After all we've been to each other, I can't believe you would.'

'No, I won't,' she said. 'But I think you will.'

He sat up in the bed, angry. 'Damn it, Clare! If you'd just give me—'

'Have you ever thought about what I'd do if something happened to you while we're on the road like this? Can you see a picture of me slinking away...shamed...not even acknowledged as the woman who's loved you through every bloody war, famine and flood for the last three years? Who will they say I am when they study the pictures of the mourners? What about the day *Newsweek* prints my name in conjunction with yours? How many lives will be disrupted by that?'

'I've told you, it wouldn't disrupt much. It would be a very slight ripple in the steady lives of—'

'Oh, crap! If Beatrice is so fucking understanding, why don't you explain to her that you can't keep up the pretense anymore. Make San Francisco your base. See your children when you're in London, as you do now, but for God's sake don't ask me to leave my own children and hide out in little rooms all over the world just so we can be together. Brandt, it's time for you to make up your mind. Six months ago you said—'

'I explained the problem then. I wasn't putting you off. Beatrice's father passed on and there was a dither over it—an estate to settle and the children home. Marc goes to university in the fall and Diedre begins her final year at Cordell. The time will be better then. Bear with me, darling. Barring death or disease, I'll have it done then. I swear!'

'It's so easy for you to consider her feelings, to go back to her again and again. I can't imagine it's only her wealth because you're wealthy, too. Is she beautiful, Brandt? Kind? Sensitive?'

'Yes, yes, she's all those things and more, but that's not what this is about. You're the woman I love! Clare, haven't you listened to me? She was a mere girl of twenty when I met her and married her and was reluctantly approved by her stricken family. She was a rich, spoiled girl, accustomed to having her way and I was what she wanted then. The poor thing realized in less than two years that she'd made a dreadful mistake, but Marc was on the way by then and she'd already hurt and shocked her family enough. She's had to become mighty wise and resilient to get through the years as well as she has. At long last we've at least become friends.

'Beatrice is more concerned with her social circle, her reputation and her family than she is with me. She's happier when I'm away than when I'm in London or at her country estate, scratching my neck under the starch of those bloody tux collars. We haven't slept in the same bedroom in fifteen years. She's asked only two things of me. She wanted children that she might have company in her old age, knowing only too well, I suppose, that she wouldn't have me. And she asked discretion, so she wouldn't be publicly humiliated by my antics.

'She's done a fine job with Marc and Diedre, so fine that they hardly expect any more of me than she does. And I love them, the both of them. They adore me in return, though they shouldn't—I'm more a visiting cousin than doting father to either of them. I admire the woman, Clare. I respect her.

I don't shrink from the talk of ending the marriage—I'm quite sure she's expecting it. But I couldn't do it while she was burying her father.'

She was quiet for a moment. Then, 'The woman sounds like a fucking saint.'

'You are evil and crass,' he said, but a smile grew slowly on his lips.

'Well, she does! I wouldn't leave a wife like that! Why should you?'

His green eyes bore into her and grew dark. 'Because I taste you in my sleep.' His hand went under the shirt she wore—his shirt. She wore it while he was away shooting, so she could smell him the whole while. The coil inside of her began to tighten and her skin became hot. He set her flesh afire. Brandt had some chemical advantage with her that no other man had. It was not the danger, nor the long absences. Could not be. She'd had other dangerous, absent men. It was something not of this world, but definitely of the flesh. No man had ever kept her sexual attention for so long, through so much, only to leave her craving more of him.

In her heart she wondered whether she was that equal match for Brandt. He said she was. 'No other woman, at no time in my life, can do for me, to me, what you can do....' But she drew herself as worldly, a woman wise to the words and seductions of the sexual male. That meant, should she learn he had lied, she would be disappointed but not surprised.

Rolling with him against the soft, sweet, hay-filled mattress in the little Irish inn in the countryside of Donnelly, thinking *once more once more once*

more, she felt the tears burn her eyes just as his
thrusts caused her body to convulse and spasm in
joy. Living without this in her life would be terrible. Giving this up, though her travels had become
perilous and fraught with tension and fear, would
be a great sacrifice.

'Tell me you love me,' he begged. 'Please.'

'I love you more than I thought possible,' she
said, kissing his lips. But he'd seen the glistening
eyes. He could sense what was ahead. 'But I'm going home to my children.'

'Clare....'

'It's July,' she said. 'Hot as hell itself in California in July....'

'Clare, don't....'

'In the fall, when the children go to school,
you'll speak to Beatrice. Call me then. Call to say
the papers are filed and the legal ties soon to be
severed. Tell me that if some biographer snaps a
picture of me sucking your ear, it's okay, that it
won't cause Marc to become suicidal or Diedre to
run away out of pure hatred of her father. It will be
a legitimate affair. Come and meet my children. I
wouldn't see you before September or October
anyway.'

'You're talking of leaving me!'

'I'm speaking of going home! Where I have a
life, a family!'

'What will change your mind and make you
come with me to London?'

'Nothing, Brandt! Go to London! Your family is
there! They're expecting you!'

'I'll tell her this week. I'll tell them all. Come to
London so that I can prove to you that I'm serious

about this, about us. Please. We've hardly had any time together this trip. You can spare three or four more days for me…and I'll prove to you that I'm not putting you last.'

She touched his cheek. 'It's *my* job to become hysterical. I'm the woman.'

'Thoughts of not having you make me hysterical.'

'Now listen to me, Brandt. Do whatever you please about your family…in your own good time for all I care. But know this. Someday, someone will notice that every time you've snapped a picture in some blighted spot, I've written an article about the women and children in that same troubled place. You can brush it off all you like, but it *will* be news. And Beatrice might be a real peach, but she would be good and pissed. Now go home to London. And do whatever you're going to do, whenever you're going to do it.'"

When Sable finished reading, she dropped the sheaf of papers into her lap. "Damn," she whispered with a tone of reverence. "How much of this have you got?"

"All of it," Elly said. "In bits and pieces. There are gaps and rough places and unfinished chapters. The biggest problem is that I have five thousand pages of it. Except for the end, as near as I can tell. I don't have the end."

"She used David's and Sarah's names," Barbara Ann said.

"For the sake of speed, I assume. That could be easily changed. She didn't use the real names of John Shelby's actual family. I found a book she has, a biography of Shelby. And pictures by the score, letters by the dozens, notes, postcards."

"Gabby was the most wonderful writer," Beth said. "What do you think? Is it publishable?"

"Not quite. It needs a little cleaning up, but it doesn't need changing. She worked on it on and off for so many years, some of it's in tatters. But if I'm not mistaken, it's the book they've always expected her to write. It's the most adventurous love story I've ever read, or I'm a sentimental old fool."

"Not if the rest of it stands up to this one chapter," Sable said. "Is this what you've been working on?"

"I wanted to be sure I had enough of it to share with the rest of you. If it was too partial, we'd have to let it go, give it to Sarah and David in its original form and call it a day. But there's enough of this novel to pull together, if there were four good heads to do it. Then, with their permission, I feel it should be sold."

"If that's what she wanted, why didn't she even mention it?" Barbara asked.

"I'm not sure I can answer that," Elly said. "Although she'd worked on it for years, she picked it up again only recently. She dates her originals. She's had this current computer for five years now and the chapters from this novel have been worked on in the past year. The earlier work on this is less objective—she was still in love and in grief. She knew that and her marginal scribbles indicate she was objective about her lack of objectivity. I think it's one of those special things that is worked on in secret until it's completely ripe. She wouldn't attempt to sell it based on a proposal or outline. She'd rather produce it suddenly, as if out of thin air, and blow their socks off with it. She was close, I think, to telling us about it."

"A posthumous blockbuster?" Beth asked. "Publishers always want to know what's next when they buy a book...and this is a loner."

"Not exactly," Sable argued. "Gabby wrote ten extremely good novels, but not very much was done with them."

"That's dead on," Barbara Ann, the recent expert in her manuscripts, said. "Writers have been shaking their heads in confusion about that for years. She was good. Used bookstores can't keep her books, people don't trade them. Everything she published should have sold huge numbers, but they were always published conservatively. We always figured it was because she couldn't stick with one 'type' of story long enough to build a category readership. That, and a not very unusual run of lousy luck."

"If you look at her work as a whole," Elly said, "it isn't as though she was floundering around, looking for a home. She always should have done better than she did. The critics loved her work, but the publishers didn't take notice. The readers loved her, but they published each title as though it was the first for her— modest print runs, no special advertising, nothing much done. If one single book of hers got the attention it deserved, the fifteen previous novels would be considered a find. Gabby never wrote as though she was just warming up. They just didn't see in New York what the rest of us saw. They're myopic, too busy looking for trends. Gabby's work transcended trends. It wasn't faddish. It was always solidly good. Versatile, creative—"

"Versatility is a dirty word in publishing—"

"We can get back the rights on at least six of those

earlier books," Beth said. That was her area of expertise.

"Nothing will ever happen to those earlier books without a blockbuster to catapult them out of obscurity," Eleanor said. "And I think this might be it. It's really smashing."

"What needs to be done?" Sable asked.

"A lot of sorting, organizing, cleaning up. Some writing, but hopefully not more than twenty percent of the novel. From her photos, letters and records, I can provide the facts for the small amount of fiction that's missing. She has outlined two missing chapters. Between the four of us, we should be able to faithfully replicate her style." She paused. "And she said there was no hidden gem!"

"Is it right for us to do that with her work? Fix it? Write it? Publish it?" Barbara asked.

"Right? I think she commissioned us to do that," Beth said.

"And if we do it well enough, Sarah and David will have pensions," Sable added.

"If we do it well enough," Elly said, "Gabby will live, which is what writers really want, I think. And what this particular writer, who was largely overlooked, deserves."

Part Three

FOURTEEN

June 30

There had to be a transformation of space. "A halfway house for insane women," Sable had best termed it. "Why didn't we think of this before?"

"I don't know how much of this dormitory living I can endure," Eleanor said. All the gang cooking, gabbing, psyche-probing, pajama-party-flopping—she had never shared her space with even one other woman, much less three. "There just better not be any childish screwing around...."

"As far as we know, Elly, you're the only one with anyone to screw," Beth pointed out. Everyone had been a bit too preoccupied to turn any attention to whether Sable's relationship with Jeff was purely professional, and she certainly hadn't offered anything on that subject. "I always secretly thought you were a lesbian." She flushed when all eyes were suddenly on her. "I mean..."

"I love the way you're learning to express yourself, Beth," Sable said. "It's like someone who's just learning the language. The most amazing things just pop out of you."

"What did I ever do to make you think—"

"Beth sees the entire world in its relationship to love, Elly," Sable said. "If you're not completely enslaved to a member of the opposite sex, you must be gay, in which case you would be hiding the fact that you're completely enslaved to a member of the same sex. Right, Beth?"

"No! I—" She paused and then said, "I guess I'm still all screwed up in love—"

"Did you think I was a lesbian, too?" Sable asked her, for any brief liaisons she had had over the years had been kept strictly secret. There were too few to even think about.

"Oh, no, Sable! I always thought you were in love with yourself! I mean—"

Only Sable did not laugh. "It could be a brain scar," she muttered, shaking her head.

They rearranged the house and began disposing of Gabby's personal effects to make room. Sarah and David took some things, from books to a sewing machine to old camping gear. Clothes were given to the women's shelter where Beth was getting counseling, Gabby's car was sold for a pittance, pictures were sorted through and given to Don and the kids and boxes of memorabilia and things that had long since lost their usefulness were divided, trashed, donated or carted over to Sarah's for a garage sale. Then, when space allowed, things could be brought in to accommodate the women. The kids' rooms, stacked high with their old things plus storage items, were cleared out so that each woman could have a bedroom. Elly had squatter's rights in Gabby's bedroom, Sable could not be budged out of the guest room, Beth got Sarah's old room and Barbara Ann got David's.

Each woman set up her own work area in her room,

hooked up a phone to the available jacks, had shelf space to put her favorite books, and her own clothes filled emptied drawers and hung in vacated closets. The four settled in as though the project of pulling together Gabby's book might take blissful months, but they knew they weren't that lucky. It would be only weeks. And then each one of them would have to decide what to do. Elly, they all thought, was the only one who could just go back to her former life as though she'd spent the summer out of town doing research. But Elly's future was as muddled as anyone's. Now that she'd brought Ben out of the closet, she would have to either go the whole distance, becoming a real significant other to his family as well, or end the relationship altogether. She was not certain she could do either.

Barbara Ann had only been gone from her house— her men—for three days when she went back there with Beth to pick up her computer and a few other things. Three days, she reminded herself on the drive over, was hardly enough time for a miracle. She remembered, from her days as a young wife and mother, how long it took her to figure out how to cook and clean and manage a family. She had to pick up tips from other women on how to keep up with things. She had to study other homes to establish her own sense of what made good housekeeping. Even though she had been an only child and didn't come in a pack, her own mother had made it seem so effortless. It was like the bathrooms were scrubbed and the floors waxed in secret.

She was not prepared for how bad it could get.

Beth could not conceal her shocked gasp, but then,

Beth had recently begun to lose the art of concealing things.

The kitchen was stacked with dirty dishes and there was a fine layer of grime on everything. Cupboard doors stood open, goop was slopped over on the walls and stove, food was not put back in the refrigerator and sat rotting on the countertops, discarded packages from snack foods and empty cereal boxes lay everywhere and she stuck to the floor in those places her step didn't crunch. She was afraid to count the empty pop cans—there could be fifty.

The laundry room was piled waist high in dirty clothes, as though someone had carted them there and then waited, amazed that they didn't wash, dry and fold themselves. It smelled like the inside of an old tennis shoe. The sad reality was that, in the case of five males who changed clothes on a whim, this was three days of wash. That's why Barbara Ann ran three loads a day, come hell or high water.

The family room was a spillover from the kitchen: plates, wrappers, glasses, cans, plus overflow from the bedrooms—shoes, socks, wadded-up T-shirts, towels, newspapers and magazines. Not surprisingly, someone was tinkering with a torn-apart stereo in the middle of the floor.

"Oh, Barbara Ann," Beth said.

"I hope you don't think I left it like this," she said.

"But look what you were up against!"

"Kind of amazing I could gain weight, huh? Come on, let's get my things. But prepare yourself, Mike's had the bedroom to himself for three days now. I'm sure it should be torched."

In her wildest dreams she hadn't expected the bed would be made, but somehow it hadn't occurred to her that the spread, sheets, mattress cover and pillows would be on the floor, exposing a mattress that had been peed on by every one of her boys at some point in their young lives. How in the world had he managed that? He must be sleeping like a spinning top. The master bath was afoul with splattered mirror, scummy basins and countertops, and clothes, towels and shoes were simply dropped where they landed.

"Come on," she said to Beth. "Let's just get my stuff together and get out of here. Now don't carry anything until I approve it. I don't want you lifting heavy things. There isn't that much I want from in here."

She had timed it so that no one should be home. Cars parked in the driveway didn't mean anything; one never knew who went off with whom. She stacked clothes from her drawers and closet on the bed for Beth to pack in two suitcases, a hang-up bag and small duffel, while she gathered books, papers and Rolodex from her work area into boxes. She began to carry things to the trunk while Beth folded and packed. She disconnected the computer and gave Beth the keyboard and cables to carry while she made several trips with the monitor, mini-tower and printer. She filled a small box with toiletries from her bathroom closet and handed it to Beth. "That's all," she said. "I'll bring down the two big suitcases and we'll be done. Go ahead. I'm going to take one quick look around and check to see if I have any mail. I'll be right behind you."

But one last look around was not at all what she wanted—she needed a little privacy. What had become of the home she had slaved over since they moved in ripped her heart out. She was not going to snivel in front of Beth, but she had earned a few painful tears over this stinking hovel. This was the impact she'd had on them. They'd done nothing but settle back and enjoy their squalor.

She heard a familiar sound. Someone had just gotten out of bed and was peeing like a racehorse in the bathroom down the hall. She should have fled. She certainly didn't stay so that one of her sons could see how the condition of her house made her cry. But she wanted to see one of them, just for a minute, because she loved them so much. That's why this killed her and why she'd done what she'd done. She couldn't take it anymore, loving them that much and feeling only their tread marks on her breaking back.

She stood in her bedroom doorway, a large suitcase on each side of her, when Joe emerged from the bathroom. She hadn't heard the toilet flush, naturally. He was wearing only his boxers, his hair spiked and goofy, and he jumped in surprise when he saw her standing there. "Mom!"

"Hi, Joey. I just came back to get a few things."

"Mom! Oh, man…. We were gonna—"

"No, it's okay. Don't say anything. I told you you can have it any way you want it now. You don't have to keep it to my standards."

"But Mom! Man, you don't know…. I mean, Dad said for me to get it together because I'm off today. And Billy gets off work at noon. We're gonna get the place all straightened up. Honest! Aw, Mom," he said, devastated.

"I've got to get going," she said, lifting her suitcases. "There is one thing you can do for me, though."

"Sure! Anything!"

"Check through the mail every day. If there's anything that's just for me—just for Barbara Ann Vaughan and not Mr. and Mrs.—bring it to me at Gabby's. And if I get any phone calls, give them Gabby's number. It's written down by the phone."

"Sure. But Mom, really—"

"It's okay," she said, hefting her suitcases.

"Aw, let me get those, Mom," he said, the sound of choking tears coming into his voice. He could not have been more humiliated if she'd seen him naked and shooting up. Even given his shame and humiliation, she doubted he and his brothers and father could make the place right. They might be able to cart off trash, but despite all her efforts to teach and supervise them, they were sadly handicapped in domestics. The only thing her men could make shine like a star was a rebuilt engine.

"I'll take it from here," she said when he got to the front door. "Beth's waiting for me and you're not dressed."

"Mom," he pleaded, tears glistening in his eyes, his lips turning red around the edges. This was the boy who had cried so hard when he lost his girl. He was losing his mother. She felt terrible for him, but not terrible enough to drop her suitcases here and now and dig out the place.

She rose up on her toes and kissed his cheek. He embraced her clumsily, his strong shoulders jerking a little as he fought back sobs. "I love you, Joey. I'll be in touch about your birthday—we'll do something special. I'll take you to dinner or something. Tell your brothers I love them. And call me at Gabby's if you need to talk to me."

"I love you, Mom. You gotta know I love you, Mom."

"I know, Joey."

"Mom...what about Dad?"

"I talk to your dad every day. He knows I love him. That house is the only thing I don't love. I'm just not up to it anymore. It's too hard and I need a rest."

"Mom, the pot wasn't ours. It was some asshole friend of Bobby's who left it there in the garage and we shouldn't have let him, but he just did it. Honest, Mom, your leaving us is *killing* us!"

"I know," she said. "I can smell it."

Sable was going to spend a day with Jeff, taking care of some business, she said. She needed to go by her house and make sure things were secure there, that nothing terrible had happened in her absence, among other things. But she was much too nervous for business to be the extent of what she was doing.

"Just tell us the truth," Barbara Ann pleaded. "Is he a boyfriend? That's all I want to know."

"No, he's not a *boyfriend*," Sable said. "Oh my God, my clothes don't fit! Oh, God, what have I done to myself? I can't button my pants! Jesus!"

"You've been eating, that's what," Eleanor pointed out. "After all these years of verging on anorexia."

"I verged on a lot of things, but not that! I used to step on the scale every morning. I exercised every day, no matter what, even if it was just sit-ups in some hotel room. I was fit and weight-conscious and not a lazy pig, that's all. Oh God, even my shoes are tight!"

"You were compulsive and obsessed," Beth said. "And you hid your true feelings in your rituals of perfection."

"Don't you just love this girl? Two weeks ago the only way she knew if she liked something was if *Jack* liked it."

"I think it's good that you're not suppressing your

feelings anymore, Beth. Isn't it nice that Beth is finally saying what she really thinks?" Barbara Ann supportively but unwisely asked.

"Well," she said, pausing in earnest consideration, "I don't think it would hurt you to give up Snicker Doodles for a while. Since you seem to want the truth."

"Remarkable," Elly observed. "Like someone coming out of a deep coma."

"Barbara Ann, do you have anything that's maybe a little *tight* on you that wouldn't be too loose on me?" Sable begged.

"Sorry, I left all my out-of-style size eights in the trash heap so they have something to wipe up blood with while I'm gone. What's the big deal? Are you going on a talk show or something? Wear one of your funny little dresses."

"I wanted to look a little more fashionable for once. It's not as though I don't plan to ever wear decent clothes again. Oh God, how much weight could I have gained in two or three weeks? What was I thinking?"

Everyone had been drawn to Sable's room by the ruckus. She'd been in and out of four or five outfits as they watched. Her sleek, tailored slacks wouldn't close; her panty line stood out like a welt across her butt; her pleats strained until they went flat. It was a good ten pounds around the middle. "This is not giving me as much pleasure as I always thought it would," Barbara Ann confessed.

Sable finally settled on a skirt that she held closed with a large safety pin, a wide belt that was moved to the last hole and a longish jacket that covered the whole mess. "I still look like a sausage," she groused. "How can I have gained weight in my shoulders and toes?"

"Fat is wondrously and fearfully distributed," Barbara Ann informed her.

The doorbell rang. "Oh my God, he's here! And I'm not ready!"

"Late, and for your first prom." Eleanor went to answer the door.

Barbara Ann trailed behind her, muttering, "There's something going on here, with Sable and this Jeff. Something interesting, I just know it."

"Well, good morning, ladies," he said cheerily. He didn't carry a bouquet or anything and was dressed casually, in slacks and a cotton shirt—no tie. It didn't appear they were running off to get married.

"Good morning to *you*," Barbara Ann gushed. "Sable's not ready yet, but nearly. Come on in, get a cup of coffee, and tell us what you two are planning to do today."

"Oh, just a little business. Tie up a few loose ends. We're going out to the house so Sable can check with Dorothy and Art, make sure they're all right alone out there."

"That can't be *all*," Barbara Ann drove on, pulling him into the kitchen and pouring him a cup of coffee. "Sable's acting so fussy about her appearance, you must have something rather special on the agenda for today!"

"Just loose ends," he insisted, smiling.

"Aren't you being awfully secretive?" Barbara whispered conspiratorially.

"Barbara Ann, if I knew of any secrets, I'd tell you at once," Jeff teased. "Sable, hurry up!" he shouted in the direction of the bedrooms. "I'm being grilled out here!"

"Oh, how tactless," she huffed.

"Oh how transparent," he replied, still smiling patiently.

Sable and Jeff had driven for a little while when he reached across the console and patted her knee. "Settle down," he said. "It's going to be a nice day."

"How can you say that? Since when is visiting a grave a nice day?"

"You'll be surprised. It's what you want to do, remember? It can be healing, restorative. Just let it happen."

"Jesus, you're sick. Do you have any graves you regularly visit?"

"Just one—my dad's. He died very suddenly when I was seventeen. We were close. I know he's not really there, but there just doesn't seem to be any other place I can feel him so strongly."

"So what do you do there? Talk to him?"

"Yeah," he said, laughing as though shocked to admit it—or maybe embarrassed. "At first, when the hurt from losing him was still fresh, I'd go there to tell him how pissed off I was at him and also to complain about how terrible my life was without him. I don't know when it happened, really, but at some point I realized I'd just been to my father's grave, musing like I do, thinking thoughts to him like he was there hearing me, and I hadn't yelled at him or complained about anything. I'd just sort of communed with his spirit, like a long-distance phone call, catching him up on events, sharing my thoughts. I rushed out there once to make sure he knew the Braves won the series. Then I felt so stupid, except that I felt better somehow. I went there to apologize for my divorce, to promise to take care of

Mom and to ask his advice about starting my own security business."

"I can't do that with my child, however," she said.

"Whatever it is you have to do, it'll come to you. You've been talking about never having seen his grave. You're ready for something. Who knows what it is, but it isn't going to be scary, Sable."

She grasped his hand. "How can you be so sweet? Shouldn't you be more cynical, given the kind of work you do?"

"Naw, just the opposite. My job is really about making people feel safe. It might involve all kinds of locks, cameras, wires and whistles, but it always starts one on one. I just listen to what people say makes them scared, then we work on handling the scary things."

"There isn't a lock you can put on this one," she said, shivering with fear that she might collapse when she saw Thomas Adam's little grave.

"I think you're missing the point here, Sable. This time we're taking the lock *off* to find safety. It'll be okay."

Two hours later they were pulling through the iron gates and into the cemetery. She had expected it to be horrid and bleak, since she hadn't had any money with which to bury him. It was a pauper's grave, for the forgotten. But it wasn't depressing. It was well-groomed and clean. There weren't many headstones, monuments or statues, which made it look a little less like a cemetery. "Is it far?" she asked nervously as Jeff drove along the winding road, farther and farther into the trees. He had found the grave for her in advance of her first visit, so they wouldn't have to go searching for it when she was finally ready to see it.

"Not far," he said. "It's pretty back here, isn't it? A nice place to rest, really."

"Oh please," she groaned, her stomach twisting inside.

"I bet it's glorious in the fall, when the leaves are changing. We'll have to come and see it then."

"Jeff, really—"

"Here we are. It's over there, about fifty yards. Come on."

"Maybe I should go alone," she suggested, already feeling as though her legs wouldn't hold her up.

"I don't think so. You've been alone long enough."

Before she knew it, she was staring down at it. It was a flat plaque. It said:

Thomas Adam Parker
Beloved Son
Rest, Little Lamb

There was a carved silhouette of a small child's head, bent in prayer on the plaque. Remarkably, it looked as Sable remembered him—a little tuft of hair in back with bangs over his forehead. Instinctively, she knelt to touch the plaque, to caress the face. Jeff knelt too, a little behind her.

"You can't imagine how precious he was," she said. "Or how smart. He would have gone so far, if I hadn't lost him."

"I bet he was beautiful."

"He was, which was a miracle in itself. I was too homely for words, and Butch wasn't that much to look at. But Tommy was incredible. Angelic. Adorable. He should have been the Gerber baby."

"You never thought about marrying again? Having more children?"

"I can't," she said. "I had pelvic inflammatory disease, one final gift from Butch, left untreated for so long that by the time it was found, it was too late. I was sterile. I struggled with the left-over symptoms for a few years and then finally had a hysterectomy. That was over ten years ago now."

"That's a shame. You should have had a second chance. Of course, there was always adoption."

"I wasn't up to it. I didn't really want more children after Thomas Adam. I think you can only survive that kind of pain once in a lifetime. I just went on to other things." Tears gathered in her eyes. "It's hard to tell what would have become of me if he had lived. Or him. What could have become of him? Years of crippling abuse that I managed, somehow, not to see?"

"You never said—did Butch beat you?"

"Sure," she said, wiping at her eyes. "But I didn't know it. He was a son of a bitch who could get ugly when he drank. Not always, but often enough that I should have been able to see it coming. He knocked me around, but I didn't know he was beating me. I thought he was losing his temper, losing his cool. I never thought he'd touch the baby. How could I have been that stupid?"

"You were young. You didn't know anything about that."

"Sometimes even when you know, you don't know. You should talk to Beth for a while. She's worse than I was. She doesn't even have the excuse that she's uneducated about battered wife syndrome. She knows about it and still thinks it has to do with other women. Oh, she's slowly coming around, changing her thinking. But I get the sense that she's staying away from Jack through sheer willpower, not because she knows in her heart that he's dangerous to her and her child.

"God, if only I could go back in time and do this differently," she said, her fingertips brushing over the silhouetted face. "If I had it to do again, smarter, I'd have run to Gabby when I found out I was pregnant. I wouldn't have even *told* Butch or my mother. I should have run for my life, to people who would have brainstormed some ideas with me, shared some survival skills. There were agencies, even then. There was help available, but you have to at least look for it. It's like trying to look up a word in the dictionary when you don't know how to spell it, a part of you thinking it just won't be there. I didn't even think there was a place to look for what I needed. I didn't know what I needed, but I should have tried. I could have found a way to stay in school, at least part-time. I could have had my baby, gotten an education, found a decent career and raised my son in some kind of safe environment.

"He would be nineteen now," she mused. "I can't even imagine how handsome, how smart. Sometimes I wish I'd run away from Butch and given Thomas Adam up for adoption. I might not know him now, but somewhere out there would be this young man who might, someday, for some reason, try to find me.

"There should have been an intervention somewhere," she said, turning to Jeff, tears streaming down her cheeks. "Somewhere along the line someone should have picked this grubby, slutty girl with the bad attitude out of the trash heap and said, 'Listen up, you idiot! You don't know how bad it will get if you don't try doing this differently!' God, how I wish someone had tried to reach me when there was still time.

"But it wasn't their fault, whoever *they* are. I was completely deaf. I didn't know my mother had a disease—I thought she was a drunk. I didn't know I was being abused—I thought Butch was a normal guy and guys hit when they're mad. And I didn't know I had a disease that complemented my mother's disease. Denial, Elly says, always ends in death. I just didn't know any of that."

"Things are getting better in that area," he said. "Kids are learning about alcoholism and abuse in school now. And birth control, et cetera."

"I know, I know, but is anyone taking that individual kid and saying, 'Come here, sit with me a while. Let's talk about it all. You can stay here the night…the weekend…sleep in clean sheets…while we figure out what it's going to take to get you out of the quicksand.' Do you think anyone is doing that?"

"I think so," he said. "But I don't think there's a surplus of them."

She looked back at the little face on the grave. "Oh, Tommy, I'm so sorry," she said. "I'm so, so sorry.…" She began to cry harder and harder, until she was wailing. She began to feel that inner collapse take her over, but yet it didn't overtake her. Jeff held her against his solid chest and she let it run out of her, like releasing the toxins of pent-up grief. She wept and wept and felt the hatred and regret and distrust leaving through her tears. Minutes passed and she did not quiet or calm. She cried so hard and for so long, only vaguely aware that Jeff didn't make her stop, that he didn't say, "All right, that's enough, now."

Finally, her wails and choking sobs began to ebb and

she wept softly. That, too, slowed to a sniffle and hic-cup. At long last she pulled away from Jeff's soaking shirt and looked at his eyes. "How long have I been crying?" she asked him.

"I'm not sure. I haven't been timing you."

"Oh God," she murmured, "I'm exhausted."

"That's all right. It's the hardest work you have to do today."

"I need to have some flowers," she said. "Can we find some flowers?"

That was easily done. They went to the car, Sable walking weakly with Jeff's support, and drove to a su-permarket in Fresno. By the time she arrived at the store, she was already feeling stronger. She purchased a bunch of fresh flowers in a vase and they took it back to the cemetery. They stayed only a little while because Jeff said, "It's hard to do it all in one visit. You'll have to come back, probably, and I'll come with you any-time."

"You're right," she agreed. "I'll have to come back because you do think of things once you're there, things you have to think to that person. It's remark-able."

She slept in the car all the way back to the Sacra-mento area and beyond. Jeff stopped at a fast-food res-taurant and woke her. He told her to take a minute to wash her face, comb her hair, and maybe have a soft drink and then they would press on to her house to see Art and Dorothy.

One look in the mirror told her she had better pull herself together; she wouldn't want to frighten the lit-tle old couple. Her eyes were red and swollen and she felt groggy. She'd had the foresight to bring along a lit-tle makeup, not because she expected to have cried all hers off, but because she planned to spend a very long day away from Gabby's. It came in handy when she realized that she'd left most of her makeup on the front of Jeff's shirt.

When she came out of the rest room she found him sitting in a booth, waiting for her with a cold drink. He'd managed to wipe off the front of his shirt so that it was hardly smudged. He seemed to know exactly what to do, no matter the circumstances. The fact that he hadn't bought food, though they hadn't eaten since breakfast, was perfect. She could hardly handle the smell of greasy food, much less the taste. But she needed the cold drink, and a moment to collect herself before seeing Dorothy and Art. "I'm nervous. Is that silly?"

"I don't think so, but you'll be fine. It'll be good for you to see that everything is all right at your house."

"I'm embarrassed to face them," she said.

"Of course you are, but you needn't be."

"But what if they think the worst of me?"

"What if they do? Whose loss would that be?"

Ah, yes, that was what he did for her. He made her feel like a valuable treasure. That he could do that while she was as slick and cool as porcelain was one thing. But he could manage that when she looked like an unmade bed and was as unstable as a house of cards.

Art came out of his cottage at the sound of the car door. As Sable walked toward him, she saw Dorothy peeking out through the curtain. Funny, she'd never been in their little house since she gave it to them. "I'm sorry about all the trouble, Art. I hope you're all right."

"It weren't that much trouble, Miss Sable. Jeff's boys

kept the place free of pests till they all lost interest and went away. And me and the missus, we been keeping it up pretty good. Just like you was off on vacation or something like that."

"I really appreciate it, Art. I don't want you to worry about it too much. I'm not going to pop in here unannounced and do an inspection. I'd like you to tell Dorothy—"

"Now wait there a minute, I'll just get her...."

"You don't have to trouble her. If you'll just—"

But he was already walking toward the house. Sable felt her spine grow tense and was conscious of her palms becoming damper at the prospect of seeing Dorothy's grim expression. And there it was, suddenly, as she came out of her little house. Dorothy protectively drew her sweater around her, though it was in the eighties and humid, and the corners of her mouth drew down in her perpetual frown. But Sable was too drained to be angry. It only made her feel more tired looking at Dorothy's scowl.

"Hello, dear," Sable said kindly. "I'm terribly sorry if you and Art have been bothered by all the publicity and fuss. I just wanted to come here personally to tell you that I'm staying with friends for the time being. I feel a lot better being around people who I know love me than I would feel here, mostly alone. Here's a number if you need anything," she said, handing Dorothy a small envelope. "Your check for June is there, too. Are things all right with the house, Dorothy?"

She nodded. "The house don't change much, day to day."

"Well, don't knock yourself out," Sable said. "As I told Art, I have no intention of popping in here unannounced and giving it a white-glove inspection. I don't expect you to spit and polish an empty house. Are the two of you all right about staying on with me, even after all the terrible publicity about me?"

"Oh my, surely yes," Art said emphatically. "That don't matter to us in any way, Miss Sable. And we don't say anything to anybody about your business, not even to our kids. We just mind our chores and worry about our own business here."

"That's very kind of you, Art," she said, though she couldn't imagine what dirt they could possibly share about her. This was where she was perfect, after all. "Then I'll be going. Call me if you need anything from me, and thank you for all your good work."

She turned to leave, taking Jeff's arm and walking toward the car.

"Sable?"

She stopped and listened for a second before turning back. Was that Dorothy? She couldn't recall Dorothy ever willingly calling her by name in the four years she'd been there.

"We been worried about you," she said. Her face still looked pinched and unhappy, but her words couldn't have sounded more sincere.

"Thank you, Dorothy. Thank you very much. I'm really getting along just fine."

When she got in the car, she was smiling. "I'm starving," she told Jeff.

"Good. There's a little steak place in Placerville. It's out of the way, old and quiet. They have good food and good wine."

She reached for his hand and pulled it toward her lips. She kissed his palm. "You are absolutely the best employee I've ever had," she said.

He threw back his head and laughed in genuine

pleasure. "Am I now? Well, just wait until you get the bill."

"Whatever it is, you're worth it." After a short pause she continued. "I think going to Tommy's grave helped me."

"Sometimes it does," he said. "Depending on what you need at the time."

"But Gabby doesn't have a grave. I wonder if we should have insisted she have a grave, if only for her ashes?"

"I wouldn't worry about that," he said. "From what I can tell, she has something even better."

FIFTEEN

Once Beth told her mother about Jack, the entire family was informed. Word traveled fast; Beth received four or five phone calls a day. It wasn't only her siblings, but brothers-in-law and sisters-in-law also called. They seemed to have created some kind of schedule, like people do about visiting the sick and infirm, so that they didn't all call her in one day, but every single day there were calls of support. Or pressure, depending on your perspective.

Her mother and oldest sister wanted to fly to Sacramento at once to see her, to assure themselves that she was all right, but she held them at bay. She explained, over and over, why she was at Gabby's house and who she was with. It would be better for everyone, especially her, if they would just be patient and wait for her to come home. "I need to stay here where I'm getting help. I have a counselor, plus I'm in a support group. I have to learn about this, Mama. There's something in me that's sick, too, that allows this abuse to happen. If I don't want it to ever happen again, I have to find out what it is."

"I'd like to know what it is, too," Sable said. "I am astonished that someone like you, who has all those people to love and support you, would endure abuse from anyone. You could have run home to your family the first time he snapped at you!"

"But I would have been running home in shame. A failure," she said.

"How could you have failed? *He* failed *you!*"

"I guess you don't know what it's like to come from a perfect family," she replied.

"Now there's an understatement!"

But that was its own burden—being one of eight children, nurtured and controlled by the soft yet iron hand of Mama. Oh, she was all love and tenderness, but she had a strong will and an absolute rule. She had God and the Church on her side. Beth grew up thinking that God had personally appointed Elba Sherman to conceive and raise the Sherman children because no one else could do it properly. Elba had proven herself to be the most remarkable woman in Kansas City, Missouri, and had been given the city council's Mother of the Year award. She had turned out eight perfect children with her gift of pride, faith, integrity and guilt— most of all guilt.

We don't have much, but what we do have we will keep clean, polished and perfect. Beth had learned to iron clothes at the age of seven. She had a school uniform and four hand-me-down dresses for Sunday church. There was not so much as a mended tear, stain or ravel on her. *Didn't Sister say that the way the paper looks is important? Isn't both the content and appearance part of the grade?* The children's schoolwork was reviewed each night and, if necessary, done over. God and Mama liked A's. *Cleanliness is next to godliness. God can hear the words you're saying and those you're thinking, so make them decent. I don't care what the other children do—in our home we live by the laws of God and the Church and I am re-*

sponsible, as God's disciple, to see that you adhere to both. That statement could have applied to short skirts, late hours or a messy room. In fact, that statement had to do with everything and ran up through college. *We must set a good example for our friends and neighbors because we are, each one of us in this family, disciples of the Lord.*

They were Mama's trophies. People turned their heads, smiled and whispered as Elba and Hank Sherman marched their brood down the street or down the aisle of the church, each child wearing spotless though well-used clothes, hair slicked back or pulled into tight braids, stockings whiter than white, faces shining and, until the age of eighteen, makeup free. Beth was mystified by the problems Barbara Ann had with her sons, she was astonished by the dirt and disorder they could live in. Not in Mama's house. *Never* in Mama's house! No one would dare leave a sock on the floor or a hairbrush on the bathroom counter. Not that Mama would be cruel or even harsh, but she was simply there, every second, like a bad dream, taking the offender by the hand and leading him or her to the untidy mistake and saying, "Is this where we leave our shoes?" "What is it we do with our towels?"

Each one of them got A's. Each one went to college, though Mama and Daddy had no money to send them. Each one excelled, kept a perfect house, ate right, slept soundly and married well. Eight college graduates, most happily married—and one of them a priest! All just as Mama had indoctrinated them all through their childhoods.

Except Beth.

Oh, she got the A's and went to college. She even got a master's degree. And her house was perfectly tidy, just as Mama would like. But she hurt inside and slept poorly. She hadn't done things according to Mama's plan, the way the others had. She was already twenty-five when she met Jack—and at a bar, no less! Her sisters had fiancés in college and married soon afterward, beginning their families right off, except Deborah, who had defiantly waited. Beth hadn't had boyfriends. She was so shy that only the very dorky ones approached her. And while she might have been panicked, she wasn't stupid. The only reason she met Jack was that one of the teachers at the junior high where Beth was the librarian manipulated Beth into going out for drinks every Friday night, mainly so Beth could drive her home if she didn't find a guy to leave with.

Beth knew when she met this smooth-talking, handsome, flirtatious airline pilot that she'd met her one chance at getting a husband. She might be an old maid, but Jack's words and touch thrilled her. Even in marrying Jack, a few concessions had to be made. Mama was concerned. (Disappointed.) He was ten years older than her for one thing, he wasn't Catholic and he'd been married twice before—something she couldn't let her family find out about. So, in an amazingly independent move, Beth married Jack, despite her parents' worries about the life-style they would have—he traveling, she staying behind—and their embarrassment that the father of Beth's future children didn't go to their church. There was, of course, no question in which faith those children would be raised. But at least she got a husband! She got something right!

The first time Jack hit her they had been married a month and her most overwhelming emotions were guilt and shame. *My God, I'm the different one again! Mama would be appalled by this! Mama will never* forgive me for getting myself into this mess! How can I keep screwing up and doing the wrong things over and over again? She didn't waste any time thinking about what a badass Jack was. She desperately plotted ways to cover up the fact that she was the only one in her family who couldn't just live the life that had been planned for her. She was riddled with guilt day and night, knowing that someday she would have to swallow her pride—pride that had been instilled in her as deeply as an organ transplant—confess her sins and do her penance. She would be the first divorce in the Sherman family.

What no one knew, except Beth herself, was that Elba Sherman's love, forgiveness and benevolence was likely to be the most painful part of her journey—surely more painful than one of Jack's left hooks.

He found her, of course. It only took him a week. Since Beth received so many phone calls from family members, male and female, the others in Gabby's house found it a challenge to screen the calls. They tried, but he got right past them.

The first time he'd called, Eleanor had answered.

"Is Beth Mahoney there, please?"

"May I ask who's calling?"

"Her husband, Jack Mahoney."

"I'm terribly sorry, but Beth isn't here. I could give her a message if I hear from her. Would you like to leave one?"

"No thanks," he said curtly, hanging up.

The second time he called, a couple of days later, Eleanor again answered.

"Is Beth there, please?" he asked.

"May I tell her who's calling?"

"Stephen Sherman, her brother."

"Just a minute, please."

She came to the phone. "Stephen?" she said.

"No, Beth, it's me. Jack. Honey, what are you doing there?"

"Jack!"

"Honey, we have to talk. I love you, baby. I know I really screwed up this time, but it doesn't mean I don't love you. You know I do. Beth, talk to me, please."

"Jack, I don't think we have anything to talk about. It's over. I'm not going to take—"

"Baby, I lost my cool. You gotta understand how a guy can overreact to some things. I've done a lot of thinking about the baby, and I've decided I was all wrong about that. We *should* have a baby! You'll be the most wonderful mother. You just hit me with it when I was worrying about money and things and I—"

"How could you be worried about money? Sell some of your toys."

"Well, that's just it. I wouldn't have spent all that money if I'd known we were going to have a baby! We'll have to get a bigger place. I don't want you walking up and down stairs in this town house if you're pregnant! And I can't be driving a stupid sports car if I have a son—there's no place for a car seat. I'll get him a sports car later. Beth, baby, I love you so much."

"Oh God, Jack," she said, tears coming.

"I need you to come home, so I can take care of you. What are you doing there? Who was that who answered the phone? Why are you there?"

Slowly, reluctantly, she began to regain her senses. "I'm here because you hit me, Jack. Hit me, knocked me down and demanded that I get an abortion before you came home from your trip. And I'm not moving back to the town house, no matter what you say."

"Beth, now listen. You're pregnant. That's the way it is. You're obviously intent on having this baby, so we'll have the baby. But you can't stay there. You have to come home—today."

She hung up on him.

A couple of days later he got through to her again, using another brother's name. The conversation went pretty much along the same lines. He wheedled and cajoled, claimed to be heartbroken at the prospect that she would take his child from him. She began to weaken. He begged her forgiveness and swore he'd never lay a hand on her again, but she stood up to him. He began to cry at the prospect of losing her and she felt herself wanting to pack a bag and go home to comfort him. Then she remembered. "No," she told him. "It's too late." And hung up. But she cried and cried, torn up inside by his pleading.

When Eleanor took to asking male callers to give her the date of Elba Sherman's birthday, Jack had a female call the house and ask for Beth. When she came to the phone, thinking it must be one of her sisters or sisters-in-law, it was Jack.

"Baby, I gotta see you. You're killing me with this. I can't take it. I want you and I want our baby. God, Beth, have some faith in me for once. Please, I'm begging you. At least *see* me. *Talk* to me. *Meet* me somewhere. Something!"

"No. You beat me up for seven years and I'm not giving you one more chance to trick me into thinking you can change. You've never changed before, even when you promised, and you won't change now."

"I'll go to counseling! I've already talked to a counselor at the company and they're going to give me a referral! Baby, I'll do anything! Anything!"

"Good, you should go to counseling. Maybe your fourth marriage will be better."

But she cried and self-doubted, rationalized and complained. "You have no idea how hard this is," she tearfully told her protective friends.

"I do," Elly said. "I stared into a glass of gin for four hours once. Four hours. Just sat there and stared. Almost got high on the fumes. I didn't stop staring until I started to sweat blood."

"But Elly, you don't think this is some kind of addiction!"

"Undoubtedly," she proclaimed. "He's in your blood. His danger has sex appeal."

"You didn't drink it, did you?" Sable asked.

"No. But I had an advantage over Beth. I *knew* gin could kill me. I knew that in choosing gin, I was choosing death. Even knowing that, it wasn't an easy choice."

"At least, for you, it was only four hours," Beth said to Elly.

"Beth, he doesn't love you," Sable said. "He only wants to be sure no one gets half his toys and investments in a divorce. Believe me."

"I believe you, I do," Beth said. But she thought that in addition to that, Jack might also love her. She couldn't help it.

Beth went to see her counselor. She went to her support group. She let everyone tell her over and over that he would hurt her, maybe kill her, that he would hurt, maybe kill the baby. No matter what he said, he was a beater. She must *not* give in. So she gritted her teeth and hung on. She was temporarily safe, with everyone holding her down, hammering her with the facts. She felt, though, like an alcoholic staring into a glass of gin.

She was temporarily safe from Jack, but there was no one there to protect her from herself.

Sable and Barbara Ann were preparing an evening meal—low-fat—while Beth and Sarah, with Lindsey in her infant seat, sat at the kitchen table and talked about babies—something that could keep the two of them going for hours. Elly was also at the table, reading her evening paper. It was seven-thirty, which wasn't late for the women because they always had a "cocktail hour" with some light snacks at five. From five o'clock on, there was no telling how many people might drop by, so they were always prepared to add lettuce and tomatoes to the salad, chicken breasts to the grill. David and Ed stopped by about once a week. Don had dropped in on them a couple of times and had been easily talked into staying for dinner. Mike Vaughan had brought some mail to Barbara Ann, and after a tentative appraisal of the situation, decided he was indeed as welcome as she claimed. The only one on a schedule was Ben, who came every Wednesday and Saturday like clockwork, and brought enough fresh fruit, vegetables and ice cream for everyone.

This was the time of day that everyone was at their happiest. The plagues of the workday were behind them, and so, it seemed, were the worries, guilts and fears of their personal lives. It was difficult to sulk or fret or whine when there was the community of food preparation, lubricated for those who were not pregnant or recovering alcoholics by a little wine. During this time of evening it was easy to pretend that the safety and security of living in a halfway house for lunatic women needn't end.

At the sudden sound of the bell, Eleanor was nominated by default to answer the door. Barbara Ann instinctively reached for another tomato to cut up; Sable went to the pantry for another envelope of instant rice. And they all grew quiet for a moment, waiting to see who had come.

"Ceola!" Eleanor said from the doorway.

The women all looked at each other for a second, thinking there must be some mistake. Beth and Sarah moved quickly toward the front door while Sable and Barbara Ann were a bit slower, pausing to set down utensils, lower the flame on the stove, dry hands.

There she stood, on the stoop, one large suitcase on each side of her, a large carry-on bag over her shoulder, her purse dangling from her forearm. She looked even shorter than her five feet because she was a step beneath them. Her hair was pink and thin—the color of cotton candy, but perfectly coifed—her eye makeup a little sloppy and her rouge too dark. She wore a rich designer suit in a pale green color with rhinestone buttons on the jacket, her pearls, her diamond rings and a green pillbox hat.

"Grandma?" Sarah asked.

"Oh, hello, dear. I didn't know you would be here, too."

"What are you doing here?" she asked.

"This is where I always come when I'm out of sorts about something. And I'm at odds with Martin. He's taken up an attitude with me."

"But why did you come *here*, Ceola?" Sable asked. "I mean, with Gabby *gone*—"

"Well, I knew you were here because Sarah and David told me you were. And, as I say, this is where I come."

They just stared at her. She'd flown in from Atlanta?

Without calling? Without notice? Expecting to stay *where?*

"Isn't anyone going to invite me in? I've had to piddle since the airport."

Still, it took a second to respond. The shock, and all. It was Sable who eventually said, "Of course, come in. I...ah...guess you know where the lavatory is."

"I guess I do," she said, entering, squeezing between them all and toddling off down the hallway like she owned the place. She left the large suitcases where they stood, but she hauled her carry-on bag with her. The size of the suitcases indicated this was not an overnight visit.

When she was around the corner and out of sight, their heads came together instantly.

"What the hell's going on here?"

"You heard her—this is where she comes when she's out of sorts."

"She can't be dumping another husband! At her age?"

"She's probably not dumping him, just leaving him until he straightens up and asks her to come home."

"I don't know about that," Sarah said. "She used to show up about once a year, for one reason or another. It wasn't like she came for a holiday or graduation or anything. I mean, it was never to see *us*. It's like she says—this is where she comes."

"Without notice? Without *asking?*"

"Yeah," Sarah said, shrugging helplessly. "Pretty much."

"What did your mother do with her?" Beth asked.

"Oh, nothing special. She made her breakfast—"

"Gabby made someone breakfast?! In the *morning?*"

"Grandma sleeps kind of late. And all she wants is

tea, half an English muffin and some fruit. Oh, and some marmalade. It has to be marmalade."

"Over my dead body," Eleanor said.

"She wouldn't mind that," Sarah replied. "What are you going to do with her?"

"What are *we* going to do with her? She's *your* grandmother!"

"Oh, we don't have a relationship. And I don't have a spare room—Lindsey's sleeping with Justin and me. She did call me a couple of weeks ago. She called David, too. She wanted to know if Mom had left her anything."

"Of all the insensitive, brutal—"

"Call David," someone suggested. "He can take her."

"David...and *Ed?*"

"Well, it's time she got with it. After all, he's her grandson."

"But David won't. He nearly hates her."

"Then he can send her home! This is nonsense."

"I don't think you'll be able to get David to do that. He barely talks to her. I guess you could call Dad."

"Call Don, Eleanor."

"Me? Hell no. You call him."

"What's Don going to do?"

"He can take her to his place. We don't have room for her here! There's barely a surface in this house that isn't being slept on or worked on!"

"I bet she won't go to Don's. *This* is where she comes."

"I can't believe this is happening."

"It's just too damn bad, that's all. That woman has been browbeating people for seventy-odd years, getting her way no matter how inconvenient it is for others. She doesn't have the least consideration for anyone but herself."

"That's true. Grandma's pretty self-centered, but she's awful old to change now."

"Go tell her she can't stay here, Sarah. Tell her she'll have to go to a hotel."

"I could tell her that, but she usually doesn't listen to me. Oops, I'd better see about Lindsey. I left her on the table."

They moved toward the kitchen in a sort of huddle, looking over their shoulders toward the hall, waiting for Ceola to appear.

"How long has this shit been going on? Ceola popping in like this because she's out of sorts?"

"All my life," Sarah said, leaning down to kiss Lindsey's head. "I'd come home from school and there would be Grandma, relaxing on the deck, or lying back on the couch."

"I've bumped into her here a few times myself," Eleanor confessed.

"So have I," said Sable. "It's not usually a short visit either."

"A couple of weeks, minimum. I don't know how Gabby did it."

"Well, she *managed* her, was her way of putting it," Sarah said. "Mom was always the only person in the world who could manage Grandma, as if catering to her was second nature for Mom. She knew just what to do and she just did it."

"Well, no one around here knows what to do," someone said.

"Where is she, anyway?"

"Piddling."

"Jesus, she must have stored up a tank. She's been in there a while."

"We're getting her out of here. She's not staying here and that's all there is to it."

"Will someone please call Don?"

"Grandma didn't like Dad very much. I don't think he'll be able to help with this."

"What does she *do* while she's here and out of sorts?"

"She mostly relaxes. She has her hair done. Mom would have to take her, of course, because she doesn't drive or anything. And she likes to go shopping...."

"God help us—"

"Basically she watches her soaps and gets a good rest."

"Why was your mother so indulgent of Ceola? I mean, didn't Ceola mainly neglect and ignore her all her life?"

"I'm surprised she made an appearance at the funeral," Sarah said. "But then, as David pointed out, mourning is one of her gifts."

"Jesus."

"Okay, we can all tell her together, or one of us can go."

"And say what?"

"How about, 'Ceola, unfortunately there is no room for you to stay here. We are all here because we're working on Gabby's writings and no one can see to your needs.'?"

"What needs? All she wants is tea and half an English muffin...."

"And hair appointments and shopping and soaps and probably a number of other things that Gabby just did as a matter of reflex. She always said that she was her mother's mother."

"Okay, how about, 'We're all delighted to see you, Ceola, but since the house is filled with crazy women who have given up their families and careers and you would probably be in mortal danger here, you'll have to go to a hotel.'?"

"That's good. I like that."

"What is *taking* her so long?"

"She probably keeled over in the bathroom. Someone better go check on her."

"Oh God, if I have to call another hearse to this house…"

"What if she grabs her heart and drops like a stone when we tell her—"

"Listen, she isn't as frail as she looks. She's browbeaten more men in her lifetime than most of us have *met!*"

"She can't stay. Are we agreed?"

"God, yes."

"Absolutely."

"Okay, so are we doing it together, as a team, or is one of us going to—"

Sable, who had crept away to peek down the hall, came back to the huddle. "Listen, she's not in the bathroom! I think she's in *my* room!"

"What the hell's she doing in there?"

"She's probably settling in," Sarah said. "And waiting for you to bring her her bags so she can unpack."

"Jesus Christ! This isn't *her house*, for God's sake."

"That never stopped her in the past."

"Don't even go back there, Sable. Just wait for her to come out here. Then we'll tell her and offer to call her a cab."

"This is Gabby's mother we're talking about," some weak-kneed coward said.

"That's too bad, isn't it? I mean, you're never too old to learn a few manners, for Christ's sake. She could have at least called and asked if we could have her."

"She wouldn't do that," Sarah said. "She doesn't bother to ask if the answer might be no. She just sort of...assumes."

"She can assume at the fucking Holiday Inn."

"This is a little old lady! Take it easy!"

"Hey, you'd better remember this is the bossiest, most presumptuous, most abusive little old lady in the free world. She's brought entire hotel staffs to their knees!"

"As I said, this is no hotel. We're packed in here like sardines anyway. And we're working. We aren't operating a home for runaway septuagenarians."

"No, indeed! We're operating a...a...what the hell are we operating here?"

"It doesn't matter. We have a mission here. Ceola cannot just come in and roost because she's out of sorts."

"Oh yeah? I think she has."

"Someone has to tell her. She obviously isn't coming out here. Who's it going to be? Elly?"

"Not me," she said. "I'm too blunt. There's no need to hurt her. We need a little tact and I don't have a tactful bone in my body. Maybe Beth."

"Beth will never get the words out of her mouth. She'll give her a pedicure or something. Barbara Ann can do it."

"Barbara Ann doesn't even know her. I'll do it," Sable said. "There's no way that woman is going to walk all over me."

"What are you going to say?"

"I don't know. That it's impossible for her to stay. That there simply isn't room. That we'll be closing up the house and putting it on the market first thing tomorrow morning and her timing just couldn't be worse. I don't know. But you can bet I'll get that little pink tuft of hair out of here, along with all her bangles and suitcases."

"Try to be nice."

"Remember, she's just a little old lady. She can only intimidate you if you let her."

"Go get her, tiger."

"Yeah, well, good luck, but my money's on Grandma."

Sable took a deep breath, straightened her spine and stomped off in the direction of her bedroom. Someone had to do the dirty work. Ceola would be fine at a hotel. Sable would make the arrangements herself, even pay for it if necessary. But she did start to feel nervous as she approached the guest-room door. She tapped lightly and heard Ceola's voice, suddenly frail, answer. "Come in."

Sable pushed open the door and saw Ceola sitting on the edge of the bed. She was wearing a flowing, expensive, purple peignoir—lots of lace and many gathers of sheer fabric. Her jewelry was stacked neatly on the bed beside her and she was rubbing lotion into her hands. Her bare feet showed off toes cruelly bent from years in fashionable shoes, but the toenails were perfectly pedicured in shiny red. She looked up at Sable as she rubbed her hands together in a wringing motion. Her lips were trembling and there were tears in her eyes.

"I can see I've put someone out," she said weakly, tearfully. "But this is where I've always stayed."

"Yes, Ceola, but I'm afraid your timing could not possibly be worse," Sable said.

"Oh, I'm sure of that. I'm sure of that. I'm a burden to most everyone in my life, come to that. I should have notified you all that I wanted to come…but I couldn't bring myself to do it. I wanted so much to be here, no matter what. I…just…miss…my little Gabby…so…."

"Now, Ceola," Sable said, moving farther into the room. "I'm sure you do. We all do. But the fact is, we're here working on her posthumous writings, and—"

"What an advantage you have over me. Being right here in her house where you can feel close to her for just a little while longer. How very, very lucky you are. All of you."

"But Ceola—"

"I apologize for not being more sociable. I should have come straight from the potty to the kitchen where you're all gathering this evening, but I began to feel so terribly weak. It was a long flight, after all. All the way from Atlanta. And I was too upset to eat anything on the plane. All I've had today was just the littlest bite of a cracker. And some club soda. Will you ask the girls to forgive my bad manners?"

"Yes, certainly, but the problem is much larger than that, Ceola. You see—"

"It's you I've put out of a room, isn't it, dear? Oh my, I wouldn't want that. It's just that this is where I've always stayed, when I came here so many other times to be with Gabby. If you'll just tell me where to go, I'll make do anywhere. Any old blanket on the rug. These old, tired, aching bones don't really care anymore. Isn't that the worst of it, when you lose someone you love? That you just don't *care* anymore? I so loved Gabby. My only child, you know."

"Yes, I know," Sable said, thinking *I'd love to tell her where to go*. "Ceola, I have to tell you something—"

"And I have to tell you something, dear. It's been left unsaid for far too long. I just want you to know how *deeply* I appreciate the devoted friendship you always showed my Gabby. She spoke about you often, you know."

"She did?"

"Oh my, yes, all the time. I think you came up in almost every conversation we had. She was so very, very proud of you...all your fabulous success. I once asked her if it was ever difficult, having a friend so rich and famous, but she said, no. Never. She said your wealth and fame had never spoiled you and that you were still the sweet, kind, generous girl she knew in college."

What bullshit, Sable thought. But then, Gabby just might have said that. She always acted as though she felt that way.

"It's so hard to lose a child, especially one you fear you failed. Gabby was always so good to me, so loving and sweet, even though I'm sure I was not the best mother. I have so much regret. I'd give anything for another chance."

"I'm sure she loved you very much, Ceola."

"She did, she did, though I didn't deserve it. How I miss my girl. I usually run to her when I'm out of sorts. I came here almost out of habit.

"Now, darling, where would you like me to sleep? Just any old chair—" She began to rise but then dropped back to the bed suddenly. "Oh. Goodness. I'm weak. Oh well, women my age should travel less and be sure to eat regular meals. I'm famished! But I'm also tired. I think I might be too tired to even walk to the kitchen."

"You just settle back, Ceola," Sable said, lifting the old woman's feet up onto the bed. Defeated, and with hardly a blow.

"Oh no, I mustn't! I think this is *your* room! Just give me a minute to catch my breath and then I'll move...."

"No, no, you stay where you are."

"But where will *you* sleep, dearest?"

"I don't know. I'll think of something."

"Oh my Lord, you are the sweetest thing. Just as kind and generous as Gabby said. Thank heavens. I don't think I could get up now if my life depended on it. I think some of it is that I've been so upset. First Gabby's death—such a shock, you know. No one expects to outlive their children. And then Martin. I've been overwrought."

"What has you so overwrought with Martin? I thought he was such a sweet man?"

"Oh, he is, in his own way. It's just that awful cardplaying at the club. Every afternoon. Day in, day out. I complained and complained about it, but my feelings just don't matter to him."

God, life can be cruel, Sable thought. First your only child dies and then you have to put up with your husband's cardplaying. Ceola probably missed a manicure or two over it all!

"Do you plan to stay long?" she heard herself ask.

"I'm afraid not, darling. Only a couple of weeks. Until I get my strength back."

Well, that should do it, Sable thought. Talk about an impetus to get your life together. What better incentive than two weeks of Ceola? Beth would probably hightail it to Kansas City, Barbara Ann would welcome the squalor of her house, Elly might cart all Gabby's papers off to her own small home and Sable thought a press conference would be preferable to this.

"I'd fall asleep this minute, if I weren't so famished," Ceola said.

"Well, we're cooking in the kitchen," Sable offered.

"Oh thank you, dearest. Just any old thing you bring me would be welcome. And a little hot tea if you have it? Oh, and if there's anything sweet... I always crave sweets when I'm depressed. But honestly, I'm not fussy. I think Gabby kept the bed tray in the pantry. Oh, and Sable, darling, I wouldn't turn down a drop of brandy. To help me settle down to sleep."

Amazing, Sable thought. She is to be studied. She has a gift. Her skills at manipulation should be written about.

"All right, Ceola. I'll bring you a tray. This one time. And then you're going to have to fend for yourself around here like the rest of us, or it's off to the Holiday Inn for you. We're all busy, working. There are no special cases around here."

"Of course, angel, of course. I don't want to be a burden to anyone."

Not much, she thought, but she thought it with some grudging appreciation.

All eyes were on Sable as she returned to the kitchen. Her expression was contrite, resigned. "Ceola's going to be staying a while," she said.

Sarah laughed. "Go Grandma! Is she good, or what?"

"Don't look at me that way," Sable said, shrinking under their glares. "After all, this is where she always comes!"

SIXTEEN

The finest sociological minds in the world could not have come up with a formula for it. It just worked. Some odd combination of qualities allowed Ceola to live there. It was an accident of fate. Or karma. Or insanity.

Beth, disabled by a long history of needing to please others, made Ceola's half English muffin with marmalade, fruit cup and tea. Then she would sit with her for a while, chatting. "I can tell you a lot about men, darling," Ceola said. "I can answer your most difficult questions. I married almost every man I ever met."

"Did you ever have one hit you?" Beth asked, half expecting to shock the old woman into silence.

"My, yes. Rupert. Number three—the handsomest one. The more attractive they are, the more brutal. At first I was so shocked that a man would hit me, I didn't even do anything about it. Of course, he may have loosened a few marbles, which made me confused about what was going on around me. He was also the best in bed," she added in a whisper, leaning closer. "I haven't figured out why that is, but it's universal. The better-looking they are, the more virile, the more violent. I didn't even bother to sue him for divorce. When I came to my senses, I ran for my life. But there was only that one. Rupert. Handsomest one, too. And the most virile, did I say that?"

Barbara Ann, forever shopping for groceries—a habit hard to break—happened to be the one available to take Ceola to the store, the hairdresser, the manicurist, wherever she needed to go. She was also the one Ceola could safely approach and say, "I have these few things for washing out, darling, if you find you're going to launder anything today."

"She has to launder," Eleanor quipped. "She's addicted to the washing machine. This is a halfway house for addicts, haven't you heard?"

Sable was mysteriously drawn to Ceola. Attention from a mother-figure, even one of the most manipulative, lured Sable. Ceola was far more refined than Sable's own mother had been. She had no hard, abusive character flaws like a quart of alcohol a day, but she had the same marvelous ability to ask without asking, need without requesting. Sable fell right into it and found herself becoming almost fond of the old woman. "Sable, my darling, are you having your cup of tea soon? Do tell me when you pour your own. I'd share a cup." And of course Sable would merely make Ceola tea rather than make her wait. Sable was fetching her a brandy, getting her reading glasses off the bureau "while she was up" and even tucking her in at night. "I'm going to just retire to my room now and let you girls have your space," Ceola would say. "Sable, I'm going to bed now, but I won't go to sleep right away, if you need anything." Of course, Sable didn't need anything. Ceola just liked it when Sable checked on her and made sure she was in for the night.

Sarah, who said she had no relationship with her grandmother, always kissed her cheek when she arrived and brought her something sweet, which Ceola craved when she was depressed. Though she never once acted depressed, she said she always was. "For half my life, at least. I've had a very hard life. Do you think it's easy to have been married eight times? The stress was sometimes unbearable."

David hated his grandmother. He called her "the old bitch." Not to her face, but in undertones behind her back. "Has the old bitch come to see if Mother left any valuables?" he'd ask. Or, "Are we serving the old bitch on her bed tray tonight, or is she up to dining with the unwashed masses?" The only problem with his unmasked hatred was Ed, his partner, who took to the old lady. "You're a big enough boy now to stop being so angry with your grandmother for not fussing over you when you were small," Ed would tell David.

Oh, and did Ceola love Ed. They sat on the couch almost like lovers or best friends. Ed was patient enough to listen to her talk about the soaps, or the latest gossip in *People* magazine. Or some fashion craze. Or movie. Ed would tease her and make her laugh. Once she delightedly said, "Oh, David, where did you *find* this dear boy?"

"He's not a boy, Grandmother, he's my *wife!*"

To which Ed, in his most effeminent whine, replied, "Now, David, I thought *you* were the wife!"

Ceola merely giggled like a girl. "Boys, boys, how you tease me. You're terrible!"

"We're not terrible, Grandmother. We're *gay!*"

She drew herself up proudly. "And so am I. Even in the very worst of times."

Later that same evening, when Sable was settling Ceola in her bed (literally, for Sable had been moved to an uncomfortable roll-away cot in Gabby's writing loft), she tried to have a heart-to-heart with Ceola. For David's sake. "Ceola, David wasn't teasing you about his relationship with Ed. And when he says 'gay' he doesn't mean happy."

"I know that, dear."

"Then why don't you acknowledge them? I think that's what David wants."

"Because I find it unpleasant. And I refuse to be co-erced into discussing things I find unpleasant. I think it's actually against the law in some places. Besides, it's time David learned he isn't going to get everything he wants."

Eleanor, it would seem, was the only member of the group who didn't have some reason to be drawn to Ceola. She certainly wasn't going to wait on her. She was the last person to discuss fashion, hairstyles or soap operas. And she was personally miffed with the way Ceola had treated Gabby and the children all those years. So, she was the only one Ceola couldn't reach. Until Ceola said, "I can tell you what it was that made Gabby decide to be a writer."

"Oh? Really?"

"She once said to me, she said, 'Ceola…' She always called me Ceola, even when she was a little bit of a thing. Because my own mother was raising her, I guess she didn't really see me as her mama. She said, 'Ceola, it's just so much easier for me to tell a story about someone else who's in love, or in trouble, or in grief than it is for me to talk about my own love or trouble or grief. In the end it's usually my story anyway.' Like that time she was in love with that world-famous pho-tographer. You were her friend then, weren't you?"

"Yes, I was," Eleanor said, immediately interested.

"Oh, that was a love. I don't think in my eight marriages I ever loved a man like Gabby loved that one. It was more than love, it was sheer passion. I think she began to lose herself a little, she loved him so much. I used to warn her about that. I used to say, 'Gabby, it's not very wise to love a man more than he loves you.' But she insisted that his passion for her was just as strong. I always wondered how that could be true, since he wouldn't divorce his wife. It's not as though it was hard to get a divorce then. I have always believed that if that man hadn't died, he would have broken Gabby's heart eventually. Just like Matthew White did, when Gabby was in her last year of college. Did she ever tell you about Matthew White?"

For someone who failed to mention to her college-freshman daughter that she'd be out of town over Christmas, it seemed that Ceola was awfully intimate with Gabby's life. Ceola had all the details about her childhood as well, from the time Gabby lost her first tooth to the time she got her first period during the week the girls' gym class had swimming. Eleanor had suspicions that Ceola could be making a lot of this stuff up, but on those things Eleanor could personally verify, she seemed to be right on. It was fascinating, Elly thought, that this woman who never gave of herself could cherish so many tiny details about her only child. It might have been nice if Ceola had even once called Gabby on her birthday. Or attended one of the childrens' graduations.

But it was the small details of Gabby's life that drew Eleanor to Ceola.

Ceola, for her part, had the instincts of a jungle cat. She knew who to approach, how to approach them, and timed it all perfectly. She would never suggest that Eleanor wash out her undies for her. Nor would she

even mention to Sable that she needed a ride somewhere, for Sable still did not have a car at the house
and only went out with Jeff. She wouldn't expect
breakfast from Barbara Ann, chats about fashion with
Beth or long conversations about her many marriages
with Sable. Yet she had someone doing for her everything she needed to have done to make her comfortable. Before she'd been there three days the women
were asking each other things like, "Has anyone fixed
a plate for Ceola's lunch?" "Does Ceola need to go
anywhere today?" "It's time for Ceola's soap operas,
where is she?"

To Ceola's credit, she knew a few things about being
a houseguest. She had developed the fine art of being
invisible so that she was only a lot of trouble some of
the time. She could spend a long time in the bathroom,
bathing, powdering, primping and perfuming, but she
seemed to do it only when no one else needed to be in
there. She took long rests on the deck while the women
were working. She kept the volume of her soaps down
low and dozed on the sofa while she watched, disturb-
ing no one. She retired early, even taking a dinner tray
to her room at times so that the women didn't feel the
constant drain of her neediness through their community meals. And she rose late. For one person to have
kept up with all her needs—her bubble bath, her afternoon sherry and then tea, her trips to the beauty parlor,
her laundry, her breakfast, lunch and dinner—would
have been exhausting, and everyone wondered how
Gabby did it. But for the four women, plus Ed and
Sarah, to cater to her was really nothing at all.

There was one danger, however. Ceola was very
comfortable with the arrangement. And her feelings
toward Martin's cardplaying were not softening.

* * *

Barbara Ann's first dinner out with her family was very uncomfortable. The boys stared at their plates and had trouble answering her questions with more than one-word replies. She figured them out pretty quickly. It wasn't their severe pain at having been abandoned by their chief cook and bottle washer. It was anxiety. They were afraid that one wrong move would set her off and she'd unload on them in the restaurant. She knew that was it the second time one of them said, 'Don't get mad, but…'' She was in the lesson-teaching mode, after all. She'd staged the big speech and walkout. Anything could happen.

The second dinner with them was better. They talked a little more. They even laughed over a couple of things. When one of them started to say something and then quickly rethought it, biting it back, she decided to console them a little. "Take it easy, guys. I'm not mad anymore.''

"You're not?" Bobby asked.

"No, I'm not mad. I was mad, but I did what I had to do and I'm not mad now."

"Then are you coming home pretty soon?"

"No," she said firmly, but nicely. "No, I'm not. I'm not mad anymore but I'm never going back to the way things were. If that upsets you, I'm sorry. But it just isn't fair for me to do all the work while everyone else enjoys what I've done."

"What if we promise to help more?" Billy asked her.

"Well, there's something to think about, Billy. Now, I know this is going to be hard to grasp, you being males poisoned by the hormone testosterone, but just try it on for size. How are *you* helping *me* by washing the plate *you* ate from? And how are *you* helping *me* by washing *your own* dirty clothes? See, you guys still have the idea that you're somehow helping me each time you do something for yourselves."

"But Mom, you've always taken care of us," Billy said pleadingly. "Don't you want to anymore?"

Something about that touched her heart. "Sure, Bill. But I want to take care of you in a new way now, a grown-up way. That's how it's always been, through all the species. I only fed you until you could feed yourself. I wiped your butt until you learned how to do it yourself—"

"In his case, longer than usual," Bobby said, laughing and punching a brother.

"Listen up, Bobby, this is also for you," Barbara Ann said. "I dressed you until you could dress yourself and I even stopped shopping for your clothes when you developed your own tastes. I drove you until you got a license and then a car. See, in all areas of your development, you gained your independence and moved on when you didn't need me to do it for you anymore. Except one area—the crud work, the stuff that's no fun. The cleaning, cooking, laundering, bill paying, yard work, painting, putting away. You're grown now. We still love each other, still need each other for lots of things—for love, emotional support, friendship. But we should have grown past the stage where one of us gets to be master and the other slave."

"Mom," Joe said earnestly, "we're *cleaning* the house. You should see it!"

"And do you want me to come home so you can stop?"

He was stuck for an answer for a second. He hesitated too long, long enough for Bobby to roll his eyes. Then he said, "No!"

"Good, then you're making great progress. You keep it up for a while, till you get used to having it nice, keeping it nice and liking it nice. Then we'll talk."

"Mom, listen, we—"

"That's enough," Mike said. "Your mother thinks we have a lot to prove and maybe she's right. Let's move on to something else. Tell her about school, Matt."

"I'm not *in* school right now! I'm working full-time this summer!"

"Good," Mike said. "Tell her about work."

At her third dinner with them, they didn't discuss the house at all. She wore a new dress, two sizes smaller than the clothes she had left in. She and Sable had been eating low-calorie food and exercising in the mornings with some trim blonde on a cable channel. Barbara Ann had been trying to lose weight for years, but had always been driven back to the Snicker Doodles by exhaustion, or frustration, or just plain inertia.

"I don't know what it is, Barbara Ann, but you just look more beautiful to me each time I see you," Mike said.

"Mom, are you *happier* now than you were with us?" Joe asked. "You look a lot happier."

"You guys are such idiots," Matt said. "She's only lost about twenty-five pounds, that's all. Jeez."

"Actually, it's only twelve. But have you ever seen twelve pounds of lard? It's massive."

"Really? Why, sure," Mike said. "Barbara Ann, honey, you look just fantastic. Like a young girl."

"Mom, what's going to happen about that pot the police caught you with?" Bobby asked. And then he looked down at his plate immediately.

"Which one of your friends left it in the garage, Bobby? Was it Jared? Brian? Seth?"

"Seth. But I really didn't know. I mean, when he said he needed to store a little pot, I thought he meant like a joint, an ounce. Mom, I had absolutely no idea—"

"An ounce here, an ounce there.... It sure isn't harmless stuff, no matter how little your doses are. But, never mind the lecture, I think I said my piece on that. On the charges, I'm still hoping to get lucky. My lawyer thinks he'll be able to get the charges reduced to a misdemeanor, if not thrown out entirely. It seems they had no probable cause to search my car. There is a technicality, however. The police are entitled to search any moving vehicle whenever they want to. And then there's that other little technicality—it was sitting right in the back seat. The bong was in plain view. It's all a little sketchy. But what I think is going on behind the scenes is this—the prosecutor knows I'm not a doper or a seller of dope. He also knows I have four sons between the ages of sixteen and twenty-one and that those sons have literally dozens of friends. The lawyer told me that the prosecutor might go after me just as an example. It seems that even if your sons are the ones in possession of a large supply of drugs, you have no excuse to keep it, hide it or transport it. You're supposed to call the police, not deliver it yourself. But, since I have an expensive lawyer who gets a lot of dealers off of far worse crimes, he thinks the prosecutor will try to cut a deal that gets me off his calendar and out of his hair. Works for me."

"Who's paying for this expensive lawyer?" Mike asked.

"Sable, of course. She also paid my bail."

"We'll repay her," he said, stiffening, his pride hurt.

He had not been prepared for how complicated and dangerous this whole thing had gotten.

"We'll work it all out, Mike. Don't worry. Sable has far greater problems than money. She knows I'd never take advantage of her and she's glad she can help. When you think about it, that's the least of our problems."

"Mom," Bobby attempted, sheepish. "Is there *any* chance you could go to jail?"

"For felony drug possession?" She took a bite of her salad, which was all she seemed to eat lately. "Uh-huh. Seven to ten. Women's federal prison."

He visibly winced. "I won't let that happen, Mom. I'll go to them myself, tell them the truth. I'll tell them it was mine, that you were trying to protect me. There is nothing, *nothing* I won't do."

"Bobby, why would you do that? I think I have this pretty well under control."

"Mom, I am not letting you go to jail over my asshole *ex*-friend's pot!"

"But why?" she persisted.

"Because that would *kill* me! It would kill me to have you go to jail!"

"What if it had been my pot, Bobby? How would you feel about me going to jail then?"

"God! Get serious! Do you think there's any way I could live with my *mother* in jail?"

"Probably not. 'Cause there's no way I could live with my son going to jail. Just so we understand each other."

He fell silent and his cheeks grew crimson. Matt elbowed him and whispered, "Dickhead." Billy glared at him, his eyes hateful. Yep, pretty dangerous stuff, that pot. It could tear up your family real good.

By the end of that dinner with Mike and the boys, Barbara Ann realized something. Her few words uttered at that weekly visitation were having more impact than twenty years of yelling. They were listening to her. They were slowly beginning to understand about the crud work, about everyone helping everyone and about the dangerous situation that had been created by some stored marijuana. Some nonverbal stuff was going on, too. They were thinking about how it was she could look so much better, be so much calmer, when she wasn't living in that house with them. Maybe they would accidentally absorb the fact that her anxiety was finally gone now that she could keep up with her workload. Or that her self-esteem was finally healthy now that she wasn't the only giver in a houseful of takers.

But the one thing she doubted they were getting was how much she missed them. God, she ached for them. Sometimes, very late at night, when Gabby's house was finally quiet, she would cry into her pillow. She found herself wanting to see how the new plane repairs were coming along. She wanted to hear that thumping noise that was a bass guitar. She wanted to see them inhale their dinner and go crazy, kissing her and whirling her around because she'd found the time to make *pies*. Mostly, she wanted to touch them. When she'd wander from her desk to the kitchen for a cup of coffee and find one of them at the breakfast bar eating cereal, just waking up at noon, she would put down her cup and give those young, smooth, strong shoulders a little rub or tousle the bed-head.

They were a very affectionate family, always had been. That was Mike. He was very physical, with her, with his sons. Mike still embraced his boys, whether they liked it or not. He still kissed their cheeks. Barbara Ann didn't have to force this physical affection on them. They still hugged her, kissed her, every time they said goodbye. It was no different when they parted after their third "date" for dinner. Each one, in his turn, embraced her very desperately, as if she were going off to the electric chair. Each one kissed her cheeks, both sides, reluctant to leave her. They told her they loved her—"Love you, Mom." "Love you, Mom." "Love you." "Love you, Mom. I miss you a lot."—and then went off in their various vehicles. Out for the evening. Or home, to forage for snacks and watch TV.

Mike had picked her up and was taking her back to Gabby's. When they were in the car alone, she noticed he just sat there behind the wheel, not starting the engine. "I gotta know, Barbara Ann," he said, staring into his lap. "*Are* you a lot happier now?"

"Well, I'm content in a lot of ways. We all help each other. No one has the lion's share of work. It's equal. Different, but equal. It's the first time since I met and married you that I haven't worked night and day. It's like going to camp."

"But are you *happier*?"

"I don't know how to answer that. I'm happier about the workload and I'm far less tense. But I miss you and the boys so much, sometimes I just cry."

He looked at her. "You do?"

"Yeah. Sure. Mike, I've talked to you every day. I've *told* you I miss you and love you. I've told you why I moved out—I can't take the mess anymore. I could somehow keep up with four little boys. Don't ask me how. I was younger, stronger, had more time, more energy. I wasn't working full-time then. But four men? Ahhh! They're more demanding, messier, eat more, want more, need more…and my *God*, they cost a fortune! I have to work just to keep up with the car insurance, much less the grocery bill. And I'm older, have less energy, less time. I was worn-out. I could have stayed, I guess, till you killed me."

"Oh, Barbara Ann…."

"Well, there was the other alternative. I could have tried to find a way to live in a constant mess, up to my nostrils in dirty clothes and dirty dishes. But Mike, I don't want to. Maybe that's an okay way for you to live, but I don't want to. Call me selfish."

"Barbara Ann, are you going to divorce me?"

"I hadn't thought that far ahead really."

"Is there…is there another…guy?"

"Another *guy?!*" Her voice was shocked, shrill. "Good Lord, are you serious? I just made my escape from five of you slobs. You think I'd want to tote that barge and lift that bale for another one?" She couldn't help herself, she laughed. The thought had never occurred to her! Jesus, maybe that was the answer! A neat, anal-retentive guy who worked out at the gym and had gourmet cooking as a hobby! With all the time she spent at the grocery store, she should have met him by now if he was out there. "Another guy. That's hysterical."

"Well, I don't think it's so goddamn hysterical. I mean, you don't seem to be suffering too much from…you know…not getting any."

She just giggled. Her head bent, she rubbed the bridge of her nose and giggled.

"Well, what's so goddamn funny? We always had a pretty good, you know, sex life."

"We sure did. I only had three periods in five years."

"Well, either you're doing pretty good without any or you got another guy!"

"To tell you the truth, I miss it a lot. But every time I remember sticking to the kitchen floor or scraping dried-on-toothpaste-spit out of a sink, the old urge just leaves me." She sighed. "That's nothing to what happens to my sex drive when I think of four boys getting stoned on pot instead of working and going to school and using those fine minds and beautiful bodies of theirs."

"Barbara Ann, are you ever coming home?"

She turned toward him and put her arms around his neck. She turned his face toward her and made him look at her. She kissed his lips. "I love you, Mike Vaughan. And I love them—enough to go to jail for them, if necessary. Are you really so completely blind to the squalor of that house that you think it would take something more than that to drive me away? Oh, Mike! How bad does it have to get?"

He kissed her. Then he chuckled against her lips. "It got pretty bad, to tell you the truth. Even *I* noticed."

"I know. I went back there to pick up a few things."

"Hey, that was only a few days. You should have seen it after a week."

She shuddered. She couldn't even think about it.

"It's okay now, though," he said.

"Yeah, I'll bet. Your idea of okay and my idea of okay are pretty different."

"No, really. They've been pretty good. I've been pretty good. It's coming around."

"I've seen the result when they've said they cleaned their rooms. Please. Don't insult me."

"I miss you."

"I miss you, too. And I do love you. You're all the man I've ever needed, Mike. You're just a slob."

"No other guy?"

She laughed again. "No other guy." She kissed him, more seriously. He couldn't help but respond. Pretty soon they were making out, in the car in the restaurant parking lot.

"Barbara Ann, will you come back to the house with me for the night? If the house isn't clean enough for you, you can leave again in the morning."

"What an offer. You're sweeping me off me feet."

"Barbara Ann, you're killing me! What am I supposed to do here?"

"You used to be a lot more inventive when we were younger, Mike."

He looked at her intensely for a minute, then started the car. He kept an arm around her as they drove, like youngsters out on a hot date. He made small talk, asking her about the book they were all working on, about the lawyer, about her diet. After about fifteen minutes, he pulled into a park and killed the lights. There were a couple of other cars parked there. It was doubtful they were middle-aged married-but-separated couples who couldn't get into a hotel because the charge cards were all maxed out.

He had a twinkle in his eye. She laughed wickedly while he tuned off the interior light so that it wouldn't come on when the car door was opened. They quickly got into the back seat and came together like red-hot illicit lovers, their mouths hungrily searching each others tongues, their hands grasping, pawing and petting.

Barbara Ann kicked off her shoes and shed her panty hose, then her panties. He unbuttoned the front of her dress and buried his face in her breasts, growling in appreciation. She held his head against her chest and scooted around on the back seat until she was under him. Mike fumbled with his belt and then his zipper. In seconds, mere seconds, he was inside her and moving. The car, she knew, must be rocking with his thrusts— Mike was not a little guy. But oh, it was good to be home; in his arms, full of him. Mike was a hungry man; it was hard to be without this in her life. He'd always wanted her often.

Mike was made to be married, that's all there was to it. He was the kind of man who liked a good woman he could depend on, and good food. Everything else in his life was secondary. The woman came before the food. He liked to know he was coming home to Barbara Ann every night, a woman he could still make purr after all these years, and he liked having her beside him when they slept. He'd damn near crush her in his sleep, never able to get close enough to the softness of her skin. He'd been waking up lately, all through the night, confused to find himself alone in the bed. And he was suffering miserably without sex, something he'd never had to beg for, something he'd never had to wonder about. The guys in the bars would joke, "Should we stay here for a sure thing or go home and take a chance?" But it hadn't been that way for Mike. For twenty-three years Barbara Ann had been a sure thing—soft, sweet-smelling, loyal, devoted and lusty for him.

He was exploding inside of her, thinking how he really couldn't give her up. He couldn't live without her anymore. He should have been thinking about how good he felt, being inside her at long last, but instead he was thinking, Those twerps are going to get that house clean and learn how to keep it clean, or I'll wring their scrawny little necks!

SEVENTEEN

"Hi, Arnie," Sable said.

"Well, how pleasant that you should call."

"I'm sorry that I've been out of touch, Arnie."

"Six weeks! Six fucking weeks! With every rag and TV tabloid program in the country calling me, hounding me, asking me what the hell's going on with you...not to even mention that you have a publisher who would like to know what to make of this shit. Six weeks, Sable!"

"Well, Arnie, didn't my doctor call you and tell you about my diverticulitis?"

"Oh, for Christ's sake, you didn't really think I'd fall for that one, did you?"

"Actually, I thought you would. Well, here I am. And incidentally, Arnie, I'm fine."

"Sable, what the hell is going on?" he asked wearily.

"I've been resting, with friends. And working on a book."

"I hope to Christ it's an autobiography."

"Well, it's not. Actually, I'm working on a collection of unpublished pages from a friend of mine who died very suddenly. But never mind that. I'm sure you have a million questions."

"You must be up to date on the trash...."

"Not at all. I saw that first program and then refused

to be subjected to the rest. That first piece was bad enough. I thought it was going to kill me."

"It was only the beginning," he said.

"So, who's behind this crap?"

"Some hotshot by the name of Robert Slatterly. He got the ball rolling and then, the way they usually do, leaked it to some of the other tabloids so there would be plenty of ruckus by the time the first television program came on. They've just about printed everything they can think of now—unless you're hiding an alien kidnapping in your past."

"Listen, Arnie, here's how it really was, okay? It's not a long story, and it's just sad. Not nearly as bad as they made out."

She ran him through the facts quickly, from childhood foster homes up to plastic surgery. He asked a few questions along the way. "Would there be records of the foster home placement? The testing? When and where did you legally change your name?"

"So, it's not that I had any reason to hide my identity—I wasn't running from the law or anything. I was devastated and ashamed. I didn't want to be that person anymore. I certainly didn't want my ex-husband or my mother to contact me."

"And you are divorced?"

"Most certainly. I have the decree in my strongbox."

"You weren't a prostitute?"

"They said *that?*"

"When you were in your teens."

"That's preposterous! If anyone had ever given me money for it, I'd have remembered. Now, they certainly can't verify something like *that!*"

"The law doesn't work that way, darling. If you're nobody, they have to prove what they print. If you're somebody, you have to prove what they printed is a lie. And the fact that you were never a prostitute would be plenty hard for you to prove. Obviously you don't need a license, if you get my drift.''

"Amazing. Isn't something about that inherently wrong, no matter who you are?''

"On this we can agree, but that doesn't change anything. Sable, I think you should make some kind of public statement about this.''

"Listen, are you still getting calls about me every day? Is there any evidence that this is dying down?''

"I think the worst is past, but you still have to—''

"Here's what I want to do, Arnie. I want to spend another few weeks recuperating and finishing up the work I'm doing—at least through the summer. I'll fax you a statement that you can read over the phone to my publisher. Did you get that? Read it to them! I don't want any paperwork about me going out anywhere right now. That's extremely important. Tell me you understand that and give me your word, or I won't send you anything at all.''

"All right, all right. But—''

"Just a minute. Within a couple of months I'll make a statement or appearance of some kind. An interview, maybe. That will be the *first time* anyone will hear from me on this subject. And it's going to be up to me, when and where. Got that?''

"Sable, listen to me, darling. You have a publisher who is almost bald from tearing his hair out over this. You have a book due in December for a June publication. You have a tour scheduled and they're scared shitless that the only people who are going to show up to see you will have bags of ripe tomatoes with them.

Some people, like the ones who pay you, need *some* reassurance from you—"

"Let them cancel," she said.

"What?"

"Tell them they can cancel my contract if they want to. If they're too fucking nervous to back me. Tell them I'll give them the goddamn money back—they didn't pay enough anyway."

"Sable, have you lost your mind!"

"No, I haven't. I found it. Along with a few other things."

"Oh my God, my God, will you listen to reason?"

"If you'll just think about this, I'm being eminently reasonable. Some very nasty people have been spreading horrible untrue trash about me all over the country. I'm a little...a little..." She paused, thinking. Then a smile came to her lips. "I'm a little 'out of sorts' with the situation. They've hurt me very badly. Hurt my feelings. And I do have them.

"Now all I want to do is rest a little bit. I'll make sure my side of the story is heard later, when I can do that with a little decorum. For now, you and the publisher can either be patient, or you can both kiss my ass. Are we clear?"

"Jesus," he said. "You're talking about a twelve-million-dollar contract!"

"I didn't ask you to give back your commission, did I? Come on, Arnie. If they don't love me anymore because I was a really poor kid, a battered wife, a young mother who lost her child, well, then they don't love me anymore. What the hell can I do about it? Huh?"

"Sable," he said, his patience strained, "it would be a good idea if *right now*—"

"Right now I'm going to run to the store for broccoli,

toilet paper and hand lotion. That's all I'm going to do *right now*. Then I'm going to work on some pages, maybe take a nap in the sun, and tonight I'm going to have dinner with my friends. That's about as far as I'm planning. Now, if I give you a phone number, can you promise not to abuse it?"

"Oh Sable, Sable...."

"That's a boy, Arnie. After all, that's why you get the big bucks, for putting up with these flaky authors. Now, here's the number." She recited the digits. "And gee whiz, Arnie, thanks for being so concerned about me."

"I'm always concerned about you, Sable."

"Uh-huh. See you later, Arnie."

She hung up the phone, borrowed Barbara Ann's car keys and went to the store—just as she had told Arnie she would. She found, when she was driving around and shopping for odds and ends, that she very much liked being out on her own again. And no one said anything at all to her except, "Plastic or paper, ma'am?"

Beth had been talking to members of her family every day for a month. She was almost weary by the time she went to the phone. Carleen, her younger sister, managed to hold her calls down to once a week. Carleen was thirty, an interior designer, mother of two. They caught up on all the family business, the babies' latest achievements, the progress on the decorating of her new home, and then Carleen said the strangest thing....

"When Phil and I were in counseling, I found out that I'm a passive-aggressive control freak."

"What?"

"I'm a passive-aggressive con—"

"No! Counseling?"

"Yeah. You knew that, when we went to counseling."

"When?"

"Um, let's see. Jeffy was nine months old or so. A couple of years ago. But you knew that."

"Did I?"

"Well, I told you," Carleen said. "And if I didn't, someone in the family must have. Everybody had an opinion, as usual. Carleen, the brat, dragging good ol' Phil to the counselor's office so she could get a little help in having her way. Or, Carleen the baby, who's always used to having everything just so. And, of course, Mother thought I shouldn't talk to anyone but a priest, who *shouldn't* have the first idea how a man and woman—"

"Carleen, I don't remember this. I mean, I vaguely remember someone saying something about how you and Phil were having some hard adjustments to having the baby, but—"

Carleen burst out laughing. "Hard adjustments! Jesus, he was *impotent!*"

"Get out!" Beth gasped.

"Limp as a dishrag. And volatile? My God, he was a volcano! All I had to do was ask him if he'd like meat loaf or chicken and he'd go through the roof. He was getting a little scary, to tell you the truth. He didn't stop shouting at me until I threatened to take the baby and go to a hotel. Thank God he never hit me or anything. I don't know what I would have done. You know how scared we all are of having an unhappy marriage. Holy shit, Mama would *die!*"

"I can't believe you're saying this," Beth said. "I

can't believe you're saying all the things I've been feeling."

"Beth, honey, where is your brain? I told you about me and Phil and marriage counseling. Did you think you'd invented marital problems?"

"In our family, yes," she said.

Carleen laughed. "Good one, Bethie. Mo has kicked Frank out twice. When they get back together they have another baby. The last time Mo let Frank back home, Mama said, 'Well, I guess I'll be a grandma again in nine months.' Bob and Sue had a couple of bad years that I predicted would be the end of them. Jody and Ted are on the skids half the time. Mama would like that to be Jody's fault, naturally, because she's not Catholic and therefore must be doing something wrong, but if you ask me, Ted's a real asshole most of the time. Wasn't he the biggest asshole when we were growing up? I mean, do you remember anyone in our family lying as much as Teddy? Really. And get this... Are you ready for this? Now this is a secret, do you swear?"

"Swear," she said.

"Father John is unhappy with the Church and is thinking of leaving the priesthood. Elba Sherman is going to shit all over herself when—if—she hears that one...."

"Carleen, no!"

"Yes! Mama doesn't know that, of course. I think John's only told me and Deb about it. Now you swear...?"

"Carleen, how long has this been going on?" Beth asked, astonished.

"Oh, I think he's been unhappy for the last—"

"No, no, no. Our family. All these things. All these

marital problems and counselors and separations and stuff."

"God, I don't know. Always, I think."

"Why didn't I know about it?" she asked.

"But you did! I know I was keeping you up to date. Jeez. Where have you been?"

"I don't know...." Beth wrinkled her brow.

"If you're counting on Mama to tell you what's going on, you know she's going to gloss it over in her way. I hate the way she does that, minimizing things, tidying 'em up. Like the way she told me about you and Jack. She said, 'It seems Jack's been a little *physical* with Beth and she's moved out of her town house for the time being....'"

"The *time being!*"

"Yeah, I know. Pathetic, isn't it? Don't you dare go back to him, Bethie. Don't you even give him a chance to—"

"Carleen, help me with this. I thought everyone in our family had perfect marriages, adorable, perfect children."

"Oh dear. Well, the children *are* perfect and adorable."

"Come on, where have I been?"

"Well, sweetie, I don't know. You have been gone a long time. Seven years. But even before you left there was trouble in Mama's paradise. Nothing earth-shattering, I guess, but it's not like we didn't all have our troubles. John was always nearly flunking out of college, Bill thought he had more than one girl pregnant—all false alarms as far as I know, but Mama's still doing her beads over them all, I think. Both Mo and Ted had to get married. I don't know, honey. Maybe you just always had your own problems."

It was a revelation. Now that Carleen mentioned a few things, she did vaguely remember some of them. John toying with the idea of leaving the seminary and Mama going crazy, so he came around. She'd heard some whispering about Bill and some girl Mama didn't like, but in the end Bill had married a girl Mama *did* like. There'd been a couple of six-month first babies, and Mama often spoke about Mo and Frank with some exasperation; she thought they quarreled too much of the time.

Had Beth not been listening? Had she been so absorbed in her own shame that she didn't think other people hurt, too?

"I thought your marital problems were about buying a new house and arguing over the floor plan and decorating," she told Carleen.

"I wish," Carleen said.

"Impotent, huh?"

"Well, obviously that's been fixed to a large degree—since we had Lauren. She pretty much proves he can get it up. *Communication* is our problem. He communicates what he wants or needs, and I fail to cooperate, but without ever standing up to him or expressing myself. Like I said, I'm passive-aggressive. Mama raised a lot of passive-aggressives. Even if we could have found the courage to stand up to Mama, we just couldn't buck God, you know?"

"I know."

"And since Mama and God were playing for the same team... I don't know about you, but I developed a lot of sneaky little ways to live my own life without letting on that I was an individual. Secret keeping, lying, manipulating, et cetera. It might have worked in dealing with Mama, but Bethie, it just doesn't work in a marriage. I think I found that out the hard way."

"Are you and Phil okay now?"

"Eh," she hedged. "I don't know. I'd give our chances fifty-fifty. I think we both want to stay together. I think we love each other. We've still got a lot of work to do, but at least we're trying to do the work now instead of trying to prove it's all the other one's fault. Things are a lot better than they were. You know, Beth, whenever you come home, you stay with Mama and we all troop over there to see you. We don't talk about all this stuff with Mama. Maybe if you stayed with me next time, or Deb or Bill, you'd hear the stuff no one has the guts to unload in front of Mama."

"I'm thinking of moving home," she said.

"So I hear. Well, you can stay with one of us while you look for a place. No one is going to make you feel like you screwed up by leaving Jack."

"Or that I screwed up by marrying him in the first place?" she asked.

"Well, the jury's still out on how many of us screwed up that one, so relax."

Barbara Ann's editor called and praised the book she had just turned in. She suggested only a few minor changes—something that could be done in a few days, if Barbara Ann agreed. And then the editor suggested, "Let's see if we can somehow put together a two-book contract from your next proposal to take up the slack for that last canceled contract. I really must take responsibility for that debacle. I was the one who pushed for the book. I really should have stopped you at the proposal stage. I had my doubts then."

"You did?" Barbara Ann asked.

"Sure. We'd talked about it. It was a fundamentally good idea, but I could see possible problems. Still, I had hoped it would come together—I mean, you usually pull off the most amazing things."

"I do?"

Her editor laughed. "Twenty-seven times now, if my count is correct. Whenever you can send me a couple of proposals, I'll see what I can do to work up a two-book contract for you. We'd like to give you a better sense of security about your future with us."

Hah! Security! She wasn't going to be tricked into that again! It could be a twelve-book contract and they still had the option of saying, "We don't find this finished product to be publishable after all." In which case, they'd want the advance money back.

"Let's make it a three-book deal," Barbara Ann said, feeling she had nothing to lose.

The editor laughed. "That's pretty ambitious. Let's see what you send me."

So Barbara Ann, who worked very fast anyway, talked it over with the other women and they all agreed—she should take some time out of her schedule to finish the revisions and put together a proposal for a trilogy. "I already have an idea," she said.

"Great," Sable said. "And this time insist on a little clause in the contract—if they refuse the finished book, you don't have to give the money back until, and if, you sell that particular book elsewhere. That takes a little of the sting out of it. You might not make as much money on the refused book, but you're not stuck with a bill."

"You think they'd go for that?" Barbara Ann asked.

"Well, I think they *have*. Ask around. You have

plenty of friends who write for that publisher—friends who have agents. Other publishers do it all the time—"

"I have it," Beth said. "I've never even had to ask for it."

"How'd I get this far without even knowing about that?" Barbara Ann wondered aloud. "Well, hey, I thought my career was over."

"It was," Sable said. "And then reborn again. I think that's what draws people to this business. Careers are destroyed one day and exhumed the next. There are a hundred ways to die in publishing—and a hundred ways to strike oil. The thing to remember is that nobody knows anything. Don't listen to anyone. The minute they tell you your idea won't work, for whatever reason, you'll find that someone else did it, successfully, the very next day. You go with your gut and cross your fingers."

"My gut is saying three books," Barbara Ann said. "Three books that I enjoy writing, for a change. After all, I'm going to have all the time in the world to write. In the Big House."

Elly walked into the room with a few manuscript pages in her hand. "Before you're sent away, I'd like everyone to have a look at this. Remember that chapter from Gabby's novel we read together?"

"When Clare was threatening to leave Brandt?" Beth asked.

"I thought it was the last Gabby had written of their love affair, but there's more. It doesn't exactly complete the story, but it comes damn close. Who will read? Sable?"

"When he dressed and left her, it was mournful. He kissed her goodbye in a long, hard, painful way. They were both a bit more desperate than other times, times when he'd known she would travel halfway around the world when he sent a set of tickets to her.

'I'm bloody goddamn tired of telling you good-bye, Clare. I swear to you—the next time I see you, I'll be a free man.'

'That's the only way you'll see me again,' she whispered against his mouth.

He squeezed her arms. 'Why'd you get into this with me if you weren't willing to stick by?' he demanded angrily.

She didn't react to the anger that burned in his green eyes. She didn't flinch from the harsh grip he had on her, rather liking the pain; it matched what she felt in her heart. He came down on her mouth hard and she pushed against him with equal strength.

When he was gone, she sobbed. The war inside her was one of pride versus pleasure. She couldn't keep following him forever knowing that, even if she dominated his time, another woman held the legal, public ties to his heart. But how could she endure life without the greatest passion ever born in her? Hadn't millions of women made that choice over the centuries—passion over propriety?

It was more than passion, more than being his chosen woman. It was her children. She wasn't about to retire her travel bags altogether, but she was done spending half her life abroad. She wanted more time with the children during this crucial stage in their development. If Brandt were free, she would even consider moving to Sydney or London with the children; the experience would be fabulous for them.

But not while her lover was married to another.

The afternoon aged, her tears dried and then, at dusk, hours after Brandt's plane had departed Londonderry, the matron of the inn brought her an enormous spray of fresh flowers, filled in with fern and grass. She had to cradle the bouquet like a nine-pound infant, it was that large. The note, scrawled in his barely legible script, read, *Come to London. Let me prove my desperate love for you is real. Then I'll go with you to Cal. B.*

At once. He had said that if she went with him to London, he'd deal with Beatrice at once. Dare she believe him? She decided to go to London, too weak with hope to stay away.

Something about this felt so wrong to Clare. She was stricken with guilt because she had demanded this—that he leave his wife and children. What had been eating at her was that million-year-old female angst—*he has two lives and I have one. He has Beatrice and me, and I am always in hiding.*

She wanted to travel openly with Brandt, to publicly write the stories to accompany some of his photos. She'd like to have her children know him; she'd like to have him come home to her and the children. She ached to have him choose her, once and for all, so she wouldn't have to be his secret indiscretion any longer. She was cursed with pride and now afraid it might cost her the greatest love of her lifetime.

London was wet and gray, overcast and oppressive. She checked into the Belvedere, having

stayed there before. It was an extravagance, but
she wanted her own bath. She ordered up tea and
soaked off the remnants of Donnelly. Then, at five,
she phoned William Berkhouse at his flat. They
had an amiable chat before she asked, 'Will you
ring Brandt and tell him where I'm staying?'

'He doesn't know you've come?'

'No, but he asked me to come when we were in
Ireland together. I was being stubborn and cruel
and refused. But in thinking about it...'

Bill laughed at her. 'You can't live without him,
I suppose. Lucky devil. Certainly I'll ring him for
you, but it's rather late in the day. Chances are I
won't catch him right off. Tell you what, love,
have dinner with me. We'll leave a message for
Brandt, and should he show his worthless face, he
can join us.'

But it was only Clare and Bill for dinner, though
Brandt had been reached. He said it was a bloody
terrible moment and he couldn't get away that
night, but to tell Clare he'd see her the next afternoon—something about the children being home.

Clare felt herself harden inside. 'I'm a damn
fool,' she told Bill.

'Oh, don't start with all that other-woman nonsense. It isn't like that with you and Brandt. It
could be any—'

'Yes, it could be anything, but it's not. It's his
wife and children. All those things he can swear to
when we're in Africa or Ireland fall away when
we're here, when he's within a hundred miles of
his marriage. He has a lot of bloody terrible moments....'

'Aw, Clare, I don't—'

'I'm a convenience, that's what. An expensive one at that.' She flipped out the credit card that she used when she traveled with Brandt. 'Dinner's on your friend.'

'Will you see him tomorrow?' Bill asked.

'Why not? I've come this far. I shouldn't leave now without saying a proper goodbye.'

The terror in the streets began the next afternoon. The noise, the sirens, the screaming and running drew Clare to the window, then to the walk in front of the Belvedere. She couldn't stand the suspense; she walked a few blocks to see what had happened. Bobbies held all spectators at bay, but the rumors circulated through the gathering throngs. A subway crash. Perhaps an IRA bomb. Smoke poured from the underground, scorching eyes and noses. Thirty dead. Hundreds injured. Then, forty dead. The numbers would only get bigger.

Clare went back to her hotel, knowing that Brandt would be delayed by both traffic and the lure of photographic opportunities. Once he knew what had happened, he would find a way to get underground. He was such a master manipulator; he'd find an emergency worker and buy off his uniform. He'd steal a fire marshal's coat and hat. He'd bribe, cajole, lie, sneak. She'd seen him do it a hundred times. Somehow, he'd shoot the wreck. Then, just about the time she'd given up hope, he'd appear at her door, dirty and disheveled and higher than a kite.

She went to the bar at seven and ordered herself a double scotch with ice, which she took to her room. The hotel bar was quiet but the streets were still crowded and tense. The sun was sinking and soon he would have to give up on the tragic accident. She heard the light tapping at the door and tried to disguise her expression; she wished to erase the signs of relief and anger she'd met him with so many times before. *Oh thank God you're alive and blast you for staying away so long!* This was not Belfast or Tehran, after all! This was London!

She faced Bill's shattered expression. His eyes were red-rimmed, his shirt rumpled and dirty, his hair tousled. She knew instantly. She knew it had happened when he was on his way to her.

'After all these wars,' he said, 'taken down by a bloody train.'''

EIGHTEEN

Mike and all the boys had dressed up for court. Sable, Eleanor and Beth had driven Barbara Ann and were going to stay through the hearing. Barbara Ann's attorney had filed some kind of motion asking for a dismissal because of illegal search and seizure of the pot found in her car, but if the judge didn't go for that, there would probably be a trial date set. This court appearance, she'd been told, could end the whole thing. The judge could throw the case out. On the other hand, this being a "readiness conference," they could affect some sort of plea bargain today and a sentence could be dispensed. It was all in the hands of the judge.

And she was a hangin' judge.

Barbara Ann had arrived and was sitting with her cheering section when the first case on the docket came before the judge. Her lawyer wasn't even there yet. "Don't worry," Sable said. "He knows exactly how long everything takes. He does this every day. He'll walk in at just the right moment."

Barbara Ann gulped. She didn't have much faith in the system.

The judge was a woman in her early fifties, Hispanic and quite attractive. She had manicured nails, shoulder-length curly hair, finely arched eyebrows and red lips that didn't smile.

The first defendant came forward wearing a yellow jumpsuit with PRISONER emblazoned on the back. "God, at least I'm not appearing in one of those," Barbara Ann whispered. "Is that what I'm going to have to wear if I get, you know, sent up?"

"It looks pretty comfortable," Sable whispered back.

"Oh God," Barbara Ann said. "I'm going to faint."

"Don't faint. It'll make you look guilty. The innocent are unafraid," Sable counseled.

"Shhh...." someone shushed.

"Young lady," the judge said, "this appears to be your third time before this court...and for the same thing. What a surprise. Cocaine. Quite a lot of it, too. Four ounces. You weren't going to use all that yourself, were you?"

"Yes, ma'am. I mean, I wasn't dealing, Your Honor. Only holding."

"You must be awfully enslaved to the stuff."

"I'd like a chance to have treatment, Your Honor. I'm really ready to kick this."

"Let's see here...you were ready once before, weren't you? Your first conviction, you went into treatment. Your second, you did some time. Four months. This is your third offense. Did anyone tell you the consequences of your possession?"

"Yes, ma'am. But I have a baby, Your Honor. I'm a single mother. I don't have anyone to take her. She's only nine months, Your Honor. I'm her sole support."

"Who's going to take her while you're in treatment?"

"I could go to outpatient. I can do it this time. I know I can."

"You're ready to get off this stuff once and for all?"

"Yes, Your Honor. I swear on my baby."

"We have AA and NA in jail, you know."

"But I have a baby!"

"How I wish you'd thought of that. The poor thing. Eighteen months. Chowchilla Women's Facility. And good luck in getting rid of this habit. Next." She banged her gavel. Barbara Ann jumped.

A young man in an identical yellow jumpsuit came forward.

"You've had quite a hard time figuring out the system, haven't you, Tony?" The young man said nothing. "Probation violation. Third time. Whew. Your original offense isn't even that bad, but these probation violations keep making it worse. What's it going to take to get your attention here?" He hung his head, defeated. "You going to talk to me today? What's the problem?"

"My PO," he said finally. "She don't make it real easy, you know?"

The judge leaned forward. "I think you might be missing the point. It isn't *she* who has to accommodate *you*. Now, my records show that you were only required to show up for one visit, once a month for six months, and pay a fifty-dollar fine each time. Six hours, three hundred dollars, and it's all over. But you can't keep the appointments."

"I had car trouble a couple a times. She wouldn't give me a break, you know?"

"We can't seem to come up with a PO you enjoy spending your time with, can we, Tony? This could have been behind you two years ago, but you just won't cooperate. That's not good at all."

"She was so mean, Your Honor. I just didn't want to see her!"

"Tony, she's the one you want to see, believe me. I'm

the one you *don't* want to see. Four months, county work program. Next." The gavel hit and Barbara Ann jumped again.

"Barbara Ann Vaughan."

The doors to the courtroom opened just as Barbara Ann stood. In strode her lawyer. She'd never gotten used to him. He was slicker than snot, so fashionable in his thousand-dollar suits, all purchased, she feared, through the payments made for his defense of drug dealers. Sable's lawyer had recommended him as "the best in this area" and Sable had insisted that she needed the kind of lawyer who knew what he was doing. That was probably true, Barbara Ann conceded, but even though she was guilty of felony drug possession, she still didn't feel she belonged in this courtroom, beside this man.

"Counsel for the defendant, Your Honor."

"Hello, Mr. Warneke," the judge said. "Good grief. Six pounds of marijuana and a bong. That's an impressive shopping list."

"We've filed a motion, Your Honor, for—"

"I have it, Mr. Warneke. Mrs. Vaughan, why did the officer stop you?"

"Your Honor, I object to testimony from my client. This isn't a trial and she hasn't been sworn."

"Relax, Mr. Warneke, this is only a hearing and with a little cooperation, maybe this whole incident can be cleared up right away. I have your motion. Now, Mrs. Vaughan?"

"I was speeding," Barbara Ann said nervously.

"Why would you be speeding with a load of marijuana like this in the car? Isn't that a little like sending the flag up the pole?"

"I wasn't paying attention," she said. She looked behind her at her gathering, then back to the judge. "I was angry."

"Oh?"

She began to tremble in fear. She couldn't speak.

"Why were you speeding, Mrs. Vaughan?"

"Your Honor—" her lawyer began to protest.

"It's all right," Barbara Ann muttered. "I'm just a little nervous. I'd just had a big blowout with my family and I was on my way to the police department to give them that stuff. I wasn't paying attention."

"You had suitcases in your car?" the judge asked, intrigued.

"Your *Honor*, I beg the court—"

"Oh, be still a minute, I'm not trying to corner your client. I just want a simple explanation. Mrs. Vaughan?"

"I was running away from home," she said.

The judge settled back in her chair and lifted a paper from the pile in front of her. "With your clothes, a couple of books, some manuscript pages and your marijuana?"

"It wasn't *my* marijuana, Your Honor."

"Oh, Jesus," her lawyer muttered. "Your Honor, I—"

"Were you running away from home because you *found* the marijuana?" the judge asked, ignoring the attorney.

"Not totally. I mean, when I found it I went over the edge, if you know what I mean. But it was a lot of things that piled up. Literally."

"Barbara Ann, we don't have to answer these questions," Bill Warneke told her.

"I don't think she's asking *you* any questions," Barbara Ann said. The courtroom chuckled.

"I have a feeling you'd like to just tell me about this, Mrs. Vaughan," the judge said.

"Well...I don't want to screw anything up. Mr. Warneke—"

"I'll take it into consideration that you're being coerced by the judge," she said, and strangely, there was a slight smile on her lips. She sat back and swiveled in her chair. "Go ahead."

Barbara Ann glanced at her attorney, who was shaking his head and tapping a pencil on the table in front of them. He was disgusted with her. She was going to jail, she just knew it. What the hell, she thought. If I'm going to end up in jail anyway, I may as well make sure my side of the story is heard.

"I had a huge fight with my family, Your Honor, because they're slobs. I mean, they're really wonderful and I love them more than my life, but they are horrible slobs. I have four sons, Your Honor. They're aged seventeen to twenty-one. Three are students. All four of them still live at home. And why shouldn't they?" she shrugged. "I go out and kill a bear for them every afternoon...." The courtroom laughed. The judge did not, but that half smile was still there.

"So, I've been begging and pleading with them for some help in keeping up the house. Like every mother does, I guess. But you cannot *imagine* how— Well, suffice it to say, they weren't making any progress. And then when I went out to the garage—" She stopped suddenly, a stricken look on her face. The judge frowned and lifted the report, glancing at it.

"You didn't find this stash of marijuana by the mailbox at the curb?"

Barbara Ann sighed deeply. Damn, was she ever a

lousy liar. Her lawyer groaned loudly and turned away from her in utter revulsion.

"We have two garages, Your Honor. One is attached to the house and the other one is a freestanding building. We have a million cars, with these boys. Anyway, the *unattached* garage is where I try to steer most of their loudest, messiest projects. It's a wreck. You can hardly walk through. I was out there digging through boxes looking for mousetraps, and I came across that stuff. And I came unglued. I mean, it's one thing to work like a farmhand to take care of these boys—these *men*—when they are living by the moral standards of my house and the laws of the land, but it's another thing if they're...you know...."

"Doing drugs?" the judge helped.

"Yes," she said, lifting her chin. "I don't think I was jumping to conclusions, Your Honor. I mean, look what I found! It was like the difference between stumbling across an empty beer can and discovering a still!" Everyone laughed. The judge's shoulders shook a little. "I think we have it pretty well established that my sons aren't drug addicts, thank God. I have to tell you, my heart was ripped out of my body and stomped on."

"Oh? So, who's taking responsibility for the marijuana?"

"No one. One of the boys thinks he's narrowed it down to one of his friends—they all have lots of friends. There were times my house was like a stadium. But, this is my fault, Your Honor. I let them treat that garage almost like a clubhouse. They worked on cars there, built things like big, huge model airplanes, played their guitars and drums out there, and there were young men coming and going all the time. There were times I'd find one of the boys' friends out there working on an engine when my boys weren't even home. We were going to run into a bad apple someday."

"So, what has you so convinced your own sons are innocent?" she asked.

"I searched their rooms. I turned over mattresses, emptied drawers, cleared out closets. I found some pretty unappetizing stuff, but I didn't find any drugs."

"But you still left?"

"It's time, Your Honor. They're grown. They can either act like the clean, decent young men I raised or they can live in that frat-house environment without me as their maid."

"But you took the marijuana with you."

"Well, I wasn't going to *leave* it there! I didn't want anyone from my family to have it or dispose of it or give it away!"

"I see. So, are you prepared to turn over the son who thinks he knows who put it there? Are you going to let someone take responsibility for what is felony drug possession?"

She hung her head. "No, Your Honor. I didn't have very good control of that household, but it was my responsibility. I take the blame."

"Jesus Christ," Bill Warneke muttered.

"Is that your gang back there? The ones you're sticking your neck out for?"

She turned and glanced at them. She nodded.

"Stand up," she instructed them. "All of you. Yes, all of you." Slowly, one by one, they came to their feet. Mike stood first. "Mr. Vaughan?" she questioned.

"Yes, Your Honor."

"Can you vouch for any of this story your wife is telling the court?"

"Yes, Your Honor," he said. "We let the house get to be a real trash heap."

The courtroom laughed. Bill Warneke sat down at the table and began to massage his temples.

"Do any of you want to step forward and take responsibility for this crime?"

"Yes, ma'am," Bobby said. "It was somebody I knew put it there."

Barbara Ann almost cried. Why couldn't he just let her handle it?

"Your Honor," Matt said, "it was one of my friends, I think."

"No it wasn't," Billy said. "I think it was someone I know."

"Your Honor, it was me. One of my friends," Joe said.

Barbara's eyes began to glisten. "Your Honor," she said, "you can't blame anyone but me. I was in charge of that household. I should have monitored everyone coming and going better than I did. I blame myself."

The judge began writing. Without looking up, she asked, "You're back at home again, Mrs. Vaughan?"

"No, ma'am."

The judge's head snapped up in surprise.

"I'm staying with friends," Barbara Ann said. "That house has gone to ruin because one person just can't do it all. And I work full-time, too. They can fend for themselves—that's what they seemed to want. At least that's what their total disregard for household responsibilities showed me."

"We're setting it right, Your Honor," Mike said.

The judge lifted her eyebrows. Clearly she was doubtful.

"I haven't seen it since I left, Your Honor," Barbara

Ann said. "I'm not up to it yet. I mean, I've seen the kitchen after they thought they'd cleaned it. Believe me, it's not that I'm overly fussy."

"When are you going to view it?" the judge asked.

Barbara Ann took a deep breath. "When I'm stronger. Right now I'm missing them all a little too much to be as tough as I want to be on this issue. It's very important to me. I don't want to get suckered into doing it all alone again…just because I miss them and love them."

"I see. So, just out of curiosity, what do you intend to do if you see your old house and find it has not improved?"

"Well, if I have somehow lost my mind and my resolve, I suppose I'll move back in and clean it up. If, on the other hand, I still feel as strongly, I've been thinking about a small, tidy, inexpensive apartment—where there are no greasy rags thrown in the washer with my lingerie."

The judge smiled. "I wish you luck, Mrs. Vaughan. Now, back to this other matter."

"I should have called the police, I know. I never thought they'd catch me with it before I could turn it over to them. What an idiot. I couldn't imagine that anyone would ever think I could be a drug dealer."

"Oh, they come in all shapes and sizes, my dear Mrs. Vaughan. Your story is compelling, but we still have the matter of six pounds of cannabis—"

"Cannabis?" Barbara Ann asked.

"Marijuana. Weed. Hemp. You with me here?"

"Oh. Yes."

"We still have the matter of six pounds of *marijuana* for which you are charged with possession."

"Your Honor, we have filed a motion for dismissal based on illegal search and—"

"Oh, give me a break, Mr. Warneke, it was sitting on the seat behind her and the officer could see it when he ticketed her. That's probable enough for me. Now, as to the matter of possession, if we could have a change of plea to guilty, I think the prosecutor could be convinced to accept a sentence, Mrs. Vaughan, and save the state a little money." Breath was inhaled all over the courtroom. "Five hundred hours of community service, which can be served by any or all members of your family."

"Your Honor, this is *felony possession*," came the very first input from the prosecutor.

"I know what it is. She was obviously not trying to hide it. I might feel differently if the officer had found it in her trunk. But I believe Mrs. Vaughan found it in a freestanding unlocked building on her property. I'll even go so far as to write a codicil to her sentence so that if she's ever before this court again on any kind of drug charge, misdemeanor included, you can safely assume she'll be hung out to dry. Done?" The judge rapped her gavel. "Mrs. Vaughan?" she asked. "Come here a minute, will you?" Barbara Ann approached the judge. "I have three sons, Mrs. Vaughan. They are now aged twenty-nine, twenty-six and twenty-three. They are largely survivable."

She smiled. "Thank you, Your Honor. Thank you very much."

"You lucked out. I could have been childless, in which case your story would have seemed preposterous." She smiled warmly. "They're very lucky to have you. I hope they come to realize that soon. See the bailiff for your instructions."

Barbara Ann turned to see her lawyer's back as he exited the courtroom. Just as well, she didn't want to have to deal with him. She went to the bailiff and signed a few papers, promising to carry out her community service and return verification to the court. Her hands were shaking almost too much to sign and lift the papers in her hand.

The next defendant had already been called and addressed by the judge. She was asked about her narcotic possession. She looked like a hooker—fluffy hair, lots of makeup, tight, short skirt, high heels... And gum in her mouth.

"Well, ye see, Yer Honor, ma'am, I have this really, really messy family..."

"Don't push me," the judge said.

Barbara Ann's knees were knocking almost uncontrollably as she left the courtroom. Her family and friends were waiting in the hallway for her and they cheered her and embraced her as she joined them.

"Way to go, Barbara Ann!"

"We'll do the community service, Mom, you're not going to have to worry about it."

"Bobby's going to do the most, though."

"The lawyer sure came in handy. Ask for a discount in his fee."

"What did the judge say to you, Barbara Ann?"

They all stopped talking for a moment and waited for her answer. She looked at each face, her mouth open as if she would speak, but before she could get the words out a lot of things rushed through her mind. The sentences issued to the two previous offenders had been harsh, ruthless. Four months for missing a couple of meetings with a probation officer? Eighteen months for a young, single mother who had requested rehabilitation? If this particular judge hadn't been the mother of three boys, she could be on her way to jail right now. After all, drug dealers must have a variety of creative stories about how they didn't really have the drugs they had.

Before she could answer, Barbara Ann fainted.

NINETEEN

By the first week of August the women were editing,
revising and reviewing chapters seventeen, eighteen,
nineteen and twenty of Gabby's book. They found the
product to be stunning, compulsively readable. Each
one was extremely excited about the prospects for its
sale and ultimate success. From page one, they believed, the book only escalated in tension and power.
These particular chapters were riveting, as had been
those chapters in Gabby's life. Trouble had been brew-
ing for her at home—her ex-husband questioning
whether it was fair for Gabby to continue these travels,
the children beginning to show signs of needing more
of her. The love affair grew only more intense, while
the locales had grown increasingly dangerous. Clare
and Brandt were beginning to fight about their future
together, as, apparently, Gabby and John had been.
Each was being torn apart by their own strife in family
and work, longing for the other's passion, fearing to
give any more to what could end as only misspent
time; an affair that began and ended away from the
mainstream of life. Tormented lives, tormented love. It
was fabulous.

But the women were tensely arguing each sentence,
each paragraph, each scene.

"Okay, hold it!" Eleanor barked, stifling the verbal

battle during one of their many story conferences. "The book is marvelous and getting better every day, despite all this bickering. Something else is going on here. What is it?"

No one answered. Sable picked at her nails. Barbara Ann looked off toward nothing in particular. Beth sipped her iced tea, eyes downcast.

"Oh Lord, that's it. It's the end."

"We don't have an ending for the book that we all agree on," Barbara Ann said.

"That wasn't the end I was talking about. None of you can face the fact that we're nearly finished here."

"Well, don't be so bloody hard on us, Eleanor. Even Ceola hasn't left—and it's been well over two weeks."

"Nor have any of us complained that she's still here," Barbara Ann said.

"At least you have school to go back to," Beth said.

"All right, now listen," Eleanor said. "If we need to talk about all that, then we'll talk about it, but let's not let it interfere with this book. It needs to be finished, finished well, and marketed to the right person. Despite our personal problems."

"It's hard to imagine what life's going to be like, that's all," Barbara Ann said. "I mean, forget about us, what about Sarah and the baby? David and Ed? Dr. Don? What's everyone going to do without this place? I think we should all pitch in and buy the house from the kids. Keep it. You know, as our meeting place."

Everyone looked at her wearily.

"I had no idea you were that scared," Elly finally said.

The logic behind keeping the house was so pitifully flawed that no one even spoke to it. Beth wasn't going to be staying in California and had no need for such a place. Even if she could convince herself that she could retreat here with the women every summer, she knew that was not likely to happen. She had no idea what she faced in Kansas City, but she'd somehow make a life there, enough of a life so that she wouldn't have to run away from it for weeks or months out of every year. Or else why go? Surely it was right that she be back there with her siblings, confusing though they still were to her.

Barbara Ann was afraid that of the three choices she had left herself, none would feed and nurture her spirit the way living with these crazy women had. She could sneak home and find that her house was unchanged, which was what she expected. That would leave her with an apartment of her own, tidy but lonely. Or perhaps her family, finally cognizant of the consequences of discourtesy, had learned something from her absence and could at long last keep house. That should fill her with joy. But it didn't. Living without the women in her life would be nearly as hard as living without her children had been. Harder, perhaps.

Sable was not anxious to go back to the sparkling, sterile, lonely Hidden Valley manse. Even though Jeff had become a significant part of her personal life, something was lacking in her. She could still the throbbing of what was to come for her when she was with the women. She was headed for change—she knew it—and could face it as long as she didn't have to face it alone. Perhaps her career as she'd known it was over, her reputation destroyed. She could certainly live happily without fame. But what would she do with herself? Could she write her stories if there was no one to read them? What was to be her purpose? Sable had always been useful. She had always had hard work and a strong mission to fulfill every single day, whether she was putting the caps on hair spray cans in order to feed and care for her child, or getting that book done on time so she could go on tour.

"I'm going to set a deadline for the book," Eleanor said. "It's the only thing to do. We're going to finish it by the end of the third week in August." She picked up the calendar she used to keep track of their progress on the book. "The twentieth," she announced. "That's a Friday. We'll have the house closed up by the following Monday morning. That gives me a week before school starts...and the rest of you? You have three weeks to decide what you're going to do. I'll help all I can."

"Come on, Elly, don't be so rigid. Your life isn't going to change, after all," Sable said.

"Isn't it?" she asked, but so softly no one bothered to argue about it. So Elly had school, as she'd had for over thirty years. And her little house. And Ben. But it was not as though the summer had had no effect on her. She was as changed by the whole thing as anyone else. And she faced at least as many uncertainties. She, too, would have to carry on without a place to go, where her friends were always there, loving her unconditionally despite the fact that she was odd and terse and homely and tactless. It would be like saying goodbye to Gabby all over again.

"What are we going to do about seeing each other?" Sable asked.

"Well, you have the room at your place. But we'll have to plan better—you're a long drive. Hell, we'll bang around town here until something feels right. Maybe we'll get really crazy and meet in Carmel in a beach house for a week every summer. There are many possibilities," Elly said. "It's not as though we'll lose touch."

"I don't know why it has to end, abruptly, with the end of summer," Barbara Ann said. "What's the matter with it just being indefinite? We're all at work here. Your commute to Berkeley is only ten minutes longer from here, Elly. Or, maybe Sable and I want to hang out a little longer than the rest of you. Maybe—"

"There are other people in all our lives," Eleanor said. "It's time, Barbara Ann. Let's make it a clean break and let Gabby's life—the life that isn't in her books, at least—be over. She was never afraid of dying. She was afraid of not living. And that's what she'd expect of us. To get on with our lives." There was silence while each one absorbed the truth to that. Sable nodded. She didn't know where she was going, but since when had she known? Beth had wanted to have a child and raise it, albeit alone. Now she had to decide how she was going to do that. Barbara Ann knew what she wanted. She was simply afraid that she would find herself in the same frustrating rut, escaping into a package of Ding Dongs when her work and her family became too demanding. "August twentieth. Where is Ceola?"

"She's in her bedroom, reading or listening to talk radio."

"I'll give her the date when she next pops out here looking for one of her servants. So she can prepare herself." The doorbell rang and Elly looked at her watch. It was six-thirty. "Good. Diversion. Someone to remind us we have to think about food." She stood up. "Don't be so down about it. You can't put off the inevitable."

"Is that what it really is?" Barbara Ann asked when

Elly had gone to the door. "Are we all scared of being on our own again?"

"I don't know about you, but I don't look forward to it," Sable said. "I spent the last twenty years trying to pretend I didn't have my past. I'm going to spend the next twenty answering questions about it. Delightful."

"At least you didn't make an arbitrary decision to get pregnant," Beth said. "You know, I had absolutely no misgivings about my ability to raise a child alone. I was positively determined. Not a single doubt in my mind—until I missed a period. Then I wondered if I'd been crazy."

"Beth?" Elly asked, taking off her glasses. "Beth, it's Jack."

"Jack?" she asked weakly.

"He says he wants to talk to you. I can tell him you're not here."

"Yes," Sable said. "Tell him she's gone home to Kansas City."

"No," Beth said. "I'll talk to him for a minute."

"Beth, *don't!*"

She stood up. "He's not going to *hurt* me, for heaven's sake. Not with all of you around here. I'm just going to talk to him."

Sable grabbed her upper arms as she would have passed. "Beth, he's going to manipulate you any way he can. He's going to try and suck you back in. Please believe me. I've been there."

"I'm just going to talk to him, Sable. I'm not going to leave with him."

Beth walked briskly toward the door, straightening her back as she went. She opened the door and walked outside. Barbara Ann, Elly and Sable all rushed to the front room the moment the door closed behind Beth.

They listened at the closed door, but couldn't hear anything. "There they are," Barbara Ann said, peeking through the front-room curtains. "Sitting on the planter box."

Jack was wearing his pilot uniform, twirling his hat in his hands. There was no denying the handsomeness of this forty-two-year-old man. He was tall and fit, trim and in possession of a healthy head of brown hair. He had a winning smile, a seductive twinkle in his eyes. All the women, even Elly, would have felt a lot better about things if Jack were a little less handsome, a little less sexy. They watched as he talked to Beth, then as he listened for a long time, head down and nodding in apparent agreement. Beth seemed to have plenty to say. He looked up at her and laughed suddenly. She laughed, too. He talked a little more while she listened. And vice versa. Five minutes passed. Ten. Fifteen. Barbara Ann gasped and covered her mouth as Jack put his arm around Beth's shoulders and covered her still-flat abdomen with his large hand.

"I saw him put that same hand up some blonde's skirt at a bar in New York," Sable said.

"Should we call to her? Make her come back in?" Barbara Ann wanted to know.

"She's an adult," Elly said. "No matter what anyone says or does, ultimately it's up to her."

Sable was biting her nails. Barbara Ann was pacing in and out of the living room. Elly went for her cigarettes and began smoking, taking fast puffs. Beth was outside with Jack for a half hour, sitting on the planter box with him. Talking, sometimes laughing. Finally they stood, facing each other. They exchanged a few more words and Beth nodded. Jack leaned toward her and kissed her cheek. "We're doomed," Sable said.

Beth had to tap on the door to be admitted; it locked itself when it closed. When she came in she wore an embarrassed smile. "I'm going to have dinner with Jack," she said.

"Have you lost your mind?" Sable demanded.

"Beth, you know he'll only try to wear you down. This is crazy," Barbara Ann said.

"He thinks we should talk about our separation, about visitation and child support payments."

"The baby isn't even going to be born for six months! Can't you see through this?"

"He's still my husband. He's still the baby's father. Even if we don't stay together, certain things have to be worked out," Beth said.

"If?" Sable questioned.

"Beth, you have months to work things out. It should be done through a lawyer, someone who can take care of you."

"You can't be saying that you intend to allow Jack to visit this baby? Maybe take him for the weekend, in case he doesn't have anything else around to punch?"

Beth's face became stern. Angry. "I doubt I can keep him from seeing his own child," she answered stiffly.

"You could if you pressed charges. He beat you. You have plenty of witnesses. He's dangerous to your baby."

"I don't think I'm going to worry about that now," Beth said. "This is only dinner. To talk a few things over."

"By all means, worry about that tomorrow," Elly said. "Scarlett." She turned her back on Beth and headed for the kitchen.

"Beth, you aren't kidding yourself that he's changed, are you?" Barbara Ann asked.

"I don't know that he's changed all the way," she said, "but I'm not afraid to go to dinner with him. He isn't going to beat me up in a restaurant."

"Maybe not tonight, at dinner," Barbara agreed. "And maybe not the next time you go to dinner, either. He might mind his manners for a whole month, in fact. But eventually he's going to—"

"Please," she said, stopping Barbara Ann. "We're just talking about dinner. I'm not going home with him, I'm just letting him buy me dinner so we can talk things over!"

"There would be nothing to talk over if you planned to get a divorce. Beth, please don't lie to us, of all people."

"I'm not lying to you!"

"Yes, you are. We saw him laugh with you. Touch the baby. Kiss you. This isn't just dinner. This is just the beginning, till he has you back in his clutches where he can—"

"He's been to counseling!" she spat, indignant. It certainly shut them up. They stared at her, gape-mouthed. "He's been to counseling," she said again, more softly. "He went for help. He knows he has a problem. He knows he has to stay in control of his temper. He wants to talk to me about it. I don't think that's too much to ask."

"Did he bring you a note from his therapist?" Sable wanted to know.

"Oh please, don't do this to me," she whined. "You know how hard I've tried. You know how much I want this baby. I wouldn't let the baby be unsafe. He's docile as a lamb! Please, I do have some common sense, some judgment. I don't think going to dinner with him could hurt any—"

"Beth," Sable said, stopping her, "will you answer me honestly? As honestly as you can?"

Beth nodded.

"If you have dinner with him and it's pleasant, would you consider having dinner again?"

"I don't know. Maybe."

"If you found out that ten dinners with him were pleasant, if you found him to be sweet and gentle and loving, would you rethink this idea of leaving him?"

"Sable, it's too soon to say whether I would. I'm not thinking that far ahead. I just agreed to go to dinner with him and talk about the plans I have for the baby."

"If he didn't hit you for, say, a year, would you think you were safe? Would you move back in with him? You and the baby?"

"Why are you doing this to me? I haven't said I'm moving back in with him!"

"I just want to know whether you believe him," Sable said.

"What?"

"Do you believe him? Believe what he says? Believe what he said to you out there on the planter box?"

"You don't even know what he said!"

"Doesn't matter," Sable said. *"Do you believe what he said to you?"*

"Yes!" she burst out. "Yes, I believe him, but he didn't say anything suspicious. He just said he was sorry. He's getting counseling. He knows where he went wrong. He'd like another chance, maybe counseling for both of us, but he'll understand if I'm not willing to try again. He just wants to take me to dinner!"

"You willing to bet on that?" Sable asked.

"Oh, Sable...."

"Really. Wanna bet?"

"No, I don't want to bet! I just want to see for myself!"

"That's just as good. Give me ten, maybe twelve minutes with him. Go back to the bedroom or up to the loft where you can hear real good and wait. Listen."

"What?" Beth asked, totally perplexed.

"Beth, do you trust me?" Sable asked.

"Of course I *trust* you. But you may be wrong about—"

"If you're right, if he's telling the truth about how much he cares, how much he loves you, and how much he's changed, he's all yours. If you do this one thing for me, I'll never ask another thing of you as long as I live. If you'll just let me have him for ten minutes and not say a word or try to butt in no matter what happens, I'll be your slave till you die. I'll baby-sit for free till I'm ninety."

"What are you going to do?" Barbara Ann asked nervously.

"I'm just going to talk to him. As Beth's most trusted friend, I'd like to assure myself that he has her best interests at heart. Just listen," Sable said. "And don't stop either one of us. Just listen for ten minutes. If I'm wrong about him, I'll apologize. I'll get down on my knees and kiss his shiny little pilot shoes. I'll take back every bad thing I ever said about Jack Mahoney, if I'm wrong."

"That's not too much to ask," Barbara Ann said cautiously. "You afraid to see what he's made of?"

"No," Beth said. "But I don't see the point in just trying to make him mad. Why stir up trouble? If Jack's—"

"If Jack's a good boy who knows where he went wrong, who's sorry and who's in counseling and who loves you, then Jack doesn't have anything to worry about, does he? Come on, Beth. Take a chance."

"This isn't smart," she said. "This isn't a good idea...."

"Why? Do you think he could be...I don't know... volatile and unpredictable? Because if you think that, you shouldn't even have dinner with him. If you think he could get mad and maybe lose his temper if someone says the wrong thing to him, you're in big trouble, aren't you? But if you think he's on the mend here, maybe learning to control his temper, then there's nothing to worry about, is there?"

"Look, even the mildest-mannered man can be pushed too far," Beth said.

"Hey, Beth, I've known a lot of men over the years and I've been brutal to a few. I've even pushed a couple with bad tempers too far. I've been called a bitch before—I can handle it. If Jack's safe enough for you and the baby, then he'll be docile and controlled and civil no matter what I say to him, right? He knows he was wrong, right? I'm not going to hit him, for gosh sakes. I'm not going to make him defend himself. Come on, Beth. Give him a chance to prove himself."

"Come on, Beth," Barbara Ann said. "What's ten minutes out of the rest of your life."

"I don't know about this, Sable." But Barbara Ann was already leading her away, already calling to Elly to join them in the loft.

"Time doesn't start till he knocks on the door, wondering where you are."

"Okay," Barbara Ann called back.

"Oh dear," Beth said as she was being dragged away.

Sable paced. She had a real gift for making a man

want to belt her, this much she knew. But that wasn't going to be enough. If Beth listened in and decided that Sable's actions were somehow outrageous, no matter what the outcome, Jack would not be indicted. A part of Beth still believed that it was all right for a man to hit a woman if she provoked him. It would be Sable's fault. About three minutes had passed when there was a knock at the door. Sable quickly ran into the family room and looked up at the loft. "You can start timing me now," she said in a stage whisper.

Barbara Ann peeked over and gave her the okay sign.

"Stay out of sight up there," Sable added. She ran to the door and opened it. He had a frown on his face. He'd been kept waiting for at least ten minutes. Sable hadn't even thought about what an advantage that was. "Oh, hello, Jack. Come in."

"Where's Beth?" he asked, stepping over the threshold.

"In her room, I'm afraid. Crying, I think. Poor thing. She's changed her mind. She asked me to tell you."

"Changed her mind about what?" he asked.

"Didn't you offer to take her to dinner? Well, she decided against it. She said to tell you."

"Go get her," he said. "She'll have to tell me herself."

"She's with Barbara Ann and Eleanor," Sable said. "We've convinced her that this would be a mistake. She's going to pass—"

"This is none of your goddamn business, you know," he said. "Now go get my wife."

Sable became heady with power. What was Beth thinking? He was already mad and nothing had even happened yet.

"Well, you know how women are. We made it our business. We feel we're in this together. We love Beth, see. We hate seeing all those bruises on her. It's revolting." She saw his eyes narrow and the muscles in his jaw begin to tense. "You ought to be ashamed of yourself, Jack. You're a lot bigger than Beth. And hitting her when she's pregnant, too. That's really low."

He inhaled sharply through his nose and glared at her. "Fine," he said. "Tell her to call me when she's ready to talk." He turned and opened the door to leave.

Sable panicked. She hadn't counted on him being unwilling to have even a verbal tussle with her. But then he didn't beat up everyone, did he? He worked with women on the job and wouldn't still be flying if he punched every one who crossed him.

"There's something I think you should know," she said. He turned around in the open door. "I was the one who told her you were fucking around. I saw you in New York. In a hotel bar. With your hand up the skirt of some young blonde. Flight attendant?"

He stared at her for a second. Then a slow, mean smile spread across his lips. "That so?" he asked, but it didn't sound like a question. "Well, thanks for nothing."

"I thought she should know. So, are you getting counseling for that, too?"

"Listen, why don't you just mind your own fucking business and stay out of mine."

"I guess with a job like yours, it's pretty easy to pick up women. Talk about a cheap date. The airline pays for the hotel and you probably get per diem checks to cover the dinner. I guess that would be a hard habit to break. What I can't figure out is, what's a guy who loves women so much doing punching them around? I don't think Beth would have complained about all your screwing around if you'd just had the good sense to keep your hands off her."

Jack glared at her for a second and then his upper body bounced with a small huff of laughter. He turned his back on her and walked out the door, slowly pulling it closed behind him.

Well, great idea, Sable, she thought. That was a bust. The gentlest man in the world would have had a hard time keeping his temper under control during a confrontation like that. She'd done everything but call him names. And she'd been as snotty as she could be. So what did she prove? Big fat zero. She proved that Jack Mahoney could be badgered by a bitchy woman and would walk away before even talking back.

She sighed in defeat and began to move away from the door. It would be hard to apologize to Beth for that.

The door swung back open behind her; he hadn't even pulled it all the way closed. "You know, I have you to thank for ruining my marriage. I love my wife. Until she got involved with you, we didn't have so many problems."

Sable turned around. He was standing there in the open door. He came in and slammed it. "Beth and I have a few things to work out, but it isn't one-sided," he said. "I'm not the only one with the temper. I'm not the only one who gets a little mad. Married people have disagreements all the time. That's how it goes."

"Getting mad and beating people up are two different things. Or didn't you learn that one in kindergarten with the rest of us."

"It's not like that happened all the time. I got pushed too far a couple of times, that's all. Maybe two times. I apologized. Under the right circumstances, anyone can make that mistake. Hell, you think Beth didn't do a lot to push it that far? It wasn't something that happened unless I was provoked."

"What about your last two wives, Jack? Did they *provoke* you into beating them, too?"

"Is that what they said? Well, let me tell you something—they're both lying whores. Both of them! All either of them ever wanted out of me was money—and the best way to go after it is to claim abuse. I never laid a hand on either one of them!"

"So, Beth is the first woman you've beaten up? I find that remarkable."

"I never beat her up! Is that what she said? It's not true. It's not true. It got a little physical a couple of times—she had as much to do with that as I did. But I *never* beat anyone up! Were the police ever called? No! Was there ever a visit to a doctor? No! We had a couple of fights—that happens to people, okay? We just have some things to work out and when she gets away from you dykes, we're going to be fine."

"Dykes?" Sable repeated, nearly laughing.

"Libbers. Bitches. We never had a single problem until she started listening to you and those other two broads. There's no way we can work anything out while she's being brainwashed by the likes of you women. She needs to come home where we can handle our problems in private. That's what a marriage is—private."

"I've been friends with Beth almost her entire marriage! When was it your relationship was so untroubled? The first two months?"

"You know, you've got one hell of a nerve, talking to

me like that. I've done for Beth and provided for her all these years and she's never wanted for anything...."

"She wanted a husband, that's what she told me."

"I've taken care of her just fine. There isn't anything I denied that woman. Not anything!"

"A baby," Sable said. "You not only forbade her to get pregnant, you warned her she'd better get an abortion before you got back from your trip 'or else.' What's 'or else' mean to you, Jack? You going to kill her next time?"

"You're blowing this all out of proportion. I'm not perfect, okay. She hit me with it when I was worrying about other things. She did it behind my back—tricked me. She didn't even talk to me about it first. But I've given that woman everything I have to—"

"Really? What have you given her? Boats and planes and lake property and ski trips and poker games and—"

"She can have anything she wants, she knows that! You've poisoned her mind against me when all we need to do is talk things over."

"Save it, Jack. You beat her. You fucked around on her, beat her up, emotionally abused her and tried to isolate her. We're the only friends she's got, because even though you weren't home, you couldn't take the risk that there would be people in her life, people who might tell her she didn't have to live with an ape like you."

"When was the last time you even had a man, huh? What do you even know about it? You married? You ever been married?"

"Oh, don't tempt me to tell you what I know about that."

"Well, you don't know shit about it, that's how

much you know. I need my wife back and I'll be god-damned if I'm going to stand by and tolerate some butch chick like you spoiling her mind against her own husband, the father of her child, when—"

"She can't work things out with you," Sable said flatly. "It's too dangerous for the child."

"She *has* to work things out with me! I'm her husband! She can't just walk away when she feels like it. We have vows. We said till death do us part!"

"She hopes to avoid that eventuality. Now get out of here."

"Go get my wife," he ground out. "Or I'll go get her myself."

"Kiss my ass."

"Don't push me, bitch. You're starting to make me really mad."

"Oh really? You mean, you're just starting to get mad? This is just the beginning? That's what I thought. When you get really mad, you—" She stopped mid-sentence and looked at him curiously. He had been far too easy to incite. This was a bad case. A lot of abusive men could hide their tempers when they had to. True, Sable knew the way to an abuser's fist—years of practice, and all. But Jack's fuse was shorter than short. "Tell me something, Jack. How young was the youngest baby you beat up?"

"Get my wife," he said, singularly emphasizing each word.

"You beat your children," she said.

"That's a lie. That's a fucking lie."

"That's why you pay child support but you don't have visitation, right? Because the court protects them from you. Because you beat them. When they were small and helpless, you beat your babies."

"That is a fucking goddamn lie!" he screamed, his hand coming out at her face so fast she didn't even have time to duck. She flew backward, her buttocks hitting the tile floor with such force that she slid about four feet. Her hand had barely come up to her cheek when he was on top of her, choking her, screaming at her and calling her obscene names. She returned to a very familiar time and place—stars swirling around in her darkening vision. She remembered sustaining a blow like that from Butch and one of her odd semiconscious thoughts being, "There really are stars."

She didn't hear the thudding of feet on the stairs as the women came running down from the loft, nor did she hear the frantic ringing of the doorbell and pounding on the door. But what she did hear, though she couldn't really respond, was the sharp report of a gun. One shot. And miraculously Jack let go of her neck. She dropped to the floor, dazed.

Sable couldn't focus. Beth knelt behind her and pulled Sable's throbbing head into her lap. Through teary vision Sable looked to her right and saw a very, very strange thing. At first she thought the angels had come for her. Soon she realized the angel had pink hair and wore a purple, lacy peignoir. Ceola. She was pointing a petite, shiny gun at Jack.

"Stand up, young man," Ceola said, "so I can get a good aim at your head. You wouldn't want to try and live with yourself after that."

"Put it away," Jack said, but he said it nervously. He was still on his knees, his hands raised as though he were being arrested.

Sable struggled to sit up. She was holding the side of her face that throbbed and she winced as she touched it. There was what appeared to be a receiving line at the door. None of it made sense to her. She feared she was hallucinating. Barbara Ann stood in the foyer in front of her husband. Her hands were on Mike's chest and she was looking up at him very earnestly. "No," she was saying. "No, Mike. I mean it. We just want him to go now."

"Barbara Ann, please, honey. *Please.*"

"No, Mike. No."

"Mom, please."

"Please, Mom. Please."

"No. I mean it now. No."

Mike stood just inside the door. His fists were clenched, his face was red, his chest was puffed out and he was *aching* to have a shot at the airline pilot. Next to him, straddling the threshold, was Matt. Equal in size, equally mad. Next to Matt was Bobby, as tall but thicker, his boyish face twisted in a grimace. Next came Joe—almost as tall, strong in his own right. And finally Billy, fists up and clenched, face twisted in outrage.

"No," Barbara Ann said to them all. "No more violence. And I mean it."

Jack Mahoney got to his feet. He looked at Beth and she averted her eyes. "Beth," he said meekly. She didn't look back at him.

"You'd better get going," Ceola said. "I shot a man once. I didn't dislike it."

Remarkably, he brushed down his pants, removing the dust of the floor from his perfectly creased uniform pants. He picked up his hat and brushed it off also. He glanced at the women and strode toward the door, walking purposefully past the Vaughan men. He almost made it, too. Billy couldn't resist. He tripped him. Jack Mahoney sprawled on the walk with a large *oomph!* and a groan. He rolled to his feet angrily, but judged the Vaughan men. Jack was a real toughie. He didn't get in fights he couldn't win. He mostly liked to smack around women and children. He brushed off his pants again, frowned at the gathering and strode down the sidewalk to his Corvette convertible.

"Put that gun away, Ceola," Eleanor said. "The only person I'm willing to have you kill is gone now."

"I could have killed him," she said, lowering the gun. "I'm a crack shot. But I left my glasses in the other room."

"Where did you get that gun?" Barbara Ann asked.

"Oh, it's mine. I keep it with me for protection."

"Protection from *what?*"

"Oh, bad manners. Inhospitality. It's a cruel world. You never know what you're going to run into." She toddled past everyone toward her room to put her weapon away.

"Did you really shoot a man once?" Beth asked her.

"Well, sort of...."

"How do you 'sort of' shoot a man?" Eleanor asked.

"I wasn't trying to kill him," Ceola said. "It was one of my husbands...Jared, the fifth one. And I only shot him in the fanny with one little bullet. I was so out of sorts." And off she went, her peignoir rustling around her.

Barbara Ann and Elly hoisted Sable to her feet. "God," she muttered thickly. "He's got one helluva punch. I think I lost a crown here."

"You need some ice. Come on. I want to check your pupils, maybe have you walk a line or tell me what day it is."

"I'm okay. It's a very hard head."

* * *

Everyone had gathered in the kitchen to go over the details of how these events had unfolded. In order to do the postmortem justice, a couple of drinks were served, a couple of beers opened, and someone called out for pizza. While Sable held an ice pack to her cheek, she sipped a little white wine.

"While Beth and Jack were sitting on the planter box, I slipped into my room for a second and called Mike," Barbara Ann said.

"She told me there was no real reason to expect trouble, but this asshole—excuse me—had shown up to talk to his wife and he was a known wife-beater. I don't much like fighting in general, but there's something about hitting a woman…"

"Dad asked if anyone wanted to go along, make sure Beth didn't get any trouble from this guy," Joe said. "And we all wanted to. It was pretty disappointing, though. We could have all taken one turn with him and maybe he wouldn't hit no one no more."

"Anymore," Barbara Ann corrected.

"I know," Joe said. "I bet he wouldn't."

"Sable pushed him pretty far," Beth said. "Did you think he'd hit you? How could you do that, thinking he'd hit you?"

"I didn't intend to let it get that far. I didn't think he'd have the balls to hit me with the rest of you in the house. I thought I could goad him into losing his cool, do a little yelling and blustering. I thought that would serve as enough of a reminder to you that he's only charming when he wants something. And that he doesn't have much control. I think he would have killed me if he could have."

"You hit a nerve," Eleanor said. "And an angle we hadn't really thought about. Beth, you need to call his ex-wife in Texas. Sable's unveiled him. He beat the children, there's no doubt about it."

"They're only fifteen and sixteen now. Jack's been divorced for ten years. That means—"

"That means they're lucky to be alive."

"Why oh why couldn't he have taken one swing at me?" Bobby asked the ceiling.

"The most remarkable discovery of this evening has been Barbara Ann's family," Elly said. "You had absolute control of these beasts even when their hormones were raging and smoke was pouring out of their nostrils. How is it you were unable to intimidate them into picking up their dirty socks?"

"I'm just not in the mood for pizza," Ceola said, rising from the kitchen table, draining her glass of brandy and putting it down on the table.

"Well, there's leftover chicken and salad fixings in the refrigerator," Barbara Ann said.

"Oh, thank you, darling. Any little thing will be all right. And I wouldn't turn down a bit of soup, if there's any. I'll just take it in my room and leave you young people to your pizza." She flowed out of the room, all purple chiffon.

"How does she do that?"

"Isn't it the most wonderful thing, the way she handles everything."

"I'll make up her tray," Beth said, standing. "I owe her."

"Mom," Joe was calling. "Mom?"

"What, Joe?"

"Come here a sec, will you?" She walked over to the counter where he stood staring down at the toaster oven. "See this here toaster? Like ours? How do you get it to shine up like that? I mean, you know, I can get all the crumbs out and all the dust and stuff off, but how do you make it so shiny? Did this one just never get real dirty?"

"S.O.S. pads," she said.

"Oh yeah? Like you use on the stove parts? Those little steel-wool and soap things?"

"Yep. Just be sure and unplug it first so you don't electrocute yourself."

"No stuff? I would'a never thought of that. S.O.S. That's great."

TWENTY

There was a talk show host named Rachael Breeze, an attractive woman in her late thirties, who had been candid with her public about her troubled youth. She came from a dysfunctional home, had spent time in foster homes, had been molested, been promiscuous, and if ever the cards had been stacked against a person, they'd been stacked against Rachael. But she rose to the top of her profession and her honesty had only endeared her to the masses. She not only had the highest ratings, she was the most altruistic. She had quite a lot in common with a certain bestselling novelist, actually.

"The most difficult part of all was the lies," Sable told Rachael. Rachael had been handpicked to be the one to get the story, should she be interested in this topic. Most of the viewers would tune in to hear the true confessions of the famous novelist, but it was for something far more important than revealing the past that made Sable choose Rachael. "The true story of my life was hard enough, but it was only a very sad story. I'll admit it took me years to look on that part of my life as only sad. I'll admit I was ashamed of the life I'd had growing up. But all things considered, it was only sad. Some of the brutal lies that accompanied the story were the most painful part of all."

"But the true part of your story was the first to come out, isn't that right? And the true parts are—?"

"Even the very first story was exaggerated unbelievably. True, I was the daughter of an alcoholic, single mother. I was raised mostly in foster homes from the time I was six years old. In some of those foster homes I was also abused—emotionally and physically battered, sexually molested by foster family members and other foster children. There were homes, however, where I was treated humanely, even if my emotional needs were not met. Then, when I was over eighteen and no longer a part of the foster care system, on my own, living again with my alcoholic mother, I met and married a man who was—it should come as no surprise—also physically and emotionally abusive...."

"And an alcoholic?" Rachael asked.

"Of course. It would have been difficult for me to have picked another kind of man to marry. But I wasn't a drunk or drug user at any time in my life, which is not at all unusual for the offspring of an alcoholic. It seems to go one of two ways—you either become another alcoholic or a codependent who is terrified of alcohol. I was the latter."

"The tabloids went to some trouble to paint a picture of you as a partyer, a wild young girl who was out of control, drinking, having sex, taking drugs...."

"I didn't say I wasn't wild," Sable said, smiling. "I was molested as a child and started having sex very indiscriminately when I was about thirteen. I was promiscuous. I did a lot of terrible things—I ran away a lot, got in fights, stole when it occurred to me. I was caught shoplifting a couple of times and held in juvenile detention several times while they decided whether to try another foster care facility or just drown me. I *tried* drugs and alcohol a couple of times, but I was a control freak—drugs and alcohol only heightened my insecurity and made me more vulnerable to whatever abuse would come my way. I was a real bad-ass, but I was always in control."

"There was a period of time when you went to college…"

"Yes, when I was nineteen. I had a chance to do some testing to see if I qualified for any training programs, since I was, you know, part of the social services system. That's welfare, for anyone who doesn't know what I'm talking about. I don't think many young people get that chance, but I had an ambitious, idealistic caseworker who was determined to save the world, or maybe just change the life of one young girl who hadn't had a break yet. I accidentally went to college, something I had never even aspired to. And I did very well while I was there, too. I met some people who had an enormous impact on me, and I started to have dreams for the first time in my life. But it was only a year of college. Intellectually, I could handle it, but emotionally, I was still stuck in that old pattern—no self-esteem, no confidence, no trust. That seems to be the problem with young women who come from dysfunctional backgrounds—even when they're faced with an opportunity, they have 'an attitude.' It comes across as total ingratitude. What it really amounts to is a lack of trust and faith. And why should they trust? Every other time they counted on someone, they were let down. Every other time they dared to have dreams of a decent life, they were beaten down and found things to be worse than ever."

"You dropped out of school…"

"No, remarkably, I didn't drop out. I didn't get

kicked out, miracle of miracles. I just failed to register for the next term. I was at home with my mother, working at a cosmetics plant so I could keep a little food on the table and a roof over her head. And I found Butch Parker...."

"You say you *found* him...."

"Like a magnet," Sable said, zapping her hand out toward the camera in a quick, snatching motion. "The most available man who could make me feel the worst about myself and threaten any chance I had of changing my path in life. That's all I knew how to deal with. My expectations were negative, and he effectively fulfilled every one. Whenever my expectations had been positive, I'd been tragically disappointed, so it was better for me to avoid disappointment. Another mind-set of the chronically abused."

"Did you love him?" she was asked.

"Of course I loved him! Like the alcoholic loves the bottle, like the drug addict loves the needle.... I needed someone like him to validate that I was no damn good and didn't deserve to rise above my miserable existence. That other business, school and all, that was a joke! I didn't belong there, among hardworking, respectable students who came from decent families and wanted to make something of themselves!"

"Why do we always think that?" Rachael asked. "That we're the only ones in the world who have some shameful secret? That all the other families are loving, caring, perfect and safe and only *we* have these terrible—"

"It's conditioning from the intense secretiveness surrounding all abuse, no matter what kind it is. The first time my mother said, 'Now, don't you tell them that I have a bottle around here or they'll take you away,' I began to take responsibility for her secret and her abuse. Every time we're abused or molested we're warned—if you think *this* is bad, telling will only make it worse. And most of the time that's true! Telling usually does make it worse! All hell breaks loose! The prophesies come true! They take you away, or they grill you—disbelieving your allegations. People call you a liar, they remove your only family, you become an outcast, everyone stares at you, people all over the place are unbelievably upset—because you *told*. Children and adolescents don't have the maturity, the experience of living, to understand that telling only makes it worse for a little while…so it can *ultimately* get better.

"So, I went back to my mother's house to guard her secrets, take care of her in her illness, and found this short-order cook who was the kind of person I deserved—a real nasty, disrespectful, insensitive brute. And I got pregnant. It turned out exactly as a lot of people would have predicted…."

"Then the most unimaginable tragedy of all struck. You had a baby—a beautiful, strong, healthy baby…."

There were a couple of times during that part of the story when Sable had to pause, collect herself and wipe the tears from her cheeks. When she looked at the tape before it aired, she was embarrassed by that—she had hoped that her voice would be clear and strong through the entire thing while she owned up to the past. It was good, however, that the emotion she had lost for twenty years was back with her now. It would have been difficult for people to relate to a woman who'd gone through so much pain without a tear to show for it.

There were a few fundamental changes in her appearance, too, though not many people would really pick up on them. She was still chic; still attractive and fashionable. Her hair was now short and honey-brown, lighter than her original color. Her nails were manicured, but no more long, red, ceramic talons; she wore short-cropped nails with clear polish. She wore a mauve dress that brought the color out in her cheeks and eyes; she had always worn creams, blacks, whites, beiges before. For some reason she had stayed away from the colors of the rainbow in her earlier life. Whether she knew it or not, she looked healthier, more like the natural beauty she was than the created beauty she'd become.

"I've seen a copy of the police report from that night," Rachael said, "and I can certainly understand how painful the retelling of that ordeal must be for you. I can't imagine...it goes beyond my comprehension what a mother might feel when she discovers her baby has been killed by the abuser in the family. But even worse than that, I think, is the fact that several tabloids alleged that there had been a party going on at the house, that *you* were involved in some big drinking and drugging binge and were neglecting the well-being of your child, when in fact you were at work that evening...."

"Yes. I didn't usually leave Tommy with my husband and mother. There was a woman down the street that took in children...I always made the excuse that it was better for Tommy to be around other children than to stay home with the adults. I suppose it's incredible to people who didn't grow up in that kind of atmosphere that I would *ever* leave my child with either of them, but they were functional alcoholics. They might not have been as sharp or quick as a nondrinking person, but they functioned normally most of the time. In fact, for a lot of alcoholics, they can't function at all without a drink. When I went to work that day, no one at my house was falling-down drunk. I think my husband was working on his car and my mother was actually playing blocks on the floor with the baby. There weren't any guests or—"

"In fact, when all this happened, it was only your mother and your husband at home?"

"That's right. So the police told me."

"So, how does it make you feel to have this story aired or printed saying that you and your husband were having some big, dangerous bash with a baby in the house? There's certainly plenty of evidence to the contrary. Did you think about suing any of the reporters or tabloids for printing something so erroneous when there is plenty of evidence that it's untrue?"

Sable took a deep breath, deciding which question to answer first. "I don't think very many people who watch those tabloid shows or buy those rags understand how the law works. I know I didn't. You don't find out how helpless you are until it happens to you, even though I know it's been explained by a number of stars-made-victims on your program and on other programs. The rule for these printed lies seems to be this— if you are an average citizen with no special notoriety of any kind and someone prints a terrible lie about you, the newspaper that printed it must prove it's true. However, if you have some special notoriety—you're an actor or politician or writer or talk show host—then *you* have to prove it's *not true.* Of the many incredible stories printed about me, one mentioned that I was a teenage prostitute." She laughed suddenly. "I was certainly too sexual for my age, but I wasn't turning tricks. But how am I going to prove that I *wasn't* something?

"You know, when somebody who hates you lashes out at you, whether you think they're justified or not, even if they're cruel and heartless, somehow you can understand a little bit of it. They hate you, after all, so why should you have expected kindness or honesty? Do you know what I mean?"

"I think so. I can tell you that it's never easy for me when someone hates me, no matter what they think the reason is...."

"But here were people who'd never met me, who'd jazzed up this already tragic story, to make me look as terrible as they possibly could, and for what? To sell papers? It takes a very long time for the shock of that alone to wear off. Why? What special power does that give a person...to create pain for someone they don't even know?"

"Well, everyone watching knows I've had more stories made up and printed about me than I can count," Rachael said.

"There's something inherently *evil* about creating a painful lie for profit," Sable said.

"I can't even comment on the pain of that, since I'm one of their favorite subjects. It's bad enough when they find out some personal thing about you that you're trying to work out for yourself so you can move on with your life, but when they invent horrific tales... There were times that hurt me so bad I thought I couldn't breathe from the pain of it."

"And, of course, people think you can't be hurt by lies because you have money and many admirers. You have famous friends, so how can horrible public vivisection hurt you?"

"Or, how about when people you know and trusted decide to take advantage of you by selling some sleazy story to the tabloids...?"

"Fortunately, I can't relate to that," Sable said. "Maybe I should say *unfortunately*. Because I kept myself so isolated and private, I had very few friends. The people who sold stories about me to the tabloids were people I don't remember ever meeting! I was told some man was paid thousands of dollars for his account of this wild weekend of drugs and orgies, and God knows what all, that was supposed to have taken place on a yacht about ten years ago. I've never heard of the man. I've never heard of the *yacht*. It blows my mind."

"Did you, or did you have someone, check out the sources and facts on these stories? Try to do anything about them?"

"I've done a lot of thinking about that. There are definitely a few things I can prove are untrue—the police report of the night Tommy died proves there was no party, for example. If I thought by suing them I could save one person from going through something like this, I'd be very eager to do something. Unfortunately, I don't think it would matter. They'd just keep doing what they're doing as long as people pay to read it. People buy those rags even knowing they're only about five percent true. And the cost of waging war against them would create a greater financial burden for me than for them. They'd probably find a way to make money on the story. And I have better things to do with my time and my money."

"I know, I know.... Let's move on past this tabloid subject if we can. I cringe every time I think I'm giving them more fuel for their fires. I know you're anxious to get back to the original subject of what happens to young women in this country when they're trapped in the welfare and foster care system, but we're not going to be able to ignore your transformation—both intellectual, emotional, and the obvious, physical. We got the picture we're about to show from a network affiliate, and even though you don't have any idea where that picture came from, we do have your permission to show it. I want to make that clear to our audience and viewers."

"Yes. You can show it. You're about the last person in America to get around to it."

"This is a picture of you when you were twelve or thirteen?"

"I don't remember when it was taken, so I'm guessing."

"Obviously, you've made some changes in your appearance."

"Improvements, I'd like to think."

"So that you wouldn't be recognized by old friends and family members?"

"No, there was hardly anyone to hide from. I was pretty intent on creating a whole new person. When I left Fresno—"

"Let's start there. After the death of your son, you left Fresno and headed south. Why Los Angeles, first of all?"

"That's exactly how much money I had when I went to the bus depot. I had to choose between Los Angeles and Redding, California. Since I had no idea what kind of work might be available in Redding, I chose the bigger, more anonymous city...."

The show went well. Sable handled even embarrassing questions from the audience with candor and cool. There wasn't any more in her past to own; nothing more to say. A very excited—and probably relieved—publisher tried to convince Sable to go on the talk show circuit and accept interviews with everyone and their brother, including the very shows that had trashed her. But she would not do it. She'd promised to come out of hiding, but she wasn't going to create fame for herself out of this story. There was something greater at stake—a larger issue. Which was what she told Rachael Breeze when they had their first, nontelevised conversation.

"I'm really not interested in cleaning up the stories, even though ninety percent of what they printed about me is total fabrication. What I am interested in doing is having a conversation about poor girls who the system has failed. There are a lot of young girls out there, right now, who aren't going to become famous novelists or talk show hosts because the system keeps them oppressed for eighteen years and then cuts them loose to find their own oppression. They have a self-fulfilling prophecy to fail."

"Your story should serve as an inspiration to a lot of young—"

"They need a lot more than inspiration, Rachael. Look, I'm afraid this can never be discussed on television, but I've contacted you because I plan to use you as my personal example. Since I can't cover up the past anymore, since I have to open up about it now in order to move on, I'm going to let this disaster make a positive impact on my life. Very Rachael Breeze style. I'm going to find a way to help young women who come from the place I came from. Maybe only a few, but if I can reach even one—"

"That's the most wonderful thing I've heard this week! I know you're going to have so much joy from that! But we should talk about your plans. We should—"

"We should be very careful," Sable said, cutting her off, "not to ever make it seem as though the actions of the tabloids—as unforgivably cruel as they can be—have created any positive outcome for anyone. They certainly never had any higher motives when they stripped me bare, so they're not going to get any credit if I can turn a nightmare into a decent reawakening. I'd like to think I might have come to this point without having been publicly humiliated first."

"If you feel that strongly, we don't have to discuss it on the air," she replied. "But will you keep me informed about your plans to help young women? And let me know if there's any way I can be involved?"

"I am letting you know," Sable replied. "When I'm brainstorming ideas of what I can do and how I can do it, I want your advice. And your support."

"You mean, you haven't even driven by?" Beth asked Barbara Ann. "Not once?"

"Nope," she said. "I was afraid to. But I have to make a decision. We're moving out of Gabby's house in ten days. If I'm going back home, it has to be because I can live with what I'm walking into. Otherwise, I have to find a small apartment somewhere."

"Do you think it's fair, Barbara Ann? Sneaking over there when you think no one will be home? Shouldn't you call them, give them a chance to spruce it up a little bit?"

"I think this is best," she said.

It was eleven in the morning. What she gathered from the boys was that everyone was working at least part-time. Billy and Joe were both working at the municipal golf course, starting at about 5:00 a.m. Thursday through Sunday, and not getting off until afternoon. Bobby was still working at the nursery, 11:00 a.m. to 9:00 p.m., potting palms and selling posies, he said. Matt had his job with UPS, delivering packages. And, of course, Mike left at seven every morning.

Eight weeks, she thought miserably as she drove toward her house. It was certainly enough time to figure out how to plug in a vacuum cleaner or operate a dishwasher. Mike had said they'd been working on it; she'd had a hint or two from the boys that they were attempting to do housework just from the questions they'd asked her. But even Barbara Ann hadn't figured out how to make a house sparkle in eight weeks. It had taken her months, even years, to fine-tune her home-making skills.

A lot had happened to her in eight weeks. She'd lost twenty-five pounds for one thing; she hadn't had much money to spend on clothes, but those few things she bought were size eights. It had been years since she'd had a size eight she could squeeze even one thigh into. Sable had opened up her suitcases and unloaded a lot of very nice, very expensive stuff on Barbara Ann; all she had to do to the pants and skirts was shorten them. Eight weeks of lettuce, diet sodas, chicken breasts and exercise with the Morning Show Lady had given her back her youthful figure. But she was not foolish enough to believe it had been willpower. It had been the summer at Gabby's house, where she had people to talk to when she became frustrated. Where she had nurturers who genuinely cared about her feelings and understood her pain. She'd had her problems during the eight weeks, but she hadn't fallen into the

Milky Ways to hold back her fears and ease her pain because she had love and understanding.

She had gotten the three-book contract in record time; the fastest response ever. And the special clause about not returning the advance money on a refused book unless it was sold to someone else. Her revised manuscript was approved and—something she'd never have thought of without Sable—she was going to spruce up that earlier refused book and use it as her tool for finding another publisher so that she wouldn't be forever betting all her hard work on the quirky tastes of one editor. She'd added up the amount of money she would soon be receiving—twenty thousand dollars plus whatever came in on her next royalty statement. After she put money aside for taxes, she'd have twenty-six thousand dollars. Even if she had to move into an apartment and start paying her own expenses, she could afford Bobby's trade school tuition plus a little money for Mike to make a healthy dent in some of the charge accounts.

This time, though, she was going to be sure that a little something was getting saved for her retirement. She was done letting Mike's retirement plan from the helicopter manufacturer be the only cushion they had for their old age.

"Are you scared?" Beth asked her.

Scared? She was terrified! What if it was worse? It well could be. After weeks of stealing matrimonial bliss in the back seat of the car, she longed to lie in bed beside her husband again. She ached to hear the sound of her sons shouting for her the moment they came in the door. She yearned for the thrill of their appreciation when she'd found the time to surprise them with some sweet dessert treat only Mom could make. The smell of their freshly laundered T-shirts as she folded them; the sound of their wild laughter; the shock of their crass, objectionable conversations that she wasn't meant to hear.

"I have to decide what I'm willing to live with," Barbara Ann told Beth. "I mean, if the house is basically picked up, but still dirty, is that acceptable? That's half the battle, really, if they'd just put away their stuff and pick up after themselves. I mean, I can *clean.* If I'm not fighting shoes, lawn-mower motors, jeans, rags, shirts, pop cans, Doritos bags, I can dust, mop, vacuum...."

"What if it's tidy, but everything is crammed in closets and under beds?" Beth asked.

"That's how they usually clean—by trying their best to hide the clutter. That's what I have to be prepared for. So, do I go back there and attempt to teach them how to do it? Part of me thinks they'd be willing to learn now...but the other part of me wonders if they're not pretty happy this way. At first they swore they were cleaning up the house and begged me to come home...but they haven't even mentioned the house in weeks. I have a feeling they *think* they've cleaned it up, but they haven't actually done it. So, do I want to move back there and fight that losing battle again?"

"Well, do you?" Beth asked.

"I don't know," she whined. "Oh God, I don't know!"

"Is that why I'm with you? As a witness? Or so someone can pick you up off the floor, pour you into your car and drive you home where it's safe?"

"As moral support," she said.

She drove right past her house.

"Barbara Ann! Jeez, you missed it! Come on, it hasn't been that long!"

She slowed to a stop and backed up. She hadn't driven past it because she'd been away so long. She'd just never realized until now that she navigated toward the messiest house on the block—the one with the brownest grass, the highest weeds, the most peeling paint and curling shingles, and the greatest number of vehicles in the driveway and on the street.

She sat for a moment staring at it. She was speechless. The house was painted. It was the same color, but it was *painted*. There were no vehicles around. Flowers had been planted in the planter boxes under the front windows. Shrubs were planted along the drive. The grass was cut and it was *green!* "I can't believe it," she whispered in awe. This was far more than she had ever dreamed of.

"This looks fantastic," Beth was saying, undoing her seat belt. "I can't wait to see how they've managed inside."

"I can't do it," Barbara Ann said. "I can't. It's too scary."

"Come on, don't be a wimp. Look what they've done out here! It's got to be an improvement inside. Come on!"

But how had he managed it? she wondered. Mike must have hired someone to paint the house, and she knew they didn't have the money for that! They'd had plenty of talks about money, over the phone and when they went out to dinner. Mike's paycheck was just about enough to cover their bills, food and a few of the surprises that came along every month no matter what. Her last advance and royalty had been eaten up on home repairs, maxed-out charges and things the boys needed. She had told him exactly how to juggle things so that he could get from paycheck to paycheck, and she'd promised him that as soon as she got any money from her publisher, she'd make sure he had some. On top of that, he'd forced fifty dollars or so on her every week when they had dinner. She had kept saying, "No, Mike, you'll need it. I know you guys aren't eating anything but pizza and junk food. And that stuff's expensive." But he had too much pride to think of his wife living off the generosity of her women friends.

"Barbara Ann, give me the keys if you can't unlock the door," Beth was saying. "The suspense is *killing* me!"

"It won't be locked," she said, trancelike. "They never learned to lock the doors or turn off the lights."

"It's locked," Beth announced. "Come on, give me your keys."

Barbara Ann handed over the keys and put a hand over her eyes. She couldn't take it. The outside looked so nice that, if the inside was a trash heap, it would break her heart. On the other hand, painting and planting was pretty easy. There was no reason to expect that much of the inside just because they'd managed to—

"Oh my God, I can't believe it!" Beth said. "Barbara Ann, get in here!"

She stepped over the threshold tentatively. It was only the entryway, the little-used formal living room to her left. It was perfectly clean. There were vacuum cleaner tracks on the rug. The wood accent tables were shiny with oil. She could smell sweet chemicals—soaps, glass cleaners, disinfectants, polish.

"Whew," Beth said. "It's really hot in here. Why do you suppose it's so hot in here?"

Barbara Ann didn't answer. She wandered into the house, her mouth standing open, her eyes darting around suspiciously. Eventually she'd run across an explanation for this—a pile of trash so big that a semi would have to be called for it. Surely they'd scraped everything from one end to another. The backyard or the garage, she guessed, would be impassable. Or, she would find a bill—thousands of dollars paid to someone to do this to her house, her family all sleeping in their cars so they wouldn't muss it.

The family room was immaculate. The cushions were all straight on the sofa, love seat and chairs. The magazines were neatly stacked in a wicker basket. The television screen was wiped clean—no fingerprints. No shoes, no pop cans, no plates or wrappers or trash. My God, the walls were painted! Not so much as a smear or scrape anywhere. She gravitated toward the thermostat for two reasons—one, it was sizzling in the house and two, there was a paper taped to the wall. She approached it and read it. 8:00 a.m. to 5:00 p.m.—90 5:00 p.m. to 8:00 a.m.—78. That's why it was hot. The temperature was turned off during the day to save money. She'd been trying to conserve for years, but someone would tinker with the temperature at will. One of the boys who had stayed up real late and wanted to sleep until 2:00 p.m. would turn the thermostat down to seventy and chill the whole house even if he was the only one at home, rather than plug in a fan. But now, either by law or consensus, the temperature was monitored.

"Hurry up," Beth was calling. "Come on."

Beth was already oohing and aahing in the kitchen. "I don't understand," Barbara Ann was muttering, "how they could have done it." The places where the wallpaper was peeling had been patched up. The scuffs and scars on the molding and floorboards had been sanded and stained. The floor shone; the countertops sparkled; the glass twinkled. Where were the dirty dishes? The cereal boxes? The rotting food? There was a new throw rug on the kitchen floor; it was clean and had been recently vacuumed or shook. There was a note on the counter.

B.V.—I had to empty your dishwasher this morning, buttface, so you got mine tonight.

B.V.

Billy to Bobby. Or Bobby to Billy.

"This is how," Beth said. "Look at this. This is incredible."

There was a chart on the side of the refrigerator, so large it took up almost the whole thing. There was a list of chores longer than a dead snake; there were five names of those responsible—Dad, Bill, Bob, Joe, Matt. There were days of the week. Some of the chores had to be done every day—dinner, shopping, empty d/w, load d/w, trash, mirrors, k.floor, l.room, water front, water back. Some things were done Monday, Wednesday and Friday—fridge, vacuum, dust, glass, bathrooms, towels. Some things were reserved for the weekend—mow, edge, trim, prune, garage 1, garage 2, pool, patio. And some things were listed for every individual—room, laundry, iron, drawers, closet, sink, toilet, car. _Drawers? Closet?_

"Unbelievable!" Beth said. "Isn't this wonderful?"

Barbara Ann couldn't absorb it. She was still reserving judgment until she saw their rooms, the garages, the backyard. She wandered from room to room, from house to yard, from yard to garage....

The entire house was freshly painted. New throw rugs were laid down in the bathrooms and laundry

rooms. New mold-free shower curtains were hung.
The deck was freshly stained and weatherall applied.
The pool shone in algae-free sky blue. The backyard
was cut, trimmed, weeded and landscaped. There
were two new pots of flowers on the patio; the patio table and chairs were scrubbed clean. Shelves had been
built in both garages; particleboard was applied to the
walls, and tools and yard equipment neatly hung
there. Bikes were suspended from ceiling hooks and
the garage walls and floors had been painted.

The boys' rooms were immaculate. Billy's bed was
unmade and someone had left a T-shirt on the bathroom floor, but Billy and Joe both had to be at the golf
course by 5:00 a.m. Jeans were folded and stacked in
space-maker shelves in the closets. The shoes sat in
neat rows. Drawers were perfectly tidy—to the extent
that a box of condoms was tucked neatly between the
socks and BVD's. The blinds were all open, letting the
sunshine flow in and there wasn't a speck of dust on
the blinds. The grout in the shower stalls and around
the toilet was scrubbed white—or perhaps replaced—
and for the first time in Barbara Ann's memory, there
was not the slightest hint of the smell of urine.

Beth was fluttering from room room, gasping, ex-
claiming, calling out—"Barbara Ann, you have to see
this!"—but by the time Barbara Ann could catch up,
she was already skittering on to another room.

When she went to her bedroom, she felt like crying.
The bed was made, the bathroom mirror sparkled, the
towels hung neatly on the rail, the toilet bowl glistened, and all of Mike's clothes hung on their hangers.
She picked through the shirts—ironed, every one. She
finally came across one that had a huge scorch on the
back and it caused her a hiccup of emotion. She lifted

the lid on the clothes hamper and saw maybe a day's worth of unlaundered clothes. Barbara Ann sat on the end of her bed, tears running down her cheeks. That's where Beth finally found her. When Beth saw that she was crying, she knelt before her.

"You must be so proud of them," Beth said in a reverent whisper.

"Oh sure, but that's not why I'm crying," she said.

"Then why, for heaven's sake?"

"Do you know that if they left for a week and I spent every minute of that time scrubbing and polishing, I could not have made it look this good?"

"I saw the house today," Barbara Ann told Mike on the phone later that day.

"Oh, honey, you should have *told* us! We wanted to be ready for you! We wanted to give you a tour!"

"Well, I was so impressed I almost fainted. Mike, it looked positively wonderful. I can't imagine how you did it. More than that, how did you have the *money* to do it? All the painting and landscaping?"

"Oh, that. Well, I did something I should'a done a long time ago, but since I never had to struggle with the bills like you did, I never thought about it. I sat down with the boys one Saturday and we went over every dime. We studied every bill. We got rid of a couple a things, things we could do without. Bobby doesn't put five slices of cheese on his sandwich anymore. We look things up in the phone book instead of calling directory assistance. Stuff like that. And then for all the supplies and new stuff around the house— we all pitched in. Bobby brought home stuff from the nursery with his discount. Matt handled most of the paint, but everyone contributed something. Bill and

Joe pitched in a little where they could, but they're part-time at the golf course so they did a lot of the work. The boys haven't had many nights out or friends over. They haven't been spending their money on toys or car parts, I can tell you that. And we all worked real hard. We worked harder than we've ever worked. No wonder you walked out on us, Barbara Ann. You should'a done it years ago. I can't believe we left all that on you."

"Even I never got it that clean," she said. "How in the world did you do it?"

"It was hell, honey, I'll tell you that. It was like going to basic training all over again. Barbara Ann, are you coming back to us? If we promise to keep it up?"

"Yes, Mike, I can't wait. But I'm going to finish the book with the girls and help close up Gabby's house. Then I'll be home."

"How long is that going to take?"

"Ten more days. We're closing up the house on Sunday night, August twenty-second. You and the boys will even be invited to our last big bash before we give up the halfway house for crazy women."

"Ten days? Ten days?"

"It's not that long. And I'll be glad to go out for a drive with you before then," she said, followed by a wicked laugh. "I think I'm going to miss that—our sneaky little sessions. It made me feel like a kid again."

"My back is killing me."

"Mike, really, I don't know how you got it that clean and perfect. When I come home you'll have to show me some of your secrets."

"I've got quite a few things I want to show you when you get home," he said. "And not much of it has to do

with housework." And he growled into the phone,
sending shivers down her spine.

They never did tell her what really happened. They
all tried to clean the house. Not one of them was stubborn about it. They wanted her back so bad they were
sick inside—and not just for the work she did for them.
They just wanted her home again. But they couldn't
get the house clean. Things kept going wrong. Laundry
turned funny colors; soapy water left streaks; wiping
down the walls took the paint off; cutting the yellowed,
tangled grass only made the yard look like a dirt patch.
That didn't even speak to the food situation—and this
was a household that loved food. Bobby cooked them a
turkey one day and served it too rare—and they all got
food poisoning. They ate out of boxes and bags until
they were weak. They were dying, for one thing. And
they were making no progress, for another, which
meant they might never get Barbara Ann back.

Mike was telling one of the guys he worked with
about his problems. Well, the guy was a retired Marine
Master Sergeant. He'd spent years whipping barracks
and grounds and young men into shape. He'd even
done some time as a base housing-inspector. He knew
things about white-glove inspections that Barbara Ann
had never heard of. His name was Chuck Mackie and
for years the boys would say, "Make it Mac," for make
it perfect.

The first two weeks of following Mac's instructions
almost killed them. But then they started to see results.
Mac showed up at about eight every evening for another inspection and a new list of chores. On the week-
ends he worked them like dogs. He was having the
best time he'd had since leaving the Marines. Pretty
soon Mrs. Mackie came around to give some simple

cooking instructions; they were going broke and getting sick on so much pizza. She gave them laundry tips and taught basic ironing. Mike was so proud of himself when he could finally iron a perfect shirt...in forty minutes. Then Andrea Mackie said, "Imagine this—first off, you're going to get a grade on it. Someone's going to say, 'Can't I even get a goddamn shirt for work around here?' Second, there are two children hanging on your legs while a third is aiming a crayon at the wallpaper. Meanwhile, something's boiling over on the stove, and the washing machine is walking. That should speed you up. Oh, and did I mention? Your period is also late." Mike learned to get his perfect shirt down to seven minutes.

Perhaps it was cruel, but Mike, Matt, Bob, Joe and Bill wanted to keep their Basic Training in Housekeeping a secret. They wanted Barbara Ann to always believe that it was sheer, devoted love that had driven them to such excellence.

Because really, it was.

TWENTY-ONE

Elly was on the phone in her room, talking to London. Barbara Ann was at her word processor. Sable was with Ceola in the kitchen, chopping tomatoes for a lunch salad. Then the screaming started.

"Nooo! Nooo! Oh, God, Oh, God. Nooo!"

Barbara Ann got there first; she had been the closest. By the time Sable, Elly and finally Ceola arrived at the bathroom doorway, Barbara Ann was kneeling on the floor, holding Beth in her arms. Beth was sobbing into Barbara Ann's shoulder. She was wearing a cotton T-shirt, sitting on a bath towel. Her shorts and panties were inside out on the floor in front of the toilet, soaked in blood. The toilet water was bloody; there was blood streaking the toilet seat and splattered inside the bowl. And Barbara Ann was saying, "It's all right, it's all right. You're going to be all right."

"Oh my God, the baby," Sable whispered.

"Should we call an ambulance?"

"Probably not," Barbara Ann said. "Beth, we have to see how heavy the bleeding is so we know what to do. Beth? Honey?"

"What's happened?"

"Barbara Ann, should we call the doctor?"

"What's going on? What's wrong with her?"

"She's having—or just had—a miscarriage. Beth, can you tell me what happened?"

"I had a stomach ache—a hard pain. It felt like I had to go to the bathroom. It felt like I couldn't make it to the toilet. There was a huge gush of blood out of me. Oh my God! The baby!"

"Beth, how many weeks along are you? Can you tell me?"

"I don't know. Twelve or so. Twelve or fourteen."

"Can you stand up, honey? Can we see how much you're bleeding?"

Beth was shaking almost too hard to get to her feet, and had to use the sink counter for support. When she was standing, Barbara Ann wiped Beth's bloody thighs with the towel. She wet a corner from the sink and washed away the bloodstains. "Do you feel that pain...or that urge to use the toilet anymore?" Barbara Ann asked.

"No. I mean, my tummy feels tender. Crampy. But not urgent."

There was the merest trickle of blood running down the inside of Beth's thigh. She asked Beth for the name of her doctor, then turned to the women in the doorway. "Sable, call Dr. Morlene's office. Tell them that Beth is miscarrying—she may have lost it in the toilet. The bleeding was very heavy for a few minutes, but has slowed down to about that of a normal menstrual flow. Ask them where we should take her—office, emergency room, whatever. Elly, find Beth some panties, shorts and shoes. And go to my room and get a sanitary napkin out of my top drawer. Ceola, go to the kitchen and get me some kind of small container with a lid. A Tupperware bowl, maybe. And a spoon with holes in it."

"What are you going to do?" Elly asked her.

"I'm going to clean Beth up, get her dressed to go to the doctor's office or hospital, and then I'm going to find out if she lost anything in that mess or if it's just blood. She's going to need a D&C, probably."

"You're going to dig around in that toilet for a *fetus*?" Elly asked, horrified.

"It's what you do, Elly. Now go on. Let's take care of our girl." The women went off about their tasks and Barbara Ann turned back to Beth, who was holding herself up by leaning on the sink counter. Her weakness was from fear and shock, not blood loss. Barbara Ann knew all about this. It had happened to her once. After Billy. "Okay, honey," she said, running water and wetting a washcloth. "Let's get you cleaned up a little and put some clothes on. You have to go to the doctor."

Beth went to the outpatient surgical center across the street from the hospital. No one would be left behind; Barbara Ann drove Beth, and Sable accompanied. Elly and Ceola followed a few minutes later in another car. The nurses who met them at the door were very calm and unhurried as Beth gingerly transferred herself from the car seat to a wheelchair. Barbara Ann presented one of them with a square Tupperware container holding a few impressive clots.

"Having some trouble?" one of the nurses asked.

"The baby," she whimpered. "I think I've lost the baby...."

"Dr. Morlene will be here in just a few minutes to have a look. Let's get you into an examining room. You're going to be fine now."

"My baby," she wept.

"It's all right, dear. It's all right."

All right? Sable thought. Didn't they know how much a woman could want the baby she was carrying? Didn't they have any idea that this was more than just a heavy period? This was a death in the family, for God's sake! What did they mean, moving so slow, being so friendly and sweet, and giving her that bullshit about it being *all right*?

The women waited for an hour. Then they were told that the doctor felt it necessary to perform a D&C and that Beth would have to stay there, lying down, for two to three hours before she could be taken home. But there were no complications and she was going to be fine. The women, the nurse said, might want to go out to lunch. Or perhaps they could go home and one of them could come back later to pick up Beth and drive her home.

"And the baby?"

"She lost the baby quickly and cleanly."

"That was a fetus in the Tupperware?"

"No, no, just some clots. She aborted spontaneously during the doctor's examination. It was a typical, uncomplicated miscarriage. She's going to be just fine. She may feel a little tired for the next couple of days and she'll have some bleeding, but she'll be fine. And the doctor told her there's no reason she won't be able to conceive again, and carry a baby to term."

"I can think of a couple," Sable said.

They were not interested in going out to lunch. Or going home, sending one of their number back to transport Beth. They all stayed in the surgical center's waiting room. They hardly spoke to each other. Elly had to go outside often, of course, where there was an ashtray at the entrance.

Two more hours had passed when the doctor came to talk to them. He said basically the same things the nurse had said. He'd like to check Beth in six weeks. And one of them could go help her get dressed.

Sable looked immediately toward Barbara Ann. "Go ahead," Barbara Ann said. "You're not going to settle down until you see her."

Beth was sitting on the edge of her bed, dangling her feet, her hospital gown open down the back under her long dark hair. Her head was bent as though she was looking at her feet. And idiotically, Sable's first words were, "It's going to be all right."

Beth turned her moist eyes to her friend. "Maybe I'm not meant to have children," she said.

Sable sat down beside her. "How can you come to that conclusion at this point in your life? You have another ten years for childbearing. Maybe more."

"I'll never get married again. It was only an accident I married Jack."

"A bad accident...."

"I never met men. I never dated. I never knew what to say...or I said something stupid. I'll end up being the old maid aunt in Kansas City. I'll sit in some little apartment and type and only go out for family functions. I'll—"

"That's enough of that. What are you doing here— setting yourself up to be lonely? Beth, you've just spent seven years with a man who didn't want you to have any friends. He kept you as isolated as he could so his power over you wouldn't be threatened. You don't have to live like that. You can change that pattern. Go out, meet people, enjoy your life—children or not."

"It's so hard for me to make friends," she said softly.

"But those friendships you've made have been

strong. Enduring. We're not the only friends you have. You knew a lot of the writers at Gabby's memorial."

"Women," she said. "I'm okay with women."

"Look, you have four brothers and three sisters in Kansas City. You graduated from high school and college there. You know the town, you know more people than you realize. You—"

"I just wanted to have a baby. That's all I've ever really wanted."

"I know, I know. But you're going to have to change your life, Beth. Look at me," Sable said. She had to physically turn her to get her attention. "Maybe this was for the best." The moisture in Beth's eyes grew thicker. One tear spilled over. "You deserve so much more than this. You deserve to have a child that isn't linked to Jack Mahoney, for one thing. It would be hell fighting him for years and years to come. Now you can make a clean break from him and his abuse and start over. Start fresh."

"I could have started fresh with—"

"I know, I know, but listen to me for a second. It was really no way to have a baby, you know? You snuck it out of him and planned to take it away and raise it alone. If you think your life is going to be solitary typing speckled with a few family parties, then what kind of life is that for a child? Were you going to make your child as reclusive and shy as you are?"

Beth blinked and tears ran down her cheeks.

"I don't think having a child without a father present is necessarily a big tragedy—lots of single moms do smashing jobs of raising kids. But growing up with a mom who doesn't want to meet people, or go out, or take those social risks…that would be sad. You're going to have to change that. You're going to have to overcome some of that terrible shyness. You sure as hell aren't shy once you know someone. I heard you tell Elly you thought she was a lesbian."

"It just takes me such a long time. It's so hard for me."

"We all do hard things. That's life. What's the old saying? Pain is mandatory—suffering is optional. You'll just have to find a way to do it even though it's hard. Ask your brothers and sisters to include you in social events with their friends. Join a couple of groups. Do some volunteer work. Take some courses."

Beth hung her head. She had surely read this much in Dear Abby. Undoubtedly, she had heard all this from her mother when she was a single, twenty-four-year-old virgin.

"You have to stop giving yourself so many negative messages. You have to stop saying 'I'm so shy' and start saying 'I love people.' You can be lonely forever if you want to, or you can change this about yourself. Beth, you're doing a very sad thing to yourself. I would hate for you to do that to your children, when you have them."

"When," she said tiredly.

"Well, I'm not very wise about things like this," Sable said. "But I do know one thing for sure. I got everything in life I ever thought I should have. If I just believed I should get it, that I deserved it, that I needed it to validate who I was, then I got it. That's what I know to be true."

"I don't really want all that success and money and fame," Beth said.

"I wasn't talking about just that," Sable said. "I was thinking further back. Like when I was getting punched in the chops."

* * *

A few days after Beth's miscarriage, Elly emerged from Gabby's bedroom wearing a summer suit. "I have to leave for a while, I have a few errands that can't wait, but I've invited company for dinner. A gentleman who has an interest in Gabby's works. Would you all be so kind as to tidy up and lay a decent table?"

"Who, Elly?" Sable wanted to know.

"You'll find out at five. Let's have drinks and hors d'oeuvres."

She left the room and them.

"Now that's a strange one...Elly with a surprise?" Barbara mused.

"She hates surprises," Beth added.

"It must be important if she's playing this out," Sable said.

Throughout the afternoon they speculated—agent, publisher, critic, academic? But none of them was even close. At 5:07 the doorbell rang and the only woman in residence who didn't rush to that portal was Ceola.

Sable, Barbara and Beth stood in the opened door, regarding the handsome young man who stood there, and as a trio they gasped and covered their mouths. For all intents and purposes, Gabby's late lover, John Shelby, stood on the stoop.

"That seems to be the only reaction I ever get from this house," the young man said. He stuck out his hand and introduced himself. "Todd Shelby. John was my father."

And they let out their breath as one.

The clopping of Elly's shoes on the walk came up behind him. "Gave you a start, did he?" she asked. "The Shelby men must come from a strong gene pool. Well, let's go inside."

First over drinks and then over dinner, Todd Shelby told them the rest of the story. They knew the beginning only too well—having lived inside Gabby's book throughout the summer. But they didn't know the end, and the end was what they were struggling with.

"I was a boy of eighteen when my father, whom I secretly worshiped, returned to London from Ireland that last summer of his life. He wasted very little time getting reacquainted with the family before he called for a conference, a family discussion. My mother, Jane Shelby, seemed to have already been informed of my father's request for a divorce. Together, they settled down to tell me and my sister.

"I was devastated by this," Todd told them. "I hated him thoroughly. He was painfully honest about the entire, sordid mess. He said that he and Mother hadn't had much of a marriage, really, and that while they were good friends and had the utmost respect for one another, there was no romance in their lives and it was time, now that we children were adults and capable of understanding adult issues, that they separate, divorce and move along with their lives.

"That Mother seemed at peace with this was horrifying to me. And it made no difference. I couldn't *comprehend* that Mother would be pleased to be divorced. It never occurred to me that perhaps she was glad about it. I saw my father as the most awful cad. He was crushing us with this terrible news. Children don't really care whether their parents have romance. What good's romance on the old folks anyway? They're supposed to perform their duties as parents, stay together amicably no matter what troubles they might have to endure, and pretend…at the very least *pretend* that all is well.

"If it wasn't terrible enough that my father was bringing this embarrassment on our household, he had to go still further and explain that there was another woman. A woman he loved. An American writer, of all things. Younger than our mother. And by implication, more beautiful, more daring, more of everything. He actually wanted to marry her! It wasn't enough that he'd obviously been sleeping with her, he wanted to make an honest woman of her."

"Was your sister equally outraged?" Sable asked him.

"My sister was *bored*. She was almost seventeen, going about with some long-haired mutt she'd met at school, more interested in clothes and parties and music than in the marriage of her parents. She wasn't at all close to Father. At that point in her life, she wasn't terribly close to our mother, either. She was close enough, though, to ask, 'Is this all right with you, Mummy?' To which Mother replied that it was, that we would all still see Father quite often and there was no real embarrassment in the fact that they'd grown apart.

"I told him I'd never forgive him if he went through with it, that he'd better drop this American tramp of his or he'd live to regret it. I think I was crying. Sobbing, perhaps. He came to my room later on that night and tried to reason with me. He was very kind about the whole thing, given the way I was carrying on. I threatened him and he consoled me. I delivered him ultimatums and he told me that one day I'd understand. I shouted that I hated him and he promised that he would see no less of me in his new circumstances.

"Of course, you know, he was killed on the train. The very next day. I buried my father when the last words between us were hateful."

"That's not entirely true," Ceola told him. It was almost as though they had forgotten she was there, forgotten this story was about her daughter. "You were filled with anger, but your father understood and didn't hold it against you. That's a parent's job, after all."

"Perhaps, but it was quite a long time before I would see that. It was at *my* insistence, my outraged insistence, that no one was ever to speak of that conversation with Father. I wasn't going to have that blight on our otherwise enviable family name when it wasn't necessary. My mother urged me to see things in a more adult way, to allow that people change and come to crossroads in their lives that are unexpected. Not vengeful or wrathful, but simply unexpected. *She*, it appeared, had no hard feelings whatsoever. In fact, she remarried within a year."

"When did you come to forgive your father?" Elly asked.

"Over the years, as I lived and was educated and married myself, I slowly began to understand that what I'd been feeling, fearing, was my father was abandoning me. Of course, he wasn't at all, but I never believed all that blather about seeing me as often. I was too young. And, of course, I was able to watch my mother blossom in her second marriage. She thrived on the attention of a man who loved her in a truly romantic way—a man who didn't keep running off to take pictures. They were tremendous grandparents to my stepfather's grandchildren and would have been to my own.

"Ten years later my mother died. She had a short, difficult, but noble fight with cancer. My stepfather, who is with us still and a very close part of our family, turned over to me some of my father's personal effects that my mother had saved all those years. She saved them for a time I might be mature enough to see him as a *man*, not some icon. Among them were letters from my father's lover, Gabrielle Marshall. There were pictures and some of the stories she'd published along with the most complete collection of my father's photos that exist to this day.

"When I read the letters, I had to meet her. Her passion for my father, for his work, his values and his courage, was a thing of purity. I found myself wishing that I'd managed a way to better appreciate all that he was, rather than wasting even a moment on any shortcoming I perceived. When she wrote to him, he came to life in my mind. When I saw the pictures of her, of him, of the two of them together, I could see why he loved her. They seemed to come to life with joy in those photos.

"But the letters were art. She was funny, warm, spontaneous. Sometimes she wrote of her love for him, sometimes she wrote furious epistles in which she maligned him for some misdeed he'd committed, most often the insensitivity of putting himself in mortal danger to snap a picture when the result might have been that she'd have to live on without him. She also wrote of daily events—her work, her children, her friends. Sometimes she used him as a sounding board for her dreams. Not just personal ambitions for herself, but rather some dream for the world, usually touched off by some heartbreaking foreign story she'd written.

"I had to know this woman," Todd said. "I could already tell from her letters and articles why he was in love with her. But I had to know her for myself. At that time I was a twenty-eight-year-old man. A young solicitor, just starting out. My wife had given birth to our first child, a son—a son who I adored and who I hoped would love me through every dreadful mistake I would make in my life."

"Gabby was then forty-five," Elly calculated for them.

"Yes, that's so. I struggled with letters, but hers were too intimidating in their greatness. I found I couldn't write to her. I impetuously flew to California and went to her door. It was the end of May. As I pulled my rented coupe up to the curb, I saw a gathering of young people come bounding out of the house, jumping in cars, shouting and laughing, and off they rode. When I went to the door, terrified to make this confrontation, you can't imagine what I found. Or perhaps you can, having known her. This tiny woman in rolled-up jeans, cotton shirt, hair all askew, feet bare came growling to the door as if she resented the intrusion. She had a wet rag in her hand—obviously she'd been cleaning.

"I had been so concerned about myself and how she might respond to me that I hadn't even thought of the impact my mere presence could have on her. The resemblance, you know. She stared at me in shock for a few moments, and when I said my name was Todd Shelby, she swooned."

"Gabby never said a word," Elly said. "I never knew Todd and Gabby had met. I am still amazed by that."

"I can't imagine why she didn't tell you. I assure you, our meeting was very nice. I found Gabby in the midst of absolute chaos—her daughter was graduating from high school that evening, her son was due home from college that very afternoon, her ex-husband's parents were coming to dinner that evening, and two days hence was her daughter's eighteenth birthday. She was cooking and cleaning, and planned to have a huge weekend full of parties and guests. It didn't look to me that she was going to make it. The place was a-tumble, actually. She was a mess. But she was indeed a lovely mess. Lovely. Had I not been mad in love with my own wife and new baby son, I'm afraid I might have fallen for her.

"Time seemed to stop for a couple of hours. With her house collapsing around us—food in preparation on the counter, electric sweeper standing ready on the rug—we sat on the divan together and talked. I wanted to know all about my father, the side of him she knew, and I wanted to tell her all about the fiasco of his confession just hours before his death. I wanted her to know that it was I who'd insisted no one ever speak of his plans, else she might have been told about his talk with us. Else, she might have been consoled at the time of his death. We could have gone on for hours and hours, but it simply wasn't possible.

"Gabby sent me on my way that day and told me to go back to London. She promised she would visit me there in the fall. And she told me I'd made her very, very happy. In her heart, she said, she had never really doubted John. He said his love for her would last forever. And indeed, it had."

"I remember her visit to London," Elly said. "I remember Sarah's graduation and birthday. I was there for all the events. And I remember that Gabby was melancholy. Tearful. I thought it was because she was launching her baby into the world, for Gabby, then, would live as a woman alone for the first time in her life. I conceded that it would make anyone sentimental."

"But I believe it was because, after all those years—

ten years—she was finally vindicated," Todd said. "My father had sworn his love for her and meant to fulfill his promises. But until I visited her that day, she was forever in doubt."

"You say she never mentioned Todd's visit, Elly?" Sable asked.

"Not once. Not even in passing. I'm not the kind of friend one talks to about romantic foibles or heartaches. Everyone, even Gabby, always considered me immune to love. But maybe it was more than that. Maybe it was something Gabby wanted all to herself. John had been dead for ten years, after all. She'd recovered from it. She didn't pine after him day and night any longer.

"In my digging, I never ran across any letters from Todd because he'd never written any."

"I was too intimidated by her wit and dash to write to Gabby, but she wrote to me. I have four years of letters—as artful and exciting as the ones she wrote my father. Only the romantic passion is missing, that's all. She wrote me long stories about Father, about their travels and time together. I've made copies and brought them for you. You have my permission to publish them in any memoir you produce. There's no longer any reason to keep John Shelby's affair secret."

"But what is equally important," Elly said, "is our—Gabby's—final chapter. I believe we found it in that photo of Gabby at the funeral...and the story we've heard from Todd. Clare and Brandt never stopped loving each other. And although it didn't come quickly, Clare did eventually have that confirmed.

"We can wrap it up. The story is finished. And so is our duty."

Despite all the best intentions, there were no reunions of four crazy women at a beach house in Carmel. It was not as though they didn't meet here and there. Sable flew to Kansas City for Beth's wedding in September, one year after Gabby's house was closed. Beth and her new husband flew to Sacramento for Matt Vaughan's wedding December of that same year. The following January, the women gathered in New York to toast the publication of *Perfect Light*. Of course, they talked all the time—local or long-distance. While the three locals in the Sacramento area didn't meet for lunch, they dropped in on each other now and then. Their lives had gone off in strange and remarkable directions; they found, once they were resettled, that they could manage by just keeping up with each other. The bond was complete, and they didn't need to fall back on the strength of that daily.

The closing of the house on Olive Street had been an affair of grand proportions. They packed the finished manuscript off to Sable's agent, Arnold Bynum. In addition to the finished, original novel, Beth had managed to retrieve the rights to seven previously pub-

lished novels and all five non-fiction books to be held
by the author's estate. The women had begun to move
their personal belongings out of the house as the closing date approached. Beth's household goods were
shipped to Kansas City to be kept in a storage facility
until she was resettled. Sable's stuff had been carted
back to Hidden Valley by some of Jeff's employees.
Ben had helped Eleanor carry boxes and boxes of
Gabby's books and papers to add to the clutter of her
packed little house. And Barbara Ann's family
couldn't move her computer, books, clothes and odds
and ends back to her sparkling home fast enough.

So, the five of them, mostly moved out except for
overnight items, had thrown a bash for all the people
who were a part of their permanent lives. The Vaughan
men came, some bringing girlfriends. Sarah, Lindsey,
and even Justin arrived. David and Ed were there. Ben,
of course. Jeff. And even Dr. Don. They ate mounds of
food, told stories of the summer, drank wine and beer,
and laughed so hard and so deeply that they cried.
Things happened that night that showed how much a
little trauma, time and healing can change the face of
the world. Justin left early, off to play with his pals.
That was the last time he ever walked out on Sarah and
the baby and was allowed to walk back into their lives.
Dr. Don dropped his arm around Ed's shoulders and
had a long conversation with him about David's un-
deniable courage in his life and his field of medicine.
David was the one to take Ceola to the airport early
Sunday morning. And Ben and Elly were caught
smooching.

The next day was a little tougher. Ceola was gone,
the women had packed up the last of their belongings
and the house was straightened up. It was to go on the

market; it would be shown with the furniture still in place. The bags were loaded into cars and the women stood at the curb to have a good, final view.

"This time we really do have to say goodbye," Barbara Ann said.

"To the house, Barbara Ann. Not to each other."

"Some of us do," said Beth, who was being taken to the airport by Sable.

"It's for the best," Elly said. "We've dragged this out long enough. Anything yet to be worked out in our personal lives, we're going to have to do alone. Or we'll cripple each other with dependence. Now, let's make it quick. I hate sentimental shit."

They hugged, wiped away tears, waved from cars, and drove away. But it was Elly who sat in front of the house for a long time, looking at it. Longing for it. "Goddamnit," she said aloud. "I'm not sure I was done."

Done or not, Eleanor faced her obligations bravely. She met Ben's family; one at a time, slowly, and then en masse. This was the day they married. Saturday, June fourth. The wedding was held at Ben's farmhouse, outdoors, where the flowers and vines and greenery had been decorated with trellises, ribbons and bows. All of Ben's family, friends and neighbors were there, of course. And all of Ben's grandchildren, especially the smaller ones, seemed to want to hang on Elly.

Sable was the maid of honor—the only attendant for Elly. She had tried, desperately, to dress Elly in some chic, designer wedding dress, but Elly wouldn't have it. She purchased a fancy dress from a department store—what to her was a fancy dress—and was done with it. "What's the difference?" she asked testily. "Ben's probably going to wear a lavender leisure suit.

Haven't you figured out that it wasn't fashion that brought us together?" Sable also tried to turn Elly's wedding into something a little more traditional—keep the bride in hiding until the wedding march is played, throw rice, throw the bouquet, take a long honeymoon, et cetera. "Nonsense," Eleanor said. "We're going to visit and enjoy ourselves, welcome our guests and friends, take a few minutes to tie the knot, and then we'll eat and party. That's it. Don't mess with it, Sable, or you'll irritate me."

"What about your honeymoon?"

"What honeymoon? There are people coming from out of town. I'm not going anywhere. Why should I miss all the fun for a silly honeymoon?"

What Elly wanted was to have the caterers serving drinks and hors d'oeurvres and have music playing while the guests arrived and had some time to socialize. Then she would have this little ceremony, which would be short and to the point. They would have a buffet dinner and enjoy the setting sun with friends and family. It would not be formal and it would not be rigidly scheduled as Sable would have planned.

It was just as well that Elly had put her foot down because it was Sable who lost all composure when Beth arrived. When she came around the flagstone walk into the backyard with her new husband, Sable dropped her wineglass and screamed. She jumped up and down, pointed and flung her arms around. Elly came running from the house and Barbara Ann flew from the other side of the lawn party to see what was happening. There stood Beth with the biggest pregnant stomach. Grinning.

"Why didn't you tell us?"

"How could you have kept it secret?"

"When did this happen?"

Beth laughed at them, clutching her husband's hand and leaning against him. She rubbed her belly fondly, proudly. "At first I kept quiet because I wanted to get past the danger zone. I didn't tell anyone but Alex for three months. And then I kept quiet because I knew I'd be seeing you here and I wanted to surprise you. And it happened about eight months ago."

"In the usual fashion," Alex added, kissing her cheek.

"This is unbelievable!" Barbara Ann proclaimed.

"No, this is natural. Unbelievable is if David and Ed make some announcement today."

"Oh, where are they! I want Alex to meet them!"

"Right over there with Sarah. Lindsey's trying to walk." Though she was two and a half, she was naturally a little behind, but still the most precious, good-natured baby on earth. "And go meet Sarah's new guy. She met him at school. He's a law student."

"New guy? Is it serious?"

"It's always serious, Beth. You should know that."

"Gamma. Gamma," a little voice was saying. They all looked down to see a tiny girl with golden ringlets pulling on Elly's dress.

"What is it, dolly?" Elly cooed, bending and scooping up the little girl.

"I want some juice, Gamma."

"Well, of course you can have some juice. Let's go get you some." She turned away from her friends and carried the little cherub toward the bartender.

"Now *that* is unbelievable," Sable said.

"Gee, I thought Eleanor only slapped small children."

"Oh, she's already a wonderful grandmother," Ben

said, elbowing into their little circle. He was wearing an old, beige, double-knit suit and the most awful bow tie. "Look at you," he said to Beth, kissing her cheek. "Is it only one, Beth?"

"It's a girl. Mama started with a girl. I'm thinking of having eight. I'll have to hurry."

"I'm thinking of having two," Alex said, squeezing her shoulders.

"Maybe we'll compromise and have seven, but it's really better if you stick to even numbers."

"I'd better check on my girls," Sable said suddenly. "I hope no one's stealing the knickknacks or smoking pot behind the barn."

"You brought the girls?" Barbara Ann asked.

"Just three of them. I have six living with me now. Two are delightful, two are sneaky and two are absolutely incorrigible. I adore them. They're awesome. Better warn your boys. They all have records. Want to meet them?"

"Sure. How'd you get them to come?"

"A little pop psychology. The three who were in the most trouble last week had to come with me to the wedding. It was marvelous. They all tried really hard. I think Dorothy got the worst end of the deal. She's armed and watching the three who were left at home."

"What about Jeff? Is Jeff here?"

"Last I saw, he was talking to Mike."

"When are you two going to make it legal?" Beth asked.

"Oh darling, wedded bliss isn't for everyone. Jeff and I work so well together as we are, we kind of hate to mess with it. Besides, I'm too busy to break in a new husband. I've got to go see about those girls. Come on, Barbara."

Elly and Ben were wed, no one objected at the crucial moment, and after the wedding toasts were made, Elly stood to make her own. "I have some friends here I'd like to thank," she said. "Most of you are very familiar with the story about how a few of us got together and weeded through our friend Gabby's office, putting together her final project for publication, *Perfect Light*, which is now enjoying its fourteenth week on the coveted *New York Times* bestseller list." There were cheers and whistles. "That was quite an ordeal, that project. It was meant to be sorting and filing—a couple of weeks' worth of work. It ended up being a full summer of four crazy women trying to get their lives and their work in some sort of order. I guess we were really five—we had Ceola with us, too. Alas, she isn't with us anymore. She was buried in her purple peignoir with her pistol at her side. Damn, I find I miss her helplessly. Now, I never thought I'd say *that*." Elly paused while people laughed, especially those who knew Ceola personally. "But the other crazy women are here. Sable, Beth— she's the one who's about to give birth any second— and Barbara Ann. You were all a lot of trouble," she said, and she was booed from some quarters. "You were impossible at times. I felt like a damn house-mother. But something happened to me in that house that summer, something I could not have planned nor willed, something for which I owe you three unstable broads a debt of gratitude till the day I die. You forced me to learn how little I enjoy being alone and allowed me to open myself up to my wonderful Ben and his marvelous family. I thank you, my friends. And I toast you. To your health!"

"And yours," the gathering said, raising glasses high and wiping tears off their cheeks.

Late in the day, when the sun was setting and stomachs were full, there were four women gathered in a small clearing on the far side of the lawn. Alone. Beth sat on a tree stump, occasionally massaging her round belly. Eleanor sat on a lawn chair, Barbara Ann stood behind her, rubbing her shoulders now and then, and Sable sat cross-legged on the grass.

"Beth, is Alex as sweet and kind as he seems?" Barbara Ann wanted to know.

"Worse. I think he lets me walk all over him. I have to stop myself and remember, sometimes, that Alex has never made a move that indicates he doesn't treasure me. I think the shadow of an abusive husband is something you struggle with for long after he's gone."

"He's adorable," Sable said.

"Isn't he? I love that bald head. I never realized how sexy I found baldness until I met Alex."

"Is he all your mother dreamed of? Is he at least Catholic?"

Beth giggled suddenly. She covered her mouth with a hand and her beautiful eyes were alive with mischief. "He used to be a priest."

"What!?"

"No way."

"How on earth…?"

"My brother John introduced us. Alex had just left the priesthood, and John had been struggling with that decision for such a long time…. I guess John had been talking to Alex about it a lot and they became good friends. John did quit, you know. Right after he married us. And you know what? Mama didn't die. But I think she's nearly worn out her beads. Since I've been home I've learned that my family is pretty normal, after all. They're wonderful, all of them, but they have the same problems in life that everyone else has. They're just people—not trophies. Sable, I'm glad you pushed me so hard. When I think that I could still be in Sacramento, ducking Jack's punches…"

"You wouldn't be," Sable said. "And besides, it was all of us. Not just me."

"It was mostly you," Barbara Ann agreed. "And it was you who took the final punch."

"I hope that's my last," Sable said. "But with these hoodlums I consort with now, one never knows…."

"How's it going with all that?" Elly asked.

"Fabulous. We have a bona fide foundation now. We're helping girls get from eighteen years old to adulthood, whatever age that is. When the foster care system dumps them on the street, penniless, at the age of eighteen, we pick them up. We make sure they have family and support that's both financial and emotional. We've got some going to school, which is something that only happened in rare cases before. We look for these girls when they're about sixteen so they can finish high school without the anxiety that they're going to be dumped by the state the minute they hit that magic number.

"All those dinner parties and trips and stuff that I did—it all paid off. I've gotten money out of every celebrity I've ever met. We're only handling about forty girls right now, but next year we'll take on a hundred. We'll grow. We're going to do a lot of good work."

"What about the ones living with you?"

"Special projects. Lost causes."

"You don't really expect to save them all by giving them quarters in that fancy white house of yours, do you?"

"Oh, you miss the point. I'm not going to save anyone. No matter how many advantages you throw at someone like that, they can't see it. They're still worthless sluts, remember? They have to come a long way to get over that mind-set. In other words, *I'm* not going to save anyone at all. They have to save themselves. It's up to them. I'm just a conduit. And besides, it's not very white anymore. Poor Dorothy."

"Speaking of white houses…?" someone asked. All eyes turned to Barbara Ann.

"Okay, we have our dust bunnies," she shrugged. "Sometimes the dishwashing crew is out sick…or maybe out playing. But I don't have any lawn-mower motors in my bedroom and things are so much better than they once were."

"And books?"

"Well, I've had all the same problems I had before. You know, they string me out for too long, they make me change too much, they hem and haw and ask me to revise books so that the characters are more complex— whatever the hell that means. But I'm just enjoying myself. I finally figured out that I'm doing what I want to do and it's not a flawless business. There are ups and downs in everything. After the experience I had a couple of years ago, thinking my career was over and then having it come back twice as big, I am just not willing to let them get that much of my soul anymore. That's my fault—creating my own problems out of fear and envy and…

"What did you ask? I'm fine. I'm happy. I'm doing what I want to do and I'm going to be a grandmother."

"Really?"

"Matt and Stacy? When?"

"October. And he gets his degree in architecture in June. We're all pretty stable."

"Elly? What are you going to do?"

"Retire."

"What?"

"You can't! All those years you said school was all you had!"

"Well, I have a lot more now. Thirteen grandchildren for one thing. And by the looks of things, we have to prepare ourselves for *great*-grandchildren."

"Elly, how can you not work?"

"I didn't say I wouldn't work. I'll do a little writing. I'm going to set up an office in what was Ben's wife's sewing room. I might be going soft, but I'm not going domestic. I'm going to do the biography. I'll take on a few reviews, an occasional article."

"I thought you hated children! You never once said a pleasant thing about a child in all the years I've known you."

"I didn't want to get involved. I didn't think I'd ever have any. I stayed away from all that mothering nonsense. It's too cloying for me. But Ben's children are different, somehow. They loved me before they knew me, as if they had decided that if I was what made Ben happy, then I would make them happy, too—even if I had a horn growing out of my head. He and his wife must have been remarkable parents. And I am left to enjoy the bounty."

"Oh Eleanor, that's beautiful," Barbara Ann said, sniffing.

"Stop it now. You know how I hate all that sentimental shit."

A bell started ringing off in the distance. *Dong, dong, dong.* "Elly!" Ben was calling. "Elly. Dr. Marshall is leaving now. Come say goodbye."

"This can't be ending already," Sable complained.

"To the contrary, it's just beginning. Remember Gabby's letter? The things she bequeathed us? Have any of you thought about that?" Elly asked them. "I have. I ask myself all the time—is it even possible she knew us that well without us knowing it? She wanted me to have a garden of virgins to tend.... Look at them," she said, throwing an arm wide to the many young children scampering around the lawn. "I always assumed children would hate me—I have so little patience and such a grumpy personality. It's the oddest thing. They're mad about me."

"And I am something of a Girl Scout leader, indeed," Sable said. "Gabby did say, a number of times, that if I had the courage to tell the truth about my past, it could help people. I don't think it's the telling that helps, but owning where I came from and looking for ways to help young girls get through that maze is giving me new purpose. Yes, I've thought about Gabby's gifts a lot. Barbara Ann certainly didn't need a lesson in how to love from that chapter in the Bible, but she needed a lesson in what kind of love she deserved in return."

"Amen," Barbara Ann said.

"And Beth," Sable said, dropping an arm around her shoulders, "needed to defend herself against the dark knight."

"We never toasted Gabby," Beth said.

"Of course we have," Elly said. "We toast her every day by doing just what she expects of us. We persevere. We carry on. Is there something more to life? I guess we're never done. I used to resent that—having something be over before I was done. I've decided that's a gift. Never getting done means there's always something left to do, some challenge yet to face, some thrill still to seek. Gabby would like that."